Collector's Library

Collector's Library

TALES AND POEMS
OF
EDGAR ALLAN POE

TALES AND POEMS OF EDGAR ALLAN POE

Edgar Allan Poe

with an Afterword by
DAVID PINCHING

BARNES
&NOBLE
BOOKS
NEW YORK

Typeset in Great Britain by Antony Gray
Printed and bound in China by Imago

Contents

5

THE POEMS

THE TALES

THE TALES

Metzengerstein

Pestis eram vivus – moriens tua mors ero.

MARTIN LUTHER

Horror and fatality have been stalking abroad in all ages. Why then give a date to this story I have to tell? Let it suffice to say, that at the period of which I speak, there existed, in the interior of Hungary, a settled although hidden belief in the doctrines of the Metempsychosis. Of the doctrines themselves – that is, of their falsity, or of their probability – I say nothing. I assert, however, that much of our incredulity – as La Bruyère says of all our unhappiness – 'vient de ne pouvoir être seuls'.*

But there are some points in the Hungarian superstition which were fast verging to absurdity. They – the Hungarians – differed very essentially from their Eastern authorities. For example, 'The soul,' said the former – I give the words of an acute and intelligent Parisian – 'ne demeure qu'une seule fois dans un corps sensible: au reste – un cheval, un chien, un homme même, n'est que la ressemblance peu tangible de ces animaux.'

The families of Berlifitzing and Metzengerstein had

* Mercier, in L'an deux mille quatre cents quarante, seriously maintains the doctrines of the Metempsychosis, and J. D'Israeli says that 'no system is so simple and so little repugnant to the understanding'. Col. Ethan Allen, the 'Green Mountain Boy', is also said to have been a serious metempsychosist.

been at variance for centuries. Never before were two houses so illustrious, mutually embittered by hostility so deadly. The origin of this enmity seems to be found in the words of an ancient prophecy – 'A lofty name shall have a fearful fall when, as the rider over his horse, the mortality of Metzengerstein shall triumph over the immortality of Berlifitzing.'

To be sure the words themselves had little or no meaning. But more trivial causes have given rise – and that no long while ago – to consequences equally eventful. Besides, the estates, which were contiguous, had long exercised a rival influence in the affairs of a busy government. Moreover, near neighbours are seldom friends; and the inhabitants of the Castle Berlifitzing might look, from their lofty buttresses, into the very windows of the palace Metzengerstein. Least of all had the more than feudal magnificence, thus discovered, a tendency to allay the irritable feelings of the less ancient and less wealthy Berlifitzings. What wonder then, that the words, however silly, of that prediction, should have succeeded in setting and keeping at variance two families already predisposed to quarrel by every instigation of hereditary jealousy? The prophecy seemed to imply – if it implied anything – a final triumph on the part of the already more powerful house; and was of course remembered with the more bitter animosity by the weaker and less influential.

Wilhelm, Count Berlifitzing, although loftily descended, was, at the epoch of this narrative, an infirm and doting old man, remarkable for nothing but an inordinate and inveterate personal antipathy to the family of his rival, and so passionate a love of horses, and of hunting, that neither bodily infirmity, great age, nor mental incapacity, prevented his daily participation in the dangers of the chase.

Frederick, Baron Metzengerstein, was, on the other hand, not yet of age. His father, the Minister G—, died young. His mother, the Lady Mary, followed him quickly after. Frederick was, at that time, in his fifteenth year. In a city, fifteen years are no long period – a child may be still a child in his third lustrum: but in a wilderness – in so magnificent a wilderness as that old principality, fifteen years have a far deeper meaning.

From some peculiar circumstances attending the administration of his father, the young Baron, at the decease of the former, entered immediately upon his vast possessions. Such estates were seldom held before by a nobleman of Hungary. His castles were without number. The chief in point of splendour and extent was the 'Chateau Metzengerstein'. The boundary line of his dominions was never clearly defined; but his principal park embraced a circuit of fifty miles.

Upon the succession of a proprietor so young, with a character so well known, to a fortune so unparalleled, little speculation was afloat in regard to his probable course of conduct. And, indeed, for the space of three days, the behaviour of the heir out-heroded Herod, and fairly surpassed the expectations of his most enthusiastic admirers. Shameful debaucheries – flagrant treacheries – unheard-of atrocities – gave his trembling vassals quickly to understand that no servile submission on their part – no punctilios of conscience on his own – were thenceforward to prove any security against the remorseless fangs of a petty Caligula. On the night of the fourth day, the stables of the castle Berlifitzing were discovered to be on fire; and the unanimous opinion of the neighbourhood added the crime of the incendiary to the already hideous list of the Baron's misdemeanours and enormities.

But during the tumult occasioned by this occurrence, the young nobleman himself sat apparently buried in meditation, in a vast and desolate upper apartment of the family palace of Metzengerstein. The rich although faded tapestry hangings which swung gloomily upon the walls, represented the shadowy and majestic forms of a thousand illustrious ancestors. *Here*, rich-ermined priests, and pontifical dignitaries, familiarly seated with the autocrat and the sovereign, put a veto on the wishes of a temporal king, or restrained with the fiat of papal supremacy the rebellious sceptre of the Arch-enemy. *There*, the dark, tall statures of the Princes Metzengerstein – their muscular war-coursers plunging over the carcasses of fallen foes – startled the steadiest nerves with their vigorous expression; and *here*, again, the voluptuous and swan-like figures of the dames of days gone by, floated away in the mazes of an unreal dance to the strains of imaginary melody.

But as the Baron listened, or affected to listen, to the gradually increasing uproar in the stables of Berlifitzing – or perhaps pondered upon some more novel, some more decided act of audacity – his eyes became unwittingly riveted to the figure of an enormous, and unnaturally coloured horse, represented in the tapestry as belonging to a Saracen ancestor of the family of his rival. The horse itself, in the foreground of the design, stood motionless and statue-like – while farther back, its discomfited rider perished by the dagger of a Metzengerstein.

On Frederick's lip arose a fiendish expression, as he became aware of the direction which his glance had, without his consciousness, assumed. Yet he did not remove it. On the contrary, he could by no means account for the overwhelming anxiety which appeared falling like a pall upon his senses. It was with difficulty that he reconciled his dreamy and incoherent feelings with the certainty of being awake. The longer he gazed the more absorbing became the spell – the more impossible did it appear that he could ever withdraw his glance from the fascination of that tapestry. But the tumult without becoming suddenly more violent, with a compulsory exertion he diverted his attention to the glare of ruddy light thrown full by the flaming stables upon the windows of the apartment.

The action, however, was but momentary; his gaze returned mechanically to the wall. To his extreme horror and astonishment, the head of the gigantic steed had, in the meantime, altered its position. The neck of the animal, before arched, as if in compassion, over the prostrate body of its lord, was now extended, at full length, in the direction of the Baron. The eyes, before invisible, now wore an energetic and human expression, while they gleamed with a fiery and unusual red; and the distended lips of the apparently enraged horse left in full view his gigantic and disgusting teeth.

Stupefied with terror, the young nobleman tottered to the door. As he threw it open, a flash of red light, streaming far into the chamber, flung his shadow with a clear outline against the quivering tapestry, and he shuddered to perceive that shadow – as he staggered awhile upon the threshold – assuming the exact position, and precisely filling up the contour, of the relentless and triumphant murderer of the Saracen Berlifitzing.

To lighten the depression of his spirits, the Baron

hurried into the open air. At the principal gate of the palace he encountered three equerries. With much difficulty, and at the imminent peril of their lives, they were restraining the convulsive plunges of a gigantic and fiery-coloured horse.

'Whose horse? Where did you get him?' demanded the youth, in a querulous and husky tone of voice, as he became instantly aware that the mysterious steed in the tapestried chamber was the very counterpart of the furious animal before his eyes.

'He is your own property, sire,' replied one of the equerries, 'at least he is claimed by no other owner. We caught him flying, all smoking and foaming with rage, from the burning stables of the Castle Berlifitzing. Supposing him to have belonged to the old Count's stud of foreign horses, we led him back as an estray. But the grooms there disclaim any title to the creature; which is strange, since he bears evident marks of having made a narrow escape from the flames.

'The letters WVB are also branded very distinctly on his forehead,' interrupted a second equerry. 'I supposed them, of course, to be the initials of Wilhelm von Berlifitzing – but all at the castle are positive in denying any knowledge of the horse.'

'Extremely singular!' said the young Baron, with a musing air, and apparently unconscious of the meaning of his words. 'He is, as you say, a remarkable horse – a prodigious horse! although, as you very justly observe, of a suspicious and untractable character; let him be mine, however,' he added, after a pause, 'perhaps a rider like Frederick of Metzengerstein may tame even the devil from the stables of Berlifitzing.'

'You are mistaken, my lord; the horse, as I think we mentioned, is *not* from the stables of the Count. If such had been the case, we know our duty better than to bring him into the presence of a noble of your family.'

'True!' observed the Baron, dryly; and at that instant a page of the bedchamber came from the palace with a heightened colour, and a precipitate step. He whispered into his master's ear an account of the sudden disappearance of a small portion of the tapestry, in an apartment which he designated; entering, at the same time, into particulars of a minute and circumstantial character; but from the low tone of voice in which these latter were communicated, nothing escaped to gratify the excited curiosity of the equerries.

The young Frederick, during the conference, seemed agitated by a variety of emotions. He soon, however, recovered his composure, and an expression of determined malignancy settled upon his countenance, as he gave peremptory orders that a certain chamber should be immediately locked up, and the key placed in his own possession.

'Have you heard of the unhappy death of the old hunter Berlifitzing?' said one of his vassals to the Baron, as, after the departure of the page, the huge steed which that nobleman had adopted as his own, plunged and curvetted, with redoubled fury, down the long avenue which extended from the chateau to the stables of Metzengerstein.

'No!' said the Baron, turning abruptly towards the speaker, 'dead! say you?'

'It is indeed true, my lord; and, to a noble of your name, will be, I imagine, no unwelcome intelligence.'

A rapid smile shot over the countenance of the listener. 'How died he?'

'In his rash exertions to rescue a favourite portion of

his hunting stud, he has himself perished miserably in the flames.'

'I-n-d-e-e-d!' ejaculated the Baron, as if slowly and deliberately impressed with the truth of some exciting idea.

'Indeed,' repeated the vassal.

'Shocking!' said the youth, calmly, and turned quietly into the chateau.

From this date a marked alteration took place in the outward demeanour of the dissolute young Baron Frederick Von Metzengerstein. Indeed, his behaviour disappointed every expectation, and proved little in accordance with the views of many a manoeuvring mama; while his habits and manner, still less than formerly, offered anything congenial with those of the neighbouring aristocracy. He was never to be seen beyond the limits of his own domain, and, in this wide and social world, was utterly companionless – unless, indeed, that unnatural, impetuous, and fiery-coloured horse, which he henceforward continually bestrode, had any mysterious right to the title of his friend.

Numerous invitations on the part of the neighbourhood for a long time, however, periodically came in. 'Will the Baron honour our festivals with his presence?' 'Will the Baron join us in a hunting of the boar?' – 'Metzengerstein does not hunt,' 'Metzengerstein will not attend,' were the haughty and laconic answers.

These repeated insults were not to be endured by an imperious nobility. Such invitations became less cordial – less frequent – in time they ceased altogether. The widow of the unfortunate Count Berlifitzing was even heard to express a hope 'that the Baron might be at home when he did not wish to be at home, since he disdained the company of his equals;

and ride when he did not wish to ride, since he preferred the society of a horse'. This to be sure was a very silly explosion of hereditary pique; and merely proved how singularly unmeaning our sayings are apt to become, when we desire to be unusually energetic.

The charitable, nevertheless, attributed the altera-tion in the conduct of the young nobleman to the natural sorrow of a son for the untimely loss of his parents – forgetting, however, his atrocious and reck-less behaviour during the short period immediately succeeding that bereavement. Some there were, indeed, who suggested a too haughty idea of self-consequence and dignity. Others again (among them may be mentioned the family physician) did not hesitate in speaking of morbid melancholy, and hereditary ill-health; while dark hints, of a more equivocal nature, were current among the multitude.

Indeed, the Baron's perverse attachment to his lately-acquired charger – an attachment which seemed to attain new strength from every fresh example of the animal's ferocious and demon-like propensities – at length became, in the eyes of all reasonable men, a hideous and unnatural fervour. In the glare of noon – at the dead hour of night – in sickness or in health – in calm or in tempest – the young Metzengerstein seemed riveted to the saddle of that colossal horse, whose intractable audacities so well accorded with his own spirit.

There were circumstances, moreover, which, coupled with late events, gave an unearthly and por-tentous character to the mania of the rider, and to the capabilities of the steed. The space passed over in a single leap had been accurately measured, and was found to exceed, by an astounding difference, the wildest expectations of the most imaginative. The Baron, besides, had no particular *name* for the animal, although all the rest in his collection were distinguished by characteristic appellations. His stable, too, was appointed at a distance from the rest; and with regard to grooming and other necessary offices, none but the owner in person had ventured to officiate, or even to enter the enclosure of that particular stall. It was also to be observed, that although the three grooms, who had caught the steed as he fled from the conflagration at Berlifitzing, had succeeded in arresting his course, by means of a chain-bridle and noose – yet no one of the three could with any certainty affirm that he had, during that dangerous struggle, or at any period thereafter, actually placed his hand upon the body of the beast. Instances of peculiar intelligence in the demeanour of a noble and high-spirited horse are not to be supposed capable of exciting unreasonable attention – especially among men who, daily trained to the labours of the chase, might appear well acquainted with the sagacity of a horse – but there were certain circumstances which intruded themselves perforce upon the most sceptical and phlegmatic; and it is said there were times when the animal caused the gaping crowd who stood around to recoil in horror from the deep and impressive meaning of his terrible stamp – times when the young Metzengerstein turned pale and shrunk away from the rapid and searching expression of his earnest and human-looking eye.

Among all the retinue of the Baron, however, none were found to doubt the ardour of that extraordinary affection which existed on the part of the young nobleman for the fiery qualities of his horse; at least, none but an insignificant and misshapen little page, whose deformities were in everybody's way, and whose opinions were of the least possible importance. He – if his ideas are worth mentioning at all – had the effrontery to assert that his master never vaulted into the saddle without an unaccountable and almost imperceptible shudder, and that, upon his return from every long-continued and habitual ride, an expression of triumphant malignity distorted every muscle in his countenance.

One tempestuous night, Metzengerstein, awaking from a heavy slumber, descended like a maniac from his chamber, and, mounting in hot haste, bounded away into the mazes of the forest. An occurrence so common attracted no particular attention, but his return was looked for with intense anxiety on the part of his domestics, when, after some hours' absence, the stupendous and magnificent battlements of the Chateau Metzengerstein were discovered crackling and rocking to their very foundation, under the influence of a dense and livid mass of ungovernable fire.

As the flames, when first seen, had already made so terrible a progress that all efforts to save any portion of the building were evidently futile, the astonished neighbourhood stood idly around in silent and pathetic wonder. But a new and fearful object soon riveted the attention of the multitude, and proved how much more intense is the excitement wrought in the feelings of a crowd by the contemplation of human agony, than that brought about by the most appalling spectacles of inanimate matter.

Up the long avenue of aged oaks which led from the forest to the main entrance of the Chateau

Metzengerstein, a steed, bearing an unbonneted and disordered rider, was seen leaping with an impetuosity which outstripped the very Demon of the Tempest.

The career of the horseman was indisputably, on his own part, uncontrollable. The agony of his countenance, the convulsive struggle of his frame, gave evidence of superhuman exertion: but no sound, save a solitary shriek, escaped from his lacerated lips, which were bitten through and through in the intensity of terror. One instant, and the clattering of hoofs resounded sharply and shrilly above the roaring of the flames and the shrieking of the winds – another, and, clearing at a single plunge the gateway and the moat, the steed bounded far up the tottering staircases of the palace, and, with its rider, disappeared amid the whirlwind of chaotic fire.

The fury of the tempest immediately died away, and a dead calm sullenly succeeded. A white flame still enveloped the building like a shroud, and, streaming far away into the quiet atmosphere, shot forth a glare of preternatural light; while a cloud of smoke settled heavily over the battlements in the distinct colossal figure of – *a horse*.

The Visionary or the Assignation

Stay for me there! I will not fail
To meet thee in that hollow vale.

Exequy on the death of his wife
by Henry King, Bishop of Chichester

Ill-fated and mysterious man! – bewildered in the brilliancy of thine own imagination, and fallen in the flames of thine own youth! Again in fancy I behold thee! Once more thy form hath risen before me! – not – oh not as thou art – in the cold valley and shadow – but as thou *shouldst be* – squandering away a life of magnificent meditation in that city of dim visions, thine own Venice – which is a star-beloved Elysium of the sea, and the wide windows of whose Palladian palaces look down with a deep and bitter meaning upon the secrets of her silent waters. Yes! I repeat it – as thou *shouldst be*. There are surely other worlds than this – other thoughts than the thoughts of the multitude – other speculations than the speculations of the sophist. Who then shall call thy conduct into question? who blame thee for thy visionary hours, or denounce those occupations as a wasting away of life, which were but the overflowings of thine everlasting energies?

It was at Venice, beneath the covered archway there called the Ponte di Sospiri, that I met for the third or fourth time the person of whom I speak. It is with a confused recollection that I bring to mind the circumstances of that meeting. Yet I remember – ah! how should I forget? – the deep midnight, the Bridge

23

of Sighs, the beauty of woman, and the Genius of Romance that stalked up and down the narrow canal.

It was a night of unusual gloom. The great clock of the Piazza had sounded the fifth hour of the Italian evening. The square of the Campanile lay silent and deserted, and the lights in the old Ducal Palace were dying fast away. I was returning home from the Piazzetta, by way of the Grand Canal. But as my gondola arrived opposite the mouth of the canal San Marco, a female voice from its recesses broke suddenly upon the night, in one wild, hysterical, and long-continued shriek. Startled at the sound, I sprang upon my feet; while the gondolier, letting slip his single oar, lost it in the pitchy darkness beyond a chance of recovery, and we were consequently left to the guidance of the current which here sets from the greater into the smaller channel. Like some huge and sable-feathered condor, we were slowly drifting down towards the Bridge of Sighs, when a thousand flambeaus flashing from the windows, and down the staircases of the Ducal Palace, turned all at once that deep gloom into a livid and preternatural day.

A child, slipping from the arms of its own mother, had fallen from an upper window of the lofty structure into the deep and dim canal. The quiet waters had closed placidly over their victim; and, although my own gondola was the only one in sight, many a stout swimmer, already in the stream, was seeking in vain upon the surface, the treasure which was to be found, alas! only within the abyss. Upon the broad black marble flagstones at the entrance of the palace, and a few steps above the water, stood a figure which none who then saw can have ever since forgotten. It was the

Marchesa Aphrodite – the adoration of all Venice – the gayest of the gay – the most lovely where all were beautiful – but still the young wife of the old and intriguing Mentoni, and the mother of that fair child, her first and only one, who now, deep beneath the murky water, was thinking in bitterness of heart upon her sweet caresses, and exhausting its little life in struggles to call upon her name.

She stood alone. Her small, bare, and silvery feet gleamed in the black mirror of marble beneath her. Her hair, not as yet more than half loosened for the night from its ballroom array, clustered, amid a shower of diamonds, round and round her classical head, in curls like those of the young hyacinth. A snowy-white and gauze-like drapery seemed to be nearly the sole covering to her delicate form; but the midsummer and midnight air was hot, sullen, and still, and no motion in the statue-like form itself, stirred even the folds of that raiment of very vapour which hung around it as the heavy marble hangs around the Niobe. Yet – strange to say! – her large lustrous eyes were not turned downwards upon that grave wherein her brightest hope lay buried – but riveted in a widely different direction! The prison of the Old Republic is, I think, the stateliest building in all Venice – but how could that lady gaze so fixedly upon it, when beneath her lay stifling her only child? Yon dark, gloomy niche, too, yawns right opposite her chamber window – what, then, *could* there be in its shadows – in its architecture – in its ivy-wreathed and solemn cornices – that the Marchesa di Mentoni had not wondered at a thousand times before? Nonsense! – Who does not remember that, at such a time as this, the eye, like a shattered mirror, multiplies the images of its sorrow, and sees in innumerable far-off places, the woe which is close at hand?

Many steps above the Marchesa, and within the arch of the water-gate, stood, in full dress, the Satyr-like figure of Mentoni himself. He was occasionally occupied in thrumming a guitar, and seemed *ennuyé* to the very death, as at intervals he gave directions for the recovery of his child. Stupefied and aghast, I had myself no power to move from the upright position I had assumed upon first hearing the shriek, and must have presented to the eyes of the agitated group a spectral and ominous appearance, as with pale countenance and rigid limbs, I floated down among them in that funereal gondola.

All efforts proved in vain. Many of the most energetic in the search were relaxing their exertions, and yielding to a gloomy sorrow. There seemed but little hope for the child; (how much less than for the mother!) but now, from the interior of that dark niche which has been already mentioned as forming a part of the Old Republican prison, and as fronting the lattice of the Marchesa, a figure muffled in a cloak, stepped out within reach of the light, and, pausing a moment upon the verge of the giddy descent, plunged headlong into the canal. As, in an instant afterwards, he stood with the still living and breathing child within his grasp, upon the marble flagstones by the side of the Marchesa, his cloak, heavy with the drenching water, became unfastened, and, falling in folds about his feet, discovered to the wonder-stricken spectators the graceful person of a very young man, with the sound of whose name the greater part of Europe was then ringing.

THE VISIONARY OR THE ASSIGNATION

No word spoke the deliverer. But the Marchesa! She will now receive her child – she will press it to her heart – she will cling to its little form, and smother it with her caresses. Alas! *another's* arms have taken it from the stranger – *another's* arms have taken it away, and borne it afar off, unnoticed, into the palace! And the Marchesa! Her lip – her beautiful lip trembles; tears are gathering in her eyes – those eyes which, like Pliny's acanthus, are 'soft and almost liquid'. Yes! tears are gathering in those eyes – and see! the entire woman thrills throughout the soul, and the statue has started into life! The pallor of the marble countenance, the swelling of the marble bosom, the very purity of the marble feet, we behold suddenly flushed over with a tide of ungovernable crimson; and a slight shudder quivers about her delicate frame, as a gentle air at Napoli about the rich silver lilies in the grass.

Why *should* that lady blush! To this demand there is no answer – except that, having left, in the eager haste and terror of a mother's heart, the privacy of her own boudoir, she has neglected to enthral her tiny feet in their slippers, and utterly forgotten to throw over her Venetian shoulders that drapery which is their due. What other possible reason could there have been for her so blushing? – for the glance of those wild appealing eyes? for the unusual tumult of that throbbing bosom? – for the convulsive pressure of that trembling hand? – that hand which fell, as Mentoni turned into the palace, accidentally, upon the hand of the stranger. What reason could there have been for the low – the singularly low tone of those unmeaning words which the lady uttered hurriedly in bidding him adieu? 'Thou hast conquered,' she said, or the murmurs of the water

27

deceived me; 'thou hast conquered – one hour after sunrise – we shall meet – so let it be!'

      *   *   *

The tumult had subsided, the lights had died away within the palace, and the stranger, whom I now recognised, stood alone upon the flags. He shook with inconceivable agitation, and his eye glanced around in search of a gondola. I could not do less than offer him the service of my own; and he accepted the civility. Having obtained an oar at the water-gate, we proceeded together to his residence, while he rapidly recovered his self-possession, and spoke of our former slight acquaintance in terms of great apparent cordiality.

There are some subjects upon which I take pleasure in being minute. The person of the stranger – let me call him by this title, who to all the world was still a stranger – the person of the stranger is one of these subjects. In height he might have been below rather than above the medium size: although there were moments of intense passion when his frame actually *expanded* and belied the assertion. The light, almost slender symmetry of his figure promised more of that ready activity which he evinced at the Bridge of Sighs, than of that Herculean strength which he has been known to wield without an effort, upon occasions of more dangerous emergency. With the mouth and chin of a deity – singular, wild, full, liquid eyes, whose shadows varied from pure hazel to intense and brilliant jet – and a profusion of curling, black hair, from which a forehead of unusual breadth gleamed forth at intervals all light and ivory – his were features than which I have seen none more classically regular, except, perhaps, the marble ones of the Emperor Commodus.

Yet his countenance was, nevertheless, one of those which all men have seen at some period of their lives, and have never afterwards seen again. It had no peculiar – it had no settled predominant expression to be fastened upon the memory; a countenance seen and instantly forgotten – but forgotten with a vague and never-ceasing desire of recalling it to mind. Not that the spirit of each rapid passion failed, at any time, to throw its own distinct image upon the mirror of that face – but that the mirror, mirror-like, retained no vestige of the passion, when the passion had departed.

Upon leaving him on the night of our adventure, he solicited me, in what I thought an urgent manner, to call upon him *very* early the next morning. Shortly after sunrise, I found myself accordingly at his Palazzo, one of those huge structures of gloomy, yet fantastic pomp, which tower above the waters of the Grand Canal in the vicinity of the Rialto. I was shown up a broad winding staircase of mosaics, into an apartment whose unparalleled splendour burst through the opening door with an actual glare, making me blind and dizzy with luxuriousness.

I knew my acquaintance to be wealthy. Report had spoken of his possessions in terms which I had even ventured to call terms of ridiculous exaggeration. But as I gazed about me, I could not bring myself to believe that the wealth of any subject in Europe could have supplied the princely magnificence which burned and blazed around.

Although, as I say, the sun had arisen, yet the room was still brilliantly lighted up. I judge from this circumstance, as well as from an air of exhaustion in the countenance of my friend, that he had not retired to bed during the whole of the preceding night. In the architecture and embellishments of the chamber, the evident design had been to dazzle and astound. Little attention had been paid to the *decora* of what is technically called *keeping*, or to the proprieties of nationality. The eye wandered from object to object, and rested upon none – neither the *grotesques* of the Greek painters, nor the sculptures of the best Italian days, nor the huge carvings of untutored Egypt. Rich draperies in every part of the room trembled to the vibration of low, melancholy music, whose origin was not to be discovered. The senses were oppressed by mingled and conflicting perfumes, reeking up from strange convolute censers, together with multitudinous flaring and flickering tongues of emerald and violet fire. The rays of the newly risen sun poured in upon the whole, through windows, formed each of a single pane of crimson-tinted glass. Glancing to and fro, in a thousand reflections, from curtains which rolled from their cornices like cataracts of molten silver, the beams of natural glory mingled at length fitfully with the artificial light, and lay weltering in subdued masses upon a carpet of rich, liquid-looking cloth of Chili gold.

'Ha! ha! ha! – ha! ha! ha!' – laughed the proprietor, motioning me to a seat as I entered the room, and throwing himself back at full-length upon an ottoman. 'I see,' said he, perceiving that I could not immediately reconcile myself to the *bienséance* of so singular a welcome – 'I see you are astonished at my apartment – at my statues – my pictures – my originality of conception in architecture and upholstery! absolutely drunk, eh, with my magnificence? But pardon me, my dear sir (here his tone of voice dropped to the very spirit of cordiality); pardon me for my uncharitable laughter.

You appeared so *utterly* astonished. Besides, some things are so completely ludicrous, that a man *must* laugh or die. To die laughing must be the most glorious of all glorious deaths! Sir Thomas More – a very fine man was Sir Thomas More – Sir Thomas More died laughing, you remember. Also in the *Absurdities* of Ravisius Textor, there is a long list of characters who came to the same magnificent end. Do you know, however,' continued he musingly, 'that at Sparta (which is now Palaeochori), at Sparta, I say, to the west of the citadel, among a chaos of scarcely visible ruins, is a kind of *socle*, upon which are still legible the letters ΛΑΞΜ. They are undoubtedly part of ΓΕΛΑΞΜΑ. Now, at Sparta were a thousand temples and shrines to a thousand different divinities. How exceedingly strange that the altar of Laughter should have survived all the others! But in the present instance,' he resumed, with a singular alteration of voice and manner, 'I have no right to be merry at your expense. You might well have been amazed. Europe cannot produce anything so fine as this, my little regal cabinet. My other apartments are by no means of the same order – mere *ultras* of fashionable insipidity. This is better than fashion – is it not? Yet this has but to be seen to become the rage – that is, with those who could afford it at the cost of their entire patrimony. I have guarded, however, against any such profanation. With one exception, you are the only human being besides myself and my *valet*, who has been admitted within the mysteries of these imperial precincts, since they have been bedizened as you see!'

I bowed in acknowledgement – for the overpowering sense of splendour and perfume, and music, together with the unexpected eccentricity of his address and manner, prevented me from expressing, in words, my appreciation of what I might have construed into a compliment.

'Here,' he resumed, arising and leaning on my arm as he sauntered around the apartment, 'here are paintings from the Greeks to Cimabue, and from Cimabue to the present hour. Many are chosen, as you see, with little deference to the opinions of Virtu. They are all, however, fitting tapestry for a chamber such as this. Here, too, are some *chefs d'oeuvre* of the unknown great; and here, unfinished designs by men, celebrated in their day, whose very names the perspicacity of the academies has left to silence and to me. What think you,' said he, turning abruptly as he spoke – 'what think you of this Madonna della Pietà?'

'It is Guido's own!' I said, with all the enthusiasm of my nature, for I had been poring intently over its surpassing loveliness. 'It is Guido's own! – how *could* you have obtained it? – she is undoubtedly in painting what the Venus is in sculpture.'

'Ha!' said he thoughtfully, 'the Venus – the beautiful Venus? – the Venus of the Medici? – she of the diminutive head and the gilded hair? Part of the left arm' (here his voice dropped so as to be heard with difficulty) 'and all the right are restorations; and in the coquetry of that right arm lies, I think, the quintessence of all affectation. Give *me* the Canova! The Apollo, too, is a copy – there can be no doubt of it – blind fool that I am, who cannot behold the boasted inspiration of the Apollo! I cannot help – pity me! – I cannot help preferring the Antinous. Was it not Socrates who said that the statuary found his statue in the block of marble? Then Michael Angelo was by no means original in his couplet:

32

Non ha l'ottimo artista alcun concetto
Che un marmo solo in se non circunscriva.'

It has been, or should be remarked, that, in the manner of the true gentleman, we are always aware of a difference from the bearing of the vulgar, without being at once precisely able to determine in what such difference consists. Allowing the remark to have applied in its full force to the outward demeanour of my acquaintance, I felt it, on that eventful morning, still more fully applicable to his moral temperament and character. Nor can I better define that peculiarity of spirit which seemed to place him so essentially apart from all other human beings, than by calling it a *habit* of intense and continual thought, pervading even his most trivial actions – intruding upon his moments of dalliance – and interweaving itself with his very flashes of merriment – like adders which writhe from out the eyes of the grinning masks in the cornices around the temples of Persepolis.

I could not help, however, repeatedly observing, through the mingled tone of levity and solemnity with which he rapidly descanted upon matters of little importance, a certain air of trepidation – a degree of nervous *unction* in action and in speech – an unquiet excitability of manner which appeared to me at all times unaccountable, and upon some occasions even filled me with alarm. Frequently, too, pausing in the middle of a sentence whose commencement he had apparently forgotten, he seemed to be listening in the deepest attention, as if either in momentary expectation of a visitor, or to sounds which must have had existence in his imagination alone.

It was during one of these reveries or pauses of

apparent abstraction, that, in turning over a page of
the poet and scholar Politian's beautiful tragedy *The
Orfeo* (the first native Italian tragedy), which lay near
me upon an ottoman, I discovered a passage under-
lined in pencil. It was a passage towards the end of
the third act – a passage of the most heart-stirring
excitement – a passage which, although tainted with
impurity, no man shall read without a thrill of novel
emotion – no woman without a sigh. The whole page
was blotted with fresh tears; and, upon the opposite
interleaf, were the following English lines, written in
a hand so very different from the peculiar characters
of my acquaintance, that I had some difficulty in
recognising it as his own:

Thou wast that all to me, love,
  For which my soul did pine –
A green isle in the sea, love,
  A fountain and a shrine,
All wreathed with fairy fruits and flowers;
  And all the flowers were mine.

Ah, dream too bright to last!
  Ah, starry Hope, that didst arise
But to be overcast!
  A voice from out the Future cries,
'Onward!' – but o'er the Past
  (Dim gulf!) my spirit hovering lies,
Mute – motionless – aghast!

For alas! alas! with me
  The light of life is o'er.
No more – no more – no more
  (Such language holds the solemn sea
To the sands upon the shore),

Shall bloom the thunder-blasted tree,
　Or the stricken eagle soar!

Now all my hours are trances;
　And all my nightly dreams
Are where the dark eye glances,
　And where thy footstep gleams
In what ethereal dances,
　By what Italian streams.

Alas! for that accursed time
　They bore thee o'er the billow,
From Love to titled age and crime,
　And an unholy pillow! –
From me, and from our misty clime,
　Where weeps the silver willow!

That these lines were written in English – a language
with which I had not believed their author acquainted
– afforded me little matter for surprise. I was too well
aware of the extent of his acquirements, and of the
singular pleasure he took in concealing them from
observation, to be astonished at any similar discovery;
but the place of date, I must confess, occasioned me
no little amazement. It had been originally written
London, and afterwards carefully overscored – not,
however, so effectually as to conceal the word from a
scrutinising eye. I say, this occasioned me no little
amazement; for I well remember that, in a former
conversation with a friend, I particularly enquired if
he had at any time met in London the Marchesa di
Mentoni (who for some years previous to her marriage
had resided in that city), when his answer, if I mistake
not, gave me to understand that he had never visited
the metropolis of Great Britain. I might as well here

mention, that I have more than once heard (without, of course, giving credit to a report involving so many improbabilities), that the person of whom I speak, was not only by birth, but in education, an *Englishman*.

* * *

'There is one painting,' said he, without being aware of my notice of the tragedy – 'there is still one painting which you have not seen.' And throwing aside a drapery, he discovered a full-length portrait of the Marchesa Aphrodite.

Human art could have done no more in the delineation of her superhuman beauty. The same ethereal figure which stood before me the preceding night upon the steps of the Ducal Palace, stood before me once again. But in the expression of the countenance, which was beaming all over with smiles, there still lurked (incomprehensible anomaly!) that fitful stain of melancholy which will ever be found inseparable from the perfection of the beautiful. Her right arm lay folded over her bosom. With her left she pointed downward to a curiously fashioned vase. One small, fairy foot, alone visible, barely touched the earth; and, scarcely discernible in the brilliant atmosphere which seemed to encircle and enshrine her loveliness, floated a pair of the most delicately imagined wings. My glance fell from the painting to the figure of my friend, and the vigorous words of Chapman's *Bussy D'Ambois* quivered instinctively upon my lips:

> He is up
> There like a Roman statue! He will stand
> Till Death hath made him marble!

'Come,' he said at length, turning towards a table

of richly enamelled and massive silver, upon which were a few goblets fantastically stained, together with two large Etruscan vases, fashioned in the same extraordinary model as that in the foreground of the portrait, and filled with what I supposed to be Johannisberger. 'Come,' he said, abruptly, 'let us drink! It is early – but let us drink. It is *indeed* early,' he continued, musingly, as a cherub with a heavy golden hammer made the apartment ring with the first hour after sunrise: 'It is *indeed* early – but what matters it? let us drink! Let us pour out an offering to yon solemn sun which these gaudy lamps and censers are so eager to subdue!' And, having made me pledge him in a bumper, he swallowed in rapid succession several goblets of the wine.

'To dream,' he continued, resuming the tone of his desultory conversation, as he held up to the rich light of a censer one of the magnificent vases – 'to dream has been the business of my life. I have therefore framed for myself, as you see, a bower of dreams. In the heart of Venice could I have erected a better? You behold around you, it is true, a medley of architectural embellishments. The chastity of Ionia is offended by antediluvian devices, and the sphinxes of Egypt are outstretched upon carpets of gold. Yet the effect is incongruous to the timid alone. Proprieties of place, and especially of time, are the bugbears which terrify mankind from the contemplation of the magnificent. Once I was myself a decorist; but that sublimation of folly has palled upon my soul. All this is now the fitter for my purpose. Like these arabesque censers, my spirit is writhing in fire, and the delirium of this scene is fashioning me for the wilder visions of that land of real dreams whither I am now rapidly departing.' He here paused abruptly, bent his head to his bosom, and seemed to listen to a sound which I could not hear. At length, erecting his frame, he looked upwards, and ejaculated the lines of the Bishop of Chichester:

> 'Stay for me there! I will not fail
> To meet thee in that hollow vale.'

In the next instant, confessing the power of the wine, he threw himself at full length upon an ottoman.

A quick step was now heard upon the staircase, and a loud knock at the door rapidly succeeded. I was hastening to anticipate a second disturbance, when a page of Mentoni's household burst into the room, and faltered out, in a voice choking with emotion, the incoherent words, 'My mistress! – my mistress! – Poisoned! – poisoned! Oh, beautiful – oh, beautiful Aphrodite!'

Bewildered, I flew to the ottoman, and endeavoured to arouse the sleeper to a sense of the startling intelligence. But his limbs were rigid – his lips were livid – his lately beaming eyes were riveted in *death*. I staggered back towards the table – my hand fell upon a cracked and blackened goblet – and a consciousness of the entire and terrible truth flashed suddenly over my soul.

Morella

Αυτο χαθ' αυτο μεθ' αυτου, μουο ειδες αιει ου.

Itself, by itself, solely, one everlasting, and single.

PLATO, *Symposium*

With a feeling of deep yet most singular affection I regarded my friend Morella. Thrown by accident into her society many years ago, my soul from our first meeting, burned with fires it had never before known; but the fires were not of Eros, and bitter and tormenting to my spirit was the gradual conviction that I could in no manner define their unusual meaning or regulate their vague intensity. Yet we met; and fate bound us together at the altar, and I never spoke of passion nor thought of love. She, however, shunned society, and, attaching herself to me alone, rendered me happy. It is a happiness to wonder; it is a happiness to dream.

Morella's erudition was profound. As I hope to live, her talents were of no common order – her powers of mind were gigantic. I felt this, and, in many matters, became her pupil. I soon, however, found that, perhaps on account of her Pressburg education, she placed before me a number of those mystical writings which are usually considered the mere dross of the early German literature. These, for what reason I could not imagine, were her favourite and constant study – and that in process of time they became my own, should be attributed to the simple but effectual influence of habit and example.

39

In all this, if I err not, my reason had little to do. My convictions, or I forget myself, were in no manner acted upon by the ideal, nor was any tincture of the mysticism which I read to be discovered, unless I am greatly mistaken, either in my deeds or in my thoughts. Persuaded of this, I abandoned myself implicitly to the guidance of my wife, and entered with an unflinching heart into the intricacies of her studies. And then – then, when poring over forbidden pages, I felt a forbidden spirit enkindling within me – would Morella place her cold hand upon my own, and rake up from the ashes of a dead philosophy some low, singular words, whose strange meaning burned themselves in upon my memory. And then, hour after hour, would I linger by her side, and dwell upon the music of her voice, until at length its melody was tainted with terror, and there fell a shadow upon my soul, and I grew pale, and shuddered inwardly at those too unearthly tones. And thus, joy suddenly faded into horror, and the most beautiful became the most hideous, as Hinnôm became Gehenna.

It is unnecessary to state the exact character of those disquisitions which, growing out of the volumes I have mentioned, formed, for so long a time, almost the sole conversation of Morella and myself. By the learned in what might be termed theological morality they will be readily conceived, and by the unlearned they would, at all events, be little understood. The wild Pantheism of Fichte; the modified Paliggenedia of the Pythagoreans; and, above all, the doctrines of Identity as urged by Schelling, were generally the points of discussion presenting the most of beauty to the imaginative Morella. That identity which is termed personal, Mr Locke, I think, truly defines to consist in the saneness of rational being. And since by person we understand an intelligent essence having reason, and since there is a consciousness which always accompanies thinking, it is this which makes us all to be that which we call *ourselves*, thereby distinguishing us from other beings that think, and giving us our personal identity. But the *principium individuationis*, the notion of that identity *which at death is or is not lost for ever*, was to me, at all times, a consideration of intense interest; not more from the perplexing and exciting nature of its consequences, than from the marked and agitated manner in which Morella mentioned them.

But, indeed, the time had now arrived when the mystery of my wife's manner oppressed me as a spell. I could no longer bear the touch of her wan fingers, nor the low tone of her musical language, nor the lustre of her melancholy eyes. And she knew all this, but did not upbraid; she seemed conscious of my weakness or my folly, and, smiling, called it fate. She seemed also conscious of a cause, to me unknown, for the gradual alienation of my regard; but she gave me no hint or token of its nature. Yet was she woman, and pined away daily. In time the crimson spot settled steadily upon the cheek, and the blue veins upon the pale forehead became prominent; and one instant my nature melted into pity, but, in the next, I met the glance of her meaning eyes, and then my soul sickened and became giddy with the giddiness of one who gazes downward into some dreary and unfathomable abyss.

Shall I then say that I longed with an earnest and consuming desire for the moment of Morella's decease? I did; but the fragile spirit clung to its tenement of clay for many days, for many weeks and irksome months, until my tortured nerves obtained the mastery over my mind, and I grew furious through delay, and, with the heart of a fiend, cursed the days and the hours and the bitter moments, which seemed to lengthen and lengthen as her gentle life declined, like shadows in the dying of the day.

But one autumnal evening, when the winds lay still in heaven, Morella called me to her bedside. There was a dim mist over all the earth, and a warm glow upon the waters, and amid the rich October leaves of the forest, a rainbow from the firmament had surely fallen.

'It is a day of days,' she said, as I approached; 'a day of all days either to live or die. It is a fair day for the sons of earth and life – ah, more fair for the daughters of heaven and death!'

I kissed her forehead, and she continued: 'I am dying, yet shall I live.'

'Morella!'

'The days have never been when thou couldst love me – but her whom in life thou didst abhor, in death thou shalt adore.'

'Morella!'

'I repeat that I am dying. But within me is a pledge of that affection – ah, how little! – which thou didst feel for me, Morella. And when my spirit departs shall the child live – thy child and mine, Morella's. But thy days shall be days of sorrow – that sorrow which is the most lasting of impressions, as the cypress is the most enduring of trees. For the hours of thy happiness are over and joy is not gathered twice in a life, as the roses of Paestum twice in a year. Thou shalt no longer, then, play the Teian with time, but, being ignorant of the myrtle and the vine, thou shalt bear about with thee thy shroud on the earth, as do the Moslemin at Mecca.'

'Morella!' I cried, 'Morella! how knowest thou

this?' but she turned away her face upon the pillow and a slight tremor coming over her limbs, she thus died, and I heard her voice no more.

Yet, as she had foretold, her child, to which in dying she had given birth, which breathed not until the mother breathed no more, her child, a daughter, lived. And she grew strangely in stature and intellect, and was the perfect resemblance of her who had departed, and I loved her with a love more fervent than I had believed it possible to feel for any denizen of earth.

But, ere long, the heaven of this pure affection became darkened, and gloom, and horror, and grief, swept over it in clouds. I said the child grew strangely in stature and intelligence. Strange, indeed, was her rapid increase in bodily size, but terrible, oh! terrible were the tumultuous thoughts which crowded upon me while watching the development of her mental being. Could it be otherwise, when I daily discovered in the conceptions of the child the adult powers and faculties of the woman? when the lessons of experience fell from the lips of infancy? and when the wisdom or the passions of maturity I found hourly gleaming from its full and speculative eye? When, I say, all this became evident to my appalled senses, when I could no longer hide it from my soul, nor throw it off from those perceptions which trembled to receive it, is it to be wondered at that suspicions, of a nature fearful and exciting, crept in upon my spirit, or that my thoughts fell back aghast upon the wild tales and thrilling theories of the entombed Morella? I snatched from the scrutiny of the world a being whom destiny compelled me to adore, and in the rigorous seclusion of my home, watched with an agonising anxiety over all which concerned the beloved.

And as years rolled away, and I gazed day after day upon her holy, and mild, and eloquent face, and pored over her maturing form, day after day did I discover new points of resemblance in the child to her mother, the melancholy and the dead. And hourly grew darker these shadows of similitude, and more full, and more definite, and more perplexing, and more hideously terrible in their aspect. For that her smile was like her mother's I could bear – but then I shuddered at its too perfect identity; that her eyes were like Morella's I could endure – but then they, too, often looked down into the depths of my soul with Morella's own intense and bewildering meaning. And in the contour of the high forehead, and in the ringlets of the silken hair, and in the wan fingers which buried themselves therein, and in the sad musical tones of her speech, and above all – oh, above all, in the phrases and expressions of the dead on the lips of the loved and the living, I found food for consuming thought and horror, for a worm that would not die.

Thus passed away two lustra of her life, and as yet my daughter remained nameless upon the earth. 'My child', and 'my love', were the designations usually prompted by a father's affection, and the rigid seclusion of her days precluded all other intercourse. Morella's name died with her at her death. Of the mother I had never spoken to the daughter; it was impossible to speak. Indeed, during the brief period of her existence, the latter had received no impressions from the outward world, save such as might have been afforded by the narrow limits of her privacy. But at length the ceremony of baptism presented to my mind, in its unnerved and agitated condition, a present deliverance from the terrors of my destiny.

And at the baptismal font I hesitated for a name. And many titles of the wise and beautiful, of old and modern times, of my own and foreign lands, came thronging to my lips, with many, many fair titles of the gentle, and the happy, and the good. What prompted me then to disturb the memory of the buried dead? What demon urged me to breathe that sound, which in its very recollection was wont to make ebb the purple blood in torrents from the temples to the heart? What fiend spoke from the recesses of my soul, when amid those dim aisles, and in the silence of the night, I whispered within the ears of the holy man the syllables – Morella? What more than fiend convulsed the features of my child, and overspread them with hues of death, as starting at that scarcely audible sound, she turned her glassy eyes from the earth to heaven, and falling prostrate on the black slabs of our ancestral vault, responded – 'I am here!'

Distinct, coldly, calmly distinct, fell those few simple sounds within my ear, and thence like molten lead rolled hissingly into my brain. Years – years may pass away, but the memory of that epoch never. Nor was I indeed ignorant of the flowers and the vine – but the hemlock and the cypress overshadowed me night and day. And I kept no reckoning of time or place, and the stars of my fate faded from heaven, and therefore the earth grew dark, and its figures passed by me like flitting shadows, and among them all I beheld only – Morella. The winds of the firmament breathed but one sound within my ears, and the ripples upon the sea murmured evermore – Morella. But she died; and with my own hands I bore her to the tomb; and I laughed with a long and bitter laugh as I found no traces of the first in the channel where I laid the second Morella.

King Pest

A TALE CONTAINING AN ALLEGORY

The gods do bear and will allow in kings
The things which they abhor in rascal routes.
BUCKHURST, *Tragedy of Ferrex and Porrex*

About twelve o'clock, one night in the month of
October, and during the chivalrous reign of the third
Edward, two seamen belonging to the crew of the
'Free and Easy', a trading schooner plying between
Sluys and the Thames, and then at anchor in that
river, were much astonished to find themselves seated
in the taproom of an alehouse in the parish of St
Andrews, London – which alehouse bore for sign the
portraiture of a 'Jolly Tar'.

The room, although ill-contrived, smoke-blackened,
low-pitched, and in every other respect agreeing with
the general character of such places at the period – was,
nevertheless, in the opinion of the grotesque groups
scattered here and there within it, sufficiently well
adapted to its purpose.

Of these groups our two seamen formed, I think,
the most interesting, if not the most conspicuous.

The one who appeared to be the elder, and whom his
companion addressed by the characteristic appellation
of 'Legs', was at the same time much the taller of the
two. He might have measured six feet and a half, and
an habitual stoop in the shoulders seemed to have
been the necessary consequence of an altitude so
enormous. Superfluities in height were, however,

more than accounted for by deficiencies in other respects. He was exceedingly thin; and might, as his associates asserted, have answered, when drunk, for a pennant at the masthead, or, when sober, have served for a jib-boom. But these jests, and others of a similar nature, had evidently produced, at no time, any effect upon the cachinnatory muscles of the tar. With high cheek-bones, a large hawk-nose, retreating chin, fallen under-jaw, and huge protruding white eyes, the expression of his countenance, although tinged with a species of dogged indifference to matters and things in general, was not the less utterly solemn and serious beyond all attempts at imitation or description.

The younger seaman was, in all outward appearance, the converse of his companion. His stature could not have exceeded four feet. A pair of stumpy bow-legs supported his squat, unwieldy figure, while his unusually short and thick arms, with no ordinary fists at their extremities, swung off dangling from his sides like the fins of a sea-turtle. Small eyes, of no particular colour, twinkled far back in his head. His nose remained buried in the mass of flesh which enveloped his round, full, and purple face; and his thick upper-lip rested upon the still thicker one beneath with an air of complacent self-satisfaction, much heightened by the owner's habit of licking them at intervals. He evidently regarded his tall shipmate with a feeling half-wondrous, half-quizzical; and stared up occasionally in his face as the red setting sun stares up at the crags of Ben Nevis.

Various and eventful, however, had been the peregrinations of the worthy couple in and about the different tap-houses of the neighbourhood during the earlier hours of the night. Funds even the most ample, are not always everlasting: and it was with empty pockets our friends had ventured upon the present hostelry.

At the precise period, then, when this history properly commences, Legs, and his fellow Hugh Tarpaulin, sat, each with both elbows resting upon the large oaken table in the middle of the floor, and with a hand upon either cheek. They were eyeing, from behind a huge flagon of unpaid-for 'humming-stuff', the portentous words, 'No Chalk', which to their indignation and astonishment were scored over the doorway by means of that very mineral whose presence they purported to deny. Not that the gift of deciphering written characters – a gift among the commonality of that day considered little less cabbalistical than the art of indicting – could, in strict justice, have been laid to the charge of either disciple of the sea; but there was, to say the truth, a certain twist in the formation of the letters – an indescribable lee-lurch about the whole – which foreboded, in the opinion of both seamen, a long run of dirty weather; and determined them at once, in the allegorical words of Legs himself, to 'pump ship, clew up all sail, and scud before the wind'.

Having accordingly disposed of what remained of the ale, and looped up the points of their short doublets, they finally made a bolt for the street. Although Tarpaulin rolled twice into the fireplace, mistaking it for the door, yet their escape was at length happily effected – and half after twelve o'clock found our heroes ripe for mischief, and running for life down a dark alley in the direction of St Andrew's Stair, hotly pursued by the landlady of the 'Jolly Tar'.

At the epoch of this eventful tale, and periodically,

for many years before and after, all England, but more especially the metropolis, resounded with the fearful cry of 'Plague!' The city was in a great measure depopulated – and in those horrible regions, in the vicinity of the Thames, where amid the dark, narrow, and filthy lanes and alleys, the Demon of Disease was supposed to have had his nativity, Awe, Terror, and Superstition were alone to be found stalking abroad.

By authority of the king such districts were placed under ban, and all persons forbidden, under pain of death, to intrude upon their dismal solitude. Yet neither the mandate of the monarch, nor the huge barriers erected at the entrances of the streets, nor the prospect of that loathsome death which, with almost absolute certainty, overwhelmed the wretch whom no peril could deter from the adventure, prevented the unfurnished and untenanted dwellings from being stripped, by the hand of nightly rapine, of every article, such as iron, brass, or lead-work, which could in any manner be turned to a profitable account.

Above all, it was usually found, upon the annual winter opening of the barriers, that locks, bolts, and secret cellars had proved but slender protection to those rich stores of wines and liquors which, in consideration of the risk and trouble of removal, many of the numerous dealers having shops in the neighbourhood had consented to trust, during the period of exile, to so insufficient a security.

But there were very few of the terror-stricken people who attributed these doings to the agency of human hands. Pest-spirits, plague-goblins, and fever-demons were the popular imps of mischief; and tales so blood-chilling were hourly told, that the whole mass of forbidden buildings was, at length, enveloped in terror as in a shroud, and the plunderer himself was often scared away by the horrors his own depredations had created; leaving the entire vast circuit of prohibited district to gloom, silence, pestilence, and death.

It was by one of the terrific barriers already mentioned, and which indicated the region beyond to be under the Pest-ban, that, in scrambling down an alley, Legs and the worthy Hugh Tarpaulin found their progress suddenly impeded. To return was out of the question, and no time was to be lost, as their pursuers were close upon their heels. With thoroughbred seamen to clamber up the roughly fashioned plank-work was a trifle; and, maddened with the twofold excitement of exercise and liquor, they leaped unhesitatingly down within the enclosure, and holding on their drunken course with shouts and yellings, were soon bewildered in its noisome and intricate recesses.

Had they not, indeed, been intoxicated beyond moral sense, their reeling footsteps must have been palsied by the horrors of their situation. The air was cold and misty. The paving-stones, loosened from their beds, lay in wild disorder amid the tall, rank grass, which sprang up around the feet and ankles. Fallen houses choked up the streets. The most fetid and poisonous smells everywhere prevailed – and by the aid of that ghastly light which, even at midnight, never fails to emanate from a vapoury and pestilential atmosphere, might be discerned lying in the by-paths and alleys, or rotting in the windowless habitations, the carcass of many a nocturnal plunderer arrested by the hand of the plague in the very perpetration of his robbery.

But it lay not in the power of images, or sensations, or impediments such as these, to stay the course of men who, naturally brave, and at that time especially, brimful of courage and of 'humming-stuff', would have reeled, as straight as their condition might have permitted, undauntedly into the very jaws of Death. Onward – still onward stalked the grim Legs, making the desolate solemnity echo and re-echo with yells like the terrific war-whoop of the Indian; and onward, still onward rolled the dumpy Tarpaulin, hanging on to the doublet of his more active companion, and far surpassing the latter's most strenuous exertions in the way of vocal music, by bull-roarings in basso, from the profundity of his stentorian lungs.

They had now evidently reached the stronghold of the pestilence. Their way at every step or plunge grew more noisome and more horrible – the paths more narrow and more intricate. Huge stones and beams falling momently from the decaying roofs above them, gave evidence, by their sullen and heavy descent, of the vast height of the surrounding houses; and while actual exertion became necessary to force a passage through frequent heaps of rubbish, it was by no means seldom that the hand fell upon a skeleton or rested upon a more fleshly corpse.

Suddenly, as the seamen stumbled against the entrance of a tall and ghastly-looking building, a yell more than usually shrill from the throat of the excited Legs, was replied to from within, in a rapid succession of wild, laughter-like, and fiendish shrieks. Nothing daunted at sounds which, of such a nature, at such a time, and in such a place, might have curdled the very blood in hearts less irrevocably on fire, the drunken couple rushed headlong against the door, burst it open, and staggered into the midst of things with a volley of curses.

The room within which they found themselves proved to be the shop of an undertaker; but an open trap-door, in a corner of the floor near the entrance, looked down upon a long range of wine-cellars, whose depths the occasional sound of bursting bottles proclaimed to be well stored with their appropriate contents. In the middle of the room stood a table – in the centre of which again arose a huge tub of what appeared to be punch. Bottles of various wines and cordials, together with jugs, pitchers, and flagons of every shape and quality, were scattered profusely upon the board. Around it, upon coffin-trestles, was seated a company of six. This company I will endeavour to delineate one by one.

Fronting the entrance, and elevated a little above his companions, sat a personage who appeared to be the president of the table. His stature was gaunt and tall, and Legs was confounded to behold in him a figure more emaciated than himself. His face was as yellow as saffron – but no feature, excepting one alone, was sufficiently marked to merit a particular description. This one consisted in a forehead so unusually and hideously lofty, as to have the appearance of a bonnet or crown of flesh superadded upon the natural head. His mouth was puckered and dimpled into an expression of ghastly affability, and his eyes, as indeed the eyes of all at table, were glazed over with the fumes of intoxication. This gentleman was clothed from head to foot in a richly embroidered black silk-velvet pall, wrapped negligently around his form after the fashion of a Spanish cloak. His head was stuck full of sable hearse-plumes, which he nodded to and fro with a jaunty and knowing air; and, in his right hand, he held a huge human thigh-bone, with which he appeared to have been just knocking down some member of the company for a song.

Opposite him, and with her back to the door, was a lady of no whit the less extraordinary character. Although quite as tall as the person just described, she had no right to complain of his unnatural emaciation. She was evidently in the last stage of a dropsy; and her figure resembled nearly that of the huge puncheon of October beer which stood, with the head driven in, close by her side, in a corner of the chamber. Her face was exceedingly round, red, and full; and the same peculiarity, or rather want of peculiarity, attached itself to her countenance, which I before mentioned in the case of the president – that is to say, only one feature of her face was sufficiently distinguished to need a separate characterisation: indeed the acute Tarpaulin immediately observed that the same remark might have applied to each individual person of the party; every one of whom seemed to possess a monopoly of some particular portion of physiognomy. With the lady in question this portion proved to be the mouth. Commencing at the right ear, it swept with a terrific chasm to the left – the short pendants which she wore in either auricle continually bobbing into the aperture. She made, however, every exertion to keep her mouth closed and look dignified, in a dress consisting of a newly starched and ironed shroud coming up close under her chin, with a crimpled ruffle of cambric muslin.

At her right hand sat a diminutive young lady whom she appeared to patronise. This delicate little creature, in the trembling of her wasted fingers, in the livid hue of her lips, and in the slight hectic spot which tinged her otherwise leaden complexion, gave evident indications of a galloping consumption. An air of extreme *haut ton*, however, pervaded her whole appearance; she wore in a graceful and *dégagé* manner, a large and beautiful winding-sheet of the finest India lawn; her hair hung in ringlets over her neck; a soft smile played about her mouth; but her nose, extremely long, thin, sinuous, flexible and pimpled, hung down far below her under-lip, and in spite of the delicate manner in which she now and then moved it to one side or the other with her tongue, gave to her countenance a somewhat equivocal expression.

Over against her, and upon the left of the dropsical lady, was seated a little puffy, wheezing, and gouty old man, whose cheeks reposed upon the shoulders of their owner, like two huge bladders of Oporto wine. With his arms folded, and with one bandaged leg deposited upon the table, he seemed to think himself entitled to some consideration. He evidently prided himself much upon every inch of his personal appearance, but took more especial delight in calling attention to his gaudy-coloured surtout. This, to say the truth, must have cost him no little money, and was made to fit him exceedingly well – being fashioned from one of the curiously embroidered silken covers appertaining to those glorious escutcheons which, in England and elsewhere, are customarily hung up, in some conspicuous place, upon the dwellings of departed aristocracy.

Next to him, and at the right hand of the president, was a gentleman in long white hose and cotton drawers. His frame shook, in a ridiculous manner, with a fit of what Tarpaulin called 'the horrors'. His jaws, which had been newly shaved, were tightly tied up by a bandage of muslin; and his arms being fastened in a similar way at the wrists, prevented him from helping himself too freely to the liquors upon the table; a precaution rendered necessary, in the opinion of Legs, by the peculiarly sottish and wine-bibbing cast of his visage. A pair of prodigious ears, nevertheless, which it was no doubt found impossible to confine, towered away into the atmosphere of the apartment, and were occasionally pricked up in a spasm, at the sound of the drawing of a cork.

Fronting him, sixthly and lastly, was situated a singularly stiff-looking personage, who, being afflicted with paralysis, must, to speak seriously, have felt very ill at ease in his unaccommodating habiliments. He was habited, somewhat uniquely, in a new and handsome mahogany coffin. Its top or head-piece pressed upon the skull of the wearer, and extended over it in the fashion of a hood, giving to the entire face an air of indescribable interest. Armholes had been cut in the sides, for the sake not more of elegance than of convenience; but the dress, nevertheless, prevented its proprietor from sitting as erect as his associates; and as he lay reclining against his trestle, at an angle of forty-five degrees, a pair of huge goggle eyes rolled up their awful whites towards the ceiling in absolute amazement at their own enormity.

Before each of the party lay a portion of a skull, which was used as a drinking cup. Overhead was suspended a human skeleton, by means of a rope tied round one of the legs and fastened to a ring in the ceiling. The other limb, confined by no such fetter, stuck off from the body at right angles, causing the whole loose and rattling frame to dangle and twirl about at the caprice of every occasional puff of wind which found its way into the apartment. In the cranium of this hideous thing lay a quantity of ignited charcoal, which threw a fitful but vivid light over the entire scene; while coffins, and other wares appertaining to the shop of an undertaker, were piled high up around the room, and against the windows, preventing any ray from escaping into the street.

At sight of this extraordinary assembly, and of their still more extraordinary paraphernalia, our two seamen did not conduct themselves with that degree of decorum which might have been expected. Legs, leaning against the wall near which he happened to be standing, dropped his lower jaw still lower than usual, and spread open his eyes to their fullest extent; while Hugh Tarpaulin, stooping down so as to bring his nose upon a level with the table, and spreading out a palm upon either knee, burst into a long, loud, and obstreperous roar of very ill-timed and immoderate laughter.

Without, however, taking offence at behaviour so excessively rude, the tall president smiled very graciously upon the intruders – nodded to them in a dignified manner with his head of sable plumes – and, arising, took each by an arm, and led him to a seat which some others of the company had placed in the meantime for his accommodation. Legs to all this offered not the slightest resistance, but sat down as he was directed; while the gallant Hugh, removing his coffin trestle from its station near the head of the table, to the vicinity of the little consumptive lady in the winding sheet, plumped down by her side in high glee, and pouring out a skull of red wine, quaffed it to their better acquaintance. But at this presumption the stiff gentleman in the coffin seemed exceedingly nettled; and serious consequences might have ensued, had not the president, rapping upon the table with his truncheon, diverted the attention of all present to the following speech: 'It becomes our duty upon the present happy occasion – '

'Avast there!' interrupted Legs, looking very serious, 'avast there a bit, I say, and tell us who the devil ye all are, and what business ye have here, rigged off like the foul fiends, and swilling the snug blue ruin stowed away for the winter by my honest shipmate, Will Wimble the undertaker!'

At this unpardonable piece of ill-breeding, all the original company half started to their feet, and uttered the same rapid succession of wild fiendish shrieks which had before caught the attention of the seamen. The president, however, was the first to recover his composure, and at length, turning to Legs with great dignity, recommended: 'Most willingly will we gratify any reasonable curiosity on the part of guests so illustrious, unbidden though they be. Know then that in these dominions I am monarch, and here rule with undivided empire under the title of "King Pest the First".

'This apartment, which you no doubt profanely suppose to be the shop of Will Wimble the undertaker – a man whom we know not, and whose plebeian appellation has never before this night thwarted our royal ears – this apartment, I say, is the Dais-Chamber of our Palace, devoted to the councils of our kingdom, and to other sacred and lofty purposes.

'The noble lady who sits opposite is Queen Pest, our Serene Consort. The other exalted personages whom you behold are all of our family, and wear the insignia of the blood royal under the respective titles of

"His Grace the Arch Duke Pest-Iferous" – "His Grace the Duke Pest-Ilential" – "His Grace the Duke Tem-Pest" – and "Her Serene Highness the Arch Duchess Ana-Pest".

'As regards,' continued he, 'your demand of the business upon which we sit here in council, we might be pardoned for replying that it concerns, and concerns alone, our own private and regal interest, and is in no manner important to any other than ourselves. But in consideration of those rights to which as guests and strangers you may feel yourselves entitled, we will furthermore explain that we are here this night, prepared by deep research and accurate investigation, to examine, analyse, and thoroughly determine the indefinable spirit – the incomprehensible qualities and nature – of those inestimable treasures of the palate, the wines, ales, and liqueurs of this goodly metropolis: by so doing to advance not more our own designs than the true welfare of that unearthly sovereign whose reign is over us all, whose dominions are unlimited, and whose name is "Death".'

'Whose name is Davy Jones!' ejaculated Tarpaulin, helping the lady by his side to a skull of liqueur, and pouring out a second for himself.

'Profane varlet!' said the president, now turning his attention to the worthy Hugh, 'profane and execrable wretch! – we have said, that in consideration of those rights which, even in thy filthy person, we feel no inclination to violate, we have condescended to make reply to thy rude and unseasonable enquiries. We nevertheless, for your unhallowed intrusion upon our councils, believe it our duty to mulct thee and thy companion in each a gallon of Black Strap – having imbibed which to the prosperity of our kingdom – at a single draught – and upon your bended knees – ye shall be forthwith free either to proceed upon your way, or remain and be admitted to the privileges of our table, according to your respective and individual pleasures.'

'It would be a matter of utter impossibility,' replied Legs, whom the assumptions and dignity of King Pest the First had evidently inspired some feelings of respect, and who arose and steadied himself by the table as he spoke – 'it would, please your majesty, be a matter of utter impossibility to stow away in my hold even one-fourth part of the same liquor which your majesty has just mentioned. To say nothing of the stuffs placed on board in the forenoon by way of ballast, and not to mention the various ales and liqueurs shipped this evening at different seaports, I have, at present, a full cargo of "humming stuff" taken in and duly paid for at the sign of the "Jolly Tar". You will, therefore, please your majesty, be so good as to take the will for the deed – for by no manner of means either can I or will I swallow another drop – least of all a drop of that villainous bilge-water that answers to the hail of "Black Strap".'

'Belay that!' interrupted Tarpaulin, astonished not more at the length of his companion's speech than at the nature of his refusal – 'Belay that, you lubber! – and I say, Legs, none of your palaver! My hull is still light, although I confess you yourself seem to be a little top-heavy; and as for the matter of your share of the cargo, why rather than raise a squall I would find stowage room for it myself, but – '

'This proceeding,' interposed the president, 'is by no means in accordance with the terms of the mulct or sentence, which is in its nature Median, and not to be altered or recalled. The conditions we have imposed must be fulfilled to the letter, and that without a moment's hesitation – in failure of which fulfilment we decree that you do here be tied neck and heels together, and duly drowned as rebels in yon hogshead of October beer!'

'A sentence! – a sentence! – a righteous and just sentence! – a glorious decree! – a most worthy and upright, and holy condemnation!' shouted the Pest family altogether. The king elevated his forehead into innumerable wrinkles; the gouty little old man puffed like a pair of bellows; the lady of the winding sheet waved her nose to and fro; the gentleman in the cotton drawers pricked up his ears; she of the shroud gasped like a dying fish; and he of the coffin looked stiff and rolled up his eyes.

'Ugh! ugh! ugh!' chuckled Tarpaulin without heeding the general excitation, 'ugh! ugh! ugh! – ugh! ugh! ugh! – ugh! ugh! ugh! – I was saying,' said he, 'I was saying when Mr King Pest poked in his marlinspike, that as for the matter of two or three gallons more or less of Black Strap, it was a trifle to a tight sea-boat like myself not over-stowed – but when it comes to drinking the health of the Devil (whom God assoilzie) and going down upon my marrow bones to his ill-favoured majesty there, whom I know, as well as I know myself to be a sinner, to be nobody in the whole world, but Tim Hurlygurly the stage-player – why! it's quite another guess sort of a thing, and utterly and altogether past my comprehension.'

He was not allowed to finish this speech in tranquillity. At the name Tim Hurlygurly the whole assembly leaped from their seats.

'Treason!' shouted his Majesty King Pest the First.

'Treason!' said the little man with the gout.

'Treason!' screamed the Arch Duchess Ana-Pest.

'Treason!' muttered the gentleman with his jaws tied up.

'Treason!' growled he of the coffin.

'Treason! treason!' shrieked her majesty of the mouth; and, seizing by the hinder part of his breeches the unfortunate Tarpaulin, who had just commenced pouring out for himself a skull of liquor, she lifted him high into the air, and let him fall without ceremony into the huge open puncheon of his beloved ale. Bobbing up and down, for a few seconds, like an apple in a bowl of toddy, he, at length, finally disappeared amid the whirlpool of foam which, in the already effervescent liquor, his struggles easily succeeded in creating.

Not tamely, however, did the tall seaman behold the discomfiture of his companion. Jostling King Pest through the open trap, the valiant Legs slammed the door down upon him with an oath, and strode towards the centre of the room. Here tearing down the skeleton which swung over the table, he laid it about him with so much energy and good will, that, as the last glimpses of light died away within the apartment, he succeeded in knocking out the brains of the little gentleman with the gout. Rushing then with all his force against the fatal hogshead full of October ale and Hugh Tarpaulin, he rolled it over and over in an instant. Out burst a deluge of liquor so fierce – so impetuous – so overwhelming – that the room was flooded from wall to wall – the loaded table was overturned – the trestles were thrown upon their backs – the tub of punch into the fireplace – and the ladies into hysterics. Piles of death-furniture floundered about. Jugs, pitchers, and carboys mingled promiscuously in the melee, and wicker flagons encountered desperately with bottles of junk. The man with the horrors was drowned upon the spot – the little stiff gentleman floated off in his coffin – and the victorious Legs, seizing by the waist the fat lady in the shroud, rushed out with her into the street, and made a bee-line for the 'Free and Easy', followed under easy sail by the redoubtable Hugh Tarpaulin, who, having sneezed three or four times, panted and puffed after him with the Arch Duchess Ana-Pest.

The Unparalleled Adventure
of One Hans Pfaall

With a heart of furious fancies,
Whereof I am commander,
With a burning spear and a horse of air,
To the wilderness I wander.

Tom o'Bedlam's Song

By late accounts from Rotterdam, that city seems to
be in a high state of philosophical excitement. Indeed,
phenomena have there occurred of a nature so
completely unexpected – so entirely novel – so utterly
at variance with preconceived opinions – as to leave
no doubt on my mind that long ere this all Europe is
in an uproar, all physics in a ferment, all reason and
astronomy together by the ears.

It appears that on the — day of — (I am not
positive about the date), a vast crowd of people, for
purposes not specifically mentioned, were assembled
in the great square of the Exchange in the well-
conditioned city of Rotterdam. The day was warm –
unusually so for the season – there was hardly a
breath of air stirring; and the multitude were in no
bad humour at being now and then besprinkled with
friendly showers of momentary duration, that fell
from large white masses of cloud which chequered in
a fitful manner the blue vault of the firmament.
Nevertheless, about noon, a slight but remarkable
agitation became apparent in the assembly: the

clattering of ten thousand tongues succeeded; and, in an instant afterwards, ten thousand faces were up-turned towards the heavens, ten thousand pipes descended simultaneously from the corners of ten thousand mouths, and a shout, which could be compared to nothing but the roaring of Niagara, resounded long, loudly, and furiously, through all the environs of Rotterdam.

The origin of this hubbub soon became sufficiently evident. From behind the huge bulk of one of those sharply defined masses of cloud already mentioned, was seen slowly to emerge into an open area of blue space, a queer, heterogeneous, but apparently solid substance, so oddly shaped, so whimsically put together, as not to be in any manner comprehended, and never to be sufficiently admired, by the host of sturdy burghers who stood open-mouthed below. What could it be? In the name of all the devils in Rotterdam, what could it possibly portend? No one knew, no one could imagine; no one – not even the burgomaster Mynheer Superbus von Underduk – had the slightest clew by which to unravel the mystery; so, as nothing more reasonable could be done, everyone to a man replaced his pipe carefully in the corner of his mouth, and cocking up his right eye towards the phenomenon, puffed, paused, waddled about, and grunted significantly – then waddled back, grunted, paused, and finally – puffed again.

In the meantime, however, lower and still lower towards the goodly city, came the object of so much curiosity, and the cause of so much smoke. In a very few minutes it arrived near enough to be accurately discerned. It appeared to be – yes! it *was* undoubtedly a species of balloon; but surely no *such* balloon had ever been seen in Rotterdam before. For who, let me ask, ever heard of a balloon manufactured entirely of dirty newspapers? No man in Holland certainly; yet here, under the very noses of the people, or rather at some distance *above* their noses was the identical thing in question, and composed, I have it on the best authority, of the precise material which no one had ever before known to be used for a similar purpose. It was an egregious insult to the good sense of the burghers of Rotterdam. As to the shape of the phenomenon, it was even still more reprehensible, being little or nothing better than a huge foolscap turned upside down. And this similitude was regarded as by no means lessened when, upon nearer inspection, there was perceived a large tassel depending from its apex, and, around the upper rim or base of the cone, a circle of little instruments, resembling sheep-bells, which kept up a continual tinkling to the tune of Betty Martin. But still worse. Suspended by blue ribbons to the end of this fantastic machine, there hung, by way of car, an enormous drab beaver hat, with a brim superlatively broad, and a hemispherical crown with a black band and a silver buckle. It is, however, somewhat remarkable that many citizens of Rotterdam swore to having seen the same hat repeatedly before; and indeed the whole assembly seemed to regard it with eyes of familiarity; while the frau Grettel Pfaall, upon sight of it, uttered an exclamation of joyful surprise, and declared it to be the identical hat of her good man himself. Now this was a circumstance the more to be observed, as Pfaall, with three companions, had actually disappeared from Rotterdam about five years before, in a very sudden and unaccountable manner, and up to the date of this narrative all attempts had failed of obtaining any intelligence concerning them whatsoever. To be sure, some bones which were thought to be human, mixed up with a quantity of odd-looking rubbish, had been lately discovered in a retired situation to the east of Rotterdam, and some people went so far as to imagine that in this spot a foul murder had been committed, and that the sufferers were in all probability Hans Pfaall and his associates. But to return.

The balloon (for such no doubt it was) had now descended to within a hundred feet of the earth, allowing the crowd below a sufficiently distinct view of the person of its occupant. This was in truth a very droll little somebody. He could not have been more than two feet in height; but this altitude, little as it was, would have been sufficient to destroy his equilibrium, and tilt him over the edge of his tiny car, but for the intervention of a circular rim reaching as high as the breast, and rigged on to the cords of the balloon. The body of the little man was more than proportionately broad, giving to his entire figure a rotundity highly absurd. His feet, of course, could not be seen at all, although a horny substance of suspicious nature was occasionally protruded through a rent in the bottom of the car, or to speak more properly, in the top of the hat. His hands were enormously large. His hair was extremely grey, and collected in a queue behind. His nose was prodigiously long, crooked, and inflammatory; his eyes full, brilliant, and acute; his chin and cheeks, although wrinkled with age, were broad, puffy, and double; but of ears of any kind or character there was not a semblance to be discovered upon any portion of his head. This odd little gentleman was dressed in a loose surtout of sky-blue satin, with tight breeches to

THE ADVENTURE OF ONE HANS PFAALL

match, fastened with silver buckles at the knees. His vest was of some bright yellow material; a white taffety cap was set jauntily on one side of his head; and, to complete his equipment, a blood-red silk handkerchief enveloped his throat, and fell down, in a dainty manner, upon his bosom, in a fantastic bow-knot of super-eminent dimensions.

Having descended, as I said before, to about one hundred feet from the surface of the earth, the little old gentleman was suddenly seized with a fit of trepidation, and appeared disinclined to make any nearer approach to *terra firma*. Throwing out, therefore, a quantity of sand from a canvas bag, which he lifted with great difficulty, he became stationary in an instant. He then proceeded, in a hurried and agitated manner, to extract from a side-pocket in his surtout a large morocco pocketbook. This he poised suspiciously in his hand, then eyed it with an air of extreme surprise, and was evidently astonished at its weight. He at length opened it, and drawing therefrom a huge letter sealed with red sealing-wax and tied carefully with red tape, let it fall precisely at the feet of the burgomaster, Superbus von Underduk. His Excellency stooped to take it up. But the aeronaut, still greatly discomposed, and having apparently no further business to detain him in Rotterdam, began at this moment to make busy preparations for departure; and it being necessary to discharge a portion of ballast to enable him to reascend, the half-dozen bags which he threw out, one after another, without taking the trouble to empty their contents, tumbled, every one of them, most unfortunately upon the back of the burgomaster, and rolled him over and over no less than one-and-twenty times, in the face of every man in Rotterdam. It is not to be supposed, however, that the great Underduk suffered this impertinence on the part of the little old man to pass off with impunity. It is said, on the contrary, that during each and every one of his one-and-twenty circumvolutions he emitted no less than one-and-twenty distinct and furious whiffs from his pipe, to which he held fast the whole time with all his might, and to which he intends holding fast until the day of his death.

In the meantime the balloon arose like a lark, and, soaring far away above the city, at length drifted quietly behind a cloud similar to that from which it had so oddly emerged, and was thus lost for ever to the wondering eyes of the good citizens of Rotterdam. All attention was now directed to the letter, the descent of which, and the consequences attending thereupon, had proved so fatally subversive of both person and personal dignity to his excellency, the illustrious Burgomaster Mynheer Superbus von Underduk. That functionary, however, had not failed, during his circumgyratory movements, to bestow a thought upon the important subject of securing the packet in question, which was seen, upon inspection, to have fallen into the most proper hands, being actually addressed to himself and Professor Rub-a-dub, in their official capacities of president and vice-president of the Rotterdam College of Astronomy.

It was accordingly opened by those dignitaries upon the spot, and found to contain the following extra-ordinary, and indeed very serious, communication:

'*To their Excellencies von Underduk and Rub-a-dub, president and vice-president of the States' College of*

Astronomers, in the city of Rotterdam.

'Your Excellencies may perhaps be able to remember an humble artisan, by name Hans Pfaall, and by occupation a mender of bellows, who, with three others, disappeared from Rotterdam, about five years ago, in a manner which must have been considered by all parties at once sudden, and extremely unaccountable. If, however, it so please your Excellencies, I, the writer of this communication, am the identical Hans Pfaall himself. It is well known to most of my fellow citizens, that for the period of forty years I continued to occupy the little square brick building, at the head of the alley called Sauerkraut, in which I resided at the time of my disappearance. My ancestors have also resided therein time out of mind – they, as well as myself, steadily following the respectable and indeed lucrative profession of mending of bellows. For, to speak the truth, until of late years, that the heads of all the people have been set agog with politics, no better business than my own could an honest citizen of Rotterdam either desire or deserve. Credit was good, employment was never wanting, and on all hands there was no lack of either money or goodwill. But, as I was saying, we soon began to feel the effects of liberty and long speeches, and radicalism, and all that sort of thing. People who were formerly the very best customers in the world, had now not a moment of time to think of us at all. They had, so they said, as much as they could do to read about the revolutions, and keep up with the march of intellect and the spirit of the age. If a fire wanted fanning, it could readily be fanned with a newspaper, and as the government grew weaker, I have no doubt that leather and iron acquired durability in proportion, for, in a very short time, there was not a pair of bellows in all Rotterdam that ever stood in need of a stitch or required the assistance of a hammer. This was a state of things not to be endured. I soon grew as poor as a rat, and, having a wife and children to provide for, my burdens at length became intolerable, and I spent hour after hour in reflecting upon the most convenient method of putting an end to my life. Duns, in the meantime, left me little leisure for contemplation. My house was literally besieged from morning till night, so that I began to rave, and foam, and fret like a caged tiger against the bars of his enclosure. There were three fellows in particular who worried me beyond endurance, keeping watch continually about my door, and threatening me with the law. Upon these three I internally vowed the bitterest revenge, if ever I should be so happy as to get them within my clutches; and I believe nothing in the world but the pleasure of this anticipation prevented me from putting my plan of suicide into immediate execution, by blowing my brains out with a blunderbuss. I thought it best, however, to dissemble my wrath, and to treat them with promises and fair words, until, by some good turn of fate, an opportunity of vengeance should be afforded me.

'One day, having given my creditors the slip, and feeling more than usually dejected, I continued for a long time to wander about the most obscure streets without object whatever, until at length I chanced to stumble against the corner of a bookseller's stall. Seeing a chair close at hand, for the use of customers, I threw myself doggedly into it, and, hardly knowing why, opened the pages of the first volume which came within my reach. It proved to be a small pamphlet treatise on Speculative Astronomy, written either by Professor Encke of Berlin or by a Frenchman of somewhat similar name. I had some little tincture of information on matters of this nature, and soon became more and more absorbed in the contents of the book, reading it actually through twice before I awoke to a recollection of what was passing around me. By this time it began to grow dark, and I directed my steps towards home. But the treatise had made an indelible impression on my mind, and, as I sauntered along the dusky streets, I revolved carefully over in my memory the wild and sometimes unintelligible reasonings of the writer. There are some particular passages which affected my imagination in a powerful and extraordinary manner. The longer I meditated upon these the more intense grew the interest which had been excited within me. The limited nature of my education in general, and more especially my ignorance on subjects connected with natural philosophy, so far from rendering me diffident of my own ability to comprehend what I had read, or inducing me to mistrust the many vague notions which had arisen in consequence, merely served as a further stimulus to imagination; and I was vain enough, or perhaps reasonable enough, to doubt whether those crude ideas which, arising in ill-regulated minds, have all the appearance, may not often in effect possess all the force, the reality, and other inherent properties, of instinct or intuition; whether, to proceed a step farther, profundity itself might not, in matters of a purely speculative nature, be detected as a legitimate source of falsity and error. In other words, I believed, and still do believe, that truth is frequently of its own essence, superficial, and that, in many cases, the depth lies more in the abysses where we seek her, than in the actual situations wherein she may be found. Nature herself seemed to afford me corroboration of these ideas. In the contemplation of the heavenly bodies it struck me forcibly that I could not distinguish a star with nearly as much precision, when I gazed on it with earnest, direct and undeviating attention, as when I suffered my eye only to glance in its vicinity alone. I was not, of course, at that time aware that this apparent paradox was occasioned by the centre of the visual area being less susceptible of feeble impressions of light than the exterior portions of the retina. This knowledge, and some of another kind, came afterwards in the course of an eventful five years, during which I have dropped the prejudices of my former humble situation in life, and forgotten the bellows-mender in far different occupations. But at the epoch of which I speak, the analogy which a casual observation of a star offered to the conclusions I had already drawn, struck me with the force of positive confirmation, and I then finally made up my mind to the course which I afterwards pursued.

'It was late when I reached home, and I went immediately to bed. My mind, however, was too much occupied to sleep, and I lay the whole night buried in meditation. Arising early in the morning, and contriving again to escape the vigilance of my creditors, I repaired eagerly to the bookseller's stall, and laid out what little ready money I possessed, in the purchase of some volumes of Mechanics and Practical Astronomy. Having arrived at home safely with these, I devoted every spare moment to their perusal, and soon made such proficiency in studies of this nature as I thought sufficient for the execution of my plan. In the intervals of this period, I made every endeavour to conciliate the three creditors who had given me so much annoyance. In this I finally succeeded – partly by selling enough of my household furniture to satisfy a moiety of their claim, and partly by a promise of paying the balance upon completion of a little project which I told them I had in view, and for assistance in which I solicited their services. By these means – for they were ignorant men – I found little difficulty in gaining them over to my purpose.

'Matters being thus arranged, I contrived, by the aid of my wife and with the greatest secrecy and caution, to dispose of what property I had remaining, and to borrow, in small sums, under various pretences, and without paying any attention to my future means of repayment, no inconsiderable quantity of ready money. With the means thus accruing I proceeded to procure at intervals, cambric muslin, very fine, in pieces of twelve yards each; twine; a lot of the varnish of caoutchouc; a large and deep basket of wickerwork, made to order; and several other articles necessary in the construction and equipment of a balloon of extra-ordinary dimensions. This I directed my wife to make up as soon as possible, and gave her all requisite information as to the particular method of proceeding. In the meantime I worked up the twine into a network of sufficient dimensions; rigged it with a hoop and the necessary cords; bought a quadrant, a compass, a spyglass, a common barometer with some important modifications, and two astronomical instruments not so generally known. I then took opportunities of conveying by night, to a retired situation east of Rotterdam, five iron-bound casks, to contain about fifty gallons each, and one of a larger size; six tin tubes, three inches in diameter, properly shaped, and ten feet in length; a quantity of a particular metallic substance, or semi-metal, which I shall not name, and a dozen demijohns of a very common acid. The gas to be formed from these latter materials is a gas never yet generated by any other person than myself – or at least never applied to any similar purpose. The secret I would make no difficulty in disclosing, but that it of right belongs to a citizen of Nantes, in France, by whom it was conditionally communicated to myself. The same individual submitted to me, without being at all aware of my intentions, a method of constructing balloons from the membrane of a certain animal, through which substance any escape of gas was nearly an impossibility. I found it, however, altogether too expensive, and was not sure, upon the whole, whether cambric muslin with a coating of gum caoutchouc, was not equally as good. I mention this circumstance, because I think it probable that hereafter the individual in question may attempt a balloon ascension with the novel gas and material I have spoken of, and I do not wish to deprive him of the honour of a very singular invention.

'On the spot which I intended each of the smaller casks to occupy respectively during the inflation of the balloon, I privately dug a hole two feet deep; the holes forming in this manner a circle twenty-five feet in diameter. In the centre of this circle, being the station designed for the large cask, I also dug a hole three feet in depth. In each of the five smaller holes, I deposited a canister containing fifty pounds, and in the larger one a keg holding one hundred and fifty pounds, of cannon powder. These – the keg and canisters – I connected in a proper manner with covered trains; and having let into one of the canisters the end of about four feet of slow match, I covered up the hole, and placed the cask over it, leaving the other end of the match protruding about an inch, and barely visible beyond the cask. I then filled up the remaining holes, and placed the barrels over them in their destined situation.

'Besides the articles above enumerated, I conveyed to the depot, and there secreted, one of M. Grimm's improvements upon the apparatus for condensation of the atmospheric air. I found this machine, however, to require considerable alteration before it could be adapted to the purposes to which I intended making it applicable. But, with severe labour and unremitting perseverance, I at length met with entire success in all my preparations. My balloon was soon completed. It would contain more than forty thousand cubic feet of gas; would take me up easily, I calculated, with all my implements, and, if I managed rightly, with one hundred and seventy-five pounds of ballast into the bargain. It had received three coats of varnish, and I found the cambric muslin to answer all the purposes of silk itself, quite as strong and a good deal less expensive.

'Everything being now ready, I exacted from my wife an oath of secrecy in relation to all my actions from the day of my first visit to the bookseller's stall; and promising, on my part, to return as soon as circumstances would permit, I gave her what little money I had left, and bade her farewell. Indeed I had no fear on her account. She was what people call a notable woman, and could manage matters in the world without my assistance. I believe, to tell the truth, she always looked upon me as an idle boy, a mere make-weight, good for nothing but building castles in the air, and was rather glad to get rid of me. It was a dark night when I bade her goodbye, and taking with me, as aides-de-camp, the three creditors who had given me so much trouble, we carried the balloon, with the car and accoutrements, by a roundabout way, to the station where the other articles were deposited. We there found them all unmolested, and I proceeded immediately to business.

'It was the first of April. The night, as I said before, was dark; there was not a star to be seen; and a drizzling rain, falling at intervals, rendered us very uncomfortable. But my chief anxiety was concerning the balloon, which, in spite of the varnish with which it was defended, began to grow rather heavy with the moisture; the powder also was liable to damage. I therefore kept my three duns working with great diligence, pounding down ice around the central cask, and stirring the acid in the others. They did not cease, however, importuning me with questions as to what I intended to do with all this apparatus, and expressed much dissatisfaction at the terrible labour I made them undergo. They could not perceive, so they said, what good was likely to result from their getting wet to the skin, merely to take a part in such horrible incantations. I began to get uneasy, and worked away with all my might, for I verily believe the idiots supposed that I had entered into a compact with the devil, and that, in short, what I was now doing was nothing better than it should be. I was, therefore, in great fear of their leaving me altogether. I contrived, however, to pacify them by promises of payment of all scores in full, as soon as I could bring the present business to a termination. To these speeches they gave, of course, their own interpretation; fancying, no doubt, that at all events I should come into possession of vast quantities of ready money; and provided I paid them all I owed, and a trifle more, in consideration of their services, I dare say they cared very little what became of either my soul or my carcass.

'In about four hours and a half I found the balloon sufficiently inflated. I attached the car, therefore, and put all my implements in it – not forgetting the condensing apparatus, a copious supply of water, and a large quantity of provisions, such as pemmican, in which much nutriment is contained in comparatively little bulk. I also secured in the car a pair of pigeons and a cat. It was now nearly daybreak, and I thought it high time to take my departure. Dropping a lighted cigar on the ground, as if by accident, I took the opportunity, in stooping to pick it up, of igniting privately the piece of slow match, whose end, as I said before, protruded a very little beyond the lower rim of one of the smaller casks. This manoeuvre was totally unperceived on the part of the three duns; and, jumping into the car, I immediately cut the single cord which held me to the earth, and was pleased to find that I shot upward, carrying with all ease one hundred and seventy-five pounds of leaden ballast, and able to have carried up as many more.

'Scarcely, however, had I attained the height of fifty yards, when, roaring and rumbling up after me in the most horrible and tumultuous manner, came so dense a hurricane of fire, and smoke, and sulphur, and legs and arms, and gravel, and burning wood, and blazing metal, that my very heart sunk within me, and I fell down in the bottom of the car, trembling with unmitigated terror. Indeed, I now perceived that I had entirely overdone the business, and that the main consequences of the shock were yet to be experienced. Accordingly, in less than a second, I felt all the blood in my body rushing to my temples, and immediately thereupon, a concussion, which I shall never forget, burst abruptly through the night and seemed to rip the very firmament asunder. When I afterwards had time for reflection, I did not fail to attribute the extreme violence of the explosion, as regarded myself, to its proper cause – my situation directly above it, and in the line of its greatest power. But at the time, I thought only of preserving my life. The balloon at first collapsed, then furiously expanded, then whirled round and round with horrible velocity, and finally, reeling and staggering like a drunken man, hurled me with great force over the rim of the car, and left me dangling, at a terrific height, with my head downwards, and my face outwards, by a piece of slender cord about three feet in length, which hung accidentally through a crevice near the bottom of the wickerwork, and in which, as I fell, my left foot became most providentially entangled. It is impossible – utterly impossible – to form any adequate idea of the horror of my situation. I gasped convulsively for breath – a shudder resembling a fit of the ague agitated every nerve and muscle of my frame – I felt my eyes starting from their sockets – a horrible nausea overwhelmed me – and at length I fainted away.

'How long I remained in this state it is impossible to say. It must, however, have been no inconsiderable time, for when I partially recovered the sense of existence, I found the day breaking, the balloon at a prodigious height over a wilderness of ocean, and not a trace of land to be discovered far and wide within the limits of the vast horizon. My sensations, however, upon thus recovering, were by no means so rife with agony as might have been anticipated. Indeed, there was much of incipient madness in the calm survey which I began to take of my situation. I drew up to my eyes each of my hands, one after the other, and wondered what occurrence could have given rise to the swelling of the veins, and the horrible blackness of the fingernails. I afterwards carefully examined my head, shaking it repeatedly, and feeling it with minute attention, until I succeeded in satisfying myself that it was not, as I had more than half suspected, larger than my balloon. Then, in a knowing manner, I felt in both my breeches pockets, and, missing therefrom a set of tablets and a toothpick case, endeavoured to account for their disappearance, and not being able to do so, felt inexpressibly chagrined. It now occurred to me that I suffered great uneasiness in the joint of my left ankle, and a dim consciousness of my situation began to glimmer through my mind. But, strange to say! I was neither astonished nor horror-stricken. If I felt any emotion at all, it was a kind of chuckling satisfaction at the cleverness I was about to display in extricating myself from this dilemma; and I never, for a moment, looked upon my ultimate safety as a question susceptible of doubt. For a few minutes I remained wrapped in the profoundest meditation. I have a distinct recollection of frequently compressing my lips, putting my forefinger to the side of my nose, and making use of other gesticulations and grimaces common to men who, at ease in their armchairs, meditate upon matters of intricacy or importance. Having, as I thought, sufficiently collected my ideas, I now, with great caution and deliberation, put my hands behind my back, and unfastened the large iron buckle which belonged to the waistband of my inexpressibles. This buckle had three teeth, which, being somewhat rusty, turned with great difficulty on their axis. I brought them, however, after some trouble, at right angles to the body of the buckle, and was glad to find them remain firm in that position. Holding the instrument thus obtained within my teeth, I now proceeded to untie the knot of my cravat. I had to rest several times before I could accomplish this manoeuvre, but it was at length accomplished. To one end of the cravat I then made fast the buckle, and the other end I tied, for greater security, tightly around my wrist. Drawing now my body upwards, with a prodigious exertion of muscular force, I succeeded, at the very first trial, in throwing the buckle over the car, and entangling it, as I had anticipated, in the circular rim of the wickerwork.

'My body was now inclined towards the side of the car, at an angle of about forty-five degrees; but it must not be understood that I was therefore only forty-five degrees below the perpendicular. So far from it, I still lay nearly level with the plane of the horizon; for the change of situation which I had acquired, had forced the bottom of the car considerably outwards from my position, which was accordingly one of the most imminent and deadly peril. It should be remembered, however, that when I fell in the first instance, from the car, if I had fallen with my face turned towards the balloon, instead of turned outwardly from it, as it actually was; or if, in the second place, the cord by which I was suspended had chanced to hang over the upper edge, instead of through a crevice near the bottom of the car – I say it may be readily conceived that, in either of these supposed cases, I should have been unable to accomplish even as much as I had now accomplished, and the wonderful adventures of Hans Pfaall would have been utterly lost to posterity. I had therefore every reason to be grateful; although, in point of fact, I was still too stupid to be anything at all, and hung for, perhaps, a quarter of an hour in that extra-ordinary manner, without making the slightest farther exertion whatsoever, and in a singularly tranquil state of idiotic enjoyment. But this feeling did not fail to die rapidly away, and thereunto succeeded horror, and dismay, and a chilling sense of utter helplessness and ruin. In fact, the blood so long accumulating in the vessels of my head and throat, and which had hitherto buoyed up my spirits with madness and delirium, had now begun to retire within their proper channels, and the distinctness which was thus added to my per-ception of the danger, merely served to deprive me of the self-possession and courage to encounter it. But this weakness was, luckily for me, of no very long duration. In good time came to my rescue the spirit of despair, and, with frantic cries and struggles, I jerked my way bodily upwards, till at length, clutching with a vice-like grip the long-desired rim, I writhed my person over it, and fell headlong and shuddering within the car.

'It was not until some time afterwards that I recov-ered myself sufficiently to attend to the ordinary cares of the balloon. I then, however, examined it with attention, and found it, to my great relief, uninjured. My implements were all safe, and, fortunately, I had lost neither ballast nor provisions. Indeed, I had so well secured them in their places, that such an accident

TALES AND POEMS OF EDGAR ALLAN POE

was entirely out of the question. Looking at my watch, I found it six o'clock. I was still rapidly ascending, and my barometer gave a present altitude of three and three-quarter miles. Immediately beneath me in the ocean, lay a small black object, slightly oblong in shape, seemingly about the size, and in every way bearing a great resemblance to one of those childish toys called a domino. Bringing my telescope to bear upon it, I plainly discerned it to be a British ninety-four-gun ship, close-hauled, and pitching heavily in the sea with her head to the west-sou'west. Besides this ship, I saw nothing but the ocean and the sky, and the sun, which had long arisen.

'It is now high time that I should explain to your Excellencies the object of my perilous voyage. Your Excellencies will bear in mind that distressed circumstances in Rotterdam had at length driven me to the resolution of committing suicide. It was not, however, that to life itself I had any positive disgust, but that I was harassed beyond endurance by the adventitious miseries attending my situation. In this state of mind, wishing to live, yet wearied with life, the treatise at the stall of the bookseller opened a resource to my imagination. I then finally made up my mind. I determined to depart, yet live – to leave the world, yet continue to exist – in short, to drop enigmas, I resolved, let what would ensue, to force a passage, if I could, to the moon. Now, lest I should be supposed more of a madman than I actually am, I will detail, as well as I am able, the considerations which led me to believe that an achievement of this nature, although without doubt difficult, and incontestably full of danger, was not absolutely, to a bold spirit, beyond the confines of the possible.

'The moon's actual distance from the earth was the

first thing to be attended to. Now, the mean or average interval between the centres of the two planets is 59.9643 of the earth's equatorial radii, or only about 237,000 miles. I say the mean or average interval. But it must be borne in mind that the form of the moon's orbit being an ellipse of eccentricity amounting to no less than 0.05484 of the major semi-axis of the ellipse itself, and the earth's centre being situated in its focus, if I could, in any manner, contrive to meet the moon, as it were, in its perigee, the above-mentioned distance would be materially diminished. But, to say nothing at present of this possibility, it was very certain that, at all events, from the 237,000 miles I would have to deduct the radius of the earth, say 4,000, and the radius of the moon, say 1,080, in all 5,080, leaving an actual interval to be traversed, under average circumstances, of 231,920 miles. Now this, I reflected, was no very extraordinary distance. Travelling on land has been repeatedly accomplished at the rate of thirty miles per hour, and indeed a much greater speed may be anticipated. But even at this velocity, it would take me no more than 322 days to reach the surface of the moon. There were, however, many particulars inducing me to believe that my average rate of travelling might possibly very much exceed that of thirty miles per hour, and, as these considerations did not fail to make a deep impression upon my mind, I will mention them more fully hereafter.

'The next point to be regarded was a matter of far greater importance. From indications afforded by the barometer, we find that, in ascensions from the surface of the earth we have, at the height of 1,000 feet, left below us about one-thirtieth of the entire mass of atmospheric air, that at 10,600 we have ascended through nearly one-third; and that at 18,000, which is not far from the elevation of Cotopaxi, we have surmounted one half of the material, or, at all events, one half of the ponderable, body of air incumbent upon our globe. It is also calculated that at an altitude not exceeding the hundredth part of the earth's diameter – that is, not exceeding eighty miles – the rarefaction would be so excessive that animal life could in no manner be sustained, and, moreover, that the most delicate means we possess of ascertaining the presence of the atmosphere would be inadequate to assure us of its existence. But I did not fail to perceive that these latter calculations are founded altogether on our experimental knowledge of the properties of air, and the mechanical laws regulating its dilation and compression, in what may be called, comparatively speaking, the immediate vicinity of the earth itself; and, at the same time, it is taken for granted that animal life is and must be essentially incapable of modification at any given unattainable distance from the surface. Now, all such reasoning and from such data must, of course, be simply analogical. The greatest height ever reached by man was that of 25,000 feet, attained in the aeronautic expedition of Messieurs Gay-Lussac and Biot. This is a moderate altitude, even when compared with the eighty miles in question; and I could not help thinking that the subject admitted room for doubt and great latitude for speculation.

'But, in point of fact, an ascension being made to any given altitude, the ponderable quantity of air surmounted in any farther ascension is by no means in proportion to the additional height ascended (as may be plainly seen from what has been stated before), but in a ratio constantly decreasing. It is therefore evident that, ascend as high as we may, we cannot, literally speaking, arrive at a limit beyond which no atmosphere is to be found. It must exist, I argued; although it may exist in a state of infinite rarefaction.

'On the other hand, I was aware that arguments have not been wanting to prove the existence of a real and definite limit to the atmosphere, beyond which there is absolutely no air whatsoever. But a circumstance which has been left out of view by those who contend for such a limit seemed to me, although no positive refutation of their creed, still a point worthy very serious investigation. On comparing the intervals between the successive arrivals of Encke's comet at its perihelion, after giving credit, in the most exact manner, for all the disturbances due to the attractions of the planets, it appears that the periods are gradually diminishing; that is to say, the major axis of the comet's ellipse is growing shorter, in a slow but perfectly regular decrease. Now, this is precisely what ought to be the case, if we suppose a resistance experienced from the comet from an extremely rare ethereal medium pervading the regions of its orbit. For it is evident that such a medium must, in retarding the comet's velocity, increase its centripetal, by weakening its centrifugal, force. In other words, the sun's attraction would be constantly attaining greater power, and the comet would be drawn nearer at every revolution. Indeed, there is no other way of accounting for the variation in question. But again: the real diameter of the same comet's nebulosity is observed to contract rapidly as it approaches the sun, and dilate with equal rapidity in its departure towards its aphelion. Was I not justified in supposing with M.

Valz, that this apparent condensation of volume has its origin in the compression of the same ethereal medium I have spoken of before, and which is only denser in proportion to its solar vicinity? The lenticular-shaped phenomenon, also called the zodiacal light, was a matter worthy of attention. This radiance, so apparent in the tropics, and which cannot be mistaken for any meteoric lustre, extends from the horizon obliquely upwards, and follows generally the direction of the sun's equator. It appeared to me evidently in the nature of a rare atmosphere extending from the sun outwards, beyond the orbit of Venus at least, and I believed indefinitely farther.* Indeed, this medium I could not suppose confined to the path of the comet's ellipse, or to the immediate neighbourhood of the sun. It was easy, on the contrary, to imagine it pervading the entire regions of our planetary system, condensed into what we call atmosphere at the planets themselves, and perhaps at some of them modified by considerations, so to speak, purely geological.

'Having adopted this view of the subject, I had little further hesitation. Granting that on my passage I should meet with atmosphere essentially the same as at the surface of the earth, I conceived that, by means of the very ingenious apparatus of M. Grimm, I should readily be enabled to condense it in sufficient quantity for the purposes of respiration. This would remove the chief obstacle in a journey to the moon. I had indeed spent some money and great labour in adapting the apparatus to the object intended, and confidently

---

* The zodiacal light is probably what the ancients called Trabes. *Emicant Trabes quas docos vocant.* Pliny, Lib. 2, p. 26.

looked forward to its successful application, if I could manage to complete the voyage within any reasonable period. This brings me back to the rate at which it might be possible to travel.

'It is true that balloons, in the first stage of their ascensions from the earth, are known to rise with a velocity comparatively moderate. Now, the power of elevation lies altogether in the superior lightness of the gas in the balloon compared with the atmospheric air; and, at first sight, it does not appear probable that, as the balloon acquires altitude, and consequently arrives successively in atmospheric strata of densities rapidly diminishing – I say, it does not appear at all reasonable that, in this its progress upwards, the original velocity should be accelerated. On the other hand, I was not aware that, in any recorded ascension, a diminution was apparent in the absolute rate of ascent; although such should have been the case, if on account of nothing else, on account of the escape of gas through balloons ill-constructed, and varnished with no better material than the ordinary varnish. It seemed, therefore, that the effect of such escape was only sufficient to counterbalance the effect of some accelerating power. I now considered that, provided in my passage I found the medium I had imagined, and provided that it should prove to be actually and essentially what we denominate atmospheric air, it could make comparatively little difference at what extreme state of rarefaction I should discover it – that is to say, in regard to my power of ascending – for the gas in the balloon would not only be itself subject to rarefaction partially similar (in proportion to the occurrence of which, I could suffer an escape of so much as would be requisite to prevent explosion), but, being what it was, would, at all events, continue specifically lighter than any compound whatever of mere nitrogen and oxygen. In the meantime, the force of gravitation would be constantly diminishing, in proportion to the squares of the distances, and thus, with a velocity prodigiously accelerating, I should at length arrive in those distant regions where the force of the earth's attraction would be superseded by that of the moon. In accordance with these ideas, I did not think it worth while to encumber myself with more provisions than would be sufficient for a period of forty days.

'There was still, however, another difficulty, which occasioned me some little disquietude. It has been observed, that, in balloon ascensions to any considerable height, besides the pain attending respiration, great uneasiness is experienced about the head and body, often accompanied with bleeding at the nose, and other symptoms of an alarming kind, and growing more and more inconvenient in proportion to the altitude attained.* This was a reflection of a nature somewhat startling. Was it not probable that these symptoms would increase indefinitely, or at least until terminated by death itself? I finally thought not. Their origin was to be looked for in the progressive removal of the customary atmospheric pressure upon the surface of the body, and consequent distention of the superficial blood-vessels – not in any positive disorganisation of the animal system, as in the case of

---

* Since the original publication of Hans Pfaall, I find that Mr Green of Nassau-balloon notoriety and other late aeronauts deny the assertions of Humboldt in this respect and speak of a *decreasing* inconvenience – precisely in accordance with the theory here urged.

difficulty in breathing, where the atmospheric density is chemically insufficient for the due renovation of blood in a ventricle of the heart. Unless for default of this renovation, I could see no reason, therefore, why life could not be sustained even in a vacuum; for the expansion and compression of chest, commonly called breathing, is action purely muscular, and the cause, not the effect, of respiration. In a word, I conceived that, as the body should become habituated to the want of atmospheric pressure, the sensations of pain would gradually diminish – and to endure them while they continued, I relied with confidence upon the iron hardihood of my constitution.

'Thus, may it please your Excellencies, I have detailed some, though by no means all, the consider-ations which led me to form the project of a lunar voyage. I shall now proceed to lay before you the result of an attempt so apparently audacious in conception, and, at all events, so utterly unparalleled in the annals of mankind.

'Having attained the altitude before mentioned, that is to say three miles and three-quarters, I threw out from the car a quantity of feathers, and found that I still ascended with sufficient rapidity; there was, therefore, no necessity for discharging any ballast. I was glad of this, for I wished to retain with me as much weight as I could carry, for reasons which will be explained in the sequel. I as yet suffered no bodily inconvenience, breathing with great freedom, and feeling no pain whatever in the head. The cat was lying very demurely upon my coat, which I had taken off, and eyeing the pigeons with an air of nonchalance. These latter being tied by the leg, to prevent their escape, were busily employed in picking up some grains of rice scattered for them in the bottom of the car.

'At twenty minutes past six o'clock, the barometer showed an elevation of 26,400 feet, or five miles to a fraction. The prospect seemed unbounded. Indeed, it is very easily calculated by means of spherical geometry, what a great extent of the earth's area I beheld. The convex surface of any segment of a sphere is, to the entire surface of the sphere itself, as the versed sine of the segment to the diameter of the sphere. Now, in my case, the versed sine – that is to say, the thickness of the segment beneath me – was about equal to my elevation, or the elevation of the point of sight above the surface. "As five miles, then, to eight thousand", would express the proportion of the earth's area seen by me. In other words, I beheld as much as a sixteen-hundredth part of the whole surface of the globe. The sea appeared unruffled as a mirror, although, by means of the spyglass, I could perceive it to be in a state of violent agitation. The ship was no longer visible, having drifted away, apparently to the eastward. I now began to experience, at intervals, severe pain in the head, especially about the ears – still, however, breathing with tolerable freedom. The cat and pigeons seemed to suffer no inconvenience whatsoever.

'At twenty minutes before seven, the balloon entered a long series of dense cloud, which put me to great trouble, by damaging my condensing apparatus and wetting me to the skin. This was, to be sure, a singular *rencontre*, for I had not believed it possible that a cloud of this nature could be sustained at so great an elevation. I thought it best, however, to throw out two five-pound pieces of ballast, reserving still a weight of one hundred and sixty-five pounds. Upon so doing, I soon rose above the difficulty, and perceived immediately, that I had obtained a great increase in my rate of ascent. In a few seconds after my leaving the cloud, a flash of vivid lightning shot from one end of it to the other, and caused it to kindle up, throughout its vast extent, like a mass of ignited and glowing charcoal. This, it must be remembered, was in the broad light of day. No fancy may picture the sublimity which might have been exhibited by a similar phenomenon taking place amid the darkness of the night. Hell itself might have been found a fitting image. Even as it was, my hair stood on end, while I gazed afar down within the yawning abysses, letting imagination descend, as it were, and stalk about in the strange vaulted halls, and ruddy gulfs, and red ghastly chasms of the hideous and unfathomable fire. I had indeed made a narrow escape. Had the balloon remained a very short while longer within the cloud – that is to say, had not the inconvenience of getting wet determined me to discharge the ballast – inevitable ruin would have been the consequence. Such perils, although little considered, are perhaps the greatest which must be encountered in balloons. I had by this time, however, attained too great an elevation to be any longer uneasy on this head.

'I was now rising rapidly, and by seven o'clock the barometer indicated an altitude of no less than nine miles and a half. I began to find great difficulty in drawing my breath. My head, too, was excessively painful; and, having felt for some time a moisture about my cheeks, I at length discovered it to be blood, which was oozing quite fast from the drums of my ears. My eyes, also, gave me great uneasiness. Upon passing the hand over them they seemed to have protruded from their sockets in no inconsiderable degree; and all objects in the car, and even the balloon itself, appeared distorted to my vision. These symptoms were more than I had expected, and occasioned me some alarm. At this juncture, very imprudently, and without consideration, I threw out from the car three five-pound pieces of ballast. The accelerated rate of ascent thus obtained carried me too rapidly, and without sufficient gradation, into a highly rarefied stratum of the atmosphere, and the result had nearly proved fatal to my expedition and to myself. I was suddenly seized with a spasm which lasted for more than five minutes, and even when this, in a measure, ceased, I could catch my breath only at long intervals, and in a gasping manner – bleeding all the while copiously at the nose and ears, and even slightly at the eyes. The pigeons appeared distressed in the extreme, and struggled to escape; while the cat mewed piteously, and, with her tongue hanging out of her mouth, staggered to and fro in the car as if under the influence of poison. I now too late discovered the great rashness of which I had been guilty in discharging the ballast, and my agitation was excessive. I anticipated nothing less than death, and death in a few minutes. The physical suffering I underwent contributed also to render me nearly incapable of making any exertion for the preservation of my life. I had, indeed, little power of reflection left, and the violence of the pain in my head seemed to be greatly on the increase. Thus I found that my senses would shortly give way altogether, and I had already clutched one of the valve ropes with the view of attempting a descent, when the recollection of the trick I had played the three creditors, and the possible consequences to myself, should I return, operated to deter me for the moment. I lay down in the bottom of the car, and endeavoured to collect my faculties. In this I so far succeeded as to determine upon the experiment of losing blood. Having no lancet, however, I was constrained to perform the operation in the best manner I was able, and finally succeeded in opening a vein in my right arm, with the blade of my penknife. The blood had hardly commenced flowing when I experienced a sensible relief, and by the time I had lost about half a moderate basin full, most of the worst symptoms had abandoned me entirely. I nevertheless did not think it expedient to attempt getting on my feet immediately; but, having tied up my arm as well as I could, I lay still for about a quarter of an hour. At the end of this time I arose, and found myself freer from absolute pain of any kind than I had been during the last hour and a quarter of my ascension. The difficulty of breathing, however, was diminished in a very slight degree, and I found that it would soon be positively necessary to make use of my condenser. In the meantime, looking towards the cat, who was again snugly stowed away upon my coat, I discovered, to my infinite surprise, that she had taken the opportunity of my indisposition to bring into light a litter of three little kittens. This was an addition to the number of passengers on my part altogether unexpected; but I was pleased at the occurrence. It would afford me a chance of bringing to a kind of test the truth of a surmise, which, more than anything else, had influenced me in attempting this ascension. I had imagined that the habitual endurance of the atmospheric pressure at the surface of the earth was the cause, or nearly so, of the pain attending animal existence at a distance above the surface.

Should the kittens be found to suffer uneasiness in an equal degree with their mother, I must consider my theory in fault, but a failure to do so I should look upon as a strong confirmation of my idea.

'By eight o'clock I had actually attained an elevation of seventeen miles above the surface of the earth. Thus it seemed to me evident that my rate of ascent was not only on the increase, but that the progression would have been apparent in a slight degree even had I not discharged the ballast which I did. The pains in my head and ears returned, at intervals, with violence, and I still continued to bleed occasionally at the nose; but, upon the whole, I suffered much less than might have been expected. I breathed, however, at every moment, with more and more difficulty, and each inhalation was attended with a troublesome spasmodic action of the chest. I now unpacked the condensing apparatus, and got it ready for immediate use.

'The view of the earth, at this period of my ascension, was beautiful indeed. To the westward, the northward, and the southward, as far as I could see, lay a boundless sheet of apparently unruffled ocean, which every moment gained a deeper and a deeper tint of blue and began already to assume a slight appearance of convexity. At a vast distance to the eastward, although perfectly discernible, extended the islands of Great Britain, the entire Atlantic coasts of France and Spain, with a small portion of the northern part of the continent of Africa. Of individual edifices not a trace could be discovered, and the proudest cities of mankind had utterly faded away from the face of the earth. From the rock of Gibraltar, now dwindled into a dim speck, the dark Mediterranean sea, dotted with shining islands as the heaven is dotted with stars, spread itself out to the eastward as far as my vision extended, until its entire mass of waters seemed at length to tumble headlong over the abyss of the horizon, and I found myself listening on tiptoe for the echoes of the mighty cataract. Overhead, the sky was of a jetty black, and the stars were brilliantly visible.

'The pigeons about this time seeming to undergo much suffering, I determined upon giving them their liberty. I first untied one of them, a beautiful grey-mottled pigeon, and placed him upon the rim of the wickerwork. He appeared extremely uneasy, looking anxiously around him, fluttering his wings, and making a loud cooing noise, but could not be persuaded to trust himself from off the car. I took him up at last, and threw him to about half a dozen yards from the balloon. He made, however, no attempt to descend as I had expected, but struggled with great vehemence to get back, uttering at the same time very shrill and piercing cries. He at length succeeded in regaining his former station on the rim, but had hardly done so when his head dropped upon his breast, and he fell dead within the car. The other one did not prove so unfortunate. To prevent his following the example of his companion, and accomplishing a return, I threw him downwards with all my force, and was pleased to find him continue his descent, with great velocity, making use of his wings with ease, and in a perfectly natural manner. In a very short time he was out of sight, and I have no doubt he reached home in safety. Puss, who seemed in a great measure recovered from her illness, now made a hearty meal of the dead bird and then went to sleep with much apparent satisfaction. Her kittens were quite lively, and so far evinced not the slightest sign of any uneasiness whatever.

'At a quarter-past eight, being no longer able to draw breath without the most intolerable pain, I proceeded forthwith to adjust around the car the apparatus belonging to the condenser. This apparatus will require some little explanation, and your Excellencies will please to bear in mind that my object, in the first place, was to surround myself and cat entirely with a barricade against the highly rarefied atmosphere in which I was existing, with the intention of introducing within this barricade, by means of my condenser, a quantity of this same atmosphere sufficiently condensed for the purposes of respiration. With this object in view I had prepared a very strong, perfectly air-tight, but flexible gum-elastic bag. In this bag, which was of sufficient dimensions, the entire car was in a manner placed. That is to say, it (the bag) was drawn over the whole bottom of the car, up its sides, and so on, along the outside of the ropes, to the upper rim or hoop where the network is attached. Having pulled the bag up in this way, and formed a complete enclosure on all sides, and at bottom, it was now necessary to fasten up its top or mouth, by passing its material over the hoop of the network – in other words, between the network and the hoop. But if the network were separated from the hoop to admit this passage, what was to sustain the car in the meantime? Now the network was not permanently fastened to the hoop, but attached by a series of running loops or nooses. I therefore undid only a few of these loops at one time, leaving the car suspended by the remainder. Having thus inserted a portion of the cloth forming the upper part of the bag, I refastened the loops – not to the hoop, for that would have been impossible, since the cloth now intervened – but to a series of large buttons, affixed to the cloth itself, about three feet below the mouth of the bag, the intervals between the buttons having been made to correspond to the intervals between the loops. This done, a few more of the loops were unfastened from the rim, a farther portion of the cloth introduced, and the disengaged loops then connected with their proper buttons. In this way it was possible to insert the whole upper part of the bag between the network and the hoop. It is evident that the hoop would now drop down within the car, while the whole weight of the car itself, with all its contents, would be held up merely by the strength of the buttons. This, at first sight, would seem an inadequate dependence; but it was by no means so, for the buttons were not only very strong in themselves, but so close together that a very slight portion of the whole weight was supported by any one of them. Indeed, had the car and contents been three times heavier than they were, I should not have been at all uneasy. I now raised up the hoop again within the covering of gum-elastic, and propped it at nearly its former height by means of three light poles prepared for the occasion. This was done, of course, to keep the bag distended at the top, and to preserve the lower part of the network in its proper situation. All that now remained was to fasten up the mouth of the enclosure; and this was readily accomplished by gathering the folds of the material together, and twisting them up very tightly on the inside by means of a kind of stationary tourniquet.

'In the sides of the covering thus adjusted round the

car, had been inserted three circular panes of thick but clear glass, through which I could see without difficulty around me in every horizontal direction. In that portion of the cloth forming the bottom was likewise a fourth window, of the same kind, and corresponding with a small aperture in the floor of the car itself. This enabled me to see perpendicularly down, but having found it impossible to place any similar contrivance overhead, on account of the peculiar manner of closing up the opening there, and the consequent wrinkles in the cloth, I could expect to see no objects situated directly in my zenith. This, of course, was a matter of little consequence; for had I even been able to place a window at top, the balloon itself would have prevented my making any use of it.

'About a foot below one of the side windows was a circular opening, eight inches in diameter, and fitted with a brass rim adapted in its inner edge to the windings of a screw. In this rim was screwed the large tube of the condenser, the body of the machine being, of course, within the chamber of gum-elastic. Through this tube a quantity of the rare atmosphere circumjacent being drawn by means of a vacuum created in the body of the machine, was thence discharged, in a state of condensation, to mingle with the thin air already in the chamber. This operation being repeated several times, at length filled the chamber with atmosphere proper for all the purposes of respiration. But in so confined a space it would, in a short time, necessarily become foul, and unfit for use from frequent contact with the lungs. It was then ejected by a small valve at the bottom of the car – the dense air readily sinking into the thinner atmosphere below. To avoid the inconvenience of making a total vacuum at any moment within the chamber, this purification was never accomplished all at once, but in a gradual manner – the valve being opened only for a few seconds, then closed again, until one or two strokes from the pump of the condenser had supplied the place of the atmosphere ejected. For the sake of experiment I had put the cat and kittens in a small basket, and suspended it outside the car to a button at the bottom, close by the valve, through which I could feed them at any moment when necessary. I did this at some little risk, and before closing the mouth of the chamber, by reaching under the car with one of the poles before mentioned to which a hook had been attached.

'By the time I had fully completed these arrangements and filled the chamber as explained, it wanted only ten minutes of nine o'clock. During the whole period of my being thus employed, I endured the most terrible distress from difficulty of respiration, and bitterly did I repent the negligence, or rather foolhardiness, of which I had been guilty, of putting off to the last moment a matter of so much importance. But having at length accomplished it, I soon began to reap the benefit of my invention. Once again I breathed with perfect freedom and ease – and indeed why should I not? I was also agreeably surprised to find myself, in a great measure, relieved from the violent pains which had hitherto tormented me. A slight headache, accompanied with a sensation of fullness or distention about the wrists, the ankles, and the throat, was nearly all of which I had now to complain. Thus it seemed evident that a greater part of the uneasiness attending the removal of atmospheric pressure had actually worn off, as I had expected, and that much of the pain endured for the last two hours should have been attributed altogether to the effects of a deficient respiration.

'At twenty minutes before nine o'clock – that is to say, a short time prior to my closing up the mouth of the chamber, the mercury attained its limit, or ran down, in the barometer, which, as I mentioned before, was one of an extended construction. It then indicated an altitude on my part of 132,000 feet, or five-and-twenty miles, and I consequently surveyed at that time an extent of the earth's area amounting to no less than the three-hundred-and-twentieth part of its entire superficies. At nine o'clock I had again lost sight of land to the eastward, but not before I became aware that the balloon was drifting rapidly to the nor'nor'-west. The convexity of the ocean beneath me was very evident indeed, although my view was often interrupted by the masses of cloud which floated to and fro. I observed now that even the lightest vapours never rose to more than ten miles above the level of the sea.

'At half-past nine I tried the experiment of throwing out a handful of feathers through the valve. They did not float as I had expected; but dropped down perpendicularly, like a bullet, *en masse*, and with the greatest velocity – being out of sight in a very few seconds. I did not at first know what to make of this extraordinary phenomenon; not being able to believe that my rate of ascent had, of a sudden, met with so prodigious an acceleration. But it soon occurred to me that the atmosphere was now far too rare to sustain even the feathers; that they actually fell, as they appeared to do, with great rapidity; and that I had been surprised by the united velocities of their descent and my own elevation.

'By ten o'clock I found that I had very little to occupy my immediate attention. Affairs went swimmingly, and I believed the balloon to be going upwards with a speed increasing momently although I had no longer any means of ascertaining the progression of the increase. I suffered no pain or uneasiness of any kind, and enjoyed better spirits than I had at any period since my departure from Rotterdam, busying myself now in examining the state of my various apparatus, and now in regenerating the atmosphere within the chamber. This latter point I determined to attend to at regular intervals of forty minutes, more on account of the preservation of my health, than from so frequent a renovation being absolutely necessary. In the meanwhile I could not help making anticipations. Fancy revelled in the wild and dreamy regions of the moon. Imagination, feeling herself for once unshackled, roamed at will among the ever-changing wonders of a shadowy and unstable land. Now there were hoary and time-honoured forests, and craggy precipices, and waterfalls tumbling with a loud noise into abysses without a bottom. Then I came suddenly into still noonday solitudes, where no wind of heaven ever intruded, and where vast meadows of poppies, and slender, lily-looking flowers spread themselves out a weary distance, all silent and motionless for ever. Then again I journeyed far down away into another country where it was all one dim and vague lake, with a boundary line of clouds. And out of this melancholy water arose a forest of tall eastern trees, like a wilderness of dreams. And I have in mind that the shadows of the trees which fell upon the lake remained not on the surface where they fell, but sunk slowly and steadily down, and commingled with the waves, while from the trunks of the trees other shadows were continually coming out, and taking the place of their brothers thus entombed. "This then," I said thoughtfully, "is the very reason why the waters of this lake grow blacker with age, and more melancholy as the hours run on." But fancies such as these were not the sole possessors of my brain. Horrors of a nature most stern and most appalling would too frequently obtrude themselves upon my mind, and shake the innermost depths of my soul with the bare supposition of their possibility. Yet I would not suffer my thoughts for any length of time to dwell upon these latter speculations, rightly judging the real and palpable dangers of the voyage sufficient for my undivided attention.

'At five o'clock p.m., being engaged in regenerating the atmosphere within the chamber, I took that opportunity of observing the cat and kittens through the valve. The cat herself appeared to suffer again very much, and I had no hesitation in attributing her uneasiness chiefly to a difficulty in breathing; but my experiment with the kittens had resulted very strangely. I had expected, of course, to see them betray a sense of pain, although in a less degree than their mother, and this would have been sufficient to confirm my opinion concerning the habitual endurance of atmospheric pressure. But I was not prepared to find them, upon close examination, evidently enjoying a high degree of health, breathing with the greatest ease and perfect regularity, and evincing not the slightest sign of any uneasiness whatever. I could only account for all this by extending my theory, and supposing that the highly rarefied atmosphere around might perhaps not be, as I had taken for granted, chemically insufficient for the purposes of life, and that a person born in such a medium might, possibly, be unaware of any inconvenience attending its inhalation, while, upon removal to the denser strata near the earth, he might endure tortures of a similar nature to those I had so lately experienced. It has since been to me a matter of deep regret that an awkward accident, at this time, occasioned me the loss of my little family of cats, and deprived me of the insight into this matter which a continued experiment might have afforded. In passing my hand through the valve, with a cup of water for the old puss, the sleeves of my shirt became entangled in the loop which sustained the basket, and thus, in a moment, loosened it from the bottom. Had the whole actually vanished into air, it could not have shot from my sight in a more abrupt and instantaneous manner. Positively, there could not have intervened the tenth part of a second between the disengagement of the basket and its absolute and total disappearance with all that it contained. My good wishes followed it to the earth, but of course, I had no hope that either cat or kittens would ever live to tell the tale of their misfortune.

'At six o'clock, I perceived a great portion of the earth's visible area to the eastward involved in thick shadow, which continued to advance with great rapidity, until, at five minutes before seven, the whole surface in view was enveloped in the darkness of night. It was not, however, until long after this time that the rays of the setting sun ceased to illumine the balloon; and this circumstance, although of course fully anticipated, did not fail to give me an infinite deal of pleasure. It was evident that, in the morning, I should behold the rising luminary many hours at least before the citizens of Rotterdam, in spite of their situation so much farther to the eastward, and thus, day after day, in proportion to the height ascended, would I enjoy the light of the sun for a longer and a longer period. I now determined to keep a journal of my passage, reckoning the days from one to twenty-four hours continuously, without taking into consideration the intervals of darkness.

'At ten o'clock, feeling sleepy, I determined to lie down for the rest of the night; but here a difficulty presented itself, which, obvious as it may appear, had escaped my attention up to the very moment of which I am now speaking. If I went to sleep as I proposed, how could the atmosphere in the chamber be regenerated in the interim? To breathe it for more than an hour, at the farthest, would be a matter of impossibility, or, if even this term could be extended to an hour and a quarter, the most ruinous consequences might ensue. The consideration of this dilemma gave me no little disquietude; and it will hardly be believed, that, after the dangers I had undergone, I should look upon this business in so serious a light, as to give up all hope of accomplishing my ultimate design, and finally make up my mind to the necessity of a descent. But this hesitation was only momentary. I reflected that man is the veriest slave of custom, and that many points in the routine of his existence are deemed essentially important, which are only so at all by his having rendered them habitual. It was very certain that I could not do without sleep; but I might easily bring myself to feel no inconvenience from being awakened at intervals of an hour during the whole period of my repose. It would require but five minutes at most to regenerate the atmosphere in the fullest manner, and the only real difficulty was to contrive a method of arousing myself at the proper moment for so doing. But this was a question which, I am willing to confess, occasioned me no little trouble in its solution. To be sure, I had heard of the student who, to prevent his falling asleep over his books, held in one hand a ball of copper, the din of whose descent into a basin of the same metal on the floor beside his chair, served effectually to startle him up, if, at any moment, he should be overcome with drowsiness. My own case, however, was very different indeed, and left me no room for any similar idea; for I did not wish to keep awake, but to be aroused from slumber at regular intervals of time. I at length hit upon the following expedient, which, simple as it may seem, was hailed by me, at the moment of discovery, as an invention fully equal to that of the telescope, the steam-engine, or the art of printing itself.

'It is necessary to premise, that the balloon, at the elevation now attained, continued its course upwards with an even and undeviating ascent, and the car consequently followed with a steadiness so perfect that it would have been impossible to detect in it the slightest vacillation whatever. This circumstance favoured me greatly in the project I now determined to adopt. My supply of water had been put on board in kegs containing five gallons each, and ranged very securely around the interior of the car. I unfastened one of these, and taking two ropes, tied them tightly across the rim of the wickerwork from one side to the other; placing them about a foot apart and parallel so as to form a kind of shelf, upon which I placed the keg, and steadied it in a horizontal position. About eight inches immediately below these ropes, and four feet from the bottom of the car, I fastened another shelf –

but made of thin plank, being the only similar piece of wood I had. Upon this latter shelf, and exactly beneath one of the rims of the keg, a small earthern pitcher was deposited. I now bored a hole in the end of the keg over the pitcher, and fitted in a plug of soft wood, cut in a tapering or conical shape. This plug I pushed in or pulled out, as might happen, until, after a few experiments, it arrived at that exact degree of tightness, at which the water, oozing from the hole, and falling into the pitcher below, would fill the latter to the brim in the period of sixty minutes. This, of course, was a matter briefly and easily ascertained, by noticing the proportion of the pitcher filled in any given time. Having arranged all this, the rest of the plan is obvious. My bed was so contrived upon the floor of the car, as to bring my head, in lying down, immediately below the mouth of the pitcher. It was evident that, at the expiration of an hour, the pitcher, getting full, would be forced to run over, and to run over at the mouth, which was somewhat lower than the rim. It was also evident that the water thus falling from a height of more than four feet could not do otherwise than fall upon my face, and that the sure consequence would be to waken me up instantaneously, even from the soundest slumber in the world.

'It was fully eleven by the time I had completed these arrangements, and I immediately betook myself to bed, with full confidence in the efficiency of my invention. Nor in this matter was I disappointed. Punctually every sixty minutes was I aroused by my trusty chronometer, when, having emptied the pitcher into the bung-hole of the keg, and performed the duties of the condenser, I retired again to bed. These regular interruptions to my slumber caused me even less discomfort than I had anticipated; and when I finally arose for the day, it was seven o'clock, and the sun had attained many degrees above the line of my horizon.

'*April 3rd*. I found the balloon at an immense height indeed, and the earth's apparent convexity increased in a material degree. Below me in the ocean lay a cluster of black specks, which undoubtedly were islands. Far away to the northward I perceived a thin, white, and exceedingly brilliant line, or streak, on the edge of the horizon, and I had no hesitation in supposing it to be the southern disc of the ices of the Polar Sea. My curiosity was greatly excited, for I had hopes of passing on much farther to the north, and might possibly, at some period, find myself placed directly above the Pole itself. I now lamented that my great elevation would, in this case, prevent my taking as accurate a survey as I could wish. Much, however, might be ascertained. Nothing else of an extraordinary nature occurred during the day. My apparatus all continued in good order, and the balloon still ascended without any perceptible vacillation. The cold was intense, and obliged me to wrap up closely in an overcoat. When darkness came over the earth, I betook myself to bed, although it was for many hours afterwards broad daylight all around my immediate situation. The wa-ter- clock was punctual in its duty, and I slept until next morning soundly, with the exception of the periodical interruption.

'*April 4th*. Arose in good health and spirits, and was astonished at the singular change which had taken place in the appearance of the sea. It had lost, in a great measure, the deep tint of blue it had hitherto worn, being now of a greyish-white, and of a lustre dazzling to the eye. The islands were no longer visible; whether they had passed down the horizon to the south east, or whether my increasing elevation had left them out of sight, it is impossible to say. I was inclined, however, to the latter opinion. The rim of ice to the northward was growing more and more apparent. Cold by no means so intense. Nothing of importance occurred, and I passed the day in reading, having taken care to supply myself with books.

'*April 5th.* Beheld the singular phenomenon of the sun rising while nearly the whole visible surface of the earth continued to be involved in darkness. In time, however, the light spread itself over all, and I again saw the line of ice to the northward. It was now very distinct, and appeared of a much darker hue than the waters of the ocean. I was evidently approaching it, and with great rapidity. Fancied I could again distinguish a strip of land to the eastward, and one also to the westward, but could not be certain. Weather moderate. Nothing of any consequence happened during the day. Went early to bed.

'*April 6th.* Was surprised at finding the rim of ice at a very moderate distance, and an immense field of the same material stretching away off to the horizon in the north. It was evident that if the balloon held its present course, it would soon arrive above the Frozen Ocean, and I had now little doubt of ultimately seeing the Pole. During the whole of the day I continued to near the ice. Towards night the limits of my horizon very suddenly and materially increased, owing undoubtedly to the earth's form being that of an oblate spheroid, and my arriving above the flattened regions in the vicinity of the Arctic circle. When darkness at length overtook me, I went to bed in great anxiety, fearing to pass over the object of so much curiosity when I should have no opportunity of observing it.

'*April 7th.* Arose early, and, to my great joy, at length beheld what there could be no hesitation in supposing the northern Pole itself. It was there, beyond a doubt, and immediately beneath my feet; but, alas! I had now ascended to so vast a distance, that nothing could with accuracy be discerned. Indeed, to judge from the progression of the numbers indicating my various altitudes, respectively, at different periods, between six o'clock on the second of April, and twenty minutes before nine of the same morning (at which time the barometer ran down), it might be fairly inferred that the balloon had now, at four o'clock in the morning of April the seventh, reached a height of not less, certainly, than 7,254 miles above the surface of the sea. This elevation may appear immense, but the estimate upon which it is calculated gave a result in all probability far inferior to the truth. At all events I undoubtedly beheld the whole of the earth's major diameter; the entire northern hemisphere lay beneath me like a chart orthographically projected: and the great circle of the equator itself formed the boundary line of my horizon. Your Excellencies may, however, readily imagine that the confined regions hitherto unexplored within the limits of the Arctic circle, although situated directly beneath me, and therefore seen without any appearance of being foreshortened, were still, in themselves, comparatively too diminutive, and at too great a distance from the point of sight, to admit of any very accurate examination. Nevertheless, what could be seen was of a nature singular and exciting. Northwardly from that huge rim before mentioned, and which, with slight qualification, may be called the limit of human discovery in these regions, one unbroken, or nearly unbroken, sheet of ice continues to extend. In the first few degrees of this its progress, its surface is very sensibly flattened, farther on depressed into a plane, and finally, becoming not a little concave, it terminates, at the Pole itself, in a circular centre, sharply defined, whose apparent diameter subtended at the balloon an angle of about sixty-five seconds, and whose dusky hue, varying in intensity, was, at all times, darker than any other spot upon the visible hemisphere, and occasionally deepened into the most absolute and impenetrable blackness. Farther than this, little could be ascertained. By twelve o'clock the circular centre had materially decreased in circumference, and by seven o'clock I lost sight of it entirely; the balloon passing over the western limb of the ice, and floating away rapidly in the direction of the equator.

'*April 8th.* Found a sensible diminution in the earth's apparent diameter, besides a material alteration in its general colour and appearance. The whole visible area partook in different degrees of a tint of pale yellow, and in some portions had acquired a brilliancy even painful to the eye. My view downwards was also considerably impeded by the dense atmosphere in the vicinity of the surface being loaded with clouds, between whose masses I could only now and then obtain a glimpse of the earth itself. This difficulty of direct vision had troubled me more or less for the last forty-eight hours; but my present enormous elevation brought closer together, as it were, the floating bodies of vapour, and the inconvenience became, of course, more and more palpable in proportion to my ascent. Nevertheless, I could easily perceive that the balloon now hovered above the range of great lakes in the continent of North

America, and was holding a course, due south, which would bring me to the tropics. This circumstance did not fail to give me the most heartfelt satisfaction, and I hailed it as a happy omen of ultimate success. Indeed, the direction I had hitherto taken had filled me with uneasiness; for it was evident that, had I continued it much longer, there would have been no possibility of my arriving at the moon at all, whose orbit is inclined to the ecliptic at only the small angle of 5° 8' 48".

'*April 9th*. Today the earth's diameter was greatly diminished, and the colour of the surface assumed hourly a deeper tint of yellow. The balloon kept steadily on her course to the southward, and arrived, at nine p.m., over the northern edge of the Mexican Gulf.

'*April 10th*. I was suddenly aroused from slumber, about five o'clock this morning, by a loud, crackling, and terrific sound, for which I could in no manner account. It was of very brief duration, but, while it lasted resembled nothing in the world of which I had any previous experience. It is needless to say that I became excessively alarmed, having, in the first instance, attributed the noise to the bursting of the balloon. I examined all my apparatus, however, with great attention, and could discover nothing out of order. Spent a great part of the day in meditating upon an occurrence so extraordinary, but could find no means whatever of accounting for it. Went to bed dissatisfied, and in a state of great anxiety and agitation.

'*April 11th*. Found a startling diminution in the apparent diameter of the earth, and a considerable increase, now observable for the first time, in that of the moon itself, which wanted only a few days of being full. It now required long and excessive labour to condense within the chamber sufficient atmospheric air for the sustenance of life.

'*April 12th.* A singular alteration took place in regard to the direction of the balloon, and although fully anticipated, afforded me the most unequivocal delight. Having reached, in its former course, about the twentieth parallel of southern latitude, it turned off suddenly, at an acute angle, to the eastward, and thus proceeded throughout the day, keeping nearly, if not altogether, in the exact plane of the lunar ellipse. What was worthy of remark, a very perceptible vacillation in the car was a consequence of this change of route – a vacillation which prevailed, in a more or less degree, for a period of many hours.

'*April 13th.* Was again very much alarmed by a repetition of the loud crackling noise which terrified me on the tenth. Thought long upon the subject, but was unable to form any satisfactory conclusion. Great decrease in the earth's apparent diameter, which now subtended from the balloon an angle of very little more than twenty-five degrees. The moon could not be seen at all, being nearly in my zenith. I still continued in the plane of the ellipse, but made little progress to the eastward.

'*April 14th.* Extremely rapid decrease in the diameter of the earth. Today I became strongly impressed with the idea that the balloon was now actually running up the line of apsides to the point of perigee – in other words, holding the direct course which would bring it immediately to the moon in that part of its orbit the nearest to the earth. The moon itself was directly overhead, and consequently hidden from my view. Great and long-continued labour necessary for the condensation of the atmosphere.

'*April 15th.* Not even the outlines of continents and seas could now be traced upon the earth with anything approaching distinctness. About twelve o'clock I became aware, for the third time, of that appalling sound which had so astonished me before. It now, however, continued for some moments, and gathered intensity as it continued. At length, while, stupefied and terror-stricken, I stood in expectation of I knew not what hideous destruction, the car vibrated with excessive violence, and a gigantic and flaming mass of some material which I could not distinguish, came with a voice of a thousand thunders, roaring and booming by the balloon. When my fears and astonishment had in some degree subsided, I had little difficulty in supposing it to be some mighty volcanic fragment ejected from that world to which I was so rapidly approaching, and, in all probability, one of that singular class of substances occasionally picked up on the earth, and termed meteoric stones for want of a better appellation.

'*April 16th.* Today, looking upwards as well as I could, through each of the side windows alternately, I beheld, to my great delight, a very small portion of the moon's disc protruding, as it were, on all sides beyond the huge circumference of the balloon. My agitation was extreme; for I had now little doubt of soon reaching the end of my perilous voyage. Indeed, the labour now required by the condenser had increased to a most oppressive degree, and allowed me scarcely any respite from exertion. Sleep was a matter nearly out of the question. I became quite ill, and my frame trembled with exhaustion. It was impossible that human nature could endure this state of intense suffering much longer. During the now brief interval of darkness a meteoric stone again passed in my vicinity, and the frequency of these phenomena began to occasion me much apprehension.

'*April 17th.* This morning proved an epoch in my voyage. It will be remembered that, on the thirteenth, the earth subtended an angular breadth of twenty-five degrees. On the fourteenth this had greatly diminished; on the fifteenth a still more remarkable decrease was observable; and, on retiring on the night of the sixteenth, I had noticed an angle of no more than about seven degrees and fifteen minutes. What, therefore, must have been my amazement, on awakening from a brief and disturbed slumber, on the morning of this day, the seventeenth, at finding the surface beneath me so suddenly and wonderfully augmented in volume, as to subtend no less than thirty-nine degrees in apparent angular diameter! I was thunderstruck! No words can give any adequate idea of the extreme, the absolute horror and astonishment, with which I was seized, possessed, and altogether overwhelmed. My knees tottered beneath me – my teeth chattered – my hair started up on end. "The balloon, then, had actually burst!" These were the first tumultuous ideas that hurried through my mind: "The balloon had positively burst! – I was falling – falling with the most impetuous, the most unparalleled velocity! To judge by the immense distance already so quickly passed over, it could not be more than ten minutes, at the farthest, before I should meet the surface of the earth, and be hurled into annihilation!" But at length reflection came to my relief. I paused; I considered; and I began to doubt. The matter was impossible. I could not in any reason have so rapidly come down. Besides, although I was evidently approaching the surface below me, it was with a speed by no means commensurate with the velocity I had at first so horribly conceived. This consideration served to calm the perturbation of my mind, and I finally succeeded in regarding the phenomenon in its proper point of view. In fact, amazement must have fairly deprived me of my senses, when I could not see the vast difference, in appearance, between the surface below me, and the surface of my mother earth. The latter was indeed over my head, and completely hidden by the balloon, while the moon – the moon itself in all its glory – lay beneath me, and at my feet.

'The stupor and surprise produced in my mind by this extraordinary change in the posture of affairs was perhaps, after all, that part of the adventure least susceptible of explanation. For the *bouleversement* in itself was not only natural and inevitable, but had been long actually anticipated as a circumstance to be expected whenever I should arrive at that exact point of my voyage where the attraction of the planet should be superseded by the attraction of the satellite – or, more precisely, where the gravitation of the balloon towards the earth should be less powerful than its gravitation towards the moon. To be sure I arose from a sound slumber, with all my senses in confusion, to the contemplation of a very startling phenomenon, and one which, although expected, was not expected at the moment. The revolution itself must, of course, have taken place in an easy and gradual manner, and it is by no means clear that, had I even been awake at the time of the occurrence, I should have been made aware of it by any internal evidence of an inversion – that is to say, by any inconvenience or disarrangement, either about my person or about my apparatus.

'It is almost needless to say that, upon coming to a due sense of my situation, and emerging from the terror which had absorbed every faculty of my soul, my attention was, in the first place, wholly directed to the contemplation of the general physical appearance of the moon. It lay beneath me like a chart – and although I judged it to be still at no inconsiderable distance, the indentures of its surface were defined to my vision with a most striking and altogether unaccountable distinctness. The entire absence of ocean or sea, and indeed of any lake or river, or body of water whatsoever, struck me, at first glance, as the most extraordinary feature in its geological condition. Yet, strange to say, I beheld vast level regions of a character decidedly alluvial, although by far the greater portion of the hemisphere in sight was covered with innumerable volcanic mountains, conical in shape, and having more the appearance of artificial than of natural protuberance. The highest among them does not exceed three and three-quarter miles in perpendicular elevation; but a map of the volcanic districts of the Campi Phlegraei would afford to your Excellencies a better idea of their general surface than any unworthy description I might think proper to attempt. The greater part of them were in a state of evident eruption, and gave me fearfully to understand their fury and their power, by the repeated thunders of the miscalled meteoric stones, which now rushed upwards by the balloon with a frequency more and more appalling.

'*April 18th*. Today I found an enormous increase in the moon's apparent bulk – and the evidently accelerated velocity of my descent began to fill me with alarm. It will be remembered that, in the earliest stage of my speculations upon the possibility of a passage to the moon, the existence, in its vicinity, of an atmosphere, dense in proportion to the bulk of the planet, had entered largely into my calculations; this too in spite of many theories to the contrary, and, it may be added, in spite of a general disbelief in the existence of any lunar atmosphere at all. But, in addition to what I have already urged in regard to Encke's comet and the zodiacal light, I had been strengthened in my opinion by certain observations of Mr Schroeter, of Lilienthal. He observed the moon when two days and a half old, in the evening soon after sunset, before the dark part was visible, and continued to watch it until it became visible. The two cusps appeared tapering in a very sharp faint prolongation, each exhibiting its farthest extremity faintly illuminated by the solar rays, before any part of the dark hemisphere was visible. Soon afterwards, the whole dark limb became illuminated. This pro- longation of the cusps beyond the semicircle, I thought, must have arisen from the refraction of the sun's rays by the moon's atmosphere. I computed, also, the height of the atmosphere (which could refract light enough into its dark hemisphere to produce a twilight more luminous than the light reflected from the earth when the moon is about 32° from the new) to be 1,356 Paris feet; in this view, I supposed the greatest height capable of refracting the solar ray to be 5,376 feet. My ideas on this topic had also received confirmation by a passage in the eighty-second volume of the Philosophical Trans- actions, in which it is stated that at an occultation of Jupiter's satellites, the third disappeared after having been about 1" or 2" of time indistinct, and the fourth became indiscernible near the limb.*

'Upon the resistance or, more properly, upon the support of an atmosphere, existing in the state of density imagined, I had, of course, entirely depended for the safety of my ultimate descent. Should I then, after all, prove to have been mistaken, I had in consequence nothing better to expect, as a finale to my adventure, than being dashed into atoms against the rugged surface of the satellite. And, indeed, I had now every reason to be terrified. My distance from the moon was comparatively trifling, while the labour required by the condenser was diminished not at all, and I could discover no indication whatever of a decreasing rarity in the air.

---

* Hevelius writes that he has several times found, in skies perfectly clear, when even stars of the sixth and seventh magnitude were conspicuous, that, at the same altitude of the moon, at the same elongation from the earth, and with one and the same excellent telescope, the moon and its maculae did not appear equally lucid at all times. From the circumstances of the observation, it is evident that the cause of this phenomenon is not either in our air, in the tube, in the moon or in the eye of the spectator, but must be looked for in something (an atmosphere?) existing about the moon.

Cassini frequently observed Saturn and Jupiter and the fixed stars, when approaching the moon to occultation, to have their circular figure changed into an oval one; and, on other occultations, he found no alteration of figure at all. Hence it might be supposed that *at some times* and not at others there is a dense matter encompassing the moon wherein the rays of the stars are refracted.

'*April 19th.* This morning, to my great joy, about nine o'clock, the surface of the moon being frightfully near, and my apprehensions excited to the utmost, the pump of my condenser at length gave evident tokens of an alteration in the atmosphere. By ten, I had reason to believe its density considerably increased. By eleven, very little labour was necessary at the apparatus; and at twelve o'clock, with some hesitation, I ventured to unscrew the tourniquet, when, finding no inconvenience from having done so, I finally threw open the gum-elastic chamber, and unrigged it from around the car. As might have been expected, spasms and violent headache were the immediate consequences of an experiment so precipitate and full of danger. But these and other difficulties attending respiration, as they were by no means so great as to put me in peril of my life, I determined to endure as I best could, in consideration of my leaving them behind me momently in my approach to the denser strata near the moon. This approach, however, was still impetuous in the extreme; and it soon became alarmingly certain that, although I had probably not been deceived in the expectation of an atmosphere dense in proportion to the mass of the satellite, still I had been wrong in supposing this density, even at the surface, at all adequate to the support of the great weight contained in the car of my balloon. Yet this should have been the case, and in an equal degree as at the surface of the earth, the actual gravity of bodies at either planet supposed in the ratio of the atmospheric condensation. That it was not the case, however, my precipitous downfall gave testimony enough; why it was not so, can only be explained by a reference to those possible geological disturbances to which I have formerly alluded. At all events I was now close upon the planet, and coming down with the most terrible impetuosity. I lost not a moment, accordingly, in throwing overboard first my ballast, then my water-kegs, then my condensing apparatus and gum-elastic chamber, and finally every article within the car. But it was all to no purpose. I still fell with horrible rapidity, and was now not more than half a mile from the surface. As a last resource, therefore, having got rid of my coat, hat, and boots, I cut loose from the balloon the car itself, which was of no inconsiderable weight, and thus, clinging with both hands to the network, I had barely time to observe that the whole country, as far as the eye could reach, was thickly interspersed with diminutive habitations, ere I tumbled headlong into the very heart of a fantastical-looking city, and into the middle of a vast crowd of ugly little people, who none of them uttered a single syllable, or gave themselves the least trouble to render me assistance, but stood, like a parcel of idiots, grinning in a ludicrous manner, and eyeing me and my balloon askant, with their arms set akimbo. I turned from them in contempt, and, gazing upward at the earth so lately left, and left perhaps for ever, beheld it like a huge, dull, copper shield, about two degrees in diameter, fixed immovably in the heavens overhead, and tipped on one of its edges with a crescent border of the most brilliant gold. No traces of land or water could be discovered, and the whole was clouded with variable spots, and belted with tropical and equatorial zones.

'Thus, may it please your Excellencies, after a series of great anxieties, unheard-of dangers, and unparalleled escapes, I had, at length, on the nineteenth day of my departure from Rotterdam, arrived in safety at the conclusion of a voyage undoubtedly the most extraordinary, and the most momentous, ever accomplished, undertaken, or conceived by any denizen of earth. But my adventures yet remain to be related. And indeed your Excellencies may well imagine that, after a residence of five years upon a planet not only deeply interesting in its own peculiar character, but rendered doubly so by its intimate connection, in capacity of satellite, with the world inhabited by man, I may have intelligence for the private ear of the States' College of Astronomers of far more importance than the details, however wonderful, of the mere voyage which so happily concluded. This is, in fact, the case. I have much – very much which it would give me the greatest pleasure to communicate. I have much to say of the climate of the planet; of its wonderful alternations of heat and cold, of unmitigated and burning sunshine for one fortnight, and more than polar frigidity for the next; of a constant transfer of moisture, by distillation like that *in vacuo*, from the point beneath the sun to the point the farthest from it; of a variable zone of running water, of the people themselves; of their manners, customs, and political institutions; of their peculiar physical construction; of their ugliness; of their want of ears, those useless appendages in an atmosphere so peculiarly modified; of their consequent ignorance of the use and properties of speech; of their substitute for speech in a singular method of intercommunication; of the incomprehensible connection between each particular individual in the moon with some particular individual on the earth – a connection analogous with, and depending upon, that of the orbs of the planet and the satellites, and by means of which the lives and destinies of the inhabitants of the one are interwoven with the lives and destinies of the inhabitants of the other; and above all, if it so please your Excellencies – above all, of those dark and hideous mysteries which lie in the outer regions of the moon – regions which, owing to the almost miraculous accordance of the satellite's rotation on its own axis with its sidereal revolution about the earth, have never yet been turned, and, by God's mercy, never shall be turned, to the scrutiny of the telescopes of man. All this, and more – much more – would I most willingly detail. But, to be brief, I must have my reward. I am pining for a return to my family and to my home, and as the price of any further communication on my part – in consideration of the light which I have it in my power to throw upon many very important branches of physical and metaphysical science – I must solicit, through the influence of your honourable body, a pardon for the crime of which I have been guilty in the death of the creditors upon my departure from Rotterdam. This, then, is the object of the present paper. Its bearer, an inhabitant of the moon, whom I have prevailed upon, and properly instructed, to be my messenger to the earth, will await your Excellencies' pleasure, and return to me with the pardon in question, if it can, in any manner, be obtained.

'I have the honour to be, etc., your Excellencies' very humble servant,

HANS PFAALL.'

Upon finishing the perusal of this very extraordinary document, Professor Rub-a-dub, it is said, dropped his pipe upon the ground in the extremity of his surprise, and Mynheer Superbus von Underduk having taken off his spectacles, wiped them, and deposited them in his pocket, so far forgot both himself and his dignity, as to turn round three times upon his heel in the quintessence of astonishment and admiration. There was no doubt about the matter – the pardon should be obtained. So at least swore, with a round oath, Professor Rub-a-dub, and so finally thought the illustrious von Underduk, as he took the arm of his brother in science, and without saying a word, began to make the best of his way home to deliberate upon the measures to be adopted. Having reached the door, however, of the burgomaster's dwelling, the professor ventured to suggest that as the messenger had thought proper to disappear – no doubt frightened to death by the savage appearance of the burghers of Rotterdam – the pardon would be of little use, as no one but a man of the moon would undertake a voyage to so vast a distance. To the truth of this observation the burgomaster assented, and the matter was therefore at an end. Not so, however, rumours and speculations. The letter, having been published, gave rise to a variety of gossip and opinion. Some of the over-wise even made themselves ridiculous by decrying the whole business as nothing better than a hoax. But hoax, with these sort of people, is, I believe, a general term for all matters above their comprehension. For my part, I cannot conceive upon what data they have founded such an accusation. Let us see what they say:

Imprimis. That certain wags in Rotterdam have certain especial antipathies to certain burgomasters and astronomers.

Don't understand at all.

Secondly. That an odd little dwarf and bottle con-
jurer, both of whose ears, for some misdemeanour,
have been cut off close to his head, has been missing
for several days from the neighbouring city of Bruges.

Well – what of that?

Thirdly. That the newspapers which were stuck all
over the little balloon were newspapers of Holland,
and therefore could not have been made in the moon.
They were dirty papers – very dirty – and Gluck, the
printer, would take his Bible oath to their having been
printed in Rotterdam.

He was mistaken – undoubtedly – mistaken.

Fourthly. That Hans Pfaall himself, the drunken
villain, and the three very idle gentlemen styled his
creditors, were all seen, no longer than two or three
days ago, in a tippling house in the suburbs, having
just returned, with money in their pockets, from a trip
beyond the sea.

Don't believe it – don't believe a word of it.

Lastly. That it is an opinion very generally received,
or which ought to be generally received, that the
College of Astronomers in the city of Rotterdam, as
well as other colleges in all other parts of the world –
not to mention colleges and astronomers in general –
are, to say the least of the matter, not a whit better,
nor greater, nor wiser than they ought to be.

NOTE – Strictly speaking, there is but little similarity
between the above sketchy trifle and the celebrated
'Moon-Story' of Mr Locke; but as both have the
character of *hoaxes* (although the one is in a tone of
banter, the other of downright earnest), and as both
hoaxes are on the same subject, the moon – moreover, as both attempt to give plausibility by scientific

detail – the author of 'Hans Pfaall' thinks it necessary to say, in *self-defence*, that his own *jeu d'esprit* was published in the *Southern Literary Messenger* about three weeks before the commencement of Mr L—'s in the *New York Sun*. Fancying a likeness which, perhaps, does not exist, some of the New York papers copied 'Hans Pfaall', and collated it with the 'Moon-Hoax', by way of detecting the writer of the one in the writer of the other.

As many more persons were actually gulled by the 'Moon-Hoax' than would be willing to acknowledge the fact, it may here afford some little amusement to show why no one should have been deceived – to point out those particulars of the story which should have been sufficient to establish its real character. Indeed, however rich the imagination displayed in this ingenious fiction, it wanted much of the force which might have been given it by a more scrupulous attention to facts and to general analogy. That the public were misled, even for an instant, merely proves the gross ignorance which is so generally prevalent upon subjects of an astronomical nature.

The moon's distance from the earth is, in round numbers, 240,000 miles. If we desire to ascertain how near, apparently, a lens would bring the satellite (or any distant object), we, of course, have but to divide the distance by the magnifying or, more strictly, by the space-penetrating power of the glass. Mr L— makes his lens have a power of 42,000 times. By this divide 240,000 (the moon's real distance), and we have five miles and five-sevenths, as the apparent distance. No animal at all could be seen so far; much less the minute points particularised in the story. Mr L— speaks about Sir John Herschel's perceiving flowers (the *Papaver rheas*, etc.), and even detecting the colour and the shape of the eyes of small birds. Shortly before, too, he has himself observed that the lens would not render perceptible objects of less than eighteen inches in diameter; but even this, as I have said, is giving the glass by far too great power. It may be observed, in passing, that this prodigious glass is said to have been moulded at the glasshouse of Messrs Hartley and Grant, in Dumbarton; but Messrs H and G's establishment had ceased operations for many years previous to the publication of the hoax.

On page 13, pamphlet edition, speaking of 'a hairy veil' over the eyes of a species of bison, the author says: 'It immediately occurred to the acute mind of Dr Herschel that this was a providential contrivance to protect the eyes of the animal from the great extremes of light and darkness to which all the inhabitants of our side of the moon are periodically subjected.' But this cannot be thought a very 'acute' observation of the doctor's. The inhabitants of our side of the moon have, evidently, no darkness at all, so there can be nothing of the 'extremes' mentioned. In the absence of the sun they have a light from the earth equal to that of thirteen full unclouded moons.

The topography throughout, even when professing to accord with Blunt's Lunar Chart, is entirely at variance with that or any other lunar chart, and even grossly at variance with itself. The points of the compass, too, are in inextricable confusion; the writer appearing to be ignorant that, on a lunar map, these are not in accordance with terrestrial points; the east being to the left, etc.

Deceived, perhaps, by the vague titles, *Mare Nubium, Mare Tranquillitatis, Mare Faecunditatis*, etc., given to the dark spots by former astronomers, Mr L— has entered into details regarding oceans and other large bodies of water in the moon; whereas there is no astronomical point more positively ascertained than that no such bodies exist there. In examining the boundary between light and darkness (in the crescent or gibbous moon) where this boundary crosses any of the dark places, the line of division is found to be rough and jagged; but, were these dark places liquid, it would evidently be even.

The description of the wings of the man-bat, on page 21, is but a literal copy of Peter Wilkins' account of the wings of his flying islanders. This simple fact should have induced suspicion, at least, it might be thought.

On page 23, we have the following: 'What a prodigious influence must our thirteen times larger globe have exercised upon this satellite when an embryo in the womb of time, the passive subject of chemical affinity!' This is very fine; but it should be observed that no astronomer would have made such remark, especially to any journal of Science; for the earth, in the sense intended, is not only thirteen, but forty-nine times larger than the moon. A similar objection applies to the whole of the concluding pages, where, by way of introduction to some discoveries in Saturn, the philosophical correspondent enters into a minute schoolboy account of that planet – this to the *Edinburgh Journal of Science*!

But there is one point, in particular, which should have betrayed the fiction. Let us imagine the power actually possessed of seeing animals upon the moon's surface – what would first arrest the attention of an observer from the earth? Certainly neither their shape, size, nor any other such peculiarity, so soon as their remarkable *situation*. They would appear to be walking, with heels up and head down, in the manner of flies on a ceiling. The *real* observer would have uttered an instant ejaculation of surprise (however prepared by previous knowledge) at the singularity of their position; the *fictitious* observer has not even mentioned the subject, but speaks of seeing the entire bodies of such creatures, when it is demonstrable that he could have seen only the diameter of their heads!

It might as well be remarked, in conclusion, that the size, and particularly the powers of the man-bats (for example, their ability to fly in so rare an atmosphere – if, indeed, the moon have any), with most of the other fancies in regard to animal and vegetable existence, are at variance, generally, with all analogical reasoning on these themes; and that analogy here will often amount to conclusive demonstration. It is, perhaps, scarcely necessary to add, that all the suggestions attributed to Brewster and Herschel, in the beginning of the article, about 'a transfusion of artificial light through the focal object of vision', etc., etc., belong to that species of figurative writing which comes, most properly, under the denomination of rigmarole.

There is a real and very definite limit to optical discovery among the stars – a limit whose nature need only be stated to be understood. If, indeed, the casting of large lenses were all that is required, man's ingenuity would ultimately prove equal to the task, and we might have them of any size demanded. But, unhappily, in proportion to the increase of size in the lens, and consequently of space-penetrating power, is the diminution of light from the object, by diffusion of its rays. And for this evil there is no remedy within human ability; for an object is seen by means of that light alone which proceeds from itself, whether direct or reflected. Thus the only 'artificial' light which could avail Mr Locke, would be some artificial light which he should be able to throw – not upon the 'focal object of vision', but upon the real object to be viewed – to wit: upon the moon. It has been easily calculated that, when the light proceeding from a star becomes so diffused as to be as weak as the natural light proceeding from the whole of the stars, in a clear and moonless night, then the star is no longer visible for any practical purpose.

The Earl of Ross's telescope, lately constructed in England, has a *speculum* with a reflecting surface of .4071 square inches; the Herschel telescope having one of only .1811. The metal of the Earl of Ross's is 6 feet in diameter; it is 5½ inches thick at the edges, and 5 at the centre. The weight is 3 tons. The focal length is 50 feet.

I have lately read a singular and somewhat ingenious little book, whose title-page runs thus: '*L'Homme dans la Lune où le Voyage Chimerique fait au Monde de la Lune, nouvellement decouvert par Dominique Gonzales, Advanturier Espagnol, autrement dit le Courier volant. Mis en notre langue par J.B.D.A., Paris, chez François Piot, près la Fontaine de Saint Benoist. Et chez J. Goignard, au premier pilier de la grand'salle du Palais, proché les Consultations,* MDCXLVII.'

The writer professes to have translated his work from the English of one Mr D'Avisson (Davidson?) although there is a terrible ambiguity in the statement. '*J'en ai eu,*' says he, '*l'original de M. D'Avisson, medecin des mieux versez qui soient aujourd'huy dans la conaissance des belles lettres, et sur tout de la philosophie naturelle. Je lui ai cette obligation entre les autres, de m'avoir non seulement mis en main ce livre en anglais, mais encore le manuscrit du Sieur Thomas D'Anan, gentilhomme Eccossais, récommandable pour sa vertu, sur la version duquel j'advoue que j'ay tiré le plan de la mienne.'*

After some irrelevant adventures, much in the manner of Gil Blas, and which occupy the first thirty pages, the author relates that, being ill during a sea voyage, the crew abandoned him, together with a negro servant, on the island of St Helena. To increase the chances of obtaining food, the two separate, and live as far apart as possible. This brings about a training of birds, to serve the purpose of carrier-pigeons between them. By and by these are taught to carry parcels of some weight – and this weight is gradually increased. At length the idea is entertained of uniting the force of a great number of the birds, with a view to raising the author himself. A machine is contrived for the purpose, and we have a minute description of it, which is materially helped out by a steel engraving. Here we perceive the Signor Gonzales, with point ruffles and a huge periwig, seated astride something which resembles very closely a broomstick, and borne aloft by a multitude of wild swans (*ganzas*) who had strings reaching from their tails to the machine.

The main event detailed in the Signor's narrative depends upon a very important fact, of which the reader is kept in ignorance until near the end of the book. The *ganzas*, with whom he had become so familiar, were not really denizens of St Helena, but of the moon. Thence it had been their custom, time out of mind, to migrate annually to some portion of the earth. In proper season, of course, they would return home; and the author, happening, one day, to require their services for a short voyage, is unexpectedly carried straight up, and in a very brief period arrives at the satellite. Here he finds, among other odd things, that the people enjoy extreme happiness; that they have no *law*; that they die without pain; that they are from ten to thirty feet in height; that they live five thousand years; that they have an emperor called Irdonozur; and that they can jump sixty feet high, when, being out of the gravitating influence, they fly about with fans.

I cannot forbear giving a specimen of the general *philosophy* of the volume.

'I must now declare to you,' says the Signor Gonzales, 'the nature of the place in which I found myself. All the clouds were beneath my feet, or, if you please, spread between me and the earth. As to the stars, *since there was no night where I was, they always had the same appearance; not brilliant, as usual, but pale, and very nearly like the moon of a morning*. But few of them were visible, and these ten times larger (as well as I could judge) than they seem to the inhabitants of the earth. The moon, which wanted two days of being full, was of a terrible bigness.

'I must not forget here, that the stars appeared only on that side of the globe turned towards the moon, and that the closer they were to it the larger they seemed. I have also to inform you that, whether it was calm weather or stormy, I found myself *always immediately between the moon and the earth*. I was convinced of this for two reasons – because my birds always flew in a straight line; and because whenever we attempted to rest, *we were carried insensibly around the globe of the earth.* For I admit the opinion of Copernicus, who maintains that it never ceases to revolve *from the east to the west,* not upon the poles of the Equinoctial, commonly called the poles of the world, but upon those of the Zodiac, a question of which I propose to speak more at length hereafter, when I shall have leisure to refresh my memory in regard to the astrology which I learned at Salamanca when young, and have since forgotten.'

Notwithstanding the blunders italicised, the book is not without some claim to attention, as affording a naive specimen of the current astronomical notions of the time. One of these assumed, that the 'gravitating power' extended but a short distance from the earth's surface, and, accordingly, we find our voyager 'carried insensibly around the globe', etc.

There have been other 'voyages to the moon', but none of higher merit than the one just mentioned. That of Bergerac is utterly meaningless. In the third volume of the *American Quarterly Review* will be found quite an elaborate criticism upon a certain 'journey' of the kind in question – a criticism in which it is difficult to say whether the critic most exposes the stupidity of the book, or his own absurd ignorance of astronomy. I forget the title of the work; but the *means* of the voyage are more deplorably ill conceived than are even the *ganzas* of our friend the Signor Gonzales. The adventurer, in digging the earth, happens to discover a peculiar metal for which the moon has a strong attraction, and straightway constructs of it a box, which, when cast loose from its terrestrial fastenings, flies with him, forthwith, to the satellite. *The Flight of Thomas O'Rourke* is a *jeu d'esprit* not altogether contemptible, and has been translated into German. Thomas, the hero, was, in fact, the gamekeeper of an Irish peer, whose eccentricities gave rise to the tale. The 'flight' is made on an eagle's back, from Hungry Hill, a lofty mountain at the end of Bantry Bay.

In these various *brochures* the aim is always satirical; the theme being a description of Lunarian customs as compared with ours. In none is there any effort at *plausibility* in the details of the voyage itself. The writers seem, in each instance, to be utterly uninformed in respect to astronomy. In 'Hans Pfaall' the design is original, inasmuch as regards an attempt at *verisimilitude*, in the application of scientific principles (so far as the whimsical nature of the subject would permit), to the actual passage between the earth and the moon.

Berenice

Dicebant mihi sodales, si sepulchrum amicae
visitarem, curas meas aliquantulum fore levatas.

Ebn Zaiat

Misery is manifold. The wretchedness of earth is
multiform. Overreaching the wide horizon as the rainbow, its hues are as various as the hues of that arch – as
distinct too, yet as intimately blended. Overreaching
the wide horizon as the rainbow! How is it that from
beauty I have derived a type of unloveliness? – from the
covenant of peace, a simile of sorrow? But as, in ethics,
evil is a consequence of good, so, in fact, out of joy is
sorrow born. Either the memory of past bliss is the
anguish of today, or the agonies which *are*, have their
origin in the ecstasies which *might have been*.

My baptismal name is Egaeus; that of my family I
will not mention. Yet there are no towers in the land
more time-honoured than my gloomy, grey, hereditary
halls. Our line has been called a race of visionaries; and
in many striking particulars – in the character of the
family mansion – in the frescos of the chief saloon – in
the tapestries of the dormitories – in the chiselling of
some buttresses in the armoury – but more especially in
the gallery of antique paintings – in the fashion of the
library chamber – and, lastly, in the very peculiar
nature of the library's contents – there is more than
sufficient evidence to warrant the belief.

The recollections of my earliest years are connected
with that chamber, and with its volumes – of which

latter I will say no more. Here died my mother. Herein was I born. But it is mere idleness to say that I had not lived before – that the soul has no previous existence. You deny it? – let us not argue the matter. Convinced myself, I seek not to convince. There is, however, a remembrance of aerial forms – of spiritual and meaning eyes – of sounds, musical yet sad – a remembrance which will not be excluded; a memory like a shadow – vague, variable, indefinite, unsteady; and like a shadow, too, in the impossibility of my getting rid of it while the sunlight of my reason shall exist.

In that chamber was I born. Thus awaking from the long night of what seemed, but was not, nonentity, at once into the very regions of fairy land – into a palace of imagination – into the wild dominions of monastic thought and erudition – it is not singular that I gazed around me with a startled and ardent eye – that I loitered away my boyhood in books, and dissipated my youth in reverie; but it *is* singular that as years rolled away, and the noon of manhood found me still in the mansion of my fathers – it is wonderful what stagnation there fell upon the springs of my life – wonderful how total an inversion took place in the character of my commonest thought. The realities of the world affected me as visions, and as visions only, while the wild ideas of the land of dreams became, in turn, not the material of my everyday existence, but in very deed that existence utterly and solely in itself.

* * *

Berenice and I were cousins, and we grew up together in my paternal halls. Yet differently we grew – I, ill of health, and buried in gloom – she, agile, graceful, and overflowing with energy; hers, the ramble on the hillside – mine, the studies of the cloister; I, living within my own heart, and addicted, body and soul, to the most intense and painful meditation – she, roaming carelessly through life, with no thought of the shadows in her path, or the silent flight of the raven-winged hours. Berenice! – I call upon her name – Berenice! – and from the grey ruins of memory a thousand tumultuous recollections are startled at the sound! Ah, vividly is her image before me now, as in the early days of her light-heartedness and joy! Oh, gorgeous yet fantastic beauty! Oh, sylph amid the shrubberies of Arnheim! Oh, Naiad among its fountains! And then – then all is mystery and terror, and a tale which should not be told. Disease – a fatal disease, fell like the simoon upon her frame; and, even while I gazed upon her, the spirit of change swept over her, pervading her mind, her habits, and her character, and, in a manner the most subtle and terrible, disturbing even the identity of her person! Alas! the destroyer came and went! – and the victim – where is she? I knew her not – or knew her no longer as Berenice.

Among the numerous train of maladies superinduced by that fatal and primary one which effected a revolution of so horrible a kind in the moral and physical being of my cousin, may be mentioned as the most distressing and obstinate in its nature, a species of epilepsy not unfrequently terminating in *trance* itself – trance very nearly resembling positive dissolution, and from which her manner of recovery was, in most instances, startlingly abrupt. In the meantime my own disease – for I have been told that I should call it by no other appellation – my own disease, then, grew rapidly upon me, and assumed finally a monomaniac character of a novel and extraordinary form – hourly and momently gaining vigour – and at length obtaining over me the most incomprehensible ascendancy. This monomania, if I must so term it, consisted in a morbid irritability of those properties of the mind in metaphysical science termed the *attentive*. It is more than probable that I am not understood; but I fear, indeed, that it is in no manner possible to convey to the mind of the merely general reader, an adequate idea of that nervous *intensity of interest* with which, in my case, the powers of meditation (not to speak technically) busied and buried themselves, in the contemplation of even the most ordinary objects of the universe.

To muse for long unwearied hours, with my attention riveted to some frivolous device on the margin, or in the typography of a book; to become absorbed, for the better part of a summer's day, in a quaint shadow falling aslant upon the tapestry or upon the floor; to lose myself, for an entire night, in watching the steady flame of a lamp, or the embers of a fire; to dream away whole days over the perfume of a flower; to repeat, monotonously, some common word, until the sound, by dint of frequent repetition, ceased to convey any idea whatever to the mind; to lose all sense of motion or physical existence, by means of absolute bodily quiescence long and obstinately persevered in: such were a few of the most common and least pernicious vagaries induced by a condition of the mental faculties, not, indeed, altogether unparalleled, but certainly bidding defiance to anything like analysis or explanation.

Yet let me not be misapprehended. The undue, earnest, and morbid attention thus excited by objects in their own nature frivolous, must not be confounded in character with that ruminating propensity common to all mankind, and more especially indulged in by persons of ardent imagination. It was not even, as might be at first supposed, an extreme condition, or exaggeration of such propensity, but primarily and essentially distinct and different. In the one instance, the dreamer, or enthusiast, being interested by an object usually *not* frivolous, imperceptibly loses sight of this object in a wilderness of deductions and suggestions issuing therefrom, until, at the conclusion of a daydream *often replete with luxury*, he finds the *incitamentum*, or first cause of his musings, entirely vanished and forgotten. In my case, the primary object was *invariably frivolous*, although assuming, through the medium of my distempered vision, a refracted and unreal importance. Few deductions, if any, were made; and those few pertinaciously returning in upon the original object as a centre. The meditations were *never* pleasurable; and, at the termination of the reverie, the first cause, so far from being out of sight, had attained that supernaturally exaggerated interest which was the prevailing feature of the disease. In a word, the powers of mind more particularly exercised were, with me, as I have said before, the *attentive*, and are, with the daydreamer, the *speculative*.

My books, at this epoch, if they did not actually serve to irritate the disorder, partook, it will be perceived, largely, in their imaginative and inconsequential nature, of the characteristic qualities of the disorder itself. I well remember, among others, the treatise of the noble Italian, Coelius Secundus Curio, *De Amplitudine Beati Regni Dei*; St Austin's great work, the *City of God*; and Tertullian's *De Carne Christi*, in which the paradoxical sentence '*Mortuus est Dei filius; credible est quia ineptum est; et sepultus resurrexit; certum est quia impossibile est*', occupied my undivided time, for many weeks of laborious and fruitless investigation.

Thus it will appear that, shaken from its balance only by trivial things, my reason bore resemblance to that ocean-crag spoken of by Ptolemy Hephestion, which steadily resisting the attacks of human violence, and the fiercer fury of the waters and the winds, trembled only to the touch of the flower called Asphodel. And although, to a careless thinker, it might appear a matter beyond doubt, that the alteration produced by her unhappy malady, in the *moral* condition of Berenice, would afford me many objects for the exercise of that intense and abnormal meditation whose nature I have been at some trouble in explaining, yet such was not in any degree the case. In the lucid intervals of my infirmity, her calamity, indeed, gave me pain, and, taking deeply to heart that total wreck of her fair and gentle life, I did not fail to ponder, frequently and bitterly, upon the wonder-working means by which so strange a revolution had been so suddenly brought to pass. But these reflections partook not of the idiosyncrasy of my disease, and were such as would have occurred, under similar circumstances, to the ordinary mass of mankind. True to its own character, my disorder revelled in the less important but more startling changes wrought in the *physical* frame of Berenice – in the singular and most appalling distortion of her personal identity.

During the brightest days of her unparalleled beauty, most surely I had never loved her. In the strange anomaly of my existence, feelings with me, *had never been* of the heart, and my passions *always were* of the mind. Through the grey of the early morning – among the trellised shadows of the forest at noonday – and in the silence of my library at night – she had flitted by my eyes, and I had seen her – not as the living and breathing Berenice, but as the Berenice of a dream; not as a being of the earth, earthy, but as the abstraction of such a being; not as a thing to admire, but to analyse; not as an object of love, but as the theme of the most abstruse although desultory speculation. And *now* – now I shuddered in her presence, and grew pale at her approach; yet, bitterly lamenting her fallen and desolate condition, I called to mind that she had loved me long, and, in an evil moment, I spoke to her of marriage.

And at length the period of our nuptials was approaching, when, upon an afternoon in the winter of the year – one of those unseasonably warm, calm, and misty days which are the nurse of the beautiful Halcyon* – I sat (and sat, as I thought, alone) in the inner apartment of the library. But, uplifting my eyes, I saw that Berenice stood before me.

Was it my own excited imagination – or the misty influence of the atmosphere – or the uncertain twilight of the chamber – or the grey draperies which fell around her figure – that caused in it so vacillating and indistinct an outline? I could not tell. She spoke no word; and I – not for worlds could I have uttered a syllable. An icy chill ran through my frame; a sense of insufferable anxiety oppressed me; a consuming

---

* For as Jove, during the winter season, gives twice seven days of warmth, men have called this clement and temperate time the nurse of the beautiful Halcyon.

SIMONIDES

curiosity pervaded my soul; and sinking back upon the chair, I remained for some time breathless and motionless, with my eyes riveted upon her person. Alas! its emaciation was excessive, and not one vestige of the former being lurked in any single line of the contour. My burning glances at length fell upon the face.

The forehead was high, and very pale, and singularly placid; and the once jetty hair fell partially over it, and overshadowed the hollow temples with innumerable ringlets, now of a vivid yellow, and jarring discordantly, in their fantastic character, with the reigning melancholy of the countenance. The eyes were lifeless, and lustreless, and seemingly pupilless, and I shrank involuntarily from their glassy stare to the contemplation of the thin and shrunken lips. They parted; and in a smile of peculiar meaning, *the teeth* of the changed Berenice disclosed themselves slowly to my view. Would to God that I had never beheld them, or that, having done so, I had died!

* * *

The shutting of a door disturbed me, and, looking up, I found that my cousin had departed from the chamber. But from the disordered chamber of my brain, had not, alas! departed, and would not be driven away, the white and ghastly *spectrum* of the teeth. Not a speck on their surface – not a shade on their enamel – not an indenture in their edges – but what that period of her smile had sufficed to brand in upon my memory. I saw them *now* even more unequivocally than I beheld them *then*. The teeth! – the teeth! – they were here, and there, and everywhere, and visibly and palpably before me; long, narrow, and excessively white, with the pale lips writhing about them, as in the very moment of their first terrible development. Then came the full fury of my *monomania*, and I struggled in vain against its strange and irresistible influence. In the multiplied objects of the external world I had no thoughts but for the teeth. For these I longed with a frenzied desire. All other matters and all different interests became absorbed in their single contemplation. They – they alone were present to the mental eye, and they, in their sole individuality, became the essence of my mental life. I held them in every light. I turned them in every attitude. I surveyed their characteristics. I dwelt upon their peculiarities. I pondered upon their conformation. I mused upon the alteration in their nature. I shuddered as I assigned to them in imagination a sensitive and sentient power, and even when unassisted by the lips, a capability of moral expression. Of Mlle Salle it has been well said, '*Que tous ses pas étaient des sentiments,*' and of Berenice I more seriously believed *que toutes ses dents étaient des idées. Des idées!* – ah here was the idiotic thought that destroyed me! *Des idées!* – ah *therefore* it was that I coveted them so madly! I felt that their possession could alone ever restore me to peace, in giving me back to reason.

And the evening closed in upon me thus – and then the darkness came, and tarried, and went – and the day again dawned – and the mists of a second night were now gathering around – and still I sat motionless in that solitary room – and still I sat buried in meditation – and still the *phantasma* of the teeth maintained its terrible ascendancy, as, with the most vivid hideous distinctness, it floated about amid the changing lights and shadows of the chamber. At length there broke in upon my dreams a cry as of horror and dismay; and thereunto, after a pause, succeeded the sound of troubled voices, intermingled with many low moanings of sorrow or of pain. I arose from my seat, and throwing open one of the doors of the library, saw standing out in the antechamber a servant maiden, all in tears, who told me that Berenice was – no more! She had been seized with epilepsy in the early morning, and now, at the closing in of the night, the grave was ready for its tenant, and all the preparations for the burial were completed.

*   *   *

I found myself sitting in the library, and again sitting there alone. It seemed that I had newly awakened from a confused and exciting dream. I knew that it was now midnight, and I was well aware, that since the setting of the sun, Berenice had been interred. But of that dreary period which intervened I had no positive, at least no definite, comprehension. Yet its memory was replete with horror – horror more horrible from being vague, and terror more terrible from ambiguity. It was a fearful page in the record of my existence, written all over with dim, and hideous, and unintelligible recollections. I strived to decipher them, but in vain; while ever and anon, like the spirit of a departed sound, the shrill and piercing shriek of a female voice seemed to be ringing in my ears. I had done a deed – what was it? I asked myself the question aloud, and the whispering echoes of the chamber answered me, '*What was it?*'

On the table beside me burned a lamp, and near it lay a little box. It was of no remarkable character, and I had seen it frequently before, for it was the property of the family physician; but how came it *there*, upon my table, and why did I shudder in regarding it? These things were in no manner to be accounted for, and my eyes at length dropped to the open pages of a book, and to a sentence underscored therein. The words were the singular but simple ones of the poet Ebn Zaiat – '*Dicebant mihi sodales si sepulchrum amicae visitarem, curas meas aliquantulum fore levatas.*' Why then, as I perused them, did the hairs of my head erect themselves on end, and the blood of my body become congealed within my veins?

There came a light tap at the library door – and, pale as the tenant of a tomb, a menial entered upon tiptoe. His looks were wild with terror, and he spoke to me in a voice tremulous, husky, and very low. What said he? – some broken sentences I heard. He told of a wild cry disturbing the silence of the night – of the gathering together of the household – of a search in the direction of the sound; and then his tones grew thrillingly distinct as he whispered me of a violated grave – of a disfigured body enshrouded, yet still breathing – still palpitating – *still alive!*

He pointed to garments – they were muddy and clotted with gore. I spoke not, and he took me gently by the hand: it was indented with the impress of human nails. He directed my attention to some object against the wall. I looked at it for some minutes: it was a spade. With a shriek I bounded to the table, and grasped the box that lay upon it. But I could not force it open; and in my tremor, it slipped from my hands, and fell heavily, and burst into pieces; and from it, with a rattling sound, there rolled out some instruments of dental surgery, intermingled with thirty-two small, white and ivory-looking substances that were scattered to and fro about the floor.

Mystification

Slid, if these be your 'passados' and
'montantes', I'll have none o' them.

NED KNOWLES

The Baron Ritzner von Jung was of a noble Hungarian
family, every member of which (at least as far back into
antiquity as any certain records extend) was more or
less remarkable for talent of some description – the
majority for that species of *grotesquerie* in conception of
which Tieck, a scion of the house, has given a vivid,
although by no means the most vivid exemplifications.
My acquaintance with Ritzner commenced at the magnificent Chateau Jung, into which a train of droll
adventures, not to be made public, threw me during the
summer months of the year 18—. Here it was that I
obtained a place in his regard, and here, with somewhat
more difficulty, a partial insight into his mental conformation. In later days this insight grew more clear, as the
intimacy which had at first permitted it became more
close; and when, after three years' separation, we met at
G—n, I knew all that it was necessary to know of the
character of the Baron Ritzner von Jung.

I remember the buzz of curiosity which his advent
excited within the college precincts on the night of the
twenty-fifth of June. I remember still more distinctly,
that while he was pronounced by all parties at first sight
'the most remarkable man in the world', no person
made any attempt at accounting for his opinion. That
he was unique appeared so undeniable that it was

145

deemed impertinent to enquire wherein the uniquity consisted. But, letting this matter pass for the present, I will merely observe that, from the first moment of his setting foot within the limits of the university, he began to exercise over the habits, manners, persons, purses, and propensities of the whole community which surrounded him, an influence the most extensive and despotic, yet at the same time the most indefinite and altogether unaccountable. Thus the brief period of his residence at the university forms an era in its annals, and is characterised by all classes of people appertaining to it or its dependencies as 'that very extraordinary epoch forming the domination of the Baron Ritzner von Jung'.

Upon his advent to G—n, he sought me out in my apartments. He was then of no particular age, by which I mean that it was impossible to form a guess respecting his age by any data personally afforded. He might have been fifteen or fifty, and *was* twenty-one years and seven months. He was by no means a handsome man – perhaps the reverse. The contour of his face was somewhat angular and harsh. His forehead was lofty and very fair; his nose a snub; his eyes large, heavy, glassy, and meaningless. About the mouth there was more to be observed. The lips were gently protruded, and rested the one upon the other, after such a fashion that it is impossible to conceive any, even the most complex, combination of human features, conveying so entirely, and so singly, the idea of unmitigated gravity, solemnity and repose.

It will be perceived, no doubt, from what I have already said, that the Baron was one of those human anomalies now and then to be found, who make the science of mystification the study and the business of their lives. For this science a peculiar turn of mind gave him instinctively the cue, while his physical appearance afforded him unusual facilities for carrying his projects into effect. I firmly believe that no student at G—n, during that renowned epoch so quaintly termed the domination of the Baron Ritzner von Jung, ever rightly entered into the mystery which overshadowed his character. I truly think that no person at the university, with the exception of myself, ever suspected him to be capable of a joke, verbal or practical – the old bulldog at the garden-gate would sooner have been accused – the ghost of Heraclitus – or the wig of the Emeritus Professor of Theology. This, too, when it was evident that the most egregious and unpardonable of all conceivable tricks, whimsicalities and buffooneries were brought about, if not directly by him, at least plainly through his intermediate agency or connivance. The beauty, if I may so call it, of his art *mystifique*, lay in that consummate ability (resulting from an almost intuitive knowledge of human nature, and a most wonderful self-possession), by means of which he never failed to make it appear that the drolleries he was occupied in bringing to a point, arose partly in spite, and partly in consequence of the laudable efforts he was making for their prevention, and for the preservation of the good order and dignity of Alma Mater. The deep, the poignant, the overwhelming mortification, which upon each such failure of his praiseworthy endeavours would suffuse every lineament of his countenance, left not the slightest room for doubt of his sincerity in the bosoms of even his most sceptical companions. The adroitness, too, was no less worthy of observation by which he contrived to shift the sense of the grotesque from the creator to the created – from his own person to the absurdities to which he had given rise. In no instance before that of which I speak, have I known the habitual mystific escape the natural consequence of his manoeuvres – an attachment of the ludicrous to his own character and person. Continually enveloped in an atmosphere of whim, my friend appeared to live only for the severities of society; and not even his own household have for a moment associated other ideas than those of the rigid and august with the memory of the Baron Ritzner von Jung.

During the epoch of his residence at G—n it really appeared that the demon of the *dolce far niente* lay like an incubus upon the university. Nothing, at least, was done beyond eating and drinking and making merry. The apartments of the students were converted into so many pot-houses, and there was no pot-house of them all more famous or more frequented than that of the Baron. Our carousals here were many, and boisterous, and long, and never unfruitful of events.

Upon one occasion we had protracted our sitting until nearly daybreak, and an unusual quantity of wine had been drunk. The company consisted of seven or eight individuals besides the Baron and myself. Most of these were young men of wealth, of high connection, of great family pride, and all alive with an exaggerated sense of honour. They abounded in the most ultra German opinions respecting the *duello*. To these Quixotic notions some recent Parisian publications, backed by three or four desperate and fatal rencounters at G—n, had given new vigour and impulse; and thus the conversation, during the greater part of the night, had run wild upon the all-engrossing topic of the times. The Baron, who had been unusually silent and abstracted in the earlier portion of the evening, at length seemed to be aroused from his apathy, took a leading part in the discourse, and dwelt upon the benefits, and more especially upon the beauties, of the received code of etiquette in passages of arms with an ardour, an eloquence, an impressiveness, and an affectionateness of manner, which elicited the warmest enthusiasm from his hearers in general, and absolutely staggered even myself, who well knew him to be at heart a ridiculer of those very points for which he contended, and especially to hold the entire *fanfaronade* of duelling etiquette in the sovereign contempt which it deserves.

Looking around me during a pause in the Baron's discourse (of which my readers may gather some faint idea when I say that it bore resemblance to the fervid, chanting, monotonous, yet musical sermonic manner of Coleridge), I perceived symptoms of even more than the general interest in the countenance of one of the party. This gentleman, whom I shall call Hermann, was an original in every respect – except, perhaps, in the single particular that he was a very great fool. He contrived to bear, however, among a particular set at the university, a reputation for deep metaphysical thinking, and, I believe, for some logical talent. As a duellist he had acquired great renown, even at G—n. I forget the precise number of victims who had fallen at his hands; but they were many. He was a man of courage undoubtedly. But it was upon his minute acquaintance with the etiquette of the *duello*, and the nicety of his sense of honour, that he most especially prided himself. These things were a hobby which he rode to the death. To Ritzner, ever upon the lookout for the grotesque, his peculiarities had for a long time past afforded food for mystification. Of this, however, I was not aware; although, in the present instance, I saw clearly that something of a whimsical nature was upon the *tapis* with my friend, and that Hermann was its especial object.

As the former proceeded in his discourse, or rather monologue, I perceived the excitement of the latter momently increasing. At length he spoke; offering some objection to a point insisted upon by R——, and giving his reasons in detail. To these the Baron replied at length (still maintaining his exaggerated tone of sentiment) and concluding, in what I thought very bad taste, with a sarcasm and a sneer. The hobby of Hermann now took the bit in his teeth. This I could discern by the studied hair-splitting *farrago* of his rejoinder. His last words I distinctly remember. 'Your opinions, allow me to say, Baron von Jung, although in the main correct, are, in many nice points, discreditable to yourself and to the university of which you are a member. In a few respects they are even unworthy of serious refutation. I would say more than this, sir, were it not for the fear of giving you offence (here the speaker smiled blandly), I would say, sir, that your opinions are not the opinions to be expected from a gentleman.'

As Hermann completed this equivocal sentence, all eyes were turned upon the Baron. He became pale, then excessively red; then, dropping his pocket-handkerchief, stooped to recover it, when I caught a glimpse of his countenance, while it could be seen by no one else at the table. It was radiant with the quizzical expression which was its natural character, but which I had never seen it assume except when we were alone together, and when he unbent himself freely. In an instant afterwards he stood erect, confronting Hermann; and so total an alteration of countenance in so short a period I certainly never saw before. For a moment I even fancied that I had misconceived him, and that he was in sober earnest. He appeared to be stifling with passion, and his face was cadaverously white. For a short time he remained silent, apparently striving to master his emotion. Having at length seemingly succeeded, he reached a decanter which stood near him, saying as he held it firmly clenched – 'The language you have thought proper to employ, Mynheer Hermann, in addressing yourself to me, is objectionable in so many particulars, that I have neither temper nor time for specification. That my opinions, however, are not the opinions to be expected from a gentleman, is an observation so directly offensive as to allow me but one line of conduct. Some courtesy, nevertheless, is due to the presence of this company, and to yourself, at this moment, as my guest. You will pardon me, therefore, if, upon this consideration, I deviate slightly from the general usage among gentlemen in similar cases of personal affront. You will forgive me for the moderate tax I shall make upon your imagination, and endeavour to consider, for an instant, the reflection of your person in yonder mirror as the living Mynheer Hermann himself. This being done, there will be no difficulty whatever. I shall discharge this decanter of wine at your image in yonder mirror, and thus fulfil all the spirit, if not the exact letter, of resentment for your insult, while the necessity of physical violence to your real person will be obviated.'

With these words he hurled the decanter, full of wine, against the mirror which hung directly opposite Hermann; striking the reflection of his person with great precision, and of course shattering the glass into fragments. The whole company at once started to their feet, and, with the exception of myself and

Ritzner, took their departure. As Hermann went out, the Baron whispered me that I should follow him and make an offer of my services. To this I agreed; not knowing precisely what to make of so ridiculous a piece of business.

The duellist accepted my aid with his stiff and *ultra recherché* air, and, taking my arm, led me to his apartment. I could hardly forbear laughing in his face while he proceeded to discuss, with the profoundest gravity, what he termed 'the refinedly peculiar character' of the insult he had received. After a tiresome harangue in his ordinary style, he took down from his book shelves a number of musty volumes on the subject of the *duello*, and entertained me for a long time with their contents; reading aloud, and commenting earnestly as he read. I can just remember the titles of some of the works. There were the *Ordonnance of Philip le Bel on Single Combat*; the *Theatre of Honour*, by Favyn, and a treatise *On the Permission of Duels*, by Andiguier. He displayed, also, with much pomposity, Brantome's *Memoirs of Duels*, published at Cologne, 1666, in the types of Elzevir – a precious and unique vellum-paper volume, with a fine margin, and bound by Derôme. But he requested my attention particularly, and with an air of mysterious sagacity, to a thick octavo, written in barbarous Latin by one Hedelin, a Frenchman, and having the quaint title, *Duelli Lex Scripta, et non; aliterque*. From this he read me one of the drollest chapters in the world concerning '*Injuriae per applicationem, per constructionem, et per se*', about half of which, he averred, was strictly applicable to his own 'refinedly peculiar' case, although not one syllable of the whole matter could I understand for the life of me. Having finished the chapter, he closed the book, and demanded what I thought necessary to be done. I replied that I had entire confidence in his superior delicacy of feeling, and would abide by what he proposed. With this answer he seemed flattered, and sat down to write a note to the Baron. It ran thus:

Sɪʀ– My friend, Mr P—, will hand you this note. I find it incumbent upon me to request, at your earliest convenience, an explanation of this evening's occurrences at your chambers. In the event of your declining this request, Mr P— will be happy to arrange, with any friend whom you may appoint, the steps preliminary to a meeting.

With sentiments of perfect respect,

Your most humble servant,

JOHANN HERMANN
To the Baron Ritzner von Jung
August 18th 18—

Not knowing what better to do, I called upon Ritzner with this epistle. He bowed as I presented it; then, with a grave countenance, motioned me to a seat. Having perused the cartel, he wrote the following reply, which I carried to Hermann.

Sɪʀ – Through our common friend, Mr P—, I have received your note of this evening. Upon due reflection I frankly admit the propriety of the explanation you suggest. This being admitted, I still find great difficulty (owing to the refinedly peculiar nature of our disagreement, and of the personal affront offered on my part) in so wording what I have to say by way of apology, as to meet all the minute exigencies, and all the variable shadows, of the case. I have great reliance, however, on that extreme delicacy of discrimination, in matters appertaining to the rules of etiquette, for which you have been so long and so pre-eminently distinguished. With perfect certainty, therefore, of being comprehended, I beg leave, in lieu of offering any sentiments of my own, to refer you to the opinions of Sieur Hedelin, as set forth in the ninth paragraph of the chapter of '*Injuriae per applicationem, per constructionem, et per se*', in his *Duelli Lex Scripta, et non; aliterque*. The nicety of your discernment in all the matters here treated, will be sufficient, I am assured, to convince you that the mere circumstance of me referring you to this admirable passage, ought to satisfy your request, as a man of honour, for explanation.

With sentiments of profound respect,

Your most obedient servant,

VON JUNG
The Herr Johann Hermann
August 18th 18—

Hermann commenced the perusal of this epistle with a scowl, which, however, was converted into a smile of the most ludicrous self-complacency as he came to the rigmarole about *Injuriae per applicationem, per constructionem, et per se*. Having finished reading, he begged me, with the blandest of all possible smiles, to be seated, while he made reference to the treatise in question. Turning to the passage specified, he read it with great care to himself, then closed the book, and desired me, in my character of confidential acquaintance, to express to the Baron von Jung his exalted sense of his chivalrous behaviour, and, in that of second, to assure him that the explanation offered was of the fullest, the most honourable, and the most unequivocally satisfactory nature.

Somewhat amazed at all this, I made my retreat to the Baron. He seemed to receive Hermann's amicable letter as a matter of course, and after a few words of general conversation, went to an inner room and brought out the everlasting treatise *Duelli Lex Scripta, et non; aliterque*. He handed me the volume and asked me to look over some portion of it. I did so, but to little purpose, not being able to gather the least particle of meaning. He then took the book himself, and read me a chapter aloud. To my surprise, what he read proved to be a most horribly absurd account of a duel between two baboons. He now explained the mystery; showing that the volume, as it appeared *prima facie*, was written upon the plan of the nonsense verses of Du Bartas; that is to say, the language was ingeniously framed so as to present to the ear all the outward signs of intelligibility, and even of profundity, while in fact not a shadow of meaning existed. The key to the whole was found in leaving out every second and third word alternately, when there appeared a series of ludicrous quizzes upon a single combat as practised in modern times.

The Baron afterwards informed me that he had purposely thrown the treatise in Hermann's way two or three weeks before the adventure, and that he was satisfied, from the general tenor of his conversation, that he had studied it with the deepest attention, and firmly believed it to be a work of unusual merit. Upon this hint he proceeded. Hermann would have died a thousand deaths rather than acknowledge his inability to understand anything and everything in the universe that had ever been written about the *duello*.

How to Write a Blackwood *Article*

'In the name of the Prophet – figs!!'
Cry of the Turkish fig-pedlar

I presume everybody has heard of me. My name is the Signora Psyche Zenobia. This I know to be a fact. Nobody but my enemies ever calls me Suky Snobbs. I have been assured that Suky is but a vulgar corruption of Psyche, which is good Greek, and means 'the soul' (that's me, I'm all soul) and sometimes 'a butterfly', which latter meaning undoubtedly alludes to my appearance in my new crimson satin dress, with the sky-blue Arabian *mantelet*, and the trimmings of green *agraffas*, and the seven flounces of orange-coloured *auriculas*. As for Snobbs – any person who should look at me would be instantly aware that my name wasn't Snobbs. Miss Tabitha Turnip propagated that report through sheer envy. Tabitha Turnip indeed! Oh the little wretch! But what can we expect from a turnip? Wonder if she remembers the old adage about 'blood out of a turnip', &c.? [Mem. put her in mind of it the first opportunity.] [Mem. again – pull her nose.] Where was I? Ah! I have been assured that Snobbs is a mere corruption of Zenobia, and that Zenobia was a queen – (So am I. Dr Moneypenny always calls me the Queen of Hearts) – and that Zenobia, as well as Psyche, is good Greek, and that my father was 'a Greek', and that consequently I have a right to our patronymic, which is Zenobia and not by any means Snobbs. Nobody but Tabitha Turnip calls me Suky Snobbs. I am the Signora Psyche Zenobia.

As I said before, everybody has heard of me. I am that very Signora Psyche Zenobia, so justly celebrated as corresponding secretary to the 'Philadelphia, Regular, Exchange, Tea, Total, Young, Belles, Lettres, Universal, Experimental, Bibliographical, Association, To, Civilise, Humanity'. Dr Moneypenny made the title for us, and says he chose it because it sounded big like an empty rum-puncheon. (A vulgar man that sometimes – but he's deep.) We all sign the initials of the society after our names, in the fashion of the RSA, Royal Society of Arts – the SDUK, Society for the Diffusion of Useful Knowledge, &c., &c. Dr Moneypenny says that S stands for stale, and that DUK spells duck (but it don't), that SDUK stands for Stale Duck and not for Lord Brougham's society – but then Dr Moneypenny is such a queer man that I am never sure when he is telling me the truth. At any rate we always add the initials PRETTYBLUEBATCH to our names – that is to say, Philadelphia, Regular, Exchange, Tea, Total, Young, Belles, Lettres, Universal, Experimental, Bibliographical, Association, To, Civilise, Humanity – one letter for each word, which is a decided improvement upon Lord Brougham. Dr Moneypenny will have it that our initials give our true character – but for my life I can't see what he means.

Notwithstanding the good offices of the doctor, and the strenuous exertions of the association to get itself into notice, it met with no very great success until I joined it. The truth is, the members indulged in too flippant a tone of discussion. The papers read every Saturday evening were characterised less by depth than buffoonery. They were all whipped syllabub.

There was no investigation of first causes, first principles. There was no investigation of anything at all. There was no attention paid to that great point, the 'fitness of things'. In short there was no fine writing like this. It was all low – very! No profundity, no reading, no metaphysics – nothing which the learned call spirituality, and which the unlearned choose to stigmatise as cant. [Dr M— says I ought to spell 'cant' with a capital K – but I know better.]

When I joined the society it was my endeavour to introduce a better style of thinking and writing, and all the world knows how well I have succeeded. We get up as good papers now in the PRETTYBLUEBATCH as any to be found even in *Blackwood*. I say, *Blackwood*, because I have been assured that the finest writing, upon every subject, is to be discovered in the pages of that justly celebrated magazine. We now take it for our model upon all themes, and are getting into rapid notice accordingly. And, after all, it's not so very difficult a matter to compose an article of the genuine *Blackwood* stamp, if one only goes properly about it. Of course I don't speak of the political articles. Everybody knows how they are managed, since Dr Moneypenny explained it. Mr Blackwood has a pair of tailor's-shears, and three apprentices who stand by him for orders. One hands him *The Times*, another the *Examiner* and a third a Gulley's *New Compendium of Slang-Whang*. Mr B— merely cuts out and intersperses. It is soon done – nothing but *Examiner*, *Slang-Whang*, and *Times* – then *Times*, *Slang-Whang*, and *Examiner* – and then *Times*, *Examiner*, and *Slang-Whang*.

But the chief merit of the magazine lies in its miscellaneous articles; and the best of these come under the head of what Dr Moneypenny calls the *bizarreries* (whatever that may mean) and what everybody else calls the intensities. This is a species of writing which I have long known how to appreciate, although it is only since my late visit to Mr Blackwood (deputed by the society) that I have been made aware of the exact method of composition. This method is very simple, but not so much so as the politics. Upon my calling at Mr B—'s, and making known to him the wishes of the society, he received me with great civility, took me into his study, and gave me a clear explanation of the whole process.

'My dear madam,' said he, evidently struck with my majestic appearance, for I had on the crimson satin, with the green *agraffas*, and orange-coloured *auriculas*. 'My dear madam,' said he, 'sit down. The matter stands thus: in the first place your writer of intensities must have very black ink, and a very big pen, with a very blunt nib. And, mark me, Miss Psyche Zenobia!' he continued, after a pause, with the most expressive energy and solemnity of manner, 'mark me! – that pen – must – never be mended! Herein, madam, lies the secret, the soul, of intensity. I assume upon myself to say, that no individual, of however great genius ever wrote with a good pen – understand me – a good article. You may take it for granted, that when manuscript can be read it is never worth reading. This is a leading principle in our faith, to which if you cannot readily assent, our conference is at an end.'

He paused. But, of course, as I had no wish to put an end to the conference, I assented to a proposition so very obvious, and one, too, of whose truth I had all along been sufficiently aware. He seemed pleased, and went on with his instructions.

'It may appear invidious in me, Miss Psyche Zenobia, to refer you to any article, or set of articles, in the way of model or study, yet perhaps I may as well call your attention to a few cases. Let me see. There was "The Dead Alive", a capital thing! – the record of a gentleman's sensations when entombed before the breath was out of his body – full of taste, terror, sentiment, metaphysics, and erudition. You would have sworn that the writer had been born and brought up in a coffin. Then we had the "Confessions of an Opium-eater" – fine, very fine! – glorious imagination – deep philosophy – acute speculation – plenty of fire and fury, and a good spicing of the decidedly unintelligible. That was a nice bit of flummery, and went down the throats of the people delightfully. They would have it that Coleridge wrote the paper – but not so. It was composed by my pet baboon, Juniper, over a rummer of Hollands and water, "hot, without sugar".' [This I could scarcely have believed had it been anybody but Mr Blackwood, who assured me of it.] 'Then there was "The Involuntary Experimentalist", all about a gentleman who got baked in an oven, and came out alive and well, although certainly done to a turn. And then there was "The Diary of a Late Physician", where the merit lay in good rant, and indifferent Greek – both of them taking things with the public. And then there was "The Man in the Bell", a paper by the by, Miss Zenobia, which I cannot sufficiently recommend to your attention. It is the history of a young person who goes to sleep under the clapper of a church bell, and is awakened by its tolling for a funeral. The sound drives him mad, and, accordingly, pulling out his tablets, he gives a record of his sensations.

Sensations are the great things after all. Should you ever be drowned or hung, be sure and make a note of your sensations – they will be worth to you ten guineas a sheet. If you wish to write forcibly, Miss Zenobia, pay minute attention to the sensations.'

'That I certainly will, Mr Blackwood,' said I.

'Good!' he replied. 'I see you are a pupil after my own heart. But I must put you *au fait* to the details necessary in composing what may be denominated a genuine *Blackwood* article of the sensation stamp – the kind which you will understand me to say I consider the best for all purposes.

'The first thing requisite is to get yourself into such a scrape as no one ever got into before. The oven, for instance, that was a good hit. But if you have no oven, or big bell, at hand, and if you cannot conveniently tumble out of a balloon, or be swallowed up in an earthquake, or get stuck fast in a chimney, you will have to be contented with simply imagining some similar misadventure. I should prefer, however, that you have the actual fact to bear you out. Nothing so well assists the fancy, as an experimental knowledge of the matter in hand. "Truth is strange", you know, "stranger than fiction" – besides being more to the purpose.'

Here I assured him I had an excellent pair of garters, and would go and hang myself forthwith.

'Good!' he replied, 'do so; although hanging is somewhat hackneyed. Perhaps you might do better. Take a dose of Brandreth's pills, and then give us your sensations. However, my instructions will apply equally well to any variety of misadventure, and in your way home you may easily get knocked in the head, or run over by an omnibus, or bitten by a mad dog, or drowned in a gutter. But to proceed.

'Having determined upon your subject, you must next consider the tone, or manner, of your narration. There is the tone didactic, the tone enthusiastic, the tone natural – all commonplace enough. But then there is the tone laconic, or curt, which has lately come much into use. It consists in short sentences. Somehow thus: Can't be too brief. Can't be too snappish. Always a full stop. And never a paragraph.

'Then there is the tone elevated, diffusive, and interjectional. Some of our best novelists patronise this tone. The words must be all in a whirl, like a humming-top, and make a noise very similar, which answers remarkably well instead of meaning. This is the best of all possible styles where the writer is in too great a hurry to think.

'The tone metaphysical is also a good one. If you know any big words this is your chance for them. Talk of the Ionic and Eleatic schools – of Archytas, Gorgias, and Alcmaeon. Say something about objectivity and subjectivity. Be sure and abuse a man named Locke. Turn up your nose at things in general, and when you let slip anything a little too absurd, you need not be at the trouble of scratching it out, but just add a footnote and say that you are indebted for the above profound observation to the *Kritik der reinem Vernunft*, or to the *Metaphysische Anfangsgründe der Naturwissenschaft*. This would look erudite and – and – and frank.

'There are various other tones of equal celebrity, but I shall mention only two more – the tone transcendental and the tone heterogeneous. In the former the merit consists in seeing into the nature of affairs a very great deal farther than anybody else. This second sight is very efficient when properly managed. A little reading of the *Dial* will carry you a great way. Eschew, in this case, big words; get them as small as possible, and write them upside down. Look over Channing's poems and quote what he says about a "fat little man with a delusive show of Can". Put in something about the supernal oneness. Don't say a syllable about the infernal twoness. Above all, study innuendo. Hint everything – assert nothing. If you feel inclined to say "bread and butter", do not by any means say it outright. You may say anything and everything approaching to "bread and butter". You may hint at buckwheat cake, or you may even go so far as to insinuate oatmeal porridge, but if bread and butter be your real meaning, be cautious, my dear Miss Psyche, not on any account to say "bread and butter"!'

I assured him that I should never say it again as long as I lived. He kissed me and continued: 'As for the tone heterogeneous, it is merely a judicious mixture, in equal proportions, of all the other tones in the world, and is consequently made up of everything deep, great, odd, piquant, pertinent, and pretty.

'Let us suppose now you have determined upon your incidents and tone. The most important portion – in fact, the soul of the whole business, is yet to be attended to – I allude to the filling up. It is not to be supposed that a lady, or gentleman either, has been leading the life of a bookworm. And yet above all things it is necessary that your article have an air of erudition, or at least afford evidence of extensive general reading. Now I'll put you in the way of accomplishing this point. See here!' (pulling down some three or four ordinary-looking volumes, and opening them at random). 'By casting your eye down almost any page of any book in the world, you will be able to perceive at once a host of little scraps of either learning or bel-espritism, which are the very thing for the spicing of a *Blackwood* article. You might as well note down a few while I read them to you. I shall make two divisions: first, "Piquant facts for the manufacture of similes"; and, second, "Piquant expressions to be introduced as occasion may require". Write now!' – and I wrote as he dictated.

'Piquant facts for similes. "There were originally but three muses – Melete, Mneme, Aoede – meditation, memory, and singing." You may make a good deal of that little fact if properly worked. You see it is not generally known, and looks *recherché*. You must be careful and give the thing with a downright *improviso* air.

'Again. "The river Alpheus passed beneath the sea, and emerged without injury to the purity of its waters." Rather stale that, to be sure, but, if properly dressed and dished up, will look quite as fresh as ever.

'Here is something better. "The Persian iris appears to some persons to possess a sweet and very powerful perfume, while to others it is perfectly scentless." Fine that, and very delicate! Turn it about a little, and it will do wonders. We'll have something else in the botanical line. There's nothing goes down so well, especially with the help of a little Latin. Write!

' "The *Epidendrum Flos Aeris*, of Java, bears a very beautiful flower, and will live when pulled up by the roots. The natives suspend it by a cord from the ceiling, and enjoy its fragrance for years." That's capital! That will do for the similes. Now for the "Piquant expressions".

'Piquant expressions. "The venerable Chinese novel *Ju-Kiao-Li*." Good! By introducing these few words with dexterity you will evince your intimate acquaintance with the language and literature of the Chinese. With the aid of this you may either get along without either Arabic, or Sanscrit, or Chickasaw. There is no passing muster, however, without Spanish, Italian, German, Latin, and Greek. I must look you out a little specimen of each. Any scrap will answer, because you must depend upon your own ingenuity to make it fit into your article. Now write!

'"*Aussi tendre que Zaïre*" – as tender as Zaïre – French. Alludes to the frequent repetition of the phrase, *la tendre Zaïre*, in the French tragedy of that name. Properly introduced, will show not only your knowledge of the language, but your general reading and wit. You can say, for instance, that the chicken you were eating (write an article about being choked to death by a chicken-bone) was not altogether *aussi tendre que Zaïre*. Write!

> *Van muerte tan escondida,*
> *Que no te sienta venir,*
> *Porque el plazer del morir,*
> *No mestorne a dar la vida.*

That's Spanish – from Miguel de Cervantes. "Come quickly, O death! but be sure and don't let me see you coming, lest the pleasure I shall feel at your appearance should unfortunately bring me back again to life." This you may slip in quite apropos when you are struggling in the last agonies with the chicken-bone. Write!

> *Il pover' huomo che non se'n era accorto,*
> *Andava combattendo, e era morto.*

That's Italian, you perceive – from Ariosto. It means that a great hero, in the heat of combat, not perceiving that he had been fairly killed, continued to fight valiantly, dead as he was. The application of this to your own case is obvious – for I trust, Miss Psyche, that you will not neglect to kick for at least an hour and a half after you have been choked to death by that chicken-bone. Please to write!

> *Und sterb' ich doch, so sterb' ich denn*
> *Durch sie – durch sie!*

That's German – from Schiller. "And if I die, at least I die – for thee – for thee!" Here it is clear that you are apostrophising the cause of your disaster, the chicken. Indeed what gentleman (or lady either) of sense, *wouldn't* die, I should like to know, for a well fattened capon of the right Molucca breed, stuffed with capers and mushrooms, and served up in a salad-bowl, with orange-jellies *en mosaïques*. Write! (You can get them that way at Tortoni's.) – Write, if you please!

'Here is a nice little Latin phrase, and rare too, (one can't be too *recherché* or brief in one's Latin, it's getting so common – *ignoratio elenchi*. He has committed an *ignoratio elenchi* – that is to say, he has understood the words of your proposition, but not the idea. The man was a fool, you see. Some poor fellow whom you address while choking with that chicken-bone, and who therefore didn't precisely understand what you were talking about. Throw the *ignoratio elenchi* in his teeth, and, at once, you have him annihilated. If he dares to reply, you can tell him from Lucan (here it is) that speeches are mere *anemonae verborum*, anemone words. The anemone, with great brilliancy, has no smell. Or, if he begins to bluster, you may be down upon him with *insomnia*

Jovis, reveries of Jupiter – a phrase which Silius Italicus (see here!) applies to thoughts pompous and inflated. This will be sure and cut him to the heart. He can do nothing but roll over and die. Will you be kind enough to write?

'In Greek we must have something pretty – from Demosthenes, for example. Ανερο φευγων και παλιν μαχεσεται. [Anero pheugoen kai palin makesetai.] There is a tolerably good translation of it in *Hudibras*:

> For he that flies may fight again,
> Which he can never do that's slain.

In a *Blackwood* article nothing makes so fine a show as your Greek. The very letters have an air of profundity about them. Only observe, madam, the astute look of that epsilon! That phi ought certainly to be a bishop! Was ever there a smarter fellow than that omicron? Just twig that tau! In short, there is nothing like Greek for a genuine sensation-paper. In the present case your application is the most obvious thing in the world. Rap out the sentence, with a huge oath, and by way of *ultimatum* at the good-for-nothing dunder-headed villain who couldn't understand your plain English in relation to the chicken-bone. He'll take the hint and be off, you may depend upon it.'

These were all the instructions Mr B— could afford me upon the topic in question, but I felt they would be entirely sufficient. I was, at length, able to write a genuine *Blackwood* article, and determined to do it forthwith. In taking leave of me, Mr B— made a proposition for the purchase of the paper when written; but as he could offer me only fifty guineas a sheet, I thought it better to let our society have it, than sacrifice it for so paltry a sum. Notwithstanding this niggardly spirit, however, the gentleman showed his consideration for me in all other respects, and indeed treated me with the greatest civility. His parting words made a deep impression upon my heart, and I hope I shall always remember them with gratitude.

'My dear Miss Zenobia,' he said, while the tears stood in his eyes, 'is there *anything* else I can do to promote the success of your laudable undertaking? Let me reflect! It is just possible that you may not be able, so soon as convenient, to – to – get yourself drowned, or – choked with a chicken-bone, or – or hung – or – bitten by a – but stay! Now I think me of it, there are a couple of very excellent bulldogs in the yard – fine fellows, I assure you – savage, and all that – indeed just the thing for your money – they'll have you eaten up, *auriculas* and all, in less than five minutes (here's my watch!) – and then only think of the sensations! Here! I say – Tom! – Peter! – Dick, you villain! – let out those – ' but as I was really in a great hurry, and had not another moment to spare, I was reluctantly forced to expedite my departure, and accordingly took leave *at once* – somewhat more abruptly, I admit, than strict courtesy would have otherwise allowed.

It was my primary object upon quitting Mr Blackwood, to get into some immediate difficulty, pursuant to his advice, and with this view I spent the greater part of the day in wandering about Edinburgh, seeking for desperate adventures – adventures adequate to the intensity of my feelings, and adapted to the vast character of the article I intended to write. In this excursion I was attended by one negro servant, Pompey, and my little lap-dog Diana, whom I had brought with me from Philadelphia. It was not, however, until late in the afternoon that I fully succeeded in my arduous undertaking. An important event then happened of which the following *Blackwood* article, in the tone heterogeneous, is the substance and result.

A Predicament

What chance, good lady, hath bereft you thus?

COMUS

It was a quiet and still afternoon when I strolled forth
in the goodly city of Edina. The confusion and bustle
in the streets were terrible. Men were talking.
Women were screaming. Children were choking.
Pigs were whistling. Carts they rattled. Bulls they
bellowed. Cows they lowed. Horses they neighed.
Cats they caterwauled. Dogs they danced. *Danced!*
Could it then be possible? *Danced!* Alas, thought I,
my dancing days are over! Thus it is ever. What a
host of gloomy recollections will ever and anon be
awakened in the mind of genius and imaginative
contemplation, especially of a genius doomed to the
everlasting and eternal, and continual, and, as one
might say, the – *continued* – yes, the *continued and
continuous*, bitter, harassing, disturbing, and, if I may
be allowed the expression, the *very* disturbing influence of the serene, and godlike, and heavenly, and
exalted, and elevated, and purifying effect of what
may be rightly termed the most enviable, the most
truly enviable – nay! the most benignly beautiful, the
most deliciously ethereal, and, as it were, the most
pretty (if I may use so bold an expression) *thing*
(pardon me, gentle reader!) in the world – but I am
always led away by my feelings. In *such* a mind, I
repeat, what a host of recollections are stirred up by a
trifle! The dogs danced! *I* – I *could* not! They frisked –

I wept. They capered – I sobbed aloud. Touching circumstances! which cannot fail to bring to the recollection of the classical reader that exquisite passage in relation to the fitness of things, which is to be found in the commencement of the third volume of that admirable and venerable Chinese novel the *Jo-Go-Slow*.

In my solitary walk through the city I had two humble but faithful companions. Diana, my poodle! sweetest of creatures! She had a quantity of hair over her one eye, and a blue ribband tied fashionably around her neck. Diana was not more than five inches in height, but her head was somewhat bigger than her body, and her tail being cut off exceedingly close, gave an air of injured innocence to the interesting animal which rendered her a favourite with all.

And Pompey, my negro! – sweet Pompey! how shall I ever forget thee? I had taken Pompey's arm. He was three feet in height (I like to be particular) and about seventy, or perhaps eighty, years of age. He had bow-legs and was corpulent. His mouth should not be called small, nor his ears short. His teeth, however, were like pearl, and his large full eyes were deliciously white. Nature had endowed him with no neck, and had placed his ankles (as usual with that race) in the middle of the upper portion of the feet. He was clad with a striking simplicity. His sole garments were a stock of nine inches in height, and a nearly-new drab overcoat which had formerly been in the service of the tall, stately, and illustrious Dr Moneypenny. It was a good overcoat. It was well cut. It was well made. The coat was nearly new. Pompey held it up out of the dirt with both hands.

There were three persons in our party, and two of

them have already been the subject of remark. There was a third – that person was myself. I am the Signora Psyche Zenobia. I am not Suky Snobbs. My appearance is commanding. On the memorable occasion of which I speak I was habited in a crimson satin dress, with a sky-blue Arabian *mantelet*. And the dress had trimmings of green *agraffas*, and seven graceful flounces of the orange-coloured *auricula*. I thus formed the third of the party. There was the poodle. There was Pompey. There was myself. We were *three*. Thus it is said there were originally but three Furies – Melty, Nimmy, and Hetty – Meditation, Memory, and Fiddling.

Leaning upon the arm of the gallant Pompey, and attended at a respectable distance by Diana, I proceeded down one of the populous and very pleasant streets of the now deserted Edina. On a sudden, there presented itself to view a church – a Gothic cathedral – vast, venerable, and with a tall steeple, which towered into the sky. What madness now possessed me? Why did I rush upon my fate? I was seized with an uncontrollable desire to ascend the giddy pinnacle, and then survey the immense extent of the city. The door of the cathedral stood invitingly open. My destiny prevailed. I entered the ominous archway. Where then was my guardian angel? – if indeed such angels there be. If! Distressing monosyllable! what world of mystery, and meaning, and doubt, and uncertainty is there involved in thy two letters! I entered the ominous archway! I entered; and, without injury to my orange-coloured *auriculas*, I passed beneath the portal, and emerged within the vestibule. Thus it is said the immense river Alfred passed, unscathed, and unwetted, beneath the sea.

I thought the staircase would never have an end. *Round!* Yes, they went round and up, and round and up and round and up, until I could not help surmising, with the sagacious Pompey, upon whose supporting arm I leaned in all the confidence of early affection – I *could* not help surmising that the upper end of the continuous spiral ladder had been accidentally, or perhaps designedly, removed. I paused for breath; and, in the meantime, an accident occurred of too momentous a nature in a moral, and also in a metaphysical point of view, to be passed over without notice. It appeared to me – indeed I was quite confident of the fact – I could not be mistaken – no! I had, for some moments, carefully and anxiously observed the motions of my Diana – I say that *I could not be* mistaken – Diana *smelt a rat!* At once I called Pompey's attention to the subject, and he – he agreed with me. There was then no longer any reasonable room for doubt. The rat had been smelled – and by Diana. Heavens! shall I ever forget the intense excitement of the moment? Alas! what is the boasted intellect of man? The rat! – it was there – that is to say, it was somewhere. Diana smelled the rat. I – I *could* not! Thus it is said the Prussian Isis has, for some persons, a sweet and very powerful perfume, while to others it is perfectly scentless.

The staircase had been surmounted, and there were now only three or four more upward steps intervening between us and the summit. We still ascended, and now only one step remained. One step! One little, little step! Upon one such little step in the great staircase of human life how vast a sum of human happiness or misery depends! I thought of myself, then of Pompey, and then of the mysterious and inexplicable destiny which surrounded us. I thought of Pompey! – alas, I thought of love! I thought of my many false *steps* which have been taken, and may be taken again. I resolved to be more cautious, more reserved. I abandoned the arm of Pompey, and, without his assistance, surmounted the one remaining step, and gained the chamber of the belfry. I was followed immediately afterwards by my poodle. Pompey alone remained behind. I stood at the head of the staircase, and encouraged him to ascend. He stretched forth to me his hand, and unfortunately in so doing was forced to abandon his firm hold upon the overcoat. Will the gods never cease their persecution? The overcoat is dropped, and, with one of his feet, Pompey stepped upon the long and trailing skirt of the overcoat. He stumbled and fell – this consequence was inevitable. He fell forward, and, with his accursed head, striking me full in the – in the breast, precipitated me headlong, together with himself, upon the hard, filthy, and detestable floor of the belfry. But my revenge was sure, sudden, and complete. Seizing him furiously by the wool with both hands, I tore out a vast quantity of black, and crisp, and curling material, and tossed it from me with every manifestation of disdain. It fell among the ropes of the belfry and remained. Pompey arose, and said no word. But he regarded me piteously with his large eyes and – sighed. Ye Gods – that sigh! It sunk into my heart. And the hair – the wool! Could I have reached that wool I would have bathed it with my tears, in testimony of regret. But alas! it was now far beyond my grasp. As it dangled among the cordage of the bell, I fancied it alive. I fancied that it stood on end with indignation. Thus the *happy-dandy Flos Aeris* of Java bears, it is said, a beautiful flower, which will live when pulled up by the roots. The natives suspend it by a cord from the ceiling and enjoy its fragrance for years.

Our quarrel was now made up, and we looked about the room for an aperture through which to survey the city of Edina. Windows there were none. The sole light admitted into the gloomy chamber proceeded from a square opening, about a foot in diameter, at a height of about seven feet from the floor. Yet what will the energy of true genius not effect? I resolved to clamber up to this hole. A vast quantity of wheels, pinions, and other cabbalistic-looking machinery stood opposite the hole, close to it; and through the hole there passed an iron rod from the machinery. Between the wheels and the wall where the hole lay there was barely room for my body – yet I was desperate, and determined to persevere. I called Pompey to my side.

'You perceive that aperture, Pompey. I wish to look through it. You will stand here just beneath the hole – so. Now, hold out one of your hands, Pompey, and let me step upon it – thus. Now, the other hand, Pompey, and with its aid I will get upon your shoulders.'

He did everything I wished, and I found, upon getting up, that I could easily pass my head and neck through the aperture. The prospect was sublime. Nothing could be more magnificent. I merely paused a moment to bid Diana behave herself, and assure Pompey that I would be considerate and bear as lightly as possible upon his shoulders. I told him I would be tender of his feelings – *ossi tender que beefsteak*. Having done this justice to my faithful friend, I gave myself up with great zest and enthusiasm to the enjoyment of the scene which so obligingly spread itself out before my eyes.

Upon this subject, however, I shall forbear to dilate. I will not describe the city of Edinburgh. Everyone has been to the city of Edinburgh. Everyone has been to Edinburgh – the classic Edina. I will confine myself to the momentous details of my own lamentable adventure. Having, in some measure, satisfied my curiosity in regard to the extent, situation, and general appearance of the city, I had leisure to survey the church in which I was, and the delicate architecture of the steeple. I observed that the aperture through which I had thrust my head was an opening in the dial-plate of a gigantic clock, and must have appeared, from the street, as a large keyhole, such as we see in the face of the French watches. No doubt the true object was to admit the arm of an attendant, to adjust, when necessary, the hands of the clock from within. I observed also, with surprise, the immense size of these hands, the longest of which could not have been less than ten feet in length, and, where broadest, eight or nine inches in breadth. They were of solid steel apparently, and their edges appeared to be sharp. Having noticed these particulars, and some others, I again turned my eyes upon the glorious prospect below, and soon became absorbed in contemplation.

From this, after some minutes, I was aroused by the voice of Pompey, who declared that he could stand it no longer, and requested that I would be so kind as to come down. This was unreasonable, and I told him so in a speech of some length. He replied, but with an evident misunderstanding of my ideas upon the subject. I accordingly grew angry, and told him in plain words, that he was a fool, that he had committed an *ignoramus e-clench-eye*, that his notions were mere *insommary Bovis*, and his words little better than an *ennemywerrybor'em*. With this he appeared satisfied, and I resumed my contemplations.

It might have been half an hour after this altercation when, as I was deeply absorbed in the heavenly scenery beneath me, I was startled by something very cold which pressed with a gentle pressure on the back of my neck. It is needless to say that I felt inexpressibly alarmed. I knew that Pompey was beneath my feet, and that Diana was sitting, according to my explicit directions, upon her hind legs, in the farthest corner of the room. What could it be? Alas! I but too soon discovered. Turning my head gently to one side, I perceived, to my extreme horror, that the huge, glittering, scimitar-like minute-hand of the clock had, in the course of its hourly revolution, *descended upon my neck*. There was, I knew, not a second to be lost. I pulled back at once – but it was too late. There was no chance of forcing my head through the mouth of that terrible trap in which it was so fairly caught, and which grew narrower and narrower with a rapidity too horrible to be conceived. The agony of that moment is not to be imagined. I threw up my hands and endeavoured, with all my strength, to force upward the ponderous iron bar. I might as well have tried to lift the cathedral itself. Down, down, down it came, closer and yet closer. I screamed to Pompey for aid; but he said that I had hurt his feelings by calling him 'an ignorant old squint-eye': I yelled to Diana; but she only said 'bow-wow-wow', and that I had told her 'on no account to stir from the corner'. Thus I had no relief to expect from my associates.

Meantime the ponderous and terrific *Scythe of Time* (for I now discovered the literal import of that classical phrase) had not stopped, nor was it likely to stop, in its career. Down and still down, it came. It had already buried its sharp edge a full inch in my flesh, and my sensations grew indistinct and confused. At one time I fancied myself in Philadelphia with the stately Dr Moneypenny, at another in the back parlour of Mr Blackwood receiving his invaluable instructions. And then again the sweet recollection of better and earlier times came over me, and I thought of that happy period when the world was not all a desert, and Pompey not altogether cruel.

The ticking of the machinery amused me. *Amused me,* I say, for my sensations now bordered upon perfect happiness, and the most trifling circumstances afforded me pleasure. The eternal *click-clack, click-clack, click-clack* of the clock was the most melodious of music in my ears, and occasionally even put me in mind of the graceful sermonic harangues of Dr Ollapod. Then there were the great figures upon the dial-plate – how intelligent, how intellectual, they all looked! And presently they took to dancing the Mazurka, and I think it was the figure V who performed the most to my satisfaction. She was evidently a lady of breeding. None of your swaggerers, and nothing at all indelicate in her motions. She did the pirouette to admiration – whirling round upon her apex. I made an endeavour to hand her a chair, for I saw that she appeared fatigued with her exertions – and it was not until then that I fully perceived my lamentable situation. Lamentable indeed! The bar had buried itself two inches in my neck. I was aroused to a sense of exquisite pain. I prayed for death, and, in the agony of the moment, could not help repeating those exquisite verses of the poet Miguel de Cervantes:

Vanny Buren, tan escondida
Query no te senty venny
Pork and pleasure, delly morry
Nommy, torny, darry, widdy!

But now a new horror presented itself, and one indeed sufficient to startle the strongest nerves. My eyes, from the cruel pressure of the machine, were absolutely starting from their sockets. While I was thinking how I should possibly manage without them, one actually tumbled out of my head, and, rolling down the steep side of the steeple, lodged in the rain gutter which ran along the eaves of the main building. The loss of the eye was not so much as the insolent air of independence and contempt with which it regarded me after it was out. There it lay in the gutter just under my nose, and the airs it gave itself would have been ridiculous had they not been disgusting. Such a winking and blinking were never before seen. This behaviour on the part of my eye in the gutter was not only irritating on account of its manifest insolence and shameful ingratitude, but was also exceedingly inconvenient on account of the sympathy which always exists between two eyes of the same head, however far apart. I was forced, in a manner, to wink and to blink, whether I would or not, in exact concert with the scoundrelly thing that lay just under my nose. I was presently relieved, however, by the dropping out of the other eye. In falling it took the same direction (possibly a concerted plot) as its fellow. Both rolled out of the gutter together, and in truth I was very glad to get rid of them.

The bar was now four inches and a half deep in my neck, and there was only a little bit of skin to cut through. My sensations were those of entire happiness, for I felt that in a few minutes, at farthest, I should be relieved from my disagreeable situation. And in this expectation I was not at all deceived. At twenty-five minutes past five in the afternoon, precisely, the huge minute-hand had proceeded sufficiently far on its terrible revolution to sever the small remainder of my neck. I was not sorry to see the head which had occasioned me so much embarrassment at length make a final separation from my body. It first rolled down the side of the steeple, then lodged, for a few seconds, in the gutter, and then made its way, with a plunge, into the middle of the street.

I will candidly confess that my feelings were now of the most singular – nay, of the most mysterious, the most perplexing and incomprehensible character. My senses were here and there at one and the same moment. With my head I imagined, at one time, that I, the head, was the real Signora Psyche Zenobia – at another I felt convinced that myself, the body, was the proper identity. To clear my ideas on this topic I felt in my pocket for my snuff-box, but, upon getting it, and endeavouring to apply a pinch of its grateful contents in the ordinary manner, I became immediately aware of my peculiar deficiency, and threw the box at once down to my head. It took a pinch with great satisfaction, and smiled me an acknowledgement in return. Shortly afterwards it made me a speech, which I could hear but indistinctly without ears. I gathered enough, however, to know that it was astonished at my wishing to remain alive under such circumstances. In the concluding sentences it quoted the noble words of Ariosto:

> *Il pover hommy che non sera corty*
> *And have a combat tenty erry morty;*

thus comparing me to the hero who, in the heat of the combat, not perceiving that he was dead, continued to contest the battle with inextinguishable valour. There was nothing now to prevent my getting down from my elevation, and I did so. What it was that Pompey saw so very peculiar in my appearance I have never yet been able to find out. The fellow opened his mouth from ear to ear, and shut his two eyes as if he were endeavouring to crack nuts between the lids. Finally, throwing off his overcoat, he made one spring for the staircase and disappeared. I hurled after the scoundrel these vehement words of Demosthenes:

> *Andrew O'Phlegethon, you really make haste to fly –*

and then turned to the darling of my heart, to the one-eyed! the shaggy-haired Diana. Alas! what a horrible vision affronted my eyes? *Was* that a rat I saw skulking into his hole? Are these the picked bones of the little angel who has been cruelly devoured by the monster? Ye gods! and what *do* I behold – is that the departed spirit, the shade, the ghost, of my beloved puppy, which I perceive sitting with a grace so melancholy, in the corner? Hearken! for she speaks, and, heavens! it is in the German of Schiller:

> '*Unt stubby duk, so stubby dun*
> *Duk she! duk she!*'

Alas! and are not her words too true?

> *And if I died, at least I died*
> *For thee – for thee.*

Sweet creature! she *too* has sacrificed herself in my behalf. Dogless, niggerless, headless, what *now* remains for the unhappy Signora Psyche Zenobia? Alas – *nothing!* I have done.

The Man that was Used Up

A TALE OF THE LATE BUGABOO
AND KICKAPOO CAMPAIGN

Pleurez, pleurez, mes yeux, et fondez vous en eau!
La moitié de ma vie a mis l'autre au tombeau.

CORNEILLE

I cannot just now remember when or where I first made the acquaintance of that truly fine-looking fellow, Brevet Brigadier General John A. B. C. Smith. Someone *did* introduce me to the gentleman, I am sure – at some public meeting, I know very well – held about something of great importance, no doubt – at some place or other, I feel convinced – whose name I have unaccountably forgotten. The truth is – that the introduction was attended, upon my part, with a degree of anxious embarrassment which operated to prevent any definite impressions of either time or place. I am constitutionally nervous – this, with me, is a family failing, and I can't help it. In especial, the slightest appearance of mystery – of any point I cannot exactly comprehend – puts me at once into a pitiable state of agitation.

There was something, as it were, remarkable – yes, *remarkable*, although this is but a feeble term to express my full meaning – about the entire individuality of the personage in question. He was, perhaps, six feet in height, and of a presence singularly commanding. There was an *air distingué* pervading the whole man, which spoke of high breeding, and hinted at high birth. Upon this topic – the topic of Smith's personal appearance – I have a kind of melancholy satisfaction in being minute. His head of hair would have done honour to a Brutus – nothing could be more richly flowing, or possess a brighter gloss. It was of a jetty black; which was also the colour, or more properly the no colour of his unimaginable whiskers. You perceive I cannot speak of these latter without enthusiasm; it is not too much to say that they were the handsomest pair of whiskers under the sun. At all events, they encircled, and at times partially overshadowed, a mouth utterly unequalled. Here were the most entirely even, and the most brilliantly white of all conceivable teeth. From between them, upon every proper occasion, issued a voice of surpassing clearness, melody, and strength. In the matter of eyes, also, my acquaintance was pre-eminently endowed. Either one of such a pair was worth a couple of the ordinary ocular organs. They were of a deep hazel, exceedingly large and lustrous; and there was perceptible about them, ever and anon, just that amount of interesting obliquity which gives pregnancy to expression.

The bust of the General was unquestionably the finest bust I ever saw. For your life you could not have found a fault with its wonderful proportion. This rare peculiarity set off to great advantage a pair of shoulders which would have called up a blush of conscious inferiority into the countenance of the marble Apollo. I have a passion for fine shoulders, and may say that I never beheld them in perfection before. The arms altogether were admirably modelled. Nor were the lower limbs less superb. These were, indeed, the *ne plus ultra* of good legs. Every connoisseur in such matters admitted the legs to be good. There was neither too much flesh, nor too little, neither rudeness nor fragility. I could not imagine a more graceful curve than that of the *os femoris*, and there was just that due gentle prominence in the rear of the *fibula* which goes to the conformation of a properly proportioned calf. I wish to God my young and talented friend Chiponchipino, the sculptor, had but seen the legs of Brevet Brigadier General John A. B. C. Smith.

But although men so absolutely fine-looking are neither as plenty as reasons or blackberries, still I could not bring myself to believe that *the remarkable* something to which I alluded just now – that the odd air of *je ne sais quoi* which hung about my new acquaintance – lay altogether, or indeed at all, in the supreme excellence of his bodily endowments. Perhaps it might be traced to the *manner* – yet here again I could not pretend to be positive. There *was* a primness, not to say stiffness, in his carriage – a degree of measured, and, if I may so express it, of rectangular precision, attending his every movement, which, observed in a more diminutive figure, would have had the least little savour in the world, of affectation, pomposity or constraint, but which noticed in a gentleman of his undoubted dimensions, was readily placed to the account of reserve, *hauteur* – of a commendable sense, in short, of what is due to the dignity of colossal proportion.

The kind friend who presented me to General Smith whispered in my ear some few words of comment upon the man. He was a *remarkable* man – a *very* remarkable man – indeed one of the *most* remarkable men of the age. He was an especial favourite, too, with the ladies – chiefly on account of his high reputation for courage.

'In *that* point he is unrivalled – indeed he is a perfect desperado – a downright fire-eater, and no mistake,' said my friend, here dropping his voice excessively low, and thrilling me with the mystery of his tone.

'A downright fire-eater, and *no* mistake. Showed *that*, I should say, to some purpose, in the late tremendous swamp-fight away down South, with the Bugaboo and Kickapoo Indians.' [Here my friend opened his eyes to some extent.] 'Bless my soul! – blood and thunder, and all that! – *prodigies* of valour! – heard of him of course? – you know he's the man – '

'Man alive, how *do* you do? why, how *are* ye? *very* glad to see ye, indeed!' here interrupted the General himself, seizing my companion by the hand as he drew near, and bowing stiffly, but profoundly, as I was presented. I then thought (and I think so still), that I never heard a clearer nor a stronger voice, nor beheld a finer set of teeth: but I *must* say that I was sorry for the interruption just at that moment, as, owing to the whispers and insinuations aforesaid, my interest had been greatly excited in the hero of the Bugaboo and Kickapoo campaign.

However, the delightfully luminous conversation of Brevet Brigadier General John A. B. C. Smith soon completely dissipated this chagrin. My friend leaving us immediately, we had quite a long *tête-à-tête*, and I was not only pleased but *really* – instructed. I never heard a more fluent talker, or a man of greater general information. With becoming modesty, he forbore, nevertheless, to touch upon the theme I had just then most at heart – I mean the mysterious circumstances attending the Bugaboo war – and, on my own part, what I conceive to be a proper sense of delicacy forbade me to broach the subject; although, in truth, I was exceedingly tempted to do so. I perceived, too, that the gallant soldier preferred topics of philosophical interest, and that he delighted, especially, in commenting upon the rapid march of mechanical invention. Indeed, lead him where I would, this was a point to which he invariably came back.

'There is nothing at all like it,' he would say; 'we are a wonderful people, and live in a wonderful age. Parachutes and railroads – mantraps and springguns! Our steamboats are upon every sea, and the Nassau balloon packet is about to run regular trips (fare either way only twenty pounds sterling) between London and Timbuktu. And who shall calculate the immense influence upon social life – upon arts – upon commerce – upon literature – which will be the immediate result of the great principles of electromagnetics! Nor is this all, let me assure you! There is really no end to the march of invention. The most wonderful – the most ingenious – and let me add, Mr – Mr – Thompson, I believe, is your name – let me add, I say, the most *useful* – the most truly *useful* mechanical contrivances, are daily springing up like mushrooms, if I may so express myself, or, more figuratively, like – ah – grasshoppers – like grasshoppers, Mr Thompson – about us and ah – ah – ah – around us!'

Thompson, to be sure, is not my name; but it is needless to say that I left General Smith with a heightened interest in the man, with an exalted opinion of his conversational powers, and a deep sense of the valuable privileges we enjoy in living in this age of mechanical invention. My curiosity, however, had not been altogether satisfied, and I resolved to prosecute immediate enquiry among my acquaintances touching the Brevet Brigadier General himself, and particularly respecting the tremendous events *quorum pars magna fuit*, during the Bugaboo and Kickapoo campaign.

The first opportunity which presented itself, and which (*horresco referens*) I did not in the least scruple to seize, occurred at the Church of the Revd Dr Drummummupp, where I found myself established, one Sunday, just at sermon time, not only in the pew, but by the side, of that worthy and communicative little friend of mine, Miss Tabitha T. Thus seated, I congratulated myself, and with much reason, upon the very flattering state of affairs. If any person knew anything about Brevet Brigadier General John A. B. C. Smith, that person, it was clear to me, was Miss Tabitha T. We telegraphed a few signals, and then commenced, *sotto voce*, a brisk *tête-à-tête*.

'Smith!' said she, in reply to my very earnest enquiry; 'Smith! – why, not General John A. B. C.? Bless me, I thought you *knew* all about *him*! This is a wonderfully inventive age! Horrid affair that! A bloody set of wretches, those Kickapoos! Fought like a hero – prodigies of valour – immortal renown. Smith! – Brevet Brigadier General John A. B. C.! why, you know he's the man –'

'Man,' here broke in Doctor Drummummupp, at the top of his voice, and with a thump that came near knocking the pulpit about our ears; 'man that is born of a woman hath but a short time to live; he cometh up and is cut down like a flower!' I started to the extremity of the pew, and perceived by the animated looks of the divine, that the wrath which had nearly proved fatal to the pulpit had been excited by the whispers of the lady and myself. There was no help for it; so I submitted with a good grace, and listened, in all the martyrdom of dignified silence, to the balance of that very capital discourse.

Next evening found me a somewhat late visitor at the Rantipole Theatre, where I felt sure of satisfying my curiosity at once, by merely stepping into the box of those exquisite specimens of affability and omniscience, the Misses Arabella and Miranda Cognoscenti. That fine tragedian, Climax, was doing Iago to a very crowded house, and I experienced some little difficulty in making my wishes understood; especially as our box was next the slips, and completely overlooked the stage.

'Smith?' said Miss Arabella, as she at length comprehended the purport of my query; 'Smith? – why, not General John A. B. C.?'

'Smith?' enquired Miranda, musingly. 'God bless me, did you ever behold a finer figure?'

'Never, madam, but *do* tell me – '

'Or so inimitable grace?'

'Never, upon my word! – But pray inform me – '

'Or so just an appreciation of stage effect?'

'Madam!'

'Or a more delicate sense of the true beauties of Shakespeare? Be so good as to look at that leg!'

'The devil!' and I turned again to her sister.

'Smith?' said she, 'why, not General John A. B. C.? Horrid affair that, wasn't it? – great wretches, those Bugaboos – savage and so on – but we live in a wonderfully inventive age! – Smith! – O yes! great man! – perfect desperado – immortal renown – prodigies of valour! *Never heard!*' [This was given in a scream.] 'Bless my soul! why, he's the man – '

'. . . mandragora
Nor all the drowsy syrups of the world
Shall ever medicine thee to that sweet sleep
Which thou ow'dst yesterday!'

here roared out Climax just in my ear, and shaking his fist in my face all the time, in a way that I *couldn't* stand, and I *wouldn't*. I left the Misses Cognoscenti immediately, went behind the scenes forthwith, and gave the beggarly scoundrel such a thrashing as I trust he will remember to the day of his death.

At the *soirée* of the lovely widow, Mrs Kathleen O'Trump, I was confident that I should meet with no similar disappointment. Accordingly, I was no sooner seated at the card-table, with my pretty hostess for a *vis-à-vis*, than I propounded those questions the solution of which had become a matter so essential to my peace.

'Smith?' said my partner, 'why, not General John A. B. C.? Horrid affair that, wasn't it? – diamonds, did you say? – terrible wretches those Kickapoos! – we are playing *whist*, if you please, Mr Tattle – however, this is the age of invention, most certainly *the* age, one may say – *the* age *par excellence* – speak French? – oh, quite a hero – perfect desperado! – *no hearts*, Mr Tattle? I don't believe it! – immortal renown and all that! – prodigies of valour! *Never heard!!* – why, bless me, he's the man – '

'Mann? – *Captain* Mann?' here screamed some little feminine interloper from the farthest corner of the room. 'Are you talking about Captain Mann and the duel? – oh, I *must* hear – do tell – go on, Mrs O'Trump! – do now go on!' And go on Mrs O'Trump did – all about a certain Captain Mann, who was either shot or hung, or should have been both shot and hung. Yes! Mrs O'Trump, she went on, and I – I went off. There was no chance of hearing anything farther that evening in regard to Brevet Brigadier General John A. B. C. Smith.

Still I consoled myself with the reflection that the tide of ill luck would not run against me for ever, and so determined to make a bold push for information at the rout of that bewitching little angel, the graceful Mrs Pirouette.

'Smith?' said Mrs P, as we twirled about together in a *pas de zephyr*, 'Smith? – why, not General John A. B. C.? Dreadful business that of the Bugaboos, wasn't it? – dreadful creatures, those Indians! – *do* turn out your toes! I really am ashamed of you – man of great courage, poor fellow! – but this is a wonderful age for invention – O dear me, I'm out of breath – quite a desperado – prodigies of valour – *never heard!!* – can't believe it – I shall have to sit down and enlighten you – Smith! why, he's the man – '

'Man-*Fred*, I tell you!' here bawled out Miss Bas-Bleu, as I led Mrs Pirouette to a seat. 'Did ever anybody hear the like? It's Man-*Fred*, I say, and not at all by any means Man-*Friday*.' Here Miss Bas-Bleu beckoned to me in a very peremptory manner; and I was obliged, willy-nilly, to leave Mrs P for the purpose of deciding a dispute touching the title of a certain poetical drama of Lord Byron's. Although I pronounced, with great promptness, that the true title was Man-*Friday*, and not by any means Man-*Fred*, yet when I returned to seek Mrs Pirouette she was not to be discovered, and I made my retreat from the house in a very bitter spirit of animosity against the whole race of the Bas-Bleus.

Matters had now assumed a really serious aspect, and I resolved to call at once upon my particular friend, Mr Theodore Sinivate; for I knew that here at least I should get something like definite information.

'Smith?' said he, in his well-known peculiar way of drawling out his syllables; 'Smith? – why, not General John A. B. C.? Savage affair that with the Kickapo–o–o–os, wasn't it? Say! don't you think so? – perfect despera–a–ado – great pity, 'pon my honour! – wonderfully inventive age! – pro–o–odigies of valour! By the by, did you ever hear about Captain Ma–a–a–a–n?'

'Captain Mann be d—d!' said I; 'please to go on with your story.'

'Hem! – oh well! – quite *la même cho–o–ose*, as we say in France. Smith, eh? Brigadier-General John A. B. C.? I say' – [here Mr S thought proper to put his finger to the side of his nose] – 'I say, you don't mean to insinuate now, really and truly, and conscientiously, that you don't know all about that affair of Smith's, as well as I do, eh? Smith? John A–B–C.? Why, bless me, he's the ma–a–an – '

'*Mr* Sinivate,' said I, imploringly, '*is* he the man in the mask?'

'No–o–o!' said he, looking wise, 'nor the man in the mo–o–on.'

This reply I considered a pointed and positive insult, and so left the house at once in high dudgeon, with a firm resolve to call my friend, Mr Sinivate, to a speedy account for his ungentlemanly conduct and ill-breeding.

In the meantime, however, I had no notion of being thwarted touching the information I desired. There was one resource left me yet. I would go to the fountain-head. I would call forthwith upon the General himself, and demand, in explicit terms, a solution of this abominable piece of mystery. Here, at least, there should be no chance for equivocation. I would be plain, positive, peremptory – as short as pie-crust – as concise as Tacitus or Montesquieu.

It was early when I called, and the General was dressing; but I pleaded urgent business, and was shown at once into his bedroom by an old negro valet, who remained in attendance during my visit. As I entered the chamber, I looked about, of course, for the occupant, but did not immediately perceive him. There was a large and exceedingly odd-looking bundle of something which lay close by my feet on the floor, and, as I was not in the best humour in the world, I gave it a kick out of the way.

'Hem! ahem! rather civil that, I should say!' said the bundle, in one of the smallest, and altogether the funniest little voices, between a squeak and a whistle, that I ever heard in all the days of my existence.

'Ahem! rather civil that, I should observe.'

I fairly shouted with terror, and made off, at a tangent, into the farthest extremity of the room.

'God bless me! my dear fellow,' here again whistled the bundle, 'what – what – what – why, what *is* the matter? I really believe you don't know me at all.'

What *could* I say to all this – what *could* I? I staggered into an armchair, and, with staring eyes and open mouth, awaited the solution of the wonder.

'Strange you shouldn't know me though, isn't it?' presently resqueaked the nondescript, which I now perceived was performing, upon the floor, some inexplicable evolution, very analogous to the drawing on of a stocking. There was only a single leg, however, apparent.

'Strange you shouldn't know me, though, isn't it? Pompey, bring me that leg!' Here Pompey handed the bundle a very capital cork leg, already dressed, which it screwed on in a trice; and then it stood up before my eyes.

'And a bloody action it *was*,' continued the thing, as if in a soliloquy; 'but then one mustn't fight with the Bugaboos and Kickapoos, and think of coming off with a mere scratch. Pompey, I'll thank you now for that arm. Thomas' [turning to me] 'is decidedly the best hand at a cork leg; but if you should ever want an arm, my dear fellow, you must really let me recommend you to Bishop.' Here Pompey screwed on an arm.

'We had rather hot work of it, that you may say. Now, you dog, slip on my shoulders and bosom! Pettit makes the best shoulders, but for a bosom you will have to go to Ducrow.'

'Bosom!' said I.

'Pompey, will you *never* be ready with that wig? Scalping is a rough process after all; but then you can procure such a capital scratch at De L'Orme's.'

'Scratch!'

'Now, you nigger, my teeth! For a *good* set of these you had better go to Parmly's at once; high prices, but excellent work. I swallowed some very capital articles, though, when the big Bugaboo rammed me down with the butt end of his rifle.'

'Butt end! ram down!! my eye!!'

'O yes, by the by, my eye – here, Pompey, you scamp, screw it in! Those Kickapoos are not so very slow at a gouge; but he's a belied man, that Dr Williams, after all; you can't imagine how well I see with the eyes of his make.'

I now began very clearly to perceive that the object before me was nothing more nor less than my new acquaintance, Brevet Brigadier General John A. B. C.

Smith. The manipulations of Pompey had made, I must confess, a very striking difference in the appearance of the personal man. The voice, however, still puzzled me no little; but even this apparent mystery was speedily cleared up.

'Pompey, you black rascal,' squeaked the General, 'I really do believe you would let me go out without my palate.'

Hereupon, the negro, grumbling out an apology, went up to his master, opened his mouth with the knowing air of a horse-jockey, and adjusted therein a somewhat singular-looking machine, in a very dexterous manner, that I could not altogether comprehend. The alteration, however, in the entire expression of the General's countenance was instantaneous and surprising. When he again spoke, his voice had resumed all that rich melody and strength which I had noticed upon our original introduction.

'D—n the vagabonds!' said he, in so clear a tone that I positively started at the change, 'D—n the vagabonds! they not only knocked in the roof of my mouth, but took the trouble to cut off at least seven-eighths of my tongue. There isn't Bonfanti's equal, however, in America, for really good articles of this description. I can recommend you to him with confidence' [here the General bowed], 'and assure you that I have the greatest pleasure in so doing.'

I acknowledged his kindness in my best manner, and took leave of him at once, with a perfect understanding of the true state of affairs – with a full comprehension of the mystery which had troubled me so long. It was evident. It was a clear case. Brevet Brigadier General John A. B. C. Smith was the man – was *the man that was used up*.

William Wilson

What say of it? what say of CONSCIENCE grim,
That spectre in my path?

Chamberlayne's *Pharronida*

Let me call myself, for the present, William Wilson. The fair page now lying before me need not be sullied with my real appellation. This has been already too much an object for the scorn – for the horror – for the detestation of my race. To the uttermost regions of the globe have not the indignant winds bruited its unparalleled infamy? Oh, outcast of all outcasts most abandoned! – to the earth art thou not forever dead? to its honours, to its flowers, to its golden aspirations? – and a cloud, dense, dismal, and limitless, does it not hang eternally between thy hopes and heaven?

I would not, if I could, here or today, embody a record of my later years of unspeakable misery, and unpardonable crime. This epoch – these later years – took unto themselves a sudden elevation in turpitude, whose origin alone it is my present purpose to assign. Men usually grow base by degrees. From me, in an instant, all virtue dropped bodily as a mantle. From comparatively trivial wickedness I passed, with the stride of a giant, into more than the enormities of an Elagabalus. What chance – what one event brought this evil thing to pass, bear with me while I relate. Death approaches; and the shadow which foreruns him has thrown a softening influence over my spirit. I long, in passing through the dim valley, for the sympathy – I had nearly said for the pity – of my fellow men. I would fain have them believe that I have been, in some measure, the slave of circumstances beyond human control. I would wish them to seek out for me, in the details I am about to give, some little oasis of fatality amid a wilderness of error. I would have them allow – what they cannot refrain from allowing – that, although temptation may have erewhile existed as great, man was never thus, at least, tempted before – certainly, never thus fell. And is it therefore that he has never thus suffered? Have I not indeed been living in a dream? And am I not now dying a victim to the horror and the mystery of the wildest of all sublunary visions?

I am the descendant of a race whose imaginative and easily excitable temperament has at all times rendered them remarkable; and, in my earliest infancy, I gave evidence of having fully inherited the family character. As I advanced in years it was more strongly developed; becoming, for many reasons, a cause of serious dis-quietude to my friends, and of positive injury to myself. I grew self-willed, addicted to the wildest caprices, and a prey to the most ungovernable passions. Weak-minded, and beset with constitutional infirmities akin to my own, my parents could do but little to check the evil propensities which distinguished me. Some feeble and ill-directed efforts resulted in complete failure on their part, and, of course, in total triumph on mine. Thenceforward my voice was a household law; and at an age when few children have abandoned their leading-strings, I was left to the guidance of my own will, and became, in all but name, the master of my own actions.

My earliest recollections of a school-life, are

connected with a large, rambling, Elizabethan house, in a misty-looking village of England, where were a vast number of gigantic and gnarled trees, and where all the houses were excessively ancient. In truth, it was a dream-like and spirit-soothing place, that venerable old town. At this moment, in fancy, I feel the refreshing chilliness of its deeply-shadowed avenues, inhale the fragrance of its thousand shrubberies, and thrill anew with undefinable delight, at the deep hollow note of the church-bell, breaking, each hour, with sullen and sudden roar, upon the stillness of the dusky atmosphere in which the fretted Gothic steeple lay embedded and asleep.

It gives me, perhaps, as much of pleasure as I can now in any manner experience, to dwell upon minute recollections of the school and its concerns. Steeped in misery as I am – misery, alas! only too real – I shall be pardoned for seeking relief, however slight and temporary, in the weakness of a few rambling details. These, moreover, utterly trivial, and even ridiculous in themselves, assume, to my fancy, adventitious importance, as connected with a period and a locality when and where I recognise the first ambiguous monitions of the destiny which afterwards so fully overshadowed me. Let me then remember.

The house, I have said, was old and irregular. The grounds were extensive, and a high and solid brick wall, topped with a bed of mortar and broken glass, encompassed the whole. This prison-like rampart formed the limit of our domain; beyond it we saw but thrice a week – once every Saturday afternoon, when, attended by two ushers, we were permitted to take brief walks in a body through some of the neighbouring fields – and twice during Sunday, when we were paraded in the same formal manner to the morning and evening service in the one church of the village. Of this church the principal of our school was pastor. With how deep a spirit of wonder and perplexity was I wont to regard him from our remote pew in the gallery, as, with step solemn and slow, he ascended the pulpit! This reverend man, with countenance so demurely benign, with robes so glossy and so clerically flowing, with wig so minutely powdered, so rigid and so vast – could this be he who, of late, with sour visage, and in snuffy habiliments, administered, ferule in hand, the Draconian laws of the academy? Oh, gigantic paradox, too utterly monstrous for solution!

At an angle of the ponderous wall frowned a more ponderous gate. It was riveted and studded with iron bolts, and surmounted with jagged iron spikes. What impressions of deep awe did it inspire! It was never opened save for the three periodical egressions and ingressions already mentioned; then, in every creak of its mighty hinges, we found a plenitude of mystery – a world of matter for solemn remark, or for more solemn meditation.

The extensive enclosure was irregular in form, having many capacious recesses. Of these, three or four of the largest constituted the playground. It was level, and covered with fine hard gravel. I well remember it had no trees, nor benches, nor anything similar within it. Of course it was in the rear of the house. In front lay a small parterre, planted with box and other shrubs; but through this sacred division we passed only upon rare occasions indeed – such as a first advent to school or final departure thence, or perhaps, when a parent or friend having called for us, we joyfully took our way home for the Christmas or Midsummer holy-days.

But the house! – how quaint an old building was this! – to me how veritably a palace of enchantment! There was really no end to its windings – to its incomprehensible subdivisions. It was difficult, at any given time, to say with certainty upon which of its two storeys one happened to be. From each room to every other there were sure to be found three or four steps either in ascent or descent. Then the lateral branches were innumerable – inconceivable – and so returning in upon themselves, that our most exact ideas in regard to the whole mansion were not very far different from those with which we pondered upon infinity. During the five years of my residence here, I was never able to ascertain with precision, in what remote locality lay the little sleeping apartment assigned to myself and some eighteen or twenty other scholars.

The schoolroom was the largest in the house – I could not help thinking, in the world. It was very long, narrow, and dismally low, with pointed Gothic windows and a ceiling of oak. In a remote and terror-inspiring angle was a square enclosure of eight or ten feet, comprising the sanctum, 'during hours', of our principal, the Revd Dr Bransby. It was a solid structure, with massy door, sooner than open which in the absence of the 'Dominie', we would all have willingly perished by the *peine forte et dure*. In other angles were two other similar boxes, far less reverenced, indeed, but still greatly matters of awe. One of these was the pulpit of the 'classical' usher, one of the 'English and mathematical'. Interspersed about the room, crossing and recrossing in endless irregularity, were innumerable benches and desks, black, ancient, and time-worn, piled desperately with much-bethumbed books, and so beseamed with initial letters, names at full length, grotesque figures, and other multiplied efforts of the knife, as to have entirely lost what little of original form might have been their portion in days long departed. A huge bucket with water stood at one extremity of the room, and a clock of stupendous dimensions at the other.

Encompassed by the massy walls of this venerable academy, I passed, yet not in tedium or disgust, the years of the third lustrum of my life. The teeming brain of childhood requires no external world of incident to occupy or amuse it; and the apparently dismal monotony of a school was replete with more intense excitement than my riper youth has derived from luxury, or my full manhood from crime. Yet I must believe that my first mental development had in it much of the uncommon – even much of the *outré*. Upon mankind at large the events of very early existence rarely leave in mature age any definite impression. All is grey shadow – a weak and irregular remembrance – an indistinct regathering of feeble pleasures and phantasmagoric pains. With me this is not so. In childhood I must have felt with the energy of a man what I now find stamped upon memory in lines as vivid, as deep, and as durable as the *exergues* of the Carthaginian medals.

Yet in fact – in the fact of the world's view – how little was there to remember! The morning's awakening, the nightly summons to bed; the connings, the recitations; the periodical half-holidays, and perambulations; the playground, with its broils, its pastimes, its intrigues; these, by a mental sorcery long forgotten, were made to involve a wilderness of sensation, a world of rich incident, an universe of varied emotion, of excitement the most passionate and spirit-stirring. '*Oh, le bon temps, que ce siècle de fer!*'

In truth, the ardour, the enthusiasm, and the imperiousness of my disposition, soon rendered me a marked character among my schoolmates, and by slow, but natural gradations, gave me an ascendancy over all not greatly older than myself – over all with a single exception. This exception was found in the person of a scholar, who, although no relation, bore the same Christian and surname as myself – a circumstance, in fact, little remarkable for, notwithstanding a noble descent, mine was one of those everyday appellations which seem, by prescriptive right, to have been, time out of mind, the common property of the mob. In this narrative I have therefore designated myself as William Wilson – a fictitious title not very dissimilar to the real. My namesake alone, of those who in school phraseology constituted 'our set', presumed to compete with me in the studies of the class – in the sports and broils of the playground – to refuse implicit belief in my assertions, and submission to my will – indeed, to interfere with my arbitrary dictation in any respect whatsoever. If there is on earth a supreme and unqualified despotism, it is the despotism of a mastermind in boyhood over the less energetic spirits of its companions.

Wilson's rebellion was to me a source of the greatest embarrassment – the more so as, in spite of the bravado with which in public I made a point of treating him and his pretensions, I secretly felt that I feared him, and could not help thinking the equality which he maintained so easily with myself, a proof of his true superiority; since not to be overcome cost me a perpetual struggle. Yet this superiority – even this equality – was in truth acknowledged by no one but myself; our associates, by some unaccountable blindness, seemed not even to suspect it. Indeed, his competition, his resistance, and especially his impertinent and dogged interference with my purposes, were not more pointed than private. He appeared to be destitute alike of the ambition which urged, and of the passionate energy of mind which enabled me to excel. In his rivalry he might have been supposed actuated solely by a whimsical desire to thwart, astonish, or mortify myself; although there were times when I could not help observing, with a feeling made up of wonder, abasement, and pique, that he mingled with his injuries, his insults, or his contradictions, a certain most inappropriate, and assuredly most unwelcome affectionateness of manner. I could only conceive this singular behaviour to arise from a consummate self-conceit assuming the vulgar airs of patronage and protection.

Perhaps it was this latter trait in Wilson's conduct, conjoined with our identity of name, and the mere accident of our having entered the school upon the same day, which set afloat the notion that we were brothers, among the senior classes in the academy. These do not usually enquire with much strictness into the affairs of their juniors. I have before said, or should have said, that Wilson was not, in the most remote degree, connected with my family. But assuredly if we had been brothers we must have been twins; for, after leaving Dr Bransby's, I casually learned that my namesake was born on the nineteenth of January, 1813 – and this is a somewhat remarkable coincidence; for the day is precisely that of my own nativity.

It may seem strange that in spite of the continual

anxiety occasioned me by the rivalry of Wilson, and his intolerable spirit of contradiction, I could not bring myself to hate him altogether. We had, to be sure, nearly every day a quarrel in which, yielding me publicly the palm of victory, he, in some manner, contrived to make me feel that it was he who had deserved it; yet a sense of pride on my part, and a veritable dignity on his own, kept us always upon what are called 'speaking terms', while there were many points of strong congeniality in our tempers, operating to awake in me a sentiment which our position alone, perhaps, prevented from ripening into friendship. It is difficult, indeed, to define, or even to describe, my real feelings towards him. They formed a motley and heterogeneous admixture – some petulant animosity, which was not yet hatred, some esteem, more respect, much fear, with a world of uneasy curiosity. To the moralist it will be unnecessary to say, in addition, that Wilson and myself were the most inseparable of companions.

It was no doubt the anomalous state of affairs existing between us, which turned all my attacks upon him (and they were many, either open or covert) into the channel of banter or practical joke (giving pain while assuming the aspect of mere fun) rather than into a more serious and determined hostility. But my endeavours on this head were by no means uniformly successful, even when my plans were the most wittily concocted; for my namesake had much about him, in character, of that unassuming and quiet austerity which, while enjoying the poignancy of its own jokes, has no heel of Achilles in itself, and absolutely refuses to be laughed at. I could find, indeed, but one vulnerable point, and that, lying in a personal peculiarity, arising, perhaps, from constitutional disease, would have been spared by any antagonist less at his wit's end than myself – my rival had a weakness in the faucial or guttural organs, which precluded him from raising his voice at any time above a very low whisper. Of this defect I did not fail to take what poor advantage lay in my power.

Wilson's retaliations in kind were many; and there was one form of his practical wit that disturbed me beyond measure. How his sagacity first discovered at all that so petty a thing would vex me, is a question I never could solve; but, having discovered, he habitually practised the annoyance. I had always felt aversion to my uncourtly patronymic, and its very common, if not plebeian *praenomen*. The words were venom in my ears; and when, upon the day of my arrival, a second William Wilson came also to the academy, I felt angry with him for bearing the name, and doubly disgusted with the name because a stranger bore it, who would be the cause of its twofold repetition, who would be constantly in my presence, and whose concerns, in the ordinary routine of the school business, must inevitably, on account of the detestable coincidence, be often confounded with my own.

The feeling of vexation thus engendered grew stronger with every circumstance tending to show resemblance, moral or physical, between my rival and myself. I had not then discovered the remarkable fact that we were of the same age; but I saw that we were of the same height, and I perceived that we were even singularly alike in general contour of person and outline of feature. I was galled, too, by the rumour touching a relationship, which had grown current in the upper forms. In a word, nothing could more seriously disturb me (although I scrupulously concealed such disturbance) than any allusion to a similarity of mind, person, or condition existing between us. But, in truth, I had no reason to believe that (with the exception of the matter of relationship, and in the case of Wilson himself) this similarity had ever been made a subject of comment, or even observed at all by our schoolfellows. That he observed it in all its bearings, and as fixedly as I, was apparent; but that he could discover in such circumstances so fruitful a field of annoyance, can only be attributed, as I said before, to his more than ordinary penetration.

His cue, which was to perfect an imitation of myself, lay both in words and in actions; and most admirably did he play his part. My dress it was an easy matter to copy; my gait and general manner were, without difficulty, appropriated; in spite of his constitutional defect, even my voice did not escape him. My louder tones were, of course, unattempted, but then the key, it was identical; and his singular whisper, it grew the very echo of my own.

How greatly this most exquisite portraiture harassed me (for it could not justly be termed a caricature) I will not now venture to describe. I had but one consolation – in the fact that the imitation, apparently, was noticed by myself alone, and that I had to endure only the knowing and strangely sarcastic smiles of my namesake himself. Satisfied with having produced in my bosom the intended effect, he seemed to chuckle in secret over the sting he had inflicted, and was characteristically disregardful of the public applause which the success of his witty endeavours might have so easily elicited. That the school, indeed, did not feel his design, perceive its accomplishment, and participate in his sneer, was, for many anxious months, a riddle I could not resolve. Perhaps the gradation of his copy rendered it not so readily perceptible; or, more possibly, I owed my security to the master air of the copyist, who, disdaining the letter (which in a painting is all the obtuse can see), gave but the full spirit of his original for my individual contemplation and chagrin.

I have already more than once spoken of the disgusting air of patronage which he assumed towards me, and of his frequent officious interference with my will. This interference often took the ungracious character of advice; advice not openly given, but hinted or insinuated. I received it with a repugnance which gained strength as I grew in years. Yet, at this distant day, let me do him the simple justice to acknowledge that I can recall no occasion when the suggestions of my rival were on the side of those errors or follies so usual to his immature age and seeming inexperience; that his moral sense, at least, if not his general talents and worldly wisdom, was far keener than my own; and that I might, today, have been a better, and thus a happier man, had I less frequently rejected the counsels embodied in those meaning whispers which I then but too cordially hated and too bitterly despised.

As it was, I at length grew restive in the extreme under his distasteful supervision, and daily resented more and more openly what I considered his intolerable arrogance. I have said that, in the first years of our connection as schoolmates, my feelings in regard to him might have been easily ripened into friendship: but, in the latter months of my residence at the academy, although the intrusion of his ordinary manner had, beyond doubt, in some measure, abated, my sentiments, in nearly similar proportion, partook very much of positive hatred. Upon one occasion he saw this, I think, and afterwards avoided, or made a show of avoiding me.

It was about the same period, if I remember aright, that, in an altercation of violence with him, in which he was more than usually thrown off his guard, and spoke and acted with an openness of demeanour rather foreign to his nature, I discovered, or fancied I discovered, in his accent, his air, and general appearance, a something which first startled, and then deeply interested me, by bringing to mind dim visions of my earliest infancy – wild, confused and thronging memories of a time when memory herself was yet unborn. I cannot better describe the sensation which oppressed me than by saying that I could with difficulty shake off the belief of my having been acquainted with the being who stood before me, at some epoch very long ago – some point of the past even infinitely remote. The delusion, however, faded rapidly as it came; and I mention it at all but to define the day of the last conversation I there held with my singular namesake.

The huge old house, with its countless subdivisions, had several large chambers communicating with each other, where slept the greater number of the students. There were, however (as must necessarily happen in a building so awkwardly planned), many little nooks or recesses, the odds and ends of the structure; and these the economic ingenuity of Dr Bransby had also fitted up as dormitories; although, being the merest closets, they were capable of accommodating but a single individual. One of these small apartments was occupied by Wilson.

One night, about the close of my fifth year at the school, and immediately after the altercation just mentioned, finding everyone wrapped in sleep, I arose from bed, and, lamp in hand, stole through a wilderness of narrow passages from my own bedroom to that of my rival. I had long been plotting one of those ill-natured pieces of practical wit at his expense in which I had hitherto been so uniformly unsuccessful. It was my intention, now, to put my scheme in operation, and I resolved to make him feel the whole extent of the malice with which I was imbued. Having reached his closet, I noiselessly entered, leaving the lamp, with a shade over it, on the outside. I advanced a step, and listened to the sound of his tranquil breathing. Assured of his being asleep, I returned, took the light, and with it again approached the bed. Close curtains were around it, which, in the prosecution of my plan, I slowly and quietly withdrew, when the bright rays fell vividly upon the sleeper, and my eyes, at the same moment, upon his countenance. I looked – and a numbness, an iciness of feeling instantly pervaded my frame. My breast heaved, my knees tottered, my whole spirit became possessed with an objectless yet intolerable horror. Gasping for breath, I lowered the lamp in still nearer proximity to the face. Were these – *these* the lineaments of William Wilson? I saw, indeed, that they were his, but I shook as if with a fit of the ague in fancying they were not. What was there about them to confound me in this manner? I gazed – while my brain reeled with a multitude of incoherent thoughts. Not thus he appeared – assuredly not thus – in the vivacity of his waking hours. The same name! the same contour of person! the same day of arrival at the academy! And then his dogged and meaningless imitation of my gait, my voice, my habits, and my manner! Was it, in truth, within the bounds of human possibility, that what I now saw was the result, merely, of the habitual practice of this sarcastic imitation? Awestricken, and with a creeping shudder, I extinguished the lamp, passed silently from the chamber, and left, at once, the halls of that old academy, never to enter them again.

After a lapse of some months, spent at home in mere idleness, I found myself a student at Eton. The brief interval had been sufficient to enfeeble my remembrance of the events at Dr Bransby's, or at least to effect a material change in the nature of the feelings with which I remembered them. The truth – the tragedy – of the drama was no more. I could now find room to doubt the evidence of my senses; and seldom called up the subject at all but with wonder at the extent of human credulity, and a smile at the vivid force of the imagination which I hereditarily possessed. Neither was this species of scepticism likely to be diminished by the character of the life I led at Eton. The vortex of thoughtless folly into which I there so immediately and so recklessly plunged, washed away all but the froth of my past hours, engulfed at once every solid or serious impression, and left to memory only the veriest levities of a former existence.

I do not wish, however, to trace the course of my miserable profligacy here – a profligacy which set at defiance the laws, while it eluded the vigilance of the institution. Three years of folly, passed without profit, had but given me rooted habits of vice, and added, in a somewhat unusual degree, to my bodily stature, when, after a week of soulless dissipation, I invited a small party of the most dissolute students to a secret carousal in my chambers. We met at a late hour of the night; for our debaucheries were to be faithfully protracted until morning. The wine flowed freely, and there were not wanting other and perhaps more dangerous seductions; so that the grey dawn had already faintly appeared in the east, while our delirious extravagance was at its height. Madly flushed with cards and intoxication, I was in the act of insisting upon a toast of more than wonted profanity, when my attention was suddenly diverted by the violent, although partial unclosing of the door of the apartment, and by the eager voice of a servant from without. He said that some person, apparently in great haste, demanded to speak with me in the hall.

Wildly excited with wine, the unexpected interruption rather delighted than surprised me. I staggered forward at once, and a few steps brought me to the vestibule of the building. In this low and small room there hung no lamp; and now no light at all was admitted, save that of the exceedingly feeble dawn which made its way through the semicircular window. As I put my foot over the threshold, I became aware of the figure of a youth about my own height, and habited in a white kerseymere morning frock, cut in the novel fashion of the one I myself wore at the moment. This the faint light enabled me to perceive; but the features of his face I could not distinguish. Upon my entering he strode hurriedly up to me, and, seizing me by the arm with a gesture of petulant impatience, whispered the words 'William Wilson!' in my ear.

I grew perfectly sober in an instant. There was that in the manner of the stranger, and in the tremulous shake of his uplifted finger, as he held it between my eyes and the light, which filled me with unqualified amazement; but it was not this which had so violently moved me. It was the pregnancy of solemn admonition in the singular, low, hissing utterance; and, above all, it was the character, the tone, the key, of those few, simple, and familiar, yet whispered syllables, which came with a thousand thronging memories of bygone days, and struck upon my soul with the shock of a galvanic battery. Ere I could recover the use of my senses he was gone.

Although this event failed not of a vivid effect upon my disordered imagination, yet was it evanescent as vivid. For some weeks, indeed, I busied myself in earnest enquiry, or was wrapped in a cloud of morbid speculation. I did not pretend to disguise from my perception the identity of the singular individual who thus perseveringly interfered with my affairs, and harassed me with his insinuated counsel. But who and what was this Wilson? – and whence came he? – and what were his purposes? Upon neither of these points could I be satisfied; merely ascertaining, in regard to him, that a sudden accident in his family had caused his removal from Dr Bransby's academy on the afternoon of the day in which I myself had eloped. But in a brief period I ceased to think upon the subject; my attention being all absorbed in a contemplated departure for Oxford. Thither I soon went; the uncalculating vanity of my parents furnishing me with an outfit and annual establishment, which would enable me to indulge at will in the luxury already so dear to my heart – to vie in profuseness of expenditure with the haughtiest heirs of the wealthiest earldoms in Great Britain.

Excited by such appliances to vice, my constitutional temperament broke forth with redoubled ardour, and I spurned even the common restraints of decency in the mad infatuation of my revels. But it were absurd to pause in the detail of my extravagance. Let it suffice, that among spendthrifts I out-Heroded Herod, and that, giving name to a multitude of novel follies, I added no brief appendix to the long catalogue of vices then usual in the most dissolute university of Europe.

It could hardly be credited, however, that I had, even here, so utterly fallen from the gentlemanly estate, as to seek acquaintance with the vilest arts of the gambler by profession, and, having become an adept in his despicable science, to practise it habitually as a means of increasing my already enormous income at the expense of the weak-minded among my fellow-collegians. Such, nevertheless, was the fact. And the very enormity of this offence against all manly and honourable sentiment proved, beyond doubt, the main if not the sole reason of the impunity with which it was committed. Who, indeed, among my most abandoned associates, would not rather have disputed the clearest evidence of his senses, than have suspected of such courses, the gay, the frank, the generous William Wilson – the noblest and most liberal commoner at Oxford – him whose follies (said his parasites) were but the follies of youth and unbridled fancy – whose errors but inimitable whim – whose darkest vice but a careless and dashing extravagance?

I had been now two years successfully busied in this way, when there came to the university a young *parvenu* nobleman, Glendinning – rich, said report, as

Herodes Atticus – his riches, too, as easily acquired. I soon found him of weak intellect, and, of course, marked him as a fitting subject for my skill. I frequently engaged him in play, and contrived, with the gambler's usual art, to let him win considerable sums, the more effectually to entangle him in my snares. At length, my schemes being ripe, I met him (with the full intention that this meeting should be final and decisive) at the chambers of a fellow-commoner (Mr Preston), equally intimate with both, but who, to do him justice, entertained not even a remote suspicion of my design. To give to this a better colouring, I had contrived to have assembled a party of some eight or ten, and was solicitously careful that the introduction of cards should appear accidental, and originate in the proposal of my contemplated dupe himself. To be brief upon a vile topic, none of the low finesse was omitted, so customary upon similar occasions that it is a just matter for wonder how any are still found so besotted as to fall its victim.

We had protracted our sitting far into the night, and I had at length effected the manoeuvre of getting Glendinning as my sole antagonist. The game, too, was my favourite *écarté*. The rest of the company, interested in the extent of our play, had abandoned their own cards, and were standing around us as spectators. The *parvenu*, who had been induced by my artifices in the early part of the evening, to drink deeply, now shuffled, dealt, or played, with a wild nervousness of manner for which his intoxication, I thought, might partially, but could not altogether account. In a very short period he had become my debtor to a large amount, when, having taken a long draught of port, he did precisely what I had been coolly anticipating – he proposed to double our already extravagant stakes. With a well-feigned show of reluctance, and not until after my repeated refusal had seduced him into some angry words which gave a colour of pique to my compliance, did I finally comply. The result, of course, did but prove how entirely the prey was in my toils; in less than an hour he had quadrupled his debt. For some time his countenance had been losing the florid tinge lent it by the wine; but now, to my astonishment, I perceived that it had grown to a pallor truly fearful. I say to my astonishment. Glendinning had been represented to my eager enquiries as immeasurably wealthy; and the sums which he had as yet lost, although in themselves vast, could not, I supposed, very seriously annoy, much less so violently affect him. That he was overcome by the wine just swallowed, was the idea which most readily presented itself; and, rather with a view to the preservation of my own character in the eyes of my associates, than from any less interested motive, I was about to insist, peremptorily, upon a discontinuance of the play, when some expressions at my elbow from among the company, and an ejaculation evincing utter despair on the part of Glendinning, gave me to understand that I had effected his total ruin under circumstances which, rendering him an object for the pity of all, should have protected him from the ill offices even of a fiend.

What now might have been my conduct it is difficult to say. The pitiable condition of my dupe had thrown an air of embarrassed gloom over all; and, for some moments, a profound silence was maintained, during which I could not help feeling my cheeks tingle with the many burning glances of scorn or reproach cast upon me by the less abandoned of the party. I will even own that an intolerable weight of anxiety was for a brief instant lifted from my bosom by the sudden and extraordinary interruption which ensued. The wide, heavy folding doors of the apartment were all at once thrown open, to their full extent, with a vigorous and rushing impetuosity that extinguished, as if by magic, every candle in the room. Their light, in dying, enabled us just to perceive that a stranger had entered, about my own height, and closely muffled in a cloak. The darkness, however, was now total; and we could only feel that he was standing in our midst. Before any one of us could recover from the extreme astonishment into which this rudeness had thrown all, we heard the voice of the intruder.

'Gentlemen,' he said, in a low, distinct, and never-to-be-forgotten whisper which thrilled to the very marrow of my bones, 'Gentlemen, I make no apology for this behaviour, because in thus behaving, I am but fulfilling a duty. You are, beyond doubt, uninformed of the true character of the person who has tonight won at *écarté* a large sum of money from Lord Glendinning. I will therefore put you upon an expeditious and decisive plan of obtaining this very necessary information. Please to examine, at your leisure, the inner linings of the cuff of his left sleeve, and the several little packages which may be found in the somewhat capacious pockets of his embroidered morning wrapper.'

While he spoke, so profound was the stillness that one might have heard a pin drop upon the floor. In ceasing, he departed at once, and as abruptly as he had entered. Can I – shall I describe my sensations? – must I say that I felt all the horrors of the damned? Most assuredly I had little time given for reflection. Many hands roughly seized me upon the spot, and lights were immediately reprocured. A search ensued. In the lining of my sleeve were found all the court cards essential in *écarté*, and, in the pockets of my wrapper, a number of packs, facsimiles of those used at our sittings, with the single exception that mine were of the species called, technically, *arrondées* – the honours being slightly convex at the ends, the lower cards slightly convex at the sides. In this disposition, the dupe who cuts, as customary, at the length of the pack, will invariably find that he cuts his antagonist an honour; while the gambler, cutting at the breadth, will, as certainly, cut nothing for his victim which may count in the records of the game.

Any burst of indignation upon this discovery would have affected me less than the silent contempt, or the sarcastic composure, with which it was received.

'Mr Wilson,' said our host, stooping to remove from beneath his feet an exceedingly luxurious cloak of rare furs, 'Mr Wilson, this is your property.' (The weather was cold; and, upon quitting my own room, I had thrown a cloak over my dressing wrapper, putting it off upon reaching the scene of play.) 'I presume it is supererogatory to seek here (eyeing the folds of the garment with a bitter smile) for any farther evidence of your skill. Indeed, we have had enough. You will see the necessity, I hope, of quitting Oxford – at all events, of quitting instantly my chambers.'

Abased, humbled to the dust as I then was, it is probable that I should have resented this galling language by immediate personal violence, had not my whole attention been at the moment arrested by a fact of the most startling character. The cloak which I had worn was of a rare description of fur; how rare, how extravagantly costly, I shall not venture to say. Its fashion, too, was of my own fantastic invention; for I was fastidious to an absurd degree of coxcombry, in matters of this frivolous nature. When, therefore, Mr Preston reached me that which he had picked up upon the floor, and near the folding doors of the apartment, it was with an astonishment nearly bordering upon terror that I perceived my own already hanging on my arm (where I had no doubt unwittingly placed it), and that the one presented me was but its exact counterpart in every, in even the minutest possible particular. The singular being who had so disastrously exposed me, had been muffled, I remembered, in a cloak; and none had been worn at all by any of the members of our party with the exception of myself. Retaining some presence of mind, I took the one offered me by Preston; placed it, unnoticed, over my own; left the apartment with a resolute scowl of defiance; and, next morning ère dawn of day, commenced a hurried journey from Oxford to the continent, in a perfect agony of horror and of shame.

I fled in vain. My evil destiny pursued me as if in exultation, and proved, indeed, that the exercise of its mysterious dominion had as yet only begun. Scarcely had I set foot in Paris ere I had fresh evidence of the detestable interest taken by this Wilson in my concerns. Years flew, while I experienced no relief. Villain! – at Rome, with how untimely, yet with how spectral an officiousness, stepped he in between me and my ambition! At Vienna, too – at Berlin – and at Moscow! Where, in truth, had I not bitter cause to curse him within my heart? From his inscrutable tyranny did I at length flee, panic-stricken, as from a pestilence; and to the very ends of the earth I fled in vain.

And again, and again, in secret communion with my own spirit, would I demand the questions 'Who is he? – whence came he? – and what are his objects?' But no answer was there found. And then I scrutinised, with a minute scrutiny, the forms, and the methods, and the leading traits of his impertinent supervision. But even here there was very little upon which to base a conjecture. It was noticeable, indeed, that, in no one of the multiplied instances in which he had of late crossed my path, had he so crossed it except to frustrate those schemes, or to disturb those actions, which, if fully carried out, might have resulted in bitter mischief. Poor justification this, in truth, for an authority so imperiously assumed! Poor indemnity for natural rights of self-agency so pertinaciously, so insultingly denied!

I had also been forced to notice that my tormentor, for a very long period of time (while scrupulously and with miraculous dexterity maintaining his whim of an identity of apparel with myself), had so contrived it, in the execution of his varied interference with my will, that I saw not, at any moment, the features of his face. Be Wilson what he might, *this*, at least, was but the veriest of affectation, or of folly. Could he, for an instant, have supposed that, in my admonisher at Eton – in the destroyer of my honour at Oxford – in him who thwarted my ambition at Rome, my revenge at Paris, my passionate love at Naples, or what he falsely termed my avarice in Egypt – that in this, my arch-enemy and evil genius, could fail to recognise the William Wilson of my schoolboy days – the namesake, the companion, the rival – the hated and dreaded rival at Dr Bransby's? Impossible! – But let me hasten to the last eventful scene of the drama.

Thus far I had succumbed supinely to this imperious domination. The sentiment of deep awe with which I habitually regarded the elevated character, the majestic wisdom, the apparent omnipresence and omnipotence of Wilson, added to a feeling of even terror, with which certain other traits in his nature and assumptions inspired me, had operated, hitherto, to impress me with an idea of my own utter weakness and helplessness, and to suggest an implicit, although bitterly reluctant submission to his arbitrary will. But, of late days, I had given myself up entirely to wine; and its maddening influence upon my hereditary temper rendered me more and more impatient of control. I began to murmur – to hesitate – to resist. And was it only fancy which induced me to believe that, with the increase of my own firmness, that of my tormentor underwent a proportional diminution? Be this as it may, I now began to feel the inspiration of a burning hope, and at length nurtured in my secret thoughts a stern and desperate resolution that I would submit no longer to be enslaved.

It was at Rome, during the Carnival of 18—, that I attended a masquerade in the palazzo of the Neapolitan Duke di Broglio. I had indulged more freely than usual in the excesses of the wine-table; and now the suffocating atmosphere of the crowded rooms irritated me beyond endurance. The difficulty, too, of forcing my way through the mazes of the company contributed not a little to the ruffling of my temper; for I was anxiously seeking (let me not say with what unworthy motive) the young, the gay, the beautiful wife of the aged and doting di Broglio. With a too unscrupulous confidence she had previously communicated to me the secret of the costume in which she would be habited, and now, having caught a glimpse of her person, I was hurrying to make my way into her presence. At this moment I felt a light hand placed upon my shoulder, and that ever-re-membered, low, damnable whisper within my ear.

In an absolute frenzy of wrath, I turned at once upon him who had thus interrupted me, and seized him violently by the collar. He was attired, as I had expected, in a costume altogether similar to my own; wearing a Spanish cloak of blue velvet, begirt about the waist with a crimson belt sustaining a rapier. A mask of black silk entirely covered his face.

'Scoundrel!' I said, in a voice husky with rage, while every syllable I uttered seemed as new fuel to my fury, 'scoundrel! impostor! accursed villain! you shall not – you shall not dog me unto death! Follow me, or I stab you where you stand!' – and I broke my way from the ballroom into a small antechamber adjoining – dragging him unresistingly with me as I went.

Upon entering, I thrust him furiously from me. He staggered against the wall, while I closed the door with an oath, and commanded him to draw. He hesitated but for an instant; then, with a slight sigh, drew in silence, and put himself upon his defence.

The contest was brief indeed. I was frantic with every species of wild excitement, and felt within my single arm the energy and power of a multitude. In a few seconds I forced him by sheer strength against the wainscoting, and thus, getting him at my mercy, plunged my sword, with brute ferocity, repeatedly through and through his bosom.

At that instant some person tried the latch of the door. I hastened to prevent an intrusion, and then immediately returned to my dying antagonist. But what human language can adequately portray that astonishment, that horror which possessed me at the spectacle then presented to view? The brief moment in which I averted my eyes had been sufficient to produce, apparently, a material change in the arrangements at the upper or farther end of the room. A large mirror – so at first it seemed to me in my confusion – now stood where none had been perceptible before; and, as I stepped up to it in extremity of terror, mine own image, but with features all pale and dabbled in blood, advanced to meet me with a feeble and tottering gait.

Thus it appeared, I say, but was not. It was my antagonist – it was Wilson, who then stood before me in the agonies of his dissolution. His mask and cloak lay, where he had thrown them, upon the floor. Not a thread in all his raiment – not a line in all the marked and singular lineaments of his face which was not, even in the most absolute identity, *mine own*!

It was Wilson; but he spoke no longer in a whisper, and I could have fancied that I myself was speaking while he said: 'You have conquered, and I yield. Yet, henceforward art thou also dead – dead to the World, to Heaven and to Hope! In me didst thou exist – and, in my death, see by this image, which is thine own, how utterly thou hast murdered thyself.'

Eleonora

Sub conservatione formae specificae salva anima.

RAYMOND LULLY

I am come of a race noted for vigour of fancy and
ardour of passion. Men have called me mad; but the
question is not yet settled, whether madness is or is
not the loftiest intelligence – whether much that is
glorious – whether all that is profound – does not
spring from disease of thought – from moods of mind
exalted at the expense of the general intellect. They
who dream by day are cognisant of many things which
escape those who dream only by night. In their grey
visions they obtain glimpses of eternity, and thrill,
in awakening, to find that they have been upon the
verge of the great secret. In snatches, they learn
something of the wisdom which is of good, and more
of the mere knowledge which is of evil. They penetrate, however, rudderless or compassless into the
vast ocean of the 'light ineffable', and again, like the
adventures of the Nubian geographer, *'agressi sunt
mare tenebrarum, quid in eo esset exploraturi'*.

We will say, then, that I am mad. I grant, at least,
that there are two distinct conditions of my mental
existence: the condition of a lucid reason – not to be
disputed, and belonging to the memory of events
forming the first epoch of my life – and a condition of
shadow and doubt, appertaining to the present, and to
the recollection of what constitutes the second great
era of my being. Therefore, what I shall tell of the

earlier period, believe; and to what I may relate of the later time, give only such credit as may seem due, or doubt it altogether; or, if doubt it ye cannot, then play unto its riddle the Oedipus.

She whom I loved in youth, and of whom I now pen calmly and distinctly these remembrances, was the sole daughter of the only sister of my mother long departed. Eleonora was the name of my cousin. We had always dwelled together, beneath a tropical sun, in the Valley of the Many-Coloured Grass. No unguided footstep ever came upon that vale; for it lay away up among a range of giant hills that hung beetling around about it, shutting out the sunlight from its sweetest recesses. No path was trodden in its vicinity; and, to reach our happy home, there was need of putting back, with force, the foliage of many thousands of forest trees, and of crushing to death the glories of many millions of fragrant flowers. Thus it was that we lived all alone, knowing nothing of the world without the valley – I, and my cousin, and her mother.

From the dim regions beyond the mountains at the upper end of our encircled domain, there crept out a narrow and deep river, brighter than all save the eyes of Eleonora; and, winding stealthily about in mazy courses, it passed away, at length, through a shadowy gorge, among hills still dimmer than those whence it had issued. We called it the 'River of Silence'; for there seemed to be a hushing influence in its flow. No murmur arose from its bed, and so gently it wandered along, that the pearly pebbles upon which we loved to gaze, far down within its bosom, stirred not at all, but lay in a motionless content, each in its own old station, shining on gloriously for ever.

The margin of the river, and of the many dazzling rivulets that glided through devious ways into its channel, as well as the spaces that extended from the margins away down into the depths of the streams until they reached the bed of pebbles at the bottom – these spots, not less than the whole surface of the valley, from the river to the mountains that girdled it in, were carpeted all by a soft green grass, thick, short, perfectly even, and vanilla-perfumed, but so besprinkled throughout with the yellow buttercup, the white daisy, the purple violet, and the ruby-red asphodel, that its exceeding beauty spoke to our hearts in loud tones, of the love and of the glory of God.

And, here and there, in groves about this grass, like wildernesses of dreams, sprang up fantastic trees, whose tall slender stems stood not upright, but slanted gracefully towards the light that peered at noonday into the centre of the valley. Their bark was speckled with the vivid alternate splendour of ebony and silver, and was smoother than all save the cheeks of Eleonora; so that, but for the brilliant green of the huge leaves that spread from their summits in long, tremulous lines, dallying with the Zephyrs, one might have fancied them giant serpents of Syria doing homage to their sovereign the Sun.

Hand in hand about this valley, for fifteen years, roamed I with Eleonora before Love entered within our hearts. It was one evening at the close of the third lustrum of her life, and of the fourth of my own, that we sat, locked in each other's embrace, beneath the serpent-like trees, and looked down within the water of the River of Silence at our images therein. We spoke no words during the rest of that sweet day, and our words even upon the morrow were tremulous and few. We had drawn the God Eros from that wave, and now we felt that he had enkindled within us the fiery souls of our forefathers. The passions which had for centuries distinguished our race, came thronging with the fancies for which they had been equally noted, and together breathed a delirious bliss over the Valley of the Many-Coloured Grass. A change fell upon all things. Strange, brilliant flowers, star-shaped, burst out upon the trees where no flowers had been known before. The tints of the green carpet deepened; and when, one by one, the white daisies shrank away, there sprang up in place of them, ten by ten of the ruby-red asphodel. And life arose in our paths; for the tall flamingo, hitherto unseen, with all gay glowing birds, flaunted his scarlet plumage before us. The golden and silver fish haunted the river, out of the bosom of which issued, little by little, a murmur that swelled, at length, into a lulling melody more divine than that of the harp of Aeolus – sweeter than all save the voice of Eleonora. And now, too, a voluminous cloud, which we had long watched in the regions of Hesper, floated out thence, all gorgeous in crimson and gold, and settling in peace above us, sank, day by day, lower and lower, until its edges rested upon the tops of the mountains, turning all their dimness into magnificence, and shutting us up, as if for ever, within a magic prison-house of grandeur and of glory.

The loveliness of Eleonora was that of the Seraphim; but she was a maiden artless and innocent as the brief life she had led among the flowers. No guile disguised the fervour of love which animated her heart, and she examined with me its inmost recesses as we walked together in the Valley of the Many-Coloured Grass, and discoursed of the mighty changes which had lately taken place therein.

At length, having spoken one day, in tears, of the last sad change which must befall Humanity, she thenceforward dwelt only upon this one sorrowful theme, interweaving it into all our converse, as, in the songs of the bard of Schiraz, the same images are found occurring, again and again, in every impressive variation of phrase.

She had seen that the finger of Death was upon her bosom – that, like the ephemeron, she had been made perfect in loveliness only to die; but the terrors of the grave to her lay solely in a consideration which she revealed to me, one evening at twilight, by the banks of the River of Silence. She grieved to think that, having entombed her in the Valley of the Many-Coloured Grass, I would quit for ever its happy recesses, transferring the love which now was so passionately her own to some maiden of the outer and everyday world. And, then and there, I threw myself hurriedly at the feet of Eleonora, and offered up a vow, to herself and to Heaven, that I would never bind myself in marriage to any daughter of Earth – that I would in no manner prove recreant to her dear memory, or to the memory of the devout affection with which she had blessed me. And I called the Mighty Ruler of the Universe to witness the pious solemnity of my vow. And the curse which I invoked of Him and of her, a saint in Helusion should I prove traitorous to that promise, involved a penalty the exceeding great horror of which will not permit me to make record of it here. And the bright eyes of Eleonora grew brighter at my words; and she sighed as if a deadly burden had been taken from her breast;

and she trembled and very bitterly wept; but she made acceptance of the vow (for what was she but a child?) and it made easy to her the bed of her death. And she said to me, not many days afterwards, tranquilly dying, that, because of what I had done for the comfort of her spirit she would watch over me in that spirit when departed, and, if so it were permitted her, return to me visibly in the watches of the night; but, if this thing were, indeed, beyond the power of the souls in Paradise, that she would, at least, give me frequent indications of her presence, sighing upon me in the evening winds, or filling the air which I breathed with perfume from the censers of the angels. And, with these words upon her lips, she yielded up her innocent life, putting an end to the first epoch of my own.

Thus far I have faithfully said. But as I pass the barrier in Time's path, formed by the death of my beloved, and proceed with the second era of my existence, I feel that a shadow gathers over my brain, and I mistrust the perfect sanity of the record. But let me on. – Years dragged themselves along heavily, and still I dwelled within the Valley of the Many-Coloured Grass; but a second change had come upon all things. The star-shaped flowers shrank into the stems of the trees, and appeared no more. The tints of the green carpet faded; and, one by one, the ruby-red asphodels withered away; and there sprang up, in place of them, ten by ten, dark, eye-like violets, that writhed uneasily and were ever encumbered with dew. And Life departed from our paths; for the tall flamingo flaunted no longer his scarlet plumage before us, but flew sadly from the vale into the hills, with all the gay glowing birds that had arrived in his company. And the golden and silver fish swam down through the gorge at the lower end of our domain and bedecked the sweet river never again. And the lulling melody that had been softer than the wind-harp of Aeolus, and more divine than all save the voice of Eleonora, it died little by little away, in murmurs growing lower and lower, until the stream returned, at length, utterly, into the solemnity of its original silence. And then, lastly, the voluminous cloud uprose, and, abandoning the tops of the mountains to the dimness of old, fell back into the regions of Hesper, and took away all its manifold golden and gorgeous glories from the Valley of the Many-Coloured Grass.

Yet the promises of Eleonora were not forgotten; for I heard the sounds of the swinging of the censers of the angels; and streams of a holy perfume floated ever and ever about the valley; and at lone hours, when my heart beat heavily, the winds that bathed my brow came unto me laden with soft sighs; and indistinct murmurs filled often the night air, and once – oh, but once only! I was awakened from a slumber, like the slumber of death, by the pressing of spiritual lips upon my own.

But the void within my heart refused, even thus, to be filled. I longed for the love which had before filled it to overflowing. At length the valley pained me through its memories of Eleonora, and I left it for ever for the vanities and the turbulent triumphs of the world.

*   *   *

I found myself within a strange city, where all things might have served to blot from recollection the sweet dreams I had dreamed so long in the Valley of the

Many-Coloured Grass. The pomps and pageantries of a stately court, and the mad clangour of arms, and the radiant loveliness of women, bewildered and intoxicated my brain. But as yet my soul had proved true to its vows, and the indications of the presence of Eleonora were still given me in the silent hours of the night. Suddenly these manifestations they ceased, and the world grew dark before mine eyes, and I stood aghast at the burning thoughts which possessed, at the terrible temptations which beset me; for there came from some far, far distant and unknown land, into the gay court of the king I served, a maiden to whose beauty my whole recreant heart yielded at once – at whose footstool I bowed down without a struggle, in the most ardent, in the most abject worship of love. What, indeed, was my passion for the young girl of the valley in comparison with the fervour, and the delirium, and the spirit-lifting ecstasy of adoration with which I poured out my whole soul in tears at the feet of the ethereal Ermengarde? – Oh, bright was the seraph Ermengarde! and in that knowledge I had room for none other. – Oh, divine was the angel Ermengarde! and as I looked down into the depths of her memorial eyes, I thought only of them – and *of her*.

I wedded – nor dreaded the curse I had invoked; and its bitterness was not visited upon me. And once – but once again in the silence of the night – there came through my lattice the soft sighs which had forsaken me; and they modelled themselves into familiar and sweet voice, saying: 'Sleep in peace! – for the spirit of love reigneth and ruleth, and, in taking to thy passionate heart her who is Ermengarde, thou art absolved, for reasons which shall be made known to thee in Heaven, of thy vows unto Eleonora.'

The Island of the Fay

Nullus enim locus sine genio est.

SERVIUS

'*La musique*,' says Marmontel, in those '*contes moraux*'* which, in all our translations, we have insisted upon calling 'moral tales', as if in mockery of their spirit – '*la musique est le seul des talents qui jouissent de lui-même; tous les autres veulent des temoins.*' He here confounds the pleasure derivable from sweet sounds with the capacity for creating them. No more than any other talent, is that for music susceptible of complete enjoyment, where there is no second party to appreciate its exercise. And it is only in common with other talents that it produces effects which may be fully enjoyed in solitude. The idea which the *raconteur* has either failed to entertain clearly, or has sacrificed in its expression to his national love of *point*, is, doubtless, the very tenable one that the higher order of music is the most thoroughly estimated when we are exclusively alone. The proposition, in this form, will be admitted at once by those who love the lyre for its own sake, and for its spiritual uses. But there is one pleasure still within the reach of fallen mortality – and perhaps only one – which owes even more than does music to the accessory sentiment of seclusion. I mean the happiness experienced in the contemplation of

* *Moraux* is here derived from *moeurs* and its meaning is 'fashionable' or more strictly 'of manners'.

natural scenery. In truth, the man who would behold aright the glory of God upon earth must in solitude behold that glory. To me, at least, the presence – not of human life only, but of life in any other form than that of the green things which grow upon the soil and are voiceless – is a stain upon the landscape – is at war with the genius of the scene. I love, indeed, to regard the dark valleys, and the grey rocks, and the waters that silently smile, and the forests that sigh in uneasy slumbers, and the proud watchful mountains that look down upon all – I love to regard these as themselves but the colossal members of one vast animate and sentient whole – a whole whose form (that of the sphere) is the most perfect and most inclusive of all; whose path is among associate planets; whose meek handmaiden is the moon, whose mediate sovereign is the sun; whose life is eternity, whose thought is that of a God; whose enjoyment is knowledge; whose destinies are lost in immensity, whose cognisance of ourselves is akin with our own cognisance of the *animalculae* which infest the brain – a being which we, in consequence, regard as purely inanimate and material, much in the same manner as these *animalculae* must thus regard us.

Our telescopes and our mathematical investigations assure us on every hand – notwithstanding the cant of the more ignorant of the priesthood – that space, and therefore that bulk, is an important consideration in the eyes of the Almighty. The cycles in which the stars move are those best adapted for the evolution, without collision, of the greatest possible number of bodies. The forms of those bodies are accurately such as, within a given surface, to include the greatest possible amount of matter – while the surfaces themselves are so disposed as to accommodate a denser population than could be accommodated on the same surfaces otherwise arranged. Nor is it any argument against bulk being an object with God, that space itself is infinite; for there may be an infinity of matter to fill it. And since we see clearly that the endowment of matter with vitality is a principle – indeed, as far as our judgements extend, the leading principle in the operations of Deity – it is scarcely logical to imagine it confined to the regions of the minute, where we daily trace it, and not extending to those of the august. As we find cycle within cycle without end – yet all revolving around one far-distant centre which is the Godhead, may we not analogically suppose in the same manner, life within life, the less within the greater, and all within the Spirit Divine? In short, we are madly erring, through self-esteem, in believing man, in either his temporal or future destinies, to be of more moment in the universe than that vast 'clod of the valley' which he tills and contemns, and to which he denies a soul for no more profound reason than that he does not behold it in operation.*

These fancies, and such as these, have always given to my meditations among the mountains and the forests, by the rivers and the ocean, a tinge of what the everyday world would not fail to term fantastic. My wanderings amid such scenes have been many, and far-searching, and often solitary; and the interest with which I have strayed through many a dim, deep valley, or gazed into the reflected Heaven of many a bright lake, has been an interest greatly deepened by the

* Speaking of the tides, Pomponius Mela, in his treatise *De Situ Orbis*, says, 'either the world is a great animal, or . . . ' etc.

thought that I have strayed and gazed alone. What flippant Frenchman* was it who said in allusion to the well-known work of Zimmerman, that, '*la solitude est une belle chose; mais il faut quelqu'un pour vous dire que la solitude est une belle chose*'? The epigram cannot be gainsaid; but the necessity is a thing that does not exist.

It was during one of my lonely journeyings, amid a far distant region of mountain locked within mountain, and sad rivers and melancholy tarn writhing or sleeping within all – that I chanced upon a certain rivulet and island. I came upon them suddenly in the leafy June, and threw myself upon the turf, beneath the branches of an unknown odorous shrub, that I might doze as I contemplated the scene. I felt that thus only should I look upon it – such was the character of phantasm which it wore.

On all sides – save to the west, where the sun was about sinking – arose the verdant walls of the forest. The little river which turned sharply in its course, and was thus immediately lost to sight, seemed to have no exit from its prison, but to be absorbed by the deep green foliage of the trees to the east – while in the opposite quarter (so it appeared to me as I lay at length and glanced upwards) there poured down noiselessly and continuously into the valley, a rich golden and crimson waterfall from the sunset fountains of the sky.

About midway in the short vista which my dreamy vision took in, one small circular island, profusely verdured, reposed upon the bosom of the stream.

* Balzac – in substance – I do not remember the words.

> So blended bank and shadow there
> That each seemed pendulous in air –

so mirror-like was the glassy water, that it was scarcely possible to say at what point upon the slope of the emerald turf its crystal dominion began.

My position enabled me to include in a single view both the eastern and western extremities of the islet; and I observed a singularly marked difference in their aspects. The latter was all one radiant harem of garden beauties. It glowed and blushed beneath the eyes of the slant sunlight, and fairly laughed with flowers. The grass was short, springy, sweet-scented, and asphodel-interspersed. The trees were lithe, mirthful, erect – bright, slender, and graceful – of eastern figure and foliage, with bark smooth, glossy, and parti-coloured. There seemed a deep sense of life and joy about all; and although no airs blew from out the heavens, yet everything had motion through the gentle sweepings to and fro of innumerable butterflies, that might have been mistaken for tulips with wings.*

The other or eastern end of the isle was whelmed in the blackest shade. A sombre, yet beautiful and peaceful gloom here pervaded all things. The trees were dark in colour, and mournful in form and attitude, wreathing themselves into sad, solemn, and spectral shapes that conveyed ideas of mortal sorrow and untimely death. The grass wore the deep tint of the cypress, and the heads of its blades hung droopingly, and hither and thither among it were many small unsightly hillocks, low and narrow, and not very long, that had the aspect of graves, but were not; although over and all about

---

* *Florem putares mare per liquidum aethera.* P. COMMIRE

them the rue and the rosemary clambered. The shade of the trees fell heavily upon the water, and seemed to bury itself therein, impregnating the depths of the element with darkness. I fancied that each shadow, as the sun descended lower and lower, separated itself sullenly from the trunk that gave it birth, and thus became absorbed by the stream; while other shadows issued momently from the trees, taking the place of their predecessors thus entombed.

This idea, having once seized upon my fancy, greatly excited it, and I lost myself forthwith in reverie. 'If ever island were enchanted,' said I to myself, 'this is it. This is the haunt of the few gentle Fays who remain from the wreck of the race. Are these green tombs theirs? – or do they yield up their sweet lives as mankind yield up their own? In dying, do they not rather waste away mournfully, rendering unto God, little by little, their existence, as these trees render up shadow after shadow, exhausting their substance unto dissolution? What the wasting tree is to the water that imbibes its shade, growing thus blacker by what it preys upon, may not the life of the Fay be to the death which engulfs it?'

As I thus mused, with half-shut eyes, while the sun sank rapidly to rest, and eddying currents careered round and round the island, bearing upon their bosom large, dazzling, white flakes of the bark of the sycamore – flakes which, in their multiform positions upon the water, a quick imagination might have converted into anything it pleased, while I thus mused, it appeared to me that the form of one of those very Fays about whom I had been pondering made its way slowly into the darkness from out the light at the western end of the island. She stood erect in a singularly fragile canoe, and urged it with the mere phantom of an oar. While within the influence of the lingering sunbeams, her attitude seemed indicative of joy – but sorrow deformed it as she passed within the shade. Slowly she glided along, and at length rounded the islet and re-entered the region of light. 'The revolution which has just been made by the Fay,' continued I, musingly, 'is the cycle of the brief year of her life. She has floated through her winter and through her summer. She is a year nearer unto Death; for I did not fail to see that, as she came into the shade, her shadow fell from her, and was swallowed up in the dark water, making its blackness more black.'

And again the boat appeared, and the Fay, but about the attitude of the latter there was more of care and uncertainty and less of elastic joy. She floated again from out the light and into the gloom (which deepened momently) and again her shadow fell from her into the ebony water, and became absorbed into its blackness. And again and again she made the circuit of the island (while the sun rushed down to his slumbers), and at each issuing into the light there was more sorrow about her person, while it grew feebler and far fainter and more indistinct, and at each passage into the gloom there fell from her a darker shade, which became whelmed in a shadow more black. But at length when the sun had utterly departed, the Fay, now the mere ghost of her former self, went disconsolately with her boat into the region of the ebony flood, and that she issued thence at all I cannot say, for darkness fell over all things and I beheld her magical figure no more.

The Balloon Hoax

Astounding news by express, via Norfolk! – The Atlantic crossed in three days! Signal triumph of Mr Monck Mason's flying machine! – Arrival at Sullivan's Island, near Charleston, SC, of Mr Mason, Mr Robert Holland, Mr Henson, Mr Harrison Ainsworth, and four others, in the steering balloon *Victoria*, after a passage of seventy-five hours from land to land! Full particulars of the voyage!

The subjoined *jeu d'esprit* with the preceding heading in magnificent capitals, well interspersed with notes of admiration, was originally published, as matter of fact, in the *New York Sun*, a daily newspaper, and therein fully subserved the purpose of creating indigestible aliment for the *quidnuncs* during the few hours intervening between a couple of the Charleston mails. The rush for the 'sole paper which had the news', was something beyond even the prodigious; and, in fact, if (as some assert) the *Victoria did* not absolutely accomplish the voyage recorded, it will be difficult to assign a reason why she *should* not have accomplished it.

The great problem is at length solved! The air, as well as the earth and the ocean, has been subdued by science, and will become a common and convenient highway for mankind. *The Atlantic has been actually crossed in a Balloon!* and this too without difficulty – without any great apparent danger – with thorough control of the machine – and in the inconceivably brief period of seventy-five hours from shore to shore! By the energy of an agent at Charleston, SC, we are enabled to be the first to furnish the public with a detailed account of this most extraordinary voyage, which was performed between Saturday, the 6th instant, at 11 a.m., and 2 p.m. on Tuesday, the 9th instant, by Sir Everard Bringhurst; Mr Osborne, a nephew of Lord Bentinck's; Mr Monck Mason and Mr Robert Holland, the well-known aeronauts; Mr Harrison Ainsworth, author of *Jack Sheppard*, etc.; and Mr Henson, the projector of the late unsuccessful flying machine – with two seamen from Woolwich – in all, eight persons. The particulars furnished below may be relied on as authentic and accurate in every respect, as, with a slight exception, they are copied verbatim from the joint diaries of Mr Monck Mason and Mr Harrison Ainsworth, to whose politeness our agent is also indebted for much verbal information respecting the balloon itself, its construction, and other matters of interest. The only alteration in the manuscript received, has been made for the purpose of throwing the hurried account of our agent, Mr Forsyth, into a connected and intelligible form.

THE BALLOON

Two very decided failures, of late – those of Mr Henson and Sir George Cayley – had much weakened the public interest in the subject of aerial navigation. Mr Henson's scheme (which at first was considered very feasible even by men of science) was founded upon the principle of an inclined plane, started from an eminence by an extrinsic force, applied and continued by the revolution of impinging vanes, in form and number resembling the vanes of a windmill. But, in all the experiments made with models at the Adelaide Gallery, it was found that the operation of these fans not only did not propel the machine, but actually impeded its flight. The only propelling force it ever exhibited was the mere *impetus* acquired from the descent of the inclined plane; and this *impetus* carried the machine farther when the vanes were at rest, than when they were in motion – a fact which sufficiently demonstrates their inutility; and in the absence of the propelling, which was also the *sustaining* power, the whole fabric would necessarily descend. This consideration led Sir George Cayley to think only of adapting a propeller to some machine having of itself an independent power of support – in a word, to a balloon; the idea, however, being novel, or original, with Sir George, only so far as regards the mode of its application to practice. He exhibited a model of his invention at the Polytechnic Institution. The propelling principle, or power, was here, also, applied to interrupted surfaces, or vanes, put in revolution. These vanes were four in number, but were found entirely ineffectual in moving the balloon, or in aiding its ascending power. The whole project was thus a complete failure.

It was at this juncture that Mr Monck Mason (whose voyage from Dover to Weilburg in the balloon, *Nassau*, occasioned so much excitement in 1837) conceived the idea of employing the principle of the Archimedean screw for the purpose of propulsion through the air – rightly attributing the failure of Mr Henson's scheme, and of Sir George Cayley's, to the interruption of surface in the independent vanes. He made the first public experiment at Willis's Rooms, but afterwards removed his model to the Adelaide Gallery.

Like Sir George Cayley's balloon, his own was an ellipsoid. Its length was thirteen feet six inches –

height, six feet eight inches. It contained about three hundred and twenty cubic feet of gas, which, if pure hydrogen, would support twenty-one pounds upon its first inflation, before the gas has time to deteriorate or escape. The weight of the whole machine and apparatus was seventeen pounds – leaving about four pounds to spare. Beneath the centre of the balloon was a frame of light wood, about nine feet long, and rigged on to the balloon itself with a network in the customary manner. From this framework was suspended a wicker basket or car.

The screw consists of an axis of hollow brass tube, eighteen inches in length, through which, upon a semi-spiral inclined at fifteen degrees, pass a series of steel wire radii, two feet long, and thus projecting a foot on either side. These radii are connected at the outer extremities by two bands of flattened wire – the whole in this manner forming the framework of the screw, which is completed by a covering of oiled silk cut into gores, and tightened so as to present a tolerably uniform surface. At each end of its axis this screw is supported by pillars of hollow brass tube descending from the hoop. In the lower ends of these tubes are holes in which the pivots of the axis revolve. From the end of the axis which is next the car, proceeds a shaft of steel, connecting the screw with the pinion of a piece of spring machinery fixed in the car. By the operation of this spring, the screw is made to revolve with great rapidity, communicating a progressive motion to the whole. By means of the rudder, the machine was readily turned in any direction. The spring was of great power, compared with its dimensions, being capable of raising forty-five pounds upon a barrel of four inches diameter, after the first turn, and gradually increasing as it was wound up. It weighed, altogether, eight pounds six ounces. The rudder was a light frame of cane covered with silk, shaped somewhat like a battledore, and was about three feet long, and at the widest, one foot. Its weight was about two ounces. It could be turned *flat*, and directed upwards or downwards, as well as to the right or left; and thus enabled the aeronaut to transfer the resistance of the air which in an inclined position it must generate in its passage, to any side upon which he might desire to act; thus determining the balloon in the opposite direction.

This model (which, through want of time, we have necessarily described in an imperfect manner) was put in action at the Adelaide Gallery, where it accomplished a velocity of five miles per hour; although, strange to say, it excited very little interest in comparison with the previous complex machine of Mr Henson – so resolute is the world to despise anything which carries with it an air of simplicity. To accomplish the great desideratum of aerial navigation, it was very generally supposed that some exceedingly complicated application must be made of some unusually profound principle in dynamics.

So well satisfied, however, was Mr Mason of the ultimate success of his invention, that he determined to construct immediately, if possible, a balloon of sufficient capacity to test the question by a voyage of some extent – the original design being to cross the British Channel, as before, in the *Nassau* balloon. To carry out his views, he solicited and obtained the patronage of Sir Everard Bringhurst and Mr Osborne, two gentlemen well known for scientific acquirement, and especially for the interest they have exhibited in the progress of aerostation. The project, at the desire of Mr Osborne, was kept a profound secret from the public – the only persons entrusted with the design being those actually engaged in the construction of the machine, which was built (under the superintendence of Mr Mason, Mr Holland, Sir Everard Bringhurst, and Mr Osborne) at the seat of the latter gentleman near Penstruthal, in Wales. Mr Henson, accompanied by his friend Mr Ainsworth, was admitted to a private view of the balloon, on Saturday last – when the two gentlemen made final arrangements to be included in the adventure. We are not informed for what reason the two seamen were also included in the party – but, in the course of a day or two, we shall put our readers in possession of the minutest particulars respecting this extraordinary voyage.

The balloon is composed of silk, varnished with the liquid gum caoutchouc. It is of vast dimensions, containing more than 40,000 cubic feet of gas; but as coal gas was employed in place of the more expensive and inconvenient hydrogen, the supporting power of the machine, when fully inflated, and immediately after inflation, is not more than about 2,500 pounds. The coal gas is not only much less costly, but is easily procured and managed.

For its introduction into common use for purposes of aerostation, we are indebted to Mr Charles Green. Up to his discovery, the process of inflation was not only exceedingly expensive, but uncertain. Two, and even three days, have frequently been wasted in futile attempts to procure a sufficiency of hydrogen to fill a balloon, from which it had great tendency to escape, owing to its extreme subtlety, and its affinity for the surrounding atmosphere. In a balloon sufficiently perfect to retain its contents of coal gas unaltered, in

243

quantity or amount, for six months, an equal quantity of hydrogen could not be maintained in equal purity for six weeks.

The supporting power being estimated at 2,500 pounds, and the united weights of the party amounting only to about 1,200, there was left a surplus of 1,300, of which again 1,200 was exhausted by ballast, arranged in bags of different sizes, with their respective weights marked upon them – by cordage, barometers, telescopes, barrels containing provision for a fortnight, water-casks, cloaks, carpet-bags, and various other indispensable matters, including a coffee-warmer, contrived for warming coffee by means of slack-lime, so as to dispense altogether with fire, if it should be judged prudent to do so. All these articles, with the exception of the ballast, and a few trifles, were suspended from the hoop overhead. The car is much smaller and lighter, in proportion, than the one appended to the model. It is formed of a light wicker, and is wonderfully strong, for so frail-looking a machine. Its rim is about four feet deep. The rudder is also very much larger, in proportion, than that of the model; and the screw is considerably smaller. The balloon is furnished besides with a grapnel, and a guide-rope; which latter is of the most indispensable importance. A few words, in explanation, will here be necessary for such of our readers as are not conversant with the details of aerostation.

As soon as the balloon quits the earth, it is subjected to the influence of many circumstances tending to create a difference in its weight; augmenting or diminishing its ascending power. For example, there may be a deposition of dew upon the silk, to the extent, even, of several hundred pounds; ballast has then to be thrown out, or the machine may descend. This ballast being discarded, and a clear sunshine evaporating the dew, and at the same time expanding the gas in the silk, the whole will again rapidly ascend. To check this ascent, the only recourse is (or rather *was*, until Mr Green's invention of the guide-rope) the permission of the escape of gas from the valve; but, in the loss of gas, is a proportionate general loss of ascending power; so that, in a comparatively brief period, the best-constructed balloon must necessarily exhaust all its resources, and come to the earth. This was the great obstacle to voyages of length.

The guide-rope remedies the difficulty in the simplest manner conceivable. It is merely a very long rope which is suffered to trail from the car, and the effect of which is to prevent the balloon from changing its level in any material degree. If, for example, there should be a deposition of moisture upon the silk, and the machine begins to descend in consequence, there will be no necessity for discharging ballast to remedy the increase of weight, for it is remedied, or counteracted, in an exactly just proportion, by the deposit on the ground of just so much of the end of the rope as is necessary. If, on the other hand, any circumstances should cause undue levity, and consequent ascent, this levity is immediately counteracted by the additional weight of rope upraised from the earth. Thus, the balloon can neither ascend or descend, except within very narrow limits, and its resources, either in gas or ballast, remain comparatively unimpaired. When passing over an expanse of water, it becomes necessary to employ small kegs of copper or wood, filled with liquid ballast of a lighter nature than water. These float, and serve all the purposes of a mere rope on land. Another most important office of the guide-rope is to point out the *direction* of the balloon. The rope *drags*, either on land or sea, while the balloon is free; the latter, consequently, is always in advance, when any progress whatever is made: a comparison, therefore, by means of the compass, of the relative positions of the two objects, will always indicate the *course*. In the same way, the angle formed by the rope with the vertical axis of the machine, indicates the *velocity*. When there is *no* angle – in other words, when the rope hangs perpendicularly, the whole apparatus is stationary; but the larger the angle, that is to say, the farther the balloon precedes the end of the rope, the greater the velocity; and the converse.

As the original design was to cross the British Channel, and alight as near Paris as possible, the voyagers had taken the precaution to prepare themselves with passports directed to all parts of the Continent, specifying the nature of the expedition, as in the case of the *Nassau* voyage, and entitling the adventurers to exemption from the usual formalities of office: unexpected events, however, rendered these passports superfluous.

The inflation was commenced very quietly at daybreak, on Saturday morning, the 6th instant, in the courtyard of Weal-Vor House, Mr Osborne's seat, about a mile from Penstruthal, in North Wales; and at seven minutes past eleven, everything being ready for departure, the balloon was set free, rising gently but steadily, in a direction nearly south; no use being made, for the first half-hour, of either the screw or the rudder. We proceed now with the journal, as transcribed by Mr Forsyth from the joint manuscripts of Mr Monck Mason, and Mr Ainsworth. The body of the journal, as given, is in the handwriting of Mr Mason, and a PS is appended, each day, by Mr Ainsworth, who has in preparation, and will shortly give the public a more minute, and no doubt, a thrillingly interesting account of the voyage.

THE JOURNAL

Saturday, April the 6th – Every preparation likely to embarrass us having been made overnight, we commenced the inflation this morning at daybreak; but owing to a thick fog, which encumbered the folds of the silk and rendered it unmanageable, we did not get through before nearly eleven o'clock. Cut loose, then, in high spirits, and rose gently but steadily, with a light breeze at north, which bore us in the direction of the British Channel. Found the ascending force greater than we had expected; and as we arose higher and so got clear of the cliffs, and more in the sun's rays, our ascent became very rapid. I did not wish, however, to lose gas at so early a period of the adventure, and so concluded to ascend for the present. We soon ran out our guide-rope; but even when we had raised it clear of the earth, we still went up very rapidly. The balloon was unusually steady, and looked beautiful. In about ten minutes after starting, the barometer indicated an altitude of 15,000 feet. The weather was remarkably fine, and the view of the subjacent country – a most romantic one when seen from any point – was now especially sublime. The numerous deep gorges presented the appearance of lakes, on account of the dense vapours with which they were filled, and the pinnacles and crags to the south east, piled in inextricable confusion, resembling nothing so much as the giant cities of Eastern fable. We were rapidly approaching the mountains in the south; but our elevation was more than sufficient to enable us to pass them in safety. In a few minutes we soared over them in fine style; and Mr Ainsworth, with the seamen, was surprised at their apparent want of altitude when viewed from the car, the tendency of great elevation in a balloon being to reduce inequalities of the surface below, to nearly a dead level. At half-past eleven still proceeding nearly south, we obtained our first view of the Bristol Channel; and, in fifteen minutes afterwards, the line of breakers on the coast appeared immediately beneath us, and we were fairly out at sea. We now resolved to let off enough gas to bring our guide-rope, with the buoys affixed, into the water. This was immediately done, and we commenced a gradual descent. In about twenty minutes our first buoy dipped, and at the touch of the second soon afterwards, we remained stationary as to elevation. We were all now anxious to test the efficiency of the rudder and screw, and we put them both into requisition forthwith, for the purpose of altering our direction more to the eastward, and in a line for Paris. By means of the rudder we instantly effected the necessary change of direction, and our course was brought nearly at right angles to that of the wind; when we set in motion the spring of the screw, and were rejoiced to find it propel us readily as desired. Upon this we gave nine hearty cheers, and dropped in the sea a bottle, enclosing a slip of parchment with a brief account of the principle of the invention. Hardly, however, had we done with our rejoicings, when an unforeseen accident occurred which discouraged us in no little degree. The steel rod connecting the spring with the propeller was suddenly jerked out of place at the car end (by a swaying of the car through some movement of one of the two seamen we had taken up) and in an instant hung dangling out of reach, from the pivot of the axis of the screw. While we were endeavouring to regain it, our attention being completely absorbed, we became involved in a strong current of wind from the east, which bore us, with rapidly increasing force, towards the Atlantic. We soon found ourselves driving out to sea at the rate of not less, certainly, than fifty or sixty miles an hour, so that we came up with Cape Clear, at some forty miles to our north, before we had secured the rod, and had time to think what we were about. It was now that Mr Ainsworth made an extraordinary, but to my fancy, a by no means unreasonable or chimerical proposition, in which he was instantly seconded by Mr Holland – viz.: that we should take advantage of the strong gale which bore us on, and in place of beating back to Paris, make an attempt to reach the coast of North America. After slight reflection I gave a willing assent to this bold proposition, which (strange to say) met with objection from the two seamen only. As the stronger party, however, we overruled their fears, and kept resolutely upon our course. We steered due west; but as the trailing of the buoys materially impeded our progress, and we had the balloon abundantly at command, either for ascent or descent, we first threw out fifty pounds of ballast, and then wound up (by means of a windlass) so much of the rope as brought it quite clear of the sea. We perceived the effect of this manoeuvre immediately, in a vastly increased rate of progress; and, as the gale freshened, we flew with a velocity nearly inconceivable; the guide-rope flying out behind the car, like a streamer from a vessel. It is needless to say that a very short time sufficed us to lose sight of the coast. We passed over innumerable vessels of all kinds, a few of which were endeavouring to beat up, but the most of them lying to. We occasioned the greatest excitement on board all – an excitement greatly relished by ourselves, and especially by our two men, who, now under the influence of a dram of Geneva, seemed resolved to give all scruple, or fear, to the wind. Many of the vessels fired signal guns; and in all we were saluted with loud cheers (which we heard with surprising distinctness) and the waving of caps and hand-kerchiefs. We kept on in this manner throughout the day, with no material incident, and, as the shades of night closed around us, we made a rough estimate of the distance traversed. It could not have been less than five hundred miles, and was probably much more. The propeller was kept in constant operation, and, no doubt, aided our progress materially. As the sun went down, the gale freshened into an absolute hurricane, and the ocean beneath was clearly visible on account of its phosphorescence. The wind was from the east all night, and gave us the brightest omen of success. We suffered no little from cold, and the dampness of the atmosphere was most unpleasant; but the ample space in the car enabled us to lie down, and by means of cloaks and a few blankets, we did sufficiently well.

PS (by Mr Ainsworth). The last nine hours have been unquestionably the most exciting of my life. I can conceive nothing more sublimating than the strange peril and novelty of an adventure such as this. May God grant that we succeed! I ask not success for mere safety to my insignificant person, but for the sake of human knowledge and – for the vastness of the triumph. And yet the feat is only so evidently feasible that the sole wonder is why men have scrupled to attempt it before. One single gale such as now befriends us – let such a tempest whirl forward a balloon for four or five days (these gales often last longer) and the voyager will be easily borne, in that period, from coast to coast. In view of such a gale the broad Atlantic becomes a mere lake. I am more struck, just now, with the supreme silence which reigns in the sea beneath us, notwithstanding its agitation, than with any other phenomenon presenting itself. The waters give up no voice to the heavens. The immense flaming ocean writhes and is tortured uncomplainingly. The mountainous surges suggest the idea of innumerable dumb gigantic fiends struggling in impotent agony. In a night such as is this to me, a man *lives* – lives a whole century of ordinary life – nor would I forgo this rapturous delight for that of a whole century of ordinary existence.

Sunday, the seventh (Mr Mason's manuscript). This morning the gale, by ten, had subsided to an eight- or nine-knot breeze (for a vessel at sea) and bears us, perhaps, thirty miles per hour, or more. It has veered, however, very considerably to the north; and now, at sundown, we are holding our course due west, principally by the screw and rudder, which answer their purposes to admiration. I regard the project as thoroughly successful, and the easy navigation of the air in any direction (not exactly in the teeth of a gale) as no longer problematical. We could not have made head against the strong wind of yesterday; but, by ascending, we might have got out of its influence, if requisite. Against a pretty stiff breeze, I feel convinced, we can make our way with the propeller. At noon, today, ascended to an elevation of nearly 25,000 feet, by discharging ballast. Did this to search for a more direct current, but found none so favourable as the one we are now in. We have an abundance of gas to take us across this small pond, even should the voyage last three weeks. I have not the slightest fear for the result. The difficulty has been strangely exaggerated and misapprehended. I can choose my current, and should I find *all* currents against me, I can make very tolerable headway with the propeller. We have had no incidents worth recording. The night promises fair.

PS (by Mr Ainsworth). I have little to record, except the fact (to me quite a surprising one) that, at an elevation equal to that of Cotopaxi, I experienced neither very intense cold, nor headache, nor difficulty of breathing; neither, I find, did Mr Mason, nor Mr Holland, nor Sir Everard. Mr Osborne complained of constriction of the chest – but this soon wore off. We have flown at a great rate during the day, and we must be more than halfway across the Atlantic. We have passed over some twenty or thirty vessels of various kinds, and all seem to be delightfully astonished. Crossing the ocean in a balloon is not so difficult a feat after all. *Omne ignotum pro magnifico. Mem.:* at 25,000 feet elevation the sky appears nearly black, and the stars are distinctly visible; while the sea does not seem convex (as one might suppose) but absolutely and most unequivocally *concave.**

* Mr Ainsworth has not attempted to account for this

Monday, the 8th (Mr Mason's manuscript). This morning we had again some little trouble with the rod of the propeller, which must be entirely remodelled, for fear of serious accident – I mean the steel rod – not the vanes. The latter could not be improved. The wind has been blowing steadily and strongly from the north east all day and so far fortune seems bent upon favouring us. Just before day, we were all somewhat alarmed at some odd noises and concussions in the balloon, accompanied with the apparent rapid subsidence of the whole machine. These phenomena were occasioned by the expansion of the gas, through increase of heat in the atmosphere, and the consequent disruption of the minute particles of ice with

---

phenomenon, which, however, is quite susceptible of explanation. A line dropped from an elevation of 25,000 feet, perpendicularly to the surface of the earth (or sea), would form the perpendicular of a right-angled triangle, of which the base would extend from the right angle to the horizon, and the hypothenuse from the horizon to the balloon. But the 25,000 feet of altitude is little or nothing, in comparison with the extent of the prospect. In other words, the base and hypothenuse of the supposed triangle would be so long when compared with the perpendicular, that the two former may be regarded as nearly parallel. In this manner the horizon of the aeronaut would appear to be *on a level* with the car. But, as the point immediately beneath him seems, and is, at a great distance below him, it seems, of course, also, at a great distance below the horizon. Hence the impression of *concavity*; and this impression must remain, until the elevation shall bear so great a proportion to the extent of prospect, that the apparent parallelism of the base and hypothenuse disappears – when the earth's real convexity must become apparent.

which the network had become encrusted during the night. Threw down several bottles to the vessels below. Saw one of them picked up by a large ship – seemingly one of the New York line packets. Endeavoured to make out her name, but could not be sure of it. Mr Osborne's telescope made it out something like *Atalanta*. It is now 12 at night and we are still going nearly west, at a rapid pace. The sea is peculiarly phosphorescent.

PS (by Mr Ainsworth). It is now 2 a.m., and nearly calm, as well as I can judge – but it is very difficult to determine this point, since we move *with* the air so completely. I have not slept since quitting Wheal-Vor, but can stand it no longer, and must take a nap. We cannot be far from the American coast.

Tuesday, the 9th (Mr Ainsworth's manuscript). 1 p.m. *We are in full view of the low coast of South Carolina.* The great problem is accomplished. We have crossed the Atlantic – fairly and *easily* crossed it in a balloon! God be praised! Who shall say that anything is impossible hereafter?

The journal here ceases. Some particulars of the descent were communicated, however, by Mr Ainsworth to Mr Forsyth. It was nearly dead calm when the voyagers first came in view of the coast, which was immediately recognised by both the seamen, and by Mr Osborne. The latter gentleman having acquaintances at Fort Moultrie, it was immediately resolved to descend in its vicinity. The balloon was brought over the beach (the tide being out and the sand hard, smooth, and admirably adapted for a descent) and the grapnel let go, which took firm hold at once. The inhabitants of the island, and of the fort, thronged out, of course, to see the balloon; but it was with the greatest difficulty that anyone could be made to credit the actual voyage – *the crossing of the Atlantic*. The grapnel caught at 2 p.m., precisely; and thus the whole voyage was completed in seventy-five hours; or rather less, counting from shore to shore. No serious accident occurred. No real danger was at any time apprehended. The balloon was exhausted and secured without trouble; and when the manuscript from which this narrative is compiled was despatched from Charleston, the party were still at Fort Moultrie. Their farther intentions were not ascertained; but we can safely promise our readers some additional information either on Monday or in the course of the next day, at farthest.

This is unquestionably the most stupendous, the most interesting, and the most important undertaking ever accomplished or even attempted by man. What magnificent events may ensue, it would be useless now to think of determining.

The System of Dr Tarr and Professor Fether

During the autumn of 18—, while on a tour through the extreme southern provinces of France, my route led me within a few miles of a certain *maison de santé* or private madhouse, about which I had heard much in Paris from my medical friends. As I had never visited a place of the kind, I thought the opportunity too good to be lost; and so proposed to my travelling companion (a gentleman with whom I had made casual acquaintance a few days before) that we should turn aside, for an hour or so, and look through the establishment. To this he objected – pleading haste in the first place, and, in the second, a very usual horror at the sight of a lunatic. He begged me, however, not to let any mere courtesy towards himself interfere with the gratification of my curiosity, and said that he would ride on leisurely, so that I might overtake him during the day, or, at all events, during the next. As he bade me goodbye, I bethought me that there might be some difficulty in obtaining access to the premises, and mentioned my fears on this point. He replied that, in fact, unless I had personal knowledge of the superintendent, M. Maillard, or some credential in the way of a letter, a difficulty might be found to exist, as the regulations of these private madhouses were more rigid than the public hospital laws. For himself, he added, he had, some years since, made the acquaintance of Maillard, and would so far assist me as to ride up to the door and introduce me; although his feelings on the subject of lunacy would not permit of his entering the house.

I thanked him, and, turning from the main road, we entered a grass-grown by-path, which, in half an hour, nearly lost itself in a dense forest, clothing the base of a mountain. Through this dank and gloomy wood we rode some two miles, when the *maison de santé* came in view. It was a fantastic chateau, much dilapidated, and indeed scarcely tenantable through age and neglect. Its aspect inspired me with absolute dread, and, checking my horse, I half resolved to turn back. I soon, however, grew ashamed of my weakness, and proceeded.

As we rode up to the gateway, I perceived it slightly open, and the visage of a man peering through. In an instant afterwards, this man came forth, accosted my companion by name, shook him cordially by the hand, and begged him to alight. It was M. Maillard himself. He was a portly, fine-looking gentleman of the old school, with a polished manner, and a certain air of gravity, dignity, and authority which was very impressive.

My friend, having presented me, mentioned my desire to inspect the establishment, and received M. Maillard's assurance that he would show me all attention, now took leave, and I saw him no more.

When he had gone, the superintendent ushered me into a small and exceedingly neat parlour, containing, among other indications of refined taste, many books, drawings, pots of flowers, and musical instruments. A cheerful fire blazed upon the hearth. At a piano, singing an aria from Bellini, sat a young and very beautiful woman, who, at my entrance, paused in her song, and received me with graceful courtesy. Her voice was low, and her whole manner subdued. I thought, too, that I perceived the traces of sorrow in her countenance, which was excessively, although to my taste, not unpleasingly, pale. She was attired in deep mourning, and excited in my bosom a feeling of mingled respect, interest, and admiration.

I had heard, at Paris, that the institution of M. Maillard was managed upon what is vulgarly termed the 'system of soothing' – that all punishments were avoided – that even confinement was seldom resorted to – that the patients, while secretly watched, were left much apparent liberty, and that most of them were permitted to roam about the house and grounds in the ordinary apparel of persons in right mind.

Keeping these impressions in view, I was cautious in what I said before the young lady; for I could not be sure that she was sane; and, in fact, there was a certain restless brilliancy about her eyes which half led me to imagine she was not. I confined my remarks, therefore, to general topics, and to such as I thought would not be displeasing or exciting even to a lunatic. She replied in a perfectly rational manner to all that I said; and even her original observations were marked with the soundest good sense, but a long acquaintance with the metaphysics of mania had taught me to put no faith in such evidence of sanity, and I continued to practise, throughout the interview, the caution with which I commenced it.

Presently a smart footman in livery brought in a tray with fruit, wine, and other refreshments, of which I partook, the lady soon afterwards leaving the room. As she departed I turned my eyes in an enquiring manner towards my host.

'No,' he said, 'oh, no – a member of my family – my niece, and a most accomplished woman.'

'I beg a thousand pardons for the suspicion,' I

replied, 'but of course you will know how to excuse me. The excellent administration of your affairs here is well understood in Paris, and I thought it just possible, you know – '

'Yes, yes – say no more – or rather it is myself who should thank you for the commendable prudence you have displayed. We seldom find so much of forethought in young men; and, more than once, some unhappy contretemps has occurred in consequence of thoughtlessness on the part of our visitors. While my former system was in operation, and my patients were permitted the privilege of roaming to and fro at will, they were often aroused to a dangerous frenzy by injudicious persons who called to inspect the house. Hence I was obliged to enforce a rigid system of exclusion; and none obtained access to the premises upon whose discretion I could not rely.'

'While your former system was in operation!' I said, repeating his words – 'do I understand you, then, to say that the "soothing system" of which I have heard so much is no longer in force?'

'It is now,' he replied, 'several weeks since we have concluded to renounce it for ever.'

'Indeed! you astonish me!'

'We found it, sir,' he said, with a sigh, 'absolutely necessary to return to the old usages. The danger of the soothing system was, at all times, appalling; and its advantages have been much overrated. I believe, sir, that in this house it has been given a fair trial, if ever in any. We did everything that rational humanity could suggest. I am sorry that you could not have paid us a visit at an earlier period, that you might have judged for yourself. But I presume you are conversant with the soothing practice – with its details.'

'Not altogether. What I have heard has been at third or fourth hand.'

'I may state the system, then, in general terms, as one in which the patients were *ménagés* – humoured. We contradicted no fancies which entered the brains of the mad. On the contrary, we not only indulged but encouraged them; and many of our most permanent cures have been thus effected. There is no argument which so touches the feeble reason of the madman as the *reductio ad absurdum*. We have had men, for example, who fancied themselves chickens. The cure was, to insist upon the thing as a fact – to accuse the patient of stupidity in not sufficiently perceiving it to be a fact – and thus to refuse him any other diet for a week than that which properly appertains to a chicken. In this manner a little corn and gravel were made to perform wonders.'

'But was this species of acquiescence all?'

'By no means. We put much faith in amusements of a simple kind, such as music, dancing, gymnastic exercises generally, cards, certain classes of books, and so forth. We affected to treat each individual as if for some ordinary physical disorder, and the word "lunacy" was never employed. A great point was to set each lunatic to guard the actions of all the others. To repose confidence in the understanding or discretion of a madman, is to gain him body and soul. In this way we were enabled to dispense with an expensive body of keepers.'

'And you had no punishments of any kind?'

'None.'

'And you never confined your patients?'

'Very rarely. Now and then, the malady of some individual growing to a crisis, or taking a sudden turn of fury, we conveyed him to a secret cell, lest his disorder should infect the rest, and there kept him until we could dismiss him to his friends – for with the raging maniac we have nothing to do. He is usually removed to the public hospitals.'

'And you have now changed all this – and you think for the better?'

'Decidedly. The system had its disadvantages, and even its dangers. It is now, happily, exploded throughout all the *maisons de santé* of France.'

'I am very much surprised,' I said, 'at what you tell me; for I made sure that, at this moment, no other method of treatment for mania existed in any portion of the country.'

'You are young yet, my friend,' replied my host, 'but the time will arrive when you will learn to judge for yourself of what is going on in the world, without trusting to the gossip of others. Believe nothing you hear, and only one half that you see. Now about our *maisons de santé*, it is clear that some ignoramus has misled you. After dinner, however, when you have sufficiently recovered from the fatigue of your ride, I will be happy to take you over the house, and introduce to you a system which, in my opinion, and in that of everyone who has witnessed its operation, is incomparably the most effectual as yet devised.'

'Your own?' I enquired – 'one of your own invention?'

'I am proud,' he replied, 'to acknowledge that it is – at least in some measure.'

In this manner I conversed with M. Maillard for an hour or two, during which he showed me the gardens and conservatories of the place.

'I cannot let you see my patients,' he said, 'just at present. To a sensitive mind there is always more or less of the shocking in such exhibitions; and I do not wish to spoil your appetite for dinner. We will dine. I can give you some veal *à la St Menehoult*, with cauliflowers in *velouté* sauce – after that a glass of Clos de Vougeôt – then your nerves will be sufficiently steadied.'

At six, dinner was announced; and my host conducted me into a large *salle à manger*, where a very numerous company were assembled – twenty-five or thirty in all. They were, apparently, people of rank – certainly of high breeding – although their habiliments, I thought, were extravagantly rich, partaking somewhat too much of the ostentatious finery of the *ville cour*. I noticed that at least two-thirds of these guests were ladies; and some of the latter were by no means accoutred in what a Parisian would consider good taste at the present day. Many females, for example, whose age could not have been less than seventy, were bedecked with a profusion of jewellery, such as rings, bracelets, and earrings, and wore their bosoms and arms shamefully bare. I observed, too, that very few of the dresses were well made – or, at least, that very few of them fitted the wearers. In looking about, I discovered the interesting girl to whom M. Maillard had presented me in the little parlour; but my surprise was great to see her wearing a hoop and farthingale, with high-heeled shoes, and a dirty cap of Brussels lace, so much too large for her that it gave her face a ridiculously diminutive expression. When I had first seen her, she was attired, most becomingly, in deep mourning. There was an air of oddity, in short, about the dress of the whole party, which, at first, caused me to recur to my original idea of the 'soothing system', and to fancy that M. Maillard had been willing to deceive me until after dinner, that I might experience no uncomfortable feelings during the repast, at finding myself dining with lunatics; but I remembered having been informed, in Paris, that the southern provincialists were a peculiarly eccentric people, with a vast number of antiquated notions; and then, too, upon conversing with several members of the company, my apprehensions were immediately and fully dispelled.

The dining room itself, although perhaps sufficiently comfortable and of good dimensions, had nothing too much of elegance about it. For example, the floor was uncarpeted; in France, however, a carpet is frequently dispensed with. The windows, too, were without curtains; the shutters, being shut, were securely fastened with iron bars, applied diagonally, after the fashion of our ordinary shop-shutters. The apartment, I observed, formed, in itself, a wing of the chateau, and thus the windows were on three sides of the parallelogram, the door being at the other. There were no less than ten windows in all.

The table was superbly set out. It was loaded with plate, and more than loaded with delicacies. The profusion was absolutely barbaric. There were meats enough to have feasted the Anakim. Never, in all my life, had I witnessed so lavish, so wasteful an expenditure of the good things of life. There seemed very little taste, however, in the arrangements; and my eyes, accustomed to quiet lights, were sadly offended by the prodigious glare of a multitude of wax candles, which, in silver candelabra, were deposited upon the table, and all about the room, wherever it was possible to find a place. There were several active servants in attendance; and, upon a large table, at the farther end of the apartment, were seated seven or eight people with fiddles, fifes, trombones, and a drum. These fellows annoyed me very much, at intervals, during the repast, by an infinite variety of noises, which were intended for music, and which appeared to afford much entertainment to all present, with the exception of myself.

Upon the whole, I could not help thinking that there was much of the bizarre about everything I saw – but then the world is made up of all kinds of persons, with all modes of thought, and all sorts of conventional customs. I had travelled, too, so much, as to be quite an adept at the *nil admirari*; so I took my seat very coolly at the right hand of my host, and, having an excellent appetite, did justice to the good cheer set before me.

The conversation, in the meantime, was spirited and general. The ladies, as usual, talked a great deal. I soon found that nearly all the company were well educated; and my host was a world of good-humoured anecdote in himself. He seemed quite willing to speak of his position as superintendent of a *maison de santé*; and, indeed, the topic of lunacy was, much to my surprise, a favourite one with all present. A great many amusing stories were told, having reference to the whims of the patients.

'We had a fellow here once,' said a fat little gentleman, who sat at my right – 'a fellow that fancied himself a teapot; and by the way, is it not especially singular how often this particular crotchet has entered the brain of the lunatic? There is scarcely an insane asylum in France which cannot supply a human teapot. *Our* gentleman was a Britannia-ware teapot, and was careful to polish himself every morning with buckskin and whiting.'

'And then,' said a tall man just opposite, 'we had here, not long ago, a person who had taken it into his head that he was a donkey – which allegorically speaking, you will say, was quite true. He was a troublesome patient; and we had much ado to keep him within bounds. For a long time he would eat nothing but thistles; but of this idea we soon cured him by insisting upon his eating nothing else. Then he was perpetually kicking out his heels – so – so – '

'M. de Kock! I will thank you to behave yourself!' here interrupted an old lady, who sat next to the speaker. 'Please keep your feet to yourself! You have spoiled my brocade! Is it necessary, pray, to illustrate a remark in so practical a style? Our friend here can surely comprehend you without all this. Upon my word, you are nearly as great a donkey as the poor unfortunate imagined himself. Your acting is very natural, as I live.'

'*Mille pardons, mademoiselle!*' replied M. de Kock, thus addressed – 'a thousand pardons! I had no intention of offending. Mlle Laplace – M. de Kock will do himself the honour of taking wine with you.'

Here M. de Kock bowed low, kissed his hand with much ceremony, and took wine with Mlle Laplace.

'Allow me, *mon ami*,' now said M. Maillard, addressing myself, 'allow me to send you a morsel of this veal *à la St Menehoult* – you will find it particularly fine.'

At this instant three sturdy waiters had just succeeded in depositing safely upon the table an enormous dish, or trencher, containing what I supposed to be the '*monstrum, horrendum, informe, ingens, cui lumen ademptum*'. A closer scrutiny assured me, however, that it was only a small calf roasted whole, and set upon its knees, with an apple in its mouth, as is the English fashion of dressing a hare.

'Thank you, no,' I replied; 'to say the truth, I am not particularly partial to veal *à la St* – what is it? – for I do not find that it altogether agrees with me. I will change my plate, however, and try some of the rabbit.'

There were several side-dishes on the table, containing what appeared to be the ordinary French rabbit – a very delicious *morceau*, which I can recommend.

'Pierre,' cried the host, 'change this gentleman's plate, and give him a side-piece of this rabbit *au-chat*.'

'This what?' said I.

'This rabbit *au-chat*.'

'Why, thank you – upon second thoughts, no. I will just help myself to some of the ham.'

There is no knowing what one eats, thought I to myself, at the tables of these people of the province. I will have none of their rabbit *au-chat* – and, for the matter of that, none of their cat *au*-rabbit either.

'And then,' said a cadaverous-looking personage, near the foot of the table, taking up the thread of the conversation where it had been broken off, 'and then, among other oddities, we had a patient, once upon a time, who very pertinaciously maintained himself to be a Cordova cheese, and went about, with a knife in his hand, soliciting his friends to try a small slice from the middle of his leg.'

'He was a great fool, beyond doubt,' interposed someone, 'but not to be compared with a certain individual whom we all know, with the exception of this strange gentleman. I mean the man who took himself for a bottle of champagne, and always went off with a pop and a fizz, in this fashion.'

Here the speaker, very rudely, as I thought, put his right thumb in his left cheek, withdrew it with a sound resembling the popping of a cork, and then, by a dexterous movement of the tongue upon the teeth, created a sharp hissing and fizzing, which lasted for several minutes, in imitation of the frothing of champagne. This behaviour, I saw plainly, was not very pleasing to M. Maillard; but that gentleman said nothing, and the conversation was resumed by a very lean little man in a big wig.

'And then there was an ignoramus,' said he, 'who mistook himself for a frog, which, by the way, he resembled in no little degree. I wish you could have seen him, sir,' – here the speaker addressed myself – 'it would have done your heart good to see the natural airs that he put on. Sir, if that man was not a frog, I can only observe that it is a pity he was not. His croak thus – o–o–o–o–gh – o–o–o–o–gh! was the finest note in the world – B flat; and when he put his elbows upon the table thus – after taking a glass or two of wine – and distended his mouth, thus, and rolled up his eyes, thus, and winked them with excessive rapidity, thus, why then, sir, I take it upon myself to say, positively, that you would have been lost in admiration of the genius of the man.'

'I have no doubt of it,' I said.

'And then,' said somebody else, 'then there was Petit Gaillard, who thought himself a pinch of snuff, and was truly distressed because he could not take himself between his own finger and thumb.'

'And then there was Jules Desoulières, who was a very singular genius, indeed, and went mad with the idea that he was a pumpkin. He persecuted the cook to make him up into pies – a thing which the cook indignantly refused to do. For my part, I am by no means sure that a pumpkin pie *à la Desoulières* would not have been very capital eating indeed!'

'You astonish me!' said I; and I looked inquisitively at M. Maillard.

'Ha! ha! ha!' said that gentleman – 'he! he! he! – hi! hi! hi! – ho! ho! ho! – hu! hu! hu! hu! – very good indeed! You must not be astonished, *mon ami*; our friend here is a wit – a *drôle* – you must not understand him to the letter.'

'And then,' said some other one of the party, 'then there was Bouffon Le Grand – another extraordinary personage in his way. He grew deranged through love, and fancied himself possessed of two heads. One of these he maintained to be the head of Cicero; the other he imagined a composite one, being Demosthenes' from the top of the forehead to the mouth, and Lord Brougham's from the mouth to the chin. It is not impossible that he was wrong; but he would have convinced you of his being in the right; for he was a man of great eloquence. He had an absolute passion for oratory, and could not refrain from display. For example, he used to leap upon the dinner-table thus, and – and – '

Here a friend, at the side of the speaker, put a hand upon his shoulder and whispered a few words in his ear, upon which he ceased talking with great suddenness, and sank back within his chair.

'And then,' said the friend who had whispered, 'there was Boullard, the tee-totum. I call him the tee-totum because, in fact, he was seized with the droll but not altogether irrational crotchet, that he had been converted into a tee-totum. You would have roared with laughter to see him spin. He would turn

round upon one heel by the hour, in this manner –
so – '

Here the friend whom he had just interrupted by a
whisper, performed an exactly similar office for himself.

'But then,' cried the old lady, at the top of her voice,
'your M. Boullard was a madman, and a very silly
madman at best; for who, allow me to ask you, ever
heard of a human tee-totum? The thing is absurd.
Mme Joyeuse was a more sensible person, as you
know. She had a crotchet, but it was instinct with
common sense, and gave pleasure to all who had the
honour of her acquaintance. She found, upon mature
deliberation, that, by some accident, she had been
turned into a chicken-cock; but, as such, she behaved
with propriety. She flapped her wings with prodigious
effect – so – so – and, as for her crow, it was delicious!
Cock-a-doodle-doo! – cock-a-doodle-doo! – cock-a-
doodle-de-doo-dooo-do-o-o-o-o-o-o!'

'Mme Joyeuse, I will thank you to behave yourself!'
here interrupted our host, very angrily. 'You can
either conduct yourself as a lady should do, or you can
quit the table forthwith – take your choice.'

The lady (whom I was much astonished to hear
addressed as Mme Joyeuse, after the description of
Mme Joyeuse she had just given) blushed up to the
eyebrows, and seemed exceedingly abashed at the
reproof. She hung down her head, and said not a
syllable in reply. But another and younger lady
resumed the theme. It was my beautiful girl of the
little parlour.

'Oh, Mme Joyeuse *was* a fool!' she exclaimed, 'but
there was really much sound sense, after all, in the
opinion of Eugénie Salsafette. She was a very beautiful
and painfully modest young lady, who thought the

ordinary mode of habiliment indecent, and wished to dress herself, always, by getting outside instead of inside of her clothes. It is a thing very easily done, after all. You have only to do so – and then so – so – so – and then so – so – so – and then so – so – and then –'

'*Mon dieu!* Mlle Salsafette!' here cried a dozen voices at once. 'What are you about? – forbear! – that is sufficient! – we see, very plainly, how it is done! – hold! hold!' and several persons were already leaping from their seats to withhold Mlle Salsafette from putting herself upon a par with the Medicean Venus, when the point was very effectually and suddenly accomplished by a series of loud screams, or yells, from some portion of the main body of the chateau.

My nerves were very much affected, indeed, by these yells; but the rest of the company I really pitied. I never saw any set of reasonable people so thoroughly frightened in my life. They all grew as pale as so many corpses, and, shrinking within their seats, sat quivering and gibbering with terror, and listening for a repetition of the sound. It came again – louder and seemingly nearer – and then a third time very loud, and then a fourth time with a vigour evidently diminished. At this apparent dying away of the noise, the spirits of the company were immediately regained, and all was life and anecdote as before. I now ventured to enquire the cause of the disturbance.

'A mere bagatelle,' said M. Maillard. 'We are used to these things, and care really very little about them. The lunatics, every now and then, get up a howl in concert; one starting another, as is sometimes the case with a bevy of dogs at night. It occasionally happens, however, that the concerto yells are succeeded by a simultaneous effort at breaking loose, when, of course, some little danger is to be apprehended.'

'And how many have you in charge?'

'At present we have not more than ten, altogether.'

'Principally females, I presume?'

'Oh, no – every one of them men, and stout fellows, too, I can tell you.'

'Indeed! I have always understood that the majority of lunatics were of the gentler sex.'

'It is generally so, but not always. Some time ago, there were about twenty-seven patients here; and, of that number, no less than eighteen were women; but, lately, matters have changed very much, as you see.'

'Yes – have changed very much, as you see,' here interrupted the gentleman who had broken the shins of Mlle Laplace.

'Yes – have changed very much, as you see!' chimed in the whole company at once.

'Hold your tongues, every one of you!' said my host, in a great rage. Whereupon the whole company maintained a dead silence for nearly a minute. As for one lady, she obeyed M. Maillard to the letter, and thrusting out her tongue, which was an excessively long one, held it very resignedly, with both hands, until the end of the entertainment.

'And this gentlewoman,' said I, to M. Maillard, bending over and addressing him in a whisper – 'this good lady who has just spoken, and who gives us the cock-a-doodle-de-doo – she, I presume, is harmless – quite harmless, eh?'

'Harmless!' ejaculated he, in unfeigned surprise, 'why – why, what can you mean?'

'Only slightly touched?' said I, touching my head. 'I take it for granted that she is not particularly – not dangerously affected, eh?'

'*Mon dieu!* what is it you imagine? This lady, my particular old friend Mme Joyeuse, is as absolutely sane as myself. She has her little eccentricities, to be sure – but then, you know, all old women – all very old women – are more or less eccentric!'

'To be sure,' said I, 'to be sure – and then the rest of these ladies and gentlemen – '

'Are my friends and keepers,' interrupted M. Maillard, drawing himself up with hauteur, 'my very good friends and assistants.'

'What! all of them?' I asked, 'the women and all?'

'Assuredly,' he said, 'we could not do at all without the women; they are the best lunatic nurses in the world; they have a way of their own, you know; their bright eyes have a marvellous effect – something like the fascination of the snake, you know.'

'To be sure,' said I, 'to be sure! They behave a little odd, eh? – they are a little queer, eh? – don't you think so?'

'Odd! – queer! – why, do you really think so? We are not very prudish, to be sure, here in the South – do pretty much as we please – enjoy life, and all that sort of thing, you know – '

'To be sure,' said I, 'to be sure.'

'And then, perhaps, this Clos de Vougeôt is a little heady, you know – a little strong – you understand, eh?'

'To be sure,' said I, 'to be sure. By the by, *monsieur*, did I understand you to say that the system you have adopted, in place of the celebrated soothing system, was one of very rigorous severity?'

'By no means. Our confinement is necessarily close; but the treatment – the medical treatment, I mean – is rather agreeable to the patients than otherwise.'

'And the new system is one of your own invention?'

'Not altogether. Some portions of it are referable to Professor Tarr, of whom you have, necessarily, heard; and, again, there are modifications in my plan which I am happy to acknowledge as belonging of right to the celebrated Fether, with whom, if I mistake not, you have the honour of an intimate acquaintance.'

'I am quite ashamed to confess,' I replied, 'that I have never even heard the names of either gentleman before.'

'Good heavens!' ejaculated my host, drawing back his chair abruptly, and uplifting his hands. 'I surely do not hear you aright! You did not intend to say, eh? that you had never heard either of the learned Doctor Tarr, or of the celebrated Professor Fether?'

'I am forced to acknowledge my ignorance,' I replied; 'but the truth should be held inviolate above all things. Nevertheless, I feel humbled to the dust, not to be acquainted with the works of these, no doubt, extraordinary men. I will seek out their writings forthwith, and peruse them with deliberate care. M. Maillard, you have really – I must confess it – you have really – made me ashamed of myself!'

And this was the fact.

'Say no more, my good young friend,' he said kindly, pressing my hand, 'join me now in a glass of Sauterne.'

We drank. The company followed our example without stint. They chatted – they jested – they laughed – they perpetrated a thousand absurdities – the fiddles shrieked – the drum row-de-dowed – the trombones bellowed like so many brazen bulls of Phalaris – and the whole scene, growing gradually worse and worse, as the wines gained the ascendancy, became at length a sort of pandemonium *in petto*. In the meantime, M. Maillard and myself, with some bottles of Sauterne and Vougeôt between us, continued our conversation at the top of the voice. A word spoken in an ordinary key stood no more chance of being heard than the voice of a fish from the bottom of Niagara Falls.

'And, sir,' said I, screaming in his ear, 'you mentioned something before dinner about the danger incurred in the old system of soothing. How is that?'

'Yes,' he replied, 'there was, occasionally, very great danger indeed. There is no accounting for the caprices of madmen; and, in my opinion as well as in that of Dr Tarr and Professor Fether, it is never safe to permit them to run at large unattended. A lunatic may be "soothed", as it is called, for a time, but, in the end, he is very apt to become obstreperous. His cunning, too, is proverbial and great. If he has a project in view, he conceals his design with a marvellous wisdom; and the dexterity with which he counterfeits sanity, presents, to the metaphysician, one of the most singular problems in the study of mind. When a madman appears thoroughly sane, indeed, it is high time to put him in a straitjacket.'

'But the danger, my dear sir, of which you were speaking, in your own experience – during your control of this house – have you had practical reason to think liberty hazardous in the case of a lunatic?'

'Here? – in my own experience? – why, I may say, yes. For example – no very long while ago, a singular circumstance occurred in this very house. The "soothing system", you know, was then in operation, and the patients were at large. They behaved remarkably well – especially so – anyone of sense might have known that some devilish scheme was brewing from that particular fact, that the fellows behaved so remarkably well. And, sure enough, one fine morning the keepers found themselves pinioned hand and foot, and thrown into the cells, where they were attended, as if they were the lunatics, by the lunatics themselves, who had usurped the offices of the keepers.'

'You don't tell me so! I never heard of anything so absurd in my life!'

'Fact – it all came to pass by means of a stupid fellow – a lunatic – who, by some means, had taken it into his head that he had invented a better system of government than any ever heard of before – of lunatic government, I mean. He wished to give his invention a trial, I suppose, and so he persuaded the rest of the patients to join him in a conspiracy for the overthrow of the reigning powers.'

'And he really succeeded?'

'No doubt of it. The keepers and kept were soon made to exchange places. Not that exactly either – for the madmen had been free, but the keepers were shut up in cells forthwith, and treated, I am sorry to say, in a very cavalier manner.'

'But I presume a counter-revolution was soon effected. This condition of things could not have long existed. The country people in the neighbourhood – visitors coming to see the establishment – would have given the alarm.'

'There you are out. The head rebel was too cunning for that. He admitted no visitors at all – with the exception, one day, of a very stupid-looking young gentleman of whom he had no reason to be afraid. He let him in to see the place – just by way of variety – to have a little fun with him. As soon as he had gammoned him sufficiently, he let him out, and sent him about his business.'

'And how long, then, did the madmen reign?'

'Oh, a very long time, indeed – a month certainly – how much longer I can't precisely say. In the meantime, the lunatics had a jolly season of it – that you may swear. They doffed their own shabby clothes, and made free with the family wardrobe and jewels. The cellars of the chateau were well stocked with wine; and these madmen are just the devils that know how to drink it. They lived well, I can tell you.'

'And the treatment – what was the particular species of treatment which the leader of the rebels put into operation?'

'Why, as for that, a madman is not necessarily a fool, as I have already observed; and it is my honest opinion that his treatment was a much better treatment than that which it superseded. It was a very capital system indeed – simple – neat – no trouble at all – in fact it was delicious – it was – '

Here my host's observations were cut short by another series of yells, of the same character as those which had previously disconcerted us. This time, however, they seemed to proceed from persons rapidly approaching.

'Gracious heavens!' I ejaculated – 'the lunatics have most undoubtedly broken loose.'

'I very much fear it is so,' replied M. Maillard, now becoming excessively pale. He had scarcely finished the sentence, before loud shouts and imprecations were heard beneath the windows; and, immediately afterwards, it became evident that some persons outside were endeavouring to gain entrance into the room. The door was beaten with what appeared to be a sledgehammer, and the shutters were wrenched and shaken with prodigious violence.

A scene of the most terrible confusion ensued. M. Maillard, to my excessive astonishment, threw himself under the sideboard. I had expected more resolution at his hands. The members of the orchestra, who, for the last fifteen minutes, had been seemingly too much intoxicated to do duty, now sprang all at once to their feet and to their instruments, and, scrambling upon their table, broke out, with one accord, into 'Yankee Doodle', which they performed, if not exactly in tune, at least with an energy superhuman, during the whole of the uproar.

Meantime, upon the main dining-table, among the bottles and glasses, leaped the gentleman who, with such difficulty, had been restrained from leaping there before. As soon as he fairly settled himself, he commenced an oration, which, no doubt, was a very capital one, if it could only have been heard. At the same moment, the man with the tee-totum predilection set himself to spinning around the apartment, with immense energy, and with arms outstretched at right angles with his body; so that he had all the air of a tee-totum in fact, and knocked everybody down that happened to get in his way. And now, too, hearing an incredible popping and fizzing of champagne, I discovered at length, that it proceeded from the person who performed the bottle of that delicate drink during dinner. And then, again, the frog-man croaked away as if the salvation of his soul depended upon every note that he uttered. And, in the midst of all this, the continuous braying of a donkey arose over all. As for my old friend, Mme Joyeuse, I really could have wept for the poor lady, she appeared so terribly perplexed. All she did, however, was to stand up in a corner, by the fireplace, and sing out incessantly at the top of her voice, 'Cock-a-doodle-de-dooooooh!'

And now came the climax – the catastrophe of the drama. As no resistance, beyond whooping and yelling and cock-a-doodling, was offered to the encroachments of the party without, the ten windows were very speedily, and almost simultaneously, broken in. But I shall never forget the emotions of wonder and horror with which I gazed, when, leaping through these windows, and down among us pell-mell, fighting, stamping, scratching, and howling, there rushed a perfect army of what I took to be chimpanzees, orang-utans, or big black baboons of the Cape of Good Hope.

I received a terrible beating – after which I rolled under a sofa and lay still. After lying there some fifteen minutes, during which time I listened with all my ears to what was going on in the room, I came to same satisfactory denouement of this tragedy. M. Maillard, it appeared, in giving me the account of the lunatic who had excited his fellows to rebellion, had been merely relating his own exploits. This gentleman had, indeed, some two or three years before, been the superintendent of the establishment, but grew crazy himself, and so became a patient. This fact was unknown to the travelling companion who introduced me. The keepers, ten in number, having been suddenly overpowered, were first well tarred, then carefully feathered, and then shut up in underground cells. They had been so imprisoned for more than a month, during which period M. Maillard had generously allowed them not only the tar and feathers (which constituted his 'system'), but some bread and abundance of water. The latter was pumped on them daily. At length, one escaping through a sewer, gave freedom to all the rest.

The 'soothing system', with important modifications, has been resumed at the chateau; yet I cannot help agreeing with M. Maillard, that his own 'treatment' was a very capital one of its kind. As he justly observed, it was 'simple – neat – and gave no trouble at all – not the least'.

I have only to add that, although I have searched every library in Europe for the works of Dr Tarr and Professor Fether, I have, up to the present day, utterly failed in my endeavours at procuring an edition.

Mesmeric Revelation

Whatever doubt may still envelop the *rationale* of mesmerism, its startling *facts* are now almost universally admitted. Of these latter, those who doubt, are your mere doubters by profession – an unprofitable and disreputable tribe. There can be no more absolute waste of time than the attempt to *prove*, at the present day, that man, by mere exercise of will, can so impress his fellow, as to cast him into an abnormal condition, of which the phenomena resemble very closely those of *death*, or at least resemble them more nearly than they do the phenomena of any other normal condition within our cognisance; that, while in this state, the person so impressed employs only with effort, and then feebly, the external organs of sense, yet perceives, with keenly refined perception, and through channels supposed unknown, matters beyond the scope of the physical organs; that, moreover, his intellectual faculties are wonderfully exalted and invigorated; that his sympathies with the person so impressing him are profound; and, finally, that his susceptibility to the impression increases with its frequency, while, in the same proportion, the peculiar phenomena elicited are more extended and more *pronounced*.

I say that these – which are the laws of mesmerism in its general features – it would be supererogation to demonstrate; nor shall I inflict upon my readers so needless a demonstration today. My purpose at present is a very different one indeed. I am impelled, even in the teeth of a world of prejudice, to detail without comment the very remarkable substance of a colloquy, occurring between a sleep-waker and myself.

I had been long in the habit of mesmerising the person in question (Mr Vankirk), and the usual acute susceptibility and exaltation of the mesmeric perception had supervened. For many months he had been labouring under confirmed phthisis, the more distressing effects of which had been relieved by my manipulations; and on the night of Wednesday, the fifteenth instant, I was summoned to his bedside.

The invalid was suffering with acute pain in the region of the heart, and breathed with great difficulty, having all the ordinary symptoms of asthma. In spasms such as these he had usually found relief from the application of mustard to the nervous centres, but tonight this had been attempted in vain.

As I entered his room he greeted me with a cheerful smile, and although evidently in much bodily pain, appeared to be, mentally, quite at ease.

'I sent for you tonight,' he said, 'not so much to administer to my bodily ailment, as to satisfy me concerning certain psychic impressions which, of late, have occasioned me much anxiety and surprise. I need not tell you how sceptical I have hitherto been on the topic of the soul's immortality. I cannot deny that there has always existed, as if in that very soul which I have been denying, a vague half-sentiment of its own existence. But this half-sentiment at no time amounted to conviction. With it my reason had nothing to do. All attempts at logical enquiry resulted, indeed, in leaving me more sceptical than before. I had been advised to study Cousin. I studied him in his own works as well as in those of his European and American echoes. The

"Charles Elwood" of Mr Brownson, for example, was placed in my hands. I read it with profound attention. Throughout I found it logical, but the portions which were not *merely* logical were unhappily the initial arguments of the disbelieving hero of the book. In his summing up it seemed evident to me that the reasoner had not even succeeded in convincing himself. His end had plainly forgotten his beginning, like the government of Trinculo. In short, I was not long in perceiving that if man is to be intellectually convinced of his own immortality, he will never be so convinced by the mere abstractions which have been so long the fashion of the moralists of England, of France, and of Germany. Abstractions may amuse and exercise, but take no hold on the mind. Here upon earth, at least, philosophy, I am persuaded, will always in vain call upon us to look upon qualities as things. The will may assent – the soul – the intellect, never.

'I repeat, then, that I only half felt, and never intellectually believed. But latterly there has been a certain deepening of the feeling, until it has come so nearly to resemble the acquiescence of reason, that I find it difficult to distinguish between the two. I am enabled, too, plainly to trace this effect to the mesmeric influence. I cannot better explain my meaning than by the hypothesis that the mesmeric exaltation enables me to perceive a train of ratiocination which, in my abnormal existence, convinces, but which, in full accordance with the mesmeric phenomena, does not extend, except through its *effect*, into my normal condition. In sleep-waking, the reasoning and its conclusion – the cause and its effect – are present together. In my natural state, the cause vanishing, the effect only, and perhaps only partially, remains.

'These considerations have led me to think that some good results might ensue from a series of well-directed questions propounded to me while mesmerised. You have often observed the profound self-cognisance evinced by the sleep-waker – the extensive knowledge he displays upon all points relating to the mesmeric condition itself; and from this self-cognisance may be deduced hints for the proper conduct of a catechism.'

I consented of course to make this experiment. A few passes threw Mr Vankirk into the mesmeric sleep. His breathing became immediately more easy, and he seemed to suffer no physical uneasiness. The following conversation then ensued – V in the dialogue representing the patient, and P myself.

P: Are you asleep?

V: Yes – no; I would rather sleep more soundly.

P: [*After a few more passes*] Do you sleep now?

V: Yes.

P: How do you think your present illness will result?

V: [*After a long hesitation and speaking as if with effort*] I must die.

P: Does the idea of death afflict you?

V: [*Very quickly*] No – no!

P: Are you pleased with the prospect?

V: If I were awake I should like to die, but now it is no matter. The mesmeric condition is so near death as to content me.

P: I wish you would explain yourself, Mr Vankirk.

V: I am willing to do so, but it requires more effort than I feel able to make. You do not question me properly.

P: What then shall I ask?

V: You must begin at the beginning.

P: The beginning! but where is the beginning?

V: You know that the beginning is GOD. [*This was said in a low, fluctuating tone, and with every sign of the most profound veneration*]

P: What then is God?

V: [*Hesitating for many minutes*] I cannot tell.

P: Is not God spirit?

V: While I was awake I knew what you meant by 'spirit', but now it seems only a word – such for instance as truth, beauty – a quality, I mean.

P: Is not God immaterial?

V: There is no immateriality – it is a mere word. That which is not matter, is not at all – unless qualities are things.

P: Is God, then, material?

V: No. [*This reply startled me very much*]

P: What then is he?

V: [*After a long pause, and mutteringly*] I see – but it is a thing difficult to tell. [*Another long pause*] He is not spirit, for he exists. Nor is he matter, *as you understand it*. But there are *gradations* of matter of which man knows nothing; the grosser impelling the finer, the finer pervading the grosser. The atmosphere, for example, impels the electric principle, while the electric principle permeates the atmosphere. These gradations of matter increase in rarity or fineness, until we arrive at a matter *unparticled* – without particles – indivisible – *one*; and here the law of impulsion and permeation is modified. The ultimate, or unparticled matter, not only permeates all things but impels all things – and thus *is* all things within itself. This matter is God. What men attempt to embody in the word 'thought', is this matter in motion.

P: The metaphysicians maintain that all action is reducible to motion and thinking, and that the latter is the origin of the former.

V: Yes; and I now see the confusion of idea. Motion is the action of *mind* – not of *thinking*. The unparticled matter, or God, in quiescence, is (as nearly as we can conceive it) what men call mind. And the power of self-movement (equivalent in effect to human volition) is, in the unparticled matter, the result of its unity and omniprevalence; *how*, I know not, and now clearly see that I shall never know. But the unparticled matter, set in motion by a law, or quality, existing within itself, is thinking.

P: Can you give me no more precise idea of what you term the unparticled matter?

V: The matters of which man is cognisant, escape the senses in gradation. We have, for example, a metal, a piece of wood, a drop of water, the atmosphere, a gas, caloric, electricity, the luminiferous ether. Now we call all these things matter, and embrace all matter in one general definition; but in spite of this, there can be no two ideas more essentially distinct than that which we attach to a metal, and that which we attach to the luminiferous ether. When we reach the latter, we feel an almost irresistible inclination to class it with spirit, or with nihility. The only consideration which restrains us is our conception of its atomic constitution; and here, even, we have to seek aid from our notion of an atom, as something possessing in infinite minuteness, solidity, palpability, weight. Destroy the idea of the atomic constitution and we should no longer be able to regard the ether as an entity, or

285

at least as matter. For want of a better word we might term it spirit. Take, now, a step beyond the luminiferous ether – conceive a matter as much more rare than the ether, as this ether is more rare than the metal, and we arrive at once (in spite of all the school dogmas) at a unique mass – an unparticled matter. For although we may admit infinite littleness in the atoms themselves, the infinitude of littleness in the spaces between them is an absurdity. There will be a point – there will be a degree of rarity, at which, if the atoms are sufficiently numerous, the interspaces must vanish, and the mass absolutely coalesce. But the consideration of the atomic constitution being now taken away, the nature of the mass inevitably glides into what we conceive of spirit. It is clear, however, that it is as fully matter as before. The truth is, it is impossible to conceive spirit, since it is impossible to imagine what is not. When we flatter ourselves that we have formed its conception, we have merely deceived our understanding by the consideration of infinitely rarefied matter.

P: There seems to me an insurmountable objection to the idea of absolute coalescence – and that is the very slight resistance experienced by the heavenly bodies in their revolutions through space – a resistance now ascertained, it is true, to exist in *some* degree, but which is, nevertheless, so slight as to have been quite overlooked by the sagacity even of Newton. We know that the resistance of bodies is, chiefly, in proportion to their density. Absolute coalescence is absolute density. Where there are no interspaces, there can be no yielding. An ether, absolutely dense, would put an infinitely more

effectual stop to the progress of a star than would
an ether of adamant or of iron.

V: Your objection is answered with an ease which is
nearly in the ratio of its apparent unanswerability.
As regards the progress of the star, it can make no
difference whether the star passes through the ether
or the ether through it. There is no astronomical error
more unaccountable than that which reconciles the
known retardation of the comets with the idea of
their passage through an ether: for, however rare
this ether be supposed, it would put a stop to all
sidereal revolution in a very far briefer period than
has been admitted by those astronomers who have
endeavoured to slur over a point which they found
it impossible to comprehend. The retardation
actually experienced is, on the other hand, about
that which might be expected from the *friction* of
the ether in the instantaneous passage through
the orb. In the one case, the retarding force is
momentary and complete within itself – in the
other it is endlessly accumulative.

P: But in all this – in this identification of mere matter
with God – is there nothing of irreverence? [*I was
forced to repeat this question before the sleep-waker fully
comprehended my meaning*]

V: Can you say *why* matter should be less reverenced
than mind? But you forget that the matter of which
I speak is, in all respects, the very 'mind' or 'spirit'
of the schools, so far as regards its high capacities,
and is, moreover, the 'matter' of these schools at
the same time. God, with all the powers attributed
to spirit, is but the perfection of matter.

P: You assert, then, that the unparticled matter, in
motion, is thought?

V: In general, this motion is the universal thought of the universal mind. This thought creates. All created things are but the thoughts of God.

P: You say, 'in general'.

V: Yes. The universal mind is God. For new individualities, *matter* is necessary.

P: But you now speak of 'mind' and 'matter' as do the metaphysicians.

V: Yes – to avoid confusion. When I say 'mind', I mean the unparticled or ultimate matter; by 'matter', I intend all else.

P: You were saying that 'for new individualities matter is necessary'.

V: Yes; for mind, existing unincorporate, is merely God. To create individual, thinking beings, it was necessary to incarnate portions of the divine mind. Thus man is individualised. Divested of corporate investiture, he were God. Now, the particular motion of the incarnated portions of the unparticled matter is the thought of man; as the motion of the whole is that of God.

P: You say that divested of the body man will be God?

V: [*After much hesitation*] I could not have said this; it is an absurdity.

P: [*Referring to my notes*] You *did* say that 'divested of corporate investiture man were God'.

V: And this is true. Man thus divested *would be* God – would be unindividualised. But he can never be thus divested – at least never *will be* – else we must imagine an action of God returning upon itself – a purposeless and futile action. Man is a creature. Creatures are thoughts of God. It is the nature of thought to be irrevocable.

P: I do not comprehend. You say that man will never put off the body?

V: I say that he will never be bodiless.

P: Explain.

V: There are two bodies – the rudimental and the complete; corresponding with the two conditions of the worm and the butterfly. What we call 'death', is but the painful metamorphosis. Our present incarnation is progressive, preparatory, temporary. Our future is perfected, ultimate, immortal. The ultimate life is the full design.

P: But of the worm's metamorphosis we are palpably cognisant.

V: *We*, certainly – but not the worm. The matter of which our rudimental body is composed, is within the ken of the organs of that body; or, more distinctly, our rudimental organs are adapted to the matter of which is formed the rudimental body; but not to that of which the ultimate is composed. The ultimate body thus escapes our rudimental senses, and we perceive only the shell which falls, in decaying, from the inner form; not that inner form itself; but this inner form, as well as the shell, is appreciable by those who have already acquired the ultimate life.

P: You have often said that the mesmeric state very nearly resembles death. How is this?

V: When I say that it resembles death, I mean that it resembles the ultimate life; for when I am entranced the senses of my rudimental life are in abeyance, and I perceive external things directly, without organs, through a medium which I shall employ in the ultimate, unorganised life.

P: Unorganised?

V: Yes; organs are contrivances by which the individual is brought into sensible relation with particular classes and forms of matter, to the exclusion of other classes and forms. The organs of man are adapted to his rudimental condition, and to that only; his ultimate condition, being unorganised, is of unlimited comprehension in all points but one – the nature of the volition of God – that is to say, the motion of the unparticled matter. You will have a distinct idea of the ultimate body by conceiving it to be entire brain. This it is *not*; but a conception of this nature will bring you near a comprehension of what it *is*. A luminous body imparts vibration to the luminiferous ether. The vibrations generate similar ones within the retina; these again communicate similar ones to the optic nerve. The nerve conveys similar ones to the brain; the brain, also, similar ones to the unparticled matter which permeates it. The motion of this latter is thought, of which perception is the first undulation. This is the mode by which the mind of the rudimental life communicates with the external world; and this external world is, to the rudimental life, limited, through the idiosyncrasy of its organs. But in the ultimate, unorganised life, the external world reaches the whole body (which is of a substance having affinity to brain, as I have said), with no other intervention than that of an infinitely rarer ether than even the luminiferous; and to this ether – in unison with it – the whole body vibrates, setting in motion the unparticled matter which permeates it. It is to the absence of idiosyncratic organs, therefore, that we must attribute the nearly unlimited perception of the ultimate life. To rudimental beings, organs are the cages necessary to confine them until fledged.

P: You speak of rudimental 'beings'. Are there other rudimental thinking beings than man?

V: The multitudinous conglomeration of rare matter into nebulae, planets, suns, and other bodies which are neither nebulae, suns, nor planets, is for the sole purpose of supplying *pabulum* for the idiosyncrasy of the organs of an infinity of rudimental beings. But for the necessity of the rudimental, prior to the ultimate life, there would have been no bodies such as these. Each of these is tenanted by a distinct variety of organic, rudimental, thinking creatures. In all, the organs vary with the features of the place tenanted. At death, or metamorphosis, these creatures, enjoying the ultimate life – immortality – and cognisant of all secrets but *the one*, act all things and pass everywhere by mere volition – indwelling, not the stars, which to us seem the sole palpabilities, and for the accommodation of which we blindly deem space created – but that SPACE itself – that infinity of which the truly substantive vastness swallows up the star-shadows – blotting them out as nonentities from the perception of the angels.

P: You say that 'but for the *necessity* of the rudimental life' there would have been no stars. But why this necessity?

V: In the inorganic life, as well as in the inorganic matter generally, there is nothing to impede the action of one simple *unique* law – the Divine Volition. With the view of producing impediment, the organic life and matter (complex, substantial, and law-encumbered) were contrived.

P: But again – why need this impediment have been produced?

V: The result of law inviolate is perfection – right – negative happiness. The result of law violate is imperfection, wrong, positive pain. Through the impediments afforded by the number, complexity, and substantiality of the laws of organic life and matter, the violation of law is rendered, to a certain extent, practicable. Thus pain, which in the inorganic life is impossible, is possible in the organic.

P: But to what good end is pain thus rendered possible?

V: All things are either good or bad by comparison. A sufficient analysis will show that pleasure, in all cases, is but the contrast of pain. *Positive* pleasure is a mere idea. To be happy at any one point we must have suffered at the same. Never to suffer would have been never to have been blessed. But it has been shown that, in the inorganic life, pain cannot be thus the necessity for the organic. The pain of the primitive life of Earth is the sole basis of the bliss of the ultimate life in Heaven.

P: Still, there is one of your expressions which I find it impossible to comprehend – 'the truly *substantive* vastness of infinity'.

V: This, probably, is because you have no sufficiently generic conception of the term '*substance*' itself. We must not regard it as a quality, but as a sentiment – it is the perception, in thinking beings, of the adaptation of matter to their organisation. There are many things on the Earth, which would be nihility to the inhabitants of Venus – many things visible and tangible in Venus, which we could not be brought to appreciate as existing at all. But to the inorganic beings – to the angels – the whole of the unparticled matter is substance; that is to say, the whole of what we term 'space' is to them the truest substantiality – the stars, meantime, through what we consider their materiality, escaping the angelic sense, just in proportion as the unparticled matter, through what we consider its immateriality, eludes the organic.

As the sleep-waker pronounced these latter words, in a feeble tone, I observed on his countenance a singular expression, which somewhat alarmed me, and induced me to awake him at once. No sooner had I done this, than, with a bright smile irradiating all his features, he fell back upon his pillow and expired. I noticed that in less than a minute afterwards his corpse had all the stern rigidity of stone. His brow was of the coldness of ice. Thus, ordinarily, should it have appeared, only after long pressure from Azrael's hand. Had the sleep-waker, indeed, during the latter portion of his discourse, been addressing me from out the region of the shadows?

A Tale of the Ragged Mountains

During the fall of the year 1827, while residing near Charlottesville, Virginia, I casually made the acquaintance of Mr Augustus Bedloe. This young gentleman was remarkable in every respect, and excited in me a profound interest and curiosity. I found it impossible to comprehend him either in his moral or his physical relations. Of his family I could obtain no satisfactory account. Whence he came, I never ascertained. Even about his age – although I call him a young gentleman – there was something which perplexed me in no little degree. He certainly seemed young – and he made a point of speaking about his youth – yet there were moments when I should have had little trouble in imagining him a hundred years of age. But in no regard was he more peculiar than in his personal appearance. He was singularly tall and thin. He stooped much. His limbs were exceedingly long and emaciated. His forehead was broad and low. His complexion was absolutely bloodless. His mouth was large and flexible, and his teeth were more wildly uneven, although sound, than I had ever before seen teeth in a human head. The expression of his smile, however, was by no means unpleasing, as might be supposed; but it had no variation whatever. It was one of profound melancholy – of a phaseless and unceasing gloom. His eyes were abnormally large, and round like those of a cat. The pupils, too, upon any accession or diminution of light, underwent contraction or dilation, just such as is observed in the feline tribe. In moments of excitement the orbs grew bright to a degree almost inconceivable; seeming to emit luminous rays, not of a reflected but of an intrinsic lustre, as does a candle or the sun; yet their ordinary condition was so totally vapid, filmy, and dull as to convey the idea of the eyes of a long-interred corpse.

These peculiarities of person appeared to cause him much annoyance, and he was continually alluding to them in a sort of half-explanatory, half-apologetic strain, which, when I first heard it, impressed me very painfully. I soon, however, grew accustomed to it, and my uneasiness wore off. It seemed to be his design rather to insinuate than directly to assert that, physically, he had not always been what he was – that a long series of neuralgic attacks had reduced him from a condition of more than usual personal beauty, to that which I saw. For many years past he had been attended by a physician, named Templeton – an old gentleman, perhaps seventy years of age – whom he had first encountered at Saratoga, and from whose attention, while there, he either received, or fancied that he received, great benefit. The result was that Bedloe, who was wealthy, had made an arrangement with Dr Templeton, by which the latter, in consideration of a liberal annual allowance, had consented to devote his time and medical experience exclusively to the care of the invalid.

Doctor Templeton had been a traveller in his younger days, and at Paris had become a convert, in great measure, to the doctrines of Mesmer. It was altogether by means of magnetic remedies that he had succeeded in alleviating the acute pains of his patient; and this success had very naturally inspired the latter with a certain degree of confidence in the opinions from which the remedies had been educed. The Doctor, however, like all enthusiasts, had struggled hard to make a thorough convert of his pupil, and finally so far gained his point as to induce the sufferer to submit to numerous experiments. By a frequent repetition of these, a result had arisen, which of late days has become so common as to attract little or no attention, but which, at the period of which I write, had very rarely been known in America. I mean to say, that between Doctor Templeton and Bedloe there had grown up, little by little, a very distinct and strongly marked rapport, or magnetic relation. I am not prepared to assert, however, that this rapport extended beyond the limits of the simple sleep-producing power, but this power itself had attained great intensity. At the first attempt to induce the magnetic somnolency, the mesmerist entirely failed. In the fifth or sixth he succeeded very partially, and after long continued effort. Only at the twelfth was the triumph complete. After this the will of the patient succumbed rapidly to that of the physician, so that, when I first became acquainted with the two, sleep was brought about almost instantaneously by the mere volition of the operator, even when the invalid was unaware of his presence. It is only now, in the year 1845, when similar miracles are witnessed daily by thousands, that I dare venture to record this apparent impossibility as a matter of serious fact.

The temperature of Bedloe was in the highest degree sensitive, excitable, enthusiastic. His imagination was singularly vigorous and creative; and no doubt it derived additional force from the habitual use of morphine, which he swallowed in great quantity, and without which he would have found it impossible to exist. It was his practice to take a very large dose of it immediately after breakfast each morning – or, rather, immediately after a cup of strong coffee, for he ate nothing in the forenoon – and then set forth alone, or attended only by a dog, upon a long ramble among the chain of wild and dreary hills that lie westward and southward of Charlottesville, and are there dignified by the title of the Ragged Mountains.

Upon a dim, warm, misty day, towards the close of November, and during the strange interregnum of the seasons which in America is termed the Indian summer, Mr Bedloe departed as usual for the hills. The day passed, and still he did not return.

About eight o'clock at night, having become seriously alarmed at his protracted absence, we were about setting out in search of him, when he unexpectedly made his appearance, in health no worse than usual, and in rather more than ordinary spirits. The account which he gave of his expedition, and of the events which had detained him, was a singular one indeed.

'You will remember,' said he, 'that it was about nine in the morning when I left Charlottesville. I bent my steps immediately to the mountains, and, about ten, entered a gorge which was entirely new to me. I followed the windings of this pass with much interest. The scenery which presented itself on all sides, although scarcely entitled to be called grand, had about it an indescribable and to me a delicious aspect of dreary desolation. The solitude seemed absolutely virgin. I could not help believing that the green sods and the grey rocks upon which I trod had been trodden never before by the foot of a human being. So entirely secluded, and in fact inaccessible, except through a series of accidents, is the entrance of the ravine, that it is by no means impossible that I was indeed the first adventurer – the very first and sole adventurer who had ever penetrated its recesses.

'The thick and peculiar mist, or smoke, which distinguishes the Indian summer, and which now hung heavily over all objects, served, no doubt, to deepen the vague impressions which these objects created. So dense was this pleasant fog that I could at no time see more than a dozen yards of the path before me. This path was excessively sinuous, and as the sun could not be seen, I soon lost all idea of the direction in which I journeyed. In the meantime the morphine had its customary effect – that of enduing all the external world with an intensity of interest. In the quivering of a leaf – in the hue of a blade of grass – in the shape of a trefoil – in the humming of a bee – in the gleaming of a dew drop – in the breathing of the wind – in the faint odours that came from the forest – there came a whole universe of suggestion – a gay and motley train of rhapsodical and immethodical thought.

'Busied in this, I walked on for several hours, during which the mist deepened around me to so great an extent that at length I was reduced to an absolute groping of the way. And now an indescribable uneasiness possessed me – a species of nervous hesitation and tremor. I feared to tread, lest I should be precipitated into some abyss. I remembered, too, strange stories told about these Ragged Hills, and of the uncouth and fierce races of men who tenanted their groves and caverns. A thousand vague fancies oppressed and disconcerted me – fancies the more distressing because vague. Very suddenly my attention was arrested by the loud beating of a drum.

'My amazement was, of course, extreme. A drum in these hills was a thing unknown. I could not have been more surprised at the sound of the trump of the Archangel. But a new and still more astounding source of interest and perplexity arose. There came a wild rattling or jingling sound, as if of a bunch of large keys, and upon the instant a dusky-visaged and half-naked man rushed past me with a shriek. He came so close to my person that I felt his hot breath upon my face. He bore in one hand an instrument composed of an assemblage of steel rings, and shook them vigorously as he ran. Scarcely had he disappeared in the mist before, panting after him, with open mouth and glaring eyes, there darted a huge beast. I could not be mistaken in its character. It was a hyena.

'The sight of this monster rather relieved than heightened my terrors – for I now made sure that I dreamed, and endeavoured to arouse myself to waking consciousness. I stepped boldly and briskly forward. I rubbed my eyes. I called aloud. I pinched my limbs. A small spring of water presented itself to my view, and here, stooping, I bathed my hands and my head and neck. This seemed to dissipate the equivocal sensations which had hitherto annoyed me. I arose, as I thought, a new man, and proceeded steadily and complacently on my unknown way.

'At length, quite overcome by exertion, and by a certain oppressive closeness of the atmosphere, I seated myself beneath a tree. Presently there came a feeble gleam of sunshine, and the shadow of the leaves of the tree fell faintly but definitely upon the grass. At this shadow I gazed wonderingly for many minutes. Its character stupefied me with astonishment. I looked upwards. The tree was a palm.

'I now arose hurriedly, and in a state of fearful agitation – for the fancy that I dreamed would serve me no longer. I saw – I felt that I had perfect command of my senses – and these senses now brought to my soul a world of novel and singular sensation. The heat became all at once intolerable. A strange odour loaded the breeze. A low, continuous murmur, like that arising from a full, but gently flowing river, came to my ears, intermingled with the peculiar hum of multitudinous human voices.

'While I listened in an extremity of astonishment which I need not attempt to describe, a strong and brief gust of wind bore off the incumbent fog as if by the wand of an enchanter.

'I found myself at the foot of a high mountain, and looking down into a vast plain, through which wound a majestic river. On the margin of this river stood an Eastern-looking city, such as we read of in the Arabian Tales, but of a character even more singular than any there described. From my position, which was far above the level of the town, I could perceive its every nook and corner, as if delineated on a map. The streets seemed innumerable, and crossed each other irregularly in all directions, but were rather long winding alleys than streets, and absolutely swarmed with inhabitants. The houses were wildly picturesque. On every hand was a wilderness of balconies, of verandas, of minarets, of shrines, and fantastically carved oriels. Bazaars abounded; and in these were displayed rich wares in infinite variety and profusion – silks, muslins, the most dazzling cutlery, the most magnificent jewels and gems. Besides these things, were seen, on all sides, banners and palanquins, litters with stately dames close veiled, elephants gorgeously caparisoned, idols grotesquely hewn, drums, banners, and gongs, spears, silver and gilded maces. And amid the crowd, and the clamour, and the general intricacy and confusion – amid the million of black and yellow men, turbaned and robed, and of flowing beard, there roamed a countless multitude of holy filleted bulls, while vast legions of the filthy but sacred ape clambered, chattering and shrieking, about the cornices of the mosques, or clung to the minarets and oriels. From the swarming streets to the banks of the river, there descended innumerable flights of steps leading to bathing places, while the river itself seemed to force a passage with difficulty through the vast fleets of deeply burdened ships that far and wide encountered its surface. Beyond the limits of the city arose, in frequent majestic groups, the palm and the cocoa, with other gigantic and weird trees of vast age, and here and there might be seen a field of rice, the thatched hut of a peasant, a tank, a stray temple, a gypsy camp, or a solitary graceful maiden taking her way, with a pitcher upon her head, to the banks of the magnificent river.

'You will say now, of course, that I dreamed; but not so. What I saw – what I heard – what I felt – what I thought – had about it nothing of the unmistakable idiosyncrasy of the dream. All was rigorously self-consistent. At first, doubting that I was really awake, I entered into a series of tests, which soon convinced me that I really was. Now, when one dreams, and, in the dream, suspects that he dreams, the suspicion never fails to confirm itself, and the sleeper is almost immediately aroused. Thus Novalis errs not in saying that "we are near waking when we dream that we dream". Had the vision occurred to me as I describe it, without my suspecting it as a dream, then a dream it might absolutely have been, but, occurring as it did, and suspected and tested as it was, I am forced to class it among other phenomena.'

'In this I am not sure that you are wrong,' observed Dr Templeton, 'but proceed. You arose and descended into the city.'

'I arose,' continued Bedloe, regarding the Doctor with an air of profound astonishment, 'I arose, as you say, and descended into the city. On my way I fell in with an immense populace, crowding through every avenue, all in the same direction, and exhibiting in every action the wildest excitement. Very suddenly, and by some inconceivable impulse, I became intensely imbued with personal interest in what was going on. I seemed to feel that I had an important part to play, without exactly understanding what it was. Against the crowd which environed me, however, I experienced a deep sentiment of animosity. I shrank from amid them, and, swiftly, by a circuitous path, reached and entered the city. Here all was the wildest tumult and contention. A small party of men, clad in garments half-Indian, half-European, and officered by gentlemen in a uniform partly British, were engaged, at great odds, with the swarming rabble of the alleys. I joined the weaker party, arming myself with the weapons of a fallen officer, and fighting I knew not whom with the nervous ferocity of despair. We were soon overpowered by numbers, and driven to seek refuge in a species of kiosk. Here we barricaded ourselves, and, for the present, were secure. From a loophole near the summit of the kiosk, I perceived a vast crowd, in furious agitation, surrounding and assaulting a gay palace that overhung the river. Presently, from an upper window of this place, there descended an effeminate-looking person, by means of a string made of the turbans of his attendants. A boat was at hand, in which he escaped to the opposite bank of the river.

'And now a new object took possession of my soul. I spoke a few hurried but energetic words to my companions, and, having succeeded in gaining over a few of them to my purpose made a frantic sally from the kiosk. We rushed amid the crowd that surrounded it. They retreated, at first, before us. They rallied, fought madly, and retreated again. In the meantime we were borne far from the kiosk, and became bewildered and entangled among the narrow streets of tall, overhanging houses, into the recesses of which the sun had never been able to shine. The rabble pressed impetuously upon us, harassing us with their spears, and overwhelming us with flights of arrows. These latter were very remarkable, and resembled in some respects the writhing *kris* of the Malay. They were made to imitate the body of a creeping serpent, and were long and black, with a poisoned barb. One of them struck me upon the right temple. I reeled and fell. An instantaneous and dreadful sickness seized me. I struggled – I gasped – I died.'

'You will hardly persist now,' said I, smiling, 'that the whole of your adventure was not a dream. You are not prepared to maintain that you are dead?'

When I said these words, I of course expected some lively sally from Bedloe in reply, but, to my astonishment, he hesitated, trembled, became fearfully pallid, and remained silent. I looked towards Templeton. He sat erect and rigid in his chair – his teeth chattered, and his eyes were starting from their sockets. 'Proceed!' he at length said hoarsely to Bedloe.

'For many minutes,' continued the latter, 'my sole sentiment – my sole feeling – was that of darkness and nonentity, with the consciousness of death. At length there seemed to pass a violent and sudden shock through my soul, as if of electricity. With it came the sense of elasticity and of light. This latter I felt – not saw. In an instant I seemed to rise from the ground. But I had no bodily, no visible, audible, or palpable presence. The crowd had departed. The tumult had ceased. The city was in comparative repose. Beneath me lay my corpse, with the arrow in my temple, the whole head greatly swollen and disfigured. But all these things I felt – not saw. I took interest in nothing. Even the corpse seemed a matter in which I had no concern. Volition I had none, but appeared to be impelled into motion, and flitted buoyantly out of the city, retracing the circuitous path by which I had entered it. When I had attained that point of the ravine in the mountains at which I had encountered the hyena, I again experienced a shock as of a galvanic battery, the sense of weight, of volition, of substance, returned. I became my original self, and bent my steps eagerly homewards – but the past had not lost the vividness of the real – and not now, even for an instant, can I compel my understanding to regard it as a dream.'

'Nor was it,' said Templeton, with an air of deep solemnity, 'yet it would be difficult to say how otherwise it should be termed. Let us suppose only, that the soul of the man of today is upon the verge of some stupendous psychic discoveries. Let us content ourselves with this supposition. For the rest I have some explanation to make. Here is a watercolour drawing, which I should have shown you before, but which an unaccountable sentiment of horror has hitherto prevented me from showing.'

We looked at the picture which he presented. I saw nothing in it of an extraordinary character, but its effect upon Bedloe was prodigious. He nearly fainted as he gazed. And yet it was but a miniature portrait – a miraculously accurate one, to be sure – of his own very remarkable features. At least this was my thought as I regarded it.

'You will perceive,' said Templeton, 'the date of this picture – it is here, scarcely visible, in this corner – 1780. In this year was the portrait taken. It is the likeness of a dead friend – a Mr Oldeb – to whom I became much attached at Calcutta, during the administration of Warren Hastings. I was then only twenty years old. When I first saw you, Mr Bedloe, at Saratoga, it was the miraculous similarity which existed between yourself and the painting which induced me to accost you, to seek your friendship, and to bring about those arrangements which resulted in my becoming your constant companion. In accomplishing this point, I was urged partly, and perhaps principally, by a regretful memory of the deceased, but also, in part, by an uneasy, and not altogether horrorless curiosity respecting yourself.

'In your detail of the vision which presented itself to you amid the hills, you have described, with the minutest accuracy, the Indian city of Benares, upon the Holy River. The riots, the combat, the massacre, were the actual events of the insurrection of Cheyte Sing, which took place in 1780, when Hastings was put in imminent peril of his life. The man escaping by the string of turbans was Cheyte Sing himself. The party in the kiosk were sepoys and British officers, headed by Hastings. Of this party I was one, and did all I could to prevent the rash and fatal sally of the officer who fell, in the crowded alleys, by the poisoned arrow of a Bengalee. That officer was my dearest friend. It was Oldeb. You will perceive by these manuscripts' (here the speaker produced a notebook in which several pages appeared to have been freshly written) 'that at the very period in which you fancied these things amid the hills, I was engaged in detailing them upon paper here at home.'

In about a week after this conversation, the following paragraphs appeared in a Charlottesville paper:

We have the painful duty of announcing the death of Mr Augustus Bedlo, a gentleman whose amiable manners and many virtues have long endeared him to the citizens of Charlottesville.

Mr B——, for some years past, has been subject to neuralgia, which has often threatened to terminate fatally; but this can be regarded only as the mediate cause of his decease. The proximate cause was one of especial singularity. In an excursion to the Ragged Mountains, a few days since, a slight cold and fever were contracted, attended with great determination of blood to the head. To relieve this, Dr Templeton resorted to topical bleeding. Leeches were applied to the temples. In a fearfully brief period the patient died, when it appeared that in the jar containing the leeches, had been introduced, by accident, one of the venomous vermicular *sangsues* which are now and then found in the neighbouring ponds. This creature fastened itself upon a small artery in the right temple. Its close resemblance to the medicinal leech caused the mistake to be overlooked until too late.

NB – The poisonous *sangsue* of Charlottesville may always be distinguished from the medicinal leech by its blackness, and especially by its writhing or vermicular motions, which very nearly resemble those of a snake.

I was speaking with the editor of the paper in question, upon the topic of this remarkable accident, when it occurred to me to ask how it happened that the name of the deceased had been given as Bedlo.

'I presume,' I said, 'you have authority for this spelling, but I have always supposed the name to be written with an e at the end.'

'Authority? – no,' he replied. 'It is a mere typographical error. The name is Bedlo with an e, all the world over, and I never knew it to be spelt otherwise in my life.'

'Then,' said I mutteringly, as I turned upon my heel, 'then indeed has it come to pass that one truth is stranger than any fiction – for Bedloe, without the e, what is it but Oldeb conversed! And this man tells me that it is a typographical error.'

The Spectacles

Many years ago, it was the fashion to ridicule the idea of 'love at first sight'; but those who think, not less than those who feel deeply, have always advocated its existence. Modern discoveries, indeed, in what may be termed ethical magnetism or magneto-aesthetics, render it probable that the most natural, and, consequently, the truest and most intense of the human affections are those which arise in the heart as if by electric sympathy – in a word, that the brightest and most enduring of the psychic fetters are those which are riveted by a glance. The confession I am about to make will add another to the already almost innumerable instances of the truth of the position.

My story requires that I should be somewhat minute. I am still a very young man – not yet twenty-two years of age. My name, at present, is a very usual and rather plebeian one – Simpson. I say 'at present'; for it is only lately that I have been so called – having legislatively adopted this surname within the last year in order to receive a large inheritance left me by a distant male relative, Adolphus Simpson, Esq. The bequest was conditioned upon my taking the name of the testator – the family, not the Christian name; my Christian name is Napoleon Bonaparte – or, more properly, these are my first and middle appellations.

I assumed the name, Simpson, with some reluctance, as in my true patronym, Froissart, I felt a very pardonable pride – believing that I could trace a descent from the immortal author of the *Chronicles*.

While on the subject of names, by the by, I may mention a singular coincidence of sound attending the names of some of my immediate predecessors. My father was a M. Froissart, of Paris. His wife – my mother, whom he married at fifteen – was a Mlle Croissart, eldest daughter of Croissart the banker, whose wife, again, being only sixteen when married, was the eldest daughter of one Victor Voissart. M. Voissart, very singularly, had married a lady of similar name – a Mlle Moissart. She, too, was quite a child when married; and her mother, also, Mme Moissart, was only fourteen when led to the altar. These early marriages are usual in France. Here, however, are Moissart, Voissart, Croissart, and Froissart, all in the direct line of descent. My own name, though, as I say, became Simpson, by act of Legislature, and with so much repugnance on my part, that, at one period, I actually hesitated about accepting the legacy with the useless and annoying proviso attached.

As to personal endowments, I am by no means deficient. On the contrary, I believe that I am well made, and possess what nine-tenths of the world would call a handsome face. In height I am five feet eleven. My hair is black and curling. My nose is sufficiently good. My eyes are large and grey; and although, in fact, they are weak to a very inconvenient degree, still no defect in this regard would be suspected from their appearance. The weakness itself, however, has always much annoyed me, and I have resorted to every remedy – short of wearing glasses. Being youthful and good-looking, I naturally dislike these, and have reso-lutely refused to employ them. I know nothing, indeed, which so disfigures the countenance of a young person, or so impresses every feature with an air of demureness, if not altogether of sanctimoniousness and of age. An eyeglass, on the other hand, has a savour of downright foppery and affectation. I have hitherto managed as well as I could without either. But something too much of these merely personal details, which, after all, are of little importance. I will content myself with saying, in addition, that my temperament is sanguine, rash, ardent, enthusiastic – and that all my life I have been a devoted admirer of the women.

One night last winter I entered a box at the P— Theatre, in company with a friend, Mr Talbot. It was an opera night, and the bills presented a very rare attraction, so that the house was excessively crowded. We were in time, however, to obtain the front seats which had been reserved for us, and into which, with some little difficulty, we elbowed our way.

For two hours my companion, who was a musical *fanatico*, gave his undivided attention to the stage; and, in the meantime, I amused myself by observing the audience, which consisted, in chief part, of the very elite of the city. Having satisfied myself upon this point, I was about turning my eyes to the prima donna, when they were arrested and riveted by a figure in one of the private boxes which had escaped my observation.

If I live a thousand years, I can never forget the intense emotion with which I regarded this figure. It was that of a female, the most exquisite I had ever beheld. The face was so far turned towards the stage that, for some minutes, I could not obtain a view of it – but the form was divine; no other word can sufficiently express its magnificent proportion – and even the term 'divine' seems ridiculously feeble as I write it.

The magic of a lovely form in woman – the necromancy of female gracefulness – was always a power which I had found it impossible to resist, but here was grace personified, incarnate, the beau ideal of my wildest and most enthusiastic visions. The figure, almost all of which the construction of the box permitted to be seen, was somewhat above the medium height, and nearly approached, without positively reaching, the majestic. Its perfect fullness and *tournure* were delicious. The head, of which only the back was visible, rivalled in outline that of the Greek Psyche, and was rather displayed than concealed by an elegant cap of *gaze aérienne*, which put me in mind of the *ventum textilem* of Apuleius. The right arm hung over the balustrade of the box, and thrilled every nerve of my frame with its exquisite symmetry. Its upper portion was draperied by one of the loose open sleeves now in fashion. This extended but little below the elbow. Beneath it was worn an under one of some frail material, close-fitting, and terminated by a cuff of rich lace, which fell gracefully over the top of the hand, revealing only the delicate fingers, upon one of which sparkled a diamond ring, which I at once saw was of extraordinary value. The admirable roundness of the wrist was well set off by a bracelet which encircled it, and which also was ornamented and clasped by a magnificent *aigrette* of jewels – telling, in words that could not be mistaken, at once of the wealth and fastidious taste of the wearer.

I gazed at this queenly apparition for at least half an hour, as if I had been suddenly converted to stone; and, during this period, I felt the full force and truth of all that has been said or sung concerning 'love at first sight'. My feelings were totally different from any which I had hitherto experienced, in the presence of even the most celebrated specimens of female loveliness. An unaccountable, and what I am compelled to consider a magnetic, sympathy of soul for soul, seemed to rivet, not only my vision, but my whole powers of thought and feeling, upon the admirable object before me. I saw – I felt – I knew that I was deeply, madly, irrevocably in love – and this even before seeing the face of the person beloved. So intense, indeed, was the passion that consumed me, that I really believe it would have received little if any abatement had the features, yet unseen, proved of merely ordinary character, so anomalous is the nature of the only true love – of the love at first sight – and so little really dependent is it upon the external conditions which only seem to create and control it.

While I was thus wrapped in admiration of this lovely vision, a sudden disturbance among the audience caused her to turn her head partially towards me, so that I beheld the entire profile of the face. Its beauty even exceeded my anticipations – and yet there was something about it which disappointed me without my being able to tell exactly what it was. I said 'disappointed', but this is not altogether the word. My sentiments were at once quieted and exalted. They partook less of transport and more of calm enthusiasm – of enthusiastic repose. This state of feeling arose, perhaps, from the Madonna-like and matronly air of the face; and yet I at once understood that it could not have arisen entirely from this. There was something else – some mystery which I could not develop – some expression about the countenance which slightly disturbed me while it greatly heightened my interest. In fact, I was just in that condition of mind which prepares a young and susceptible man for any act of extravagance. Had the lady been alone,

I should undoubtedly have entered her box and accosted her at all hazards; but, fortunately, she was attended by two companions – a gentleman, and a strikingly beautiful woman, to all appearance a few years younger than herself.

I revolved in my mind a thousand schemes by which I might obtain, hereafter, an introduction to the elder lady, or, for the present, at all events, a more distinct view of her beauty. I would have removed my position to one nearer her own, but the crowded state of the theatre rendered this impossible; and the stern decrees of Fashion had, of late, imperatively prohibited the use of the opera-glass in a case such as this, even had I been so fortunate as to have one with me – but I had not – and was thus in despair.

At length I bethought me of applying to my companion.

'Talbot,' I said, 'you have an opera-glass. Let me have it.'

'An opera-glass! – no! – what do you suppose I would be doing with an opera-glass?' Here he turned impatiently towards the stage.

'But, Talbot,' I continued, pulling him by the shoulder, 'listen to me, will you? Do you see the stage-box? – there! – no, the next. – Did you ever behold as lovely a woman?'

'She is very beautiful, no doubt,' he said.

'I wonder who she can be?'

'Why, in the name of all that is angelic, don't you *know* who she is? "Not to know her argues yourself unknown." She is the celebrated Mme Lalande – the beauty of the day *par excellence*, and the talk of the whole town. Immensely wealthy too – a widow, and a great match. She has just arrived from Paris.'

'Do you know her?'

'Yes; I have the honour.'

'Will you introduce me?'

'Assuredly, with the greatest pleasure; when shall it be?'

'Tomorrow, at one, I will call upon you at B—'s.'

'Very good; and now *do* hold your tongue, *if* you can.'

In this latter respect I was forced to take Talbot's advice; for he remained obstinately deaf to every further question or suggestion, and occupied himself exclusively for the rest of the evening with what was transacting upon the stage.

In the meantime I kept my eyes riveted on Mme Lalande, and at length had the good fortune to obtain a full front view of her face. It was exquisitely lovely – this, of course, my heart had told me before, even had not Talbot fully satisfied me upon the point – but still the unintelligible something disturbed me. I finally concluded that my senses were impressed by a certain air of gravity, sadness, or, still more properly, of weariness, which took something from the youth and freshness of the countenance, only to endow it with a seraphic tenderness and majesty, and thus, of course, to my enthusiastic and romantic temperament, with an interest tenfold.

While I thus feasted my eyes, I perceived, at last, to my great trepidation, by an almost imperceptible start on the part of the lady, that she had become suddenly aware of the intensity of my gaze. Still, I was absolutely fascinated, and could not withdraw it, even for an instant. She turned aside her face, and again I saw only the chiselled contour of the back portion of the head. After some minutes, as if urged by curiosity to see if I was still looking, she gradually brought her face again around and again encountered my burning gaze. Her large dark eyes fell instantly, and a deep blush mantled her cheek. But what was my astonishment at perceiving that she not only did not a second time avert her head, but that she actually took from her girdle a double eyeglass – elevated it – adjusted it – and then regarded me through it, intently and deliberately, for the space of several minutes.

Had a thunderbolt fallen at my feet I could not have been more thoroughly astounded – astounded only – not offended or disgusted in the slightest degree; although an action so bold in any other woman would have been likely to offend or disgust. But the whole thing was done with so much quietude – so much nonchalance – so much repose – with so evident an air of the highest breeding, in short – that nothing of mere effrontery was perceptible, and my sole sentiments were those of admiration and surprise.

I observed that, upon her first elevation of the glass, she had seemed satisfied with a momentary inspection of my person, and was withdrawing the instrument, when, as if struck by a second thought, she resumed it, and so continued to regard me with fixed attention for the space of several minutes – for five minutes, at the very least, I am sure.

This action, so remarkable in an American theatre, attracted very general observation, and gave rise to an indefinite movement, or buzz, among the audience, which for a moment filled me with confusion, but produced no visible effect upon the countenance of Mme Lalande.

Having satisfied her curiosity – if such it was – she dropped the glass, and quietly gave her attention again to the stage; her profile now being turned towards myself, as before. I continued to watch her unremittingly, although I was fully conscious of my rudeness in so doing. Presently I saw the head slowly and slightly change its position; and soon I became convinced that the lady, while pretending to look at the stage was, in fact, attentively regarding myself. It is needless to say what effect this conduct, on the part of so fascinating a woman, had upon my excitable mind.

Having thus scrutinised me for perhaps a quarter of an hour, the fair object of my passion addressed the gentleman who attended her, and while she spoke, I saw distinctly, by the glances of both, that the conversation had reference to myself.

Upon its conclusion, Mme Lalande again turned towards the stage, and, for a few minutes, seemed absorbed in the performance. At the expiration of this period, however, I was thrown into an extremity of agitation by seeing her unfold, for the second time, the eyeglass which hung at her side, fully confront me as before, and, disregarding the renewed buzz of the audience, survey me, from head to foot, with the same miraculous composure which had previously so delighted and confounded my soul.

This extraordinary behaviour, by throwing me into a perfect fever of excitement – into an absolute delirium of love – served rather to embolden than to disconcert me. In the mad intensity of my devotion, I forgot everything but the presence and the majestic loveliness of the vision which confronted my gaze. Watching my opportunity, when I thought the audience were fully engaged with the opera, I at length caught the eyes of Mme Lalande, and, upon the instant, made a slight but unmistakable bow.

She blushed very deeply – then averted her eyes – then slowly and cautiously looked around, apparently to see if my rash action had been noticed – then leaned over towards the gentleman who sat by her side.

I now felt a burning sense of the impropriety I had committed, and expected nothing less than instant exposure; while a vision of pistols upon the morrow floated rapidly and uncomfortably through my brain. I was greatly and immediately relieved, however, when I saw the lady merely hand the gentleman a playbill, without speaking; but the reader may form some feeble conception of my astonishment – of my profound amazement – my delirious bewilderment of heart and soul – when, instantly afterwards, having again glanced furtively around, she allowed her bright eyes to set fully and steadily upon my own, and then, with a faint smile, disclosing a bright line of her pearly teeth, made two distinct, pointed, and unequivocal affirmative inclinations of the head.

It is useless, of course, to dwell upon my joy – upon my transport – upon my illimitable ecstasy of heart. If ever man was mad with excess of happiness, it was myself at that moment. I loved. This was my first love – so I felt it to be. It was love supreme – indescribable. It was 'love at first sight'; and at first sight, too, it had been appreciated and returned.

Yes, returned. How and why should I doubt it for an instant. What other construction could I possibly put upon such conduct, on the part of a lady so beautiful – so wealthy – evidently so accomplished – of so high breeding – of so lofty a position in society – in every regard so entirely respectable as I felt assured was Mme Lalande? Yes, she loved me – she returned the enthusiasm of my love, with an enthusiasm as blind – as uncompromising – as uncalculating – as abandoned – and as utterly unbounded as my own! These delicious fancies and reflections, however, were now interrupted by the falling of the drop-curtain. The audience arose; and the usual tumult immediately supervened. Quitting Talbot abruptly, I made every effort to force my way into closer proximity with Mme Lalande. Having failed in this, on account of the crowd, I at length gave up the chase, and bent my steps homewards; consoling myself for my disappointment in not having been able to touch even the hem of her robe by the reflection that I should be introduced by Talbot, in due form, upon the morrow.

This morrow at last came; that is to say, a day finally dawned upon a long and weary night of impatience; and then the hours until 'one' were snail-paced, dreary, and innumerable. But even Stamboul, it is said, shall have an end, and there came an end to this long delay. The clock struck. As the last echo ceased, I stepped into B—'s and enquired for Talbot.

'Out,' said the footman – Talbot's own.

'Out!' I replied, staggering back half a dozen paces – 'let me tell you, my fine fellow, that this thing is thoroughly impossible and impracticable; Mr Talbot is not out. What do you mean?'

'Nothing, sir; only Mr Talbot is not in, that's all. He rode over to S—, immediately after breakfast, and left word that he would not be in town again for a week.'

I stood petrified with horror and rage. I endeavoured to reply, but my tongue refused its office. At length I turned on my heel, livid with wrath, and inwardly consigning the whole tribe of the Talbots to the innermost regions of Erebus. It was evident that my considerate friend, *il fanatico*, had quite forgotten his appointment with myself – had forgotten it as soon as it was made. At no time was he a very scrupulous man of his word. There was no help for it; so smothering my vexation as well as I could, I strolled moodily up the street, propounding futile enquiries about Mme Lalande to every male acquaintance I met. By report she was known, I found, to all – to many by sight – but she had been in town only a few weeks, and there were very few, therefore, who claimed her personal acquaintance. These few, being still comparatively strangers, could not, or would not, take the liberty of introducing me through the formality of a morning call. While I stood thus in despair, conversing with a trio of friends upon the all-absorbing subject of my heart, it so happened that the subject itself passed by.

'As I live, there she is!' cried one.

'Surprisingly beautiful!' exclaimed a second.

'An angel upon earth!' ejaculated a third.

I looked; and in an open carriage which approached us, passing slowly down the street, sat the enchanting vision of the opera, accompanied by the younger lady who had occupied a portion of her box.

'Her companion also wears remarkably well,' said the one of my trio who had spoken first.

'Astonishingly,' said the second; 'still quite a brilliant air, but art will do wonders. Upon my word, she looks better than she did at Paris five years ago. A beautiful woman still – don't you think so, Froissart? – Simpson, I mean.'

'Still!' said I, 'and why shouldn't she be? But compared with her friend she is as a rush-light to the evening star – a glow-worm to Antares.'

'Ha! ha! ha! – why, Simpson, you have an astonishing

tact at making discoveries – original ones, I mean.' And here we separated, while one of the trio began humming a gay vaudeville, of which I caught only the lines:

> Ninon, Ninon, Ninon à bas –
> À bas Ninon de L'Enclos!

During this little scene, however, one thing had served greatly to console me, although it fed the passion by which I was consumed. As the carriage of Mme Lalande rolled by our group, I had observed that she recognised me; and more than this, she had blessed me, by the most seraphic of all imaginable smiles, with no equivocal mark of the recognition.

As for an introduction, I was obliged to abandon all hope of it until such time as Talbot should think proper to return from the country. In the meantime I perseveringly frequented every reputable place of public amusement; and, at length, at the theatre, where I first saw her, I had the supreme bliss of meeting her, and of exchanging glances with her once again. This did not occur, however, until the lapse of a fortnight. Every day, in the interim, I had enquired for Talbot at his hotel, and every day had been thrown into a spasm of wrath by the everlasting 'Not come home yet' of his footman.

Upon the evening in question, therefore, I was in a condition little short of madness. Mme Lalande, I had been told, was a Parisian – had lately arrived from Paris – might she not suddenly return? – return before Talbot came back – and might she not be thus lost to me for ever? The thought was too terrible to bear. Since my future happiness was at issue, I resolved to act with a manly decision. In a word, upon the breaking up of the play, I traced the lady to her residence, noted the address, and the next morning sent her a full and elaborate letter, in which I poured out my whole heart.

I spoke boldly, freely – in a word, I spoke with passion. I concealed nothing – nothing even of my weakness. I alluded to the romantic circumstances of our first meeting – even to the glances which had passed between us. I went so far as to say that I felt assured of her love; while I offered this assurance, and my own intensity of devotion, as two excuses for my otherwise unpardonable conduct. As a third, I spoke of my fear that she might quit the city before I could have the opportunity of a formal introduction. I concluded the most wildly enthusiastic epistle ever penned, with a frank declaration of my worldly circumstances – of my affluence – and with an offer of my heart and of my hand.

In an agony of expectation I awaited the reply. After what seemed the lapse of a century it came.

Yes, actually came. Romantic as all this may appear, I really received a letter from Mme Lalande – the beautiful, the wealthy, the idolised Mme Lalande. Her eyes – her magnificent eyes, had not belied her noble heart. Like a true Frenchwoman as she was she had obeyed the frank dictates of her reason – the generous impulses of her nature – despising the conventional pruderies of the world. She had not scorned my proposals. She had not sheltered herself in silence. She had not returned my letter unopened. She had even sent me, in reply, one penned by her own exquisite fingers. It ran thus:

M. Simpson vill pardonne me for not compose de butefulle tong of his contrée so vell as might. It is only de late dat I am arrive, and not yet ave do opportunité for to – l'étudier.

Vid dis apologie for the manière, I vill now say dat, hélas! – M. Simpson ave guess but de too true. Need I say de more? Hélas! am I not ready speak de too moshe?

EUGÉNIE LALANDE

This noble-spirited note I kissed a million times, and committed, no doubt, on its account, a thousand other extravagances that have now escaped my memory. Still Talbot would not return. Alas! could he have formed even the vaguest idea of the suffering his absence had occasioned his friend, would not his sympathising nature have flown immediately to my relief? Still, however, he came not. I wrote. He replied. He was detained by urgent business – but would shortly return. He begged me not to be impatient – to moderate my transports – to read soothing books – to drink nothing stronger than Hock – and to bring the consolations of philosophy to my aid. The fool! if he could not come himself, why, in the name of everything rational, could he not have enclosed me a letter of presentation? I wrote him again, entreating him to forward one forthwith. My letter was returned by that footman, with the following endorsement in pencil. The scoundrel had joined his master in the country:

Left S— yesterday, for parts unknown – did not say where – or when be back – so thought best to return letter, knowing your handwriting, and as how you is always, more or less, in a hurry.

Yours sincerely,

STUBBS

322

After this, it is needless to say that I devoted to the infernal deities both master and valet – but there was little use in anger, and no consolation at all in complaint.

But I had yet a resource left, in my constitutional audacity. Hitherto it had served me well, and I now resolved to make it avail me to the end. Besides, after the correspondence which had passed between us, what act of mere informality could I commit, within bounds, that ought to be regarded as indecorous by Mme Lalande? Since the affair of the letter, I had been in the habit of watching her house, and thus discovered that, about twilight, it was her custom to promenade, attended only by a negro in livery, in a public square overlooked by her windows. Here, amid the luxuriant and shadowing groves, in the grey gloom of a sweet midsummer evening, I observed my opportunity and accosted her.

The better to deceive the servant in attendance, I did this with the assured air of an old and familiar acquaintance. With a presence of mind truly Parisian, she took the cue at once, and, to greet me, held out the most bewitchingly little of hands. The valet at once fell into the rear, and now, with hearts full to overflowing, we discoursed long and unreservedly of our love.

As Mme Lalande spoke English even less fluently than she wrote it, our conversation was necessarily in French. In this sweet tongue, so adapted to passion, I gave loose to the impetuous enthusiasm of my nature, and, with all the eloquence I could command, besought her to consent to an immediate marriage.

At this impatience she smiled. She urged the old story of decorum – that bugbear which deters so many from bliss until the opportunity for bliss has forever gone by. I had most imprudently made it known

323

among my friends, she observed, that I desired her acquaintance – thus that I did not possess it – thus, again, there was no possibility of concealing the date of our first knowledge of each other. And then she adverted, with a blush, to the extreme recency of this date. To wed immediately would be improper – would be indecorous – would be *outré*. All this she said with a charming air of *naïveté* which enraptured while it grieved and convinced me. She went even so far as to accuse me, laughingly, of rashness – of imprudence. She bade me remember that I really even knew not who she was – what were her prospects, her connections, her standing in society. She begged me, but with a sigh, to reconsider my proposal, and termed my love an infatuation – a will o' the wisp – a fancy or fantasy of the moment – a baseless and unstable creation rather of the imagination than of the heart. These things she uttered as the shadows of the sweet twilight gathered darkly and more darkly around us – and then, with a gentle pressure of her fairy-like hand, overthrew, in a single sweet instant, all the argumentative fabric she had reared.

I replied as best I could – as only a true lover can. I spoke at length, and perseveringly of my devotion, of my passion – of her exceeding beauty, and of my own enthusiastic admiration. In conclusion, I dwelt, with a convincing energy, upon the perils that encompass the course of love – that course of true love that never did run smooth – and thus deduced the manifest danger of rendering that course unnecessarily long.

This latter argument seemed finally to soften the rigour of her determination. She relented; but there was yet an obstacle, she said, which she felt assured I had not properly considered. This was a delicate point

– for a woman to urge, especially so; in mentioning it, she saw that she must make a sacrifice of her feelings; still, for me, every sacrifice should be made. She alluded to the topic of age. Was I aware – was I fully aware of the discrepancy between us? That the age of the husband should surpass by a few years – even by fifteen or twenty – the age of the wife, was regarded by the world as admissible, and, indeed, as even proper, but she had always entertained the belief that the years of the wife should never exceed in number those of the husband. A discrepancy of this unnatural kind gave rise, too frequently, alas! to a life of unhappiness. Now she was aware that my own age did not exceed two and twenty; and I, on the contrary, perhaps, was not aware that the years of my Eugénie extended very considerably beyond that sum.

About all this there was a nobility of soul – a dignity of candour – which delighted – which enchanted me – which eternally riveted my chains. I could scarcely restrain the excessive transport which possessed me.

'My sweetest Eugénie,' I cried, 'what is all this about which you are discoursing? Your years surpass in some measure my own. But what then? The customs of the world are so many conventional follies. To those who love as ourselves, in what respect differs a year from an hour? I am twenty-two, you say; granted: indeed, you may as well call me, at once, twenty-three. Now you yourself, my dearest Eugénie, can have numbered no more than – can have numbered no more than – no more than – than – than – than – '

Here I paused for an instant, in the expectation that Mme Lalande would interrupt me by supplying her true age. But a Frenchwoman is seldom direct, and has always, by way of answer to an embarrassing query, some little practical reply of her own. In the present instance, Eugénie, who for a few moments past had seemed to be searching for something in her bosom, at length let fall upon the grass a miniature, which I immediately picked up and presented to her.

'Keep it!' she said, with one of her most ravishing smiles. 'Keep it for my sake – for the sake of her whom it too flatteringly represents. Besides, upon the back of the trinket you may discover, perhaps, the very information you seem to desire. It is now, to be sure, growing rather dark – but you can examine it at your leisure in the morning. In the meantime, you shall be my escort home tonight. My friends are about holding a little musical *levée*. I can promise you, too, some good singing. We French are not nearly so punctilious as you Americans, and I shall have no difficulty in smuggling you in, in the character of an old acquaintance.'

With this, she took my arm, and I attended her home. The mansion was quite a fine one, and, I believe, furnished in good taste. Of this latter point, however, I am scarcely qualified to judge; for it was just dark as we arrived; and in American mansions of the better sort lights seldom, during the heat of summer, make their appearance at this, the most pleasant period of the day. In about an hour after my arrival, to be sure, a single shaded solar lamp was lit in the principal drawing room; and this apartment, I could thus see, was arranged with unusual good taste and even splendour; but two other rooms of the suite, and in which the company chiefly assembled, remained, during the whole evening, in a very agreeable shadow. This is a well-conceived custom, giving the party at least a choice of light or shade, and one which our friends over the water could not do better than immediately adopt.

The evening thus spent was unquestionably the most delicious of my life. Mme Lalande had not overrated the musical abilities of her friends; and the singing I here heard I had never heard excelled in any private circle out of Vienna. The instrumental performers were many and of superior talents. The vocalists were chiefly ladies, and no individual sang less than well. At length, upon a peremptory call for 'Mme Lalande', she arose at once, without affectation or demur, from the *chaise longue* upon which she had sat by my side, and, accompanied by one or two gentlemen and her female friend of the opera, repaired to the piano in the main drawing room. I would have escorted her myself, but felt that, under the circumstances of my introduction to the house, I had better remain unobserved where I was. I was thus deprived of the pleasure of seeing, although not of hearing, her sing.

The impression she produced upon the company seemed electrical – but the effect upon myself was something even more. I know not how adequately to describe it. It arose in part, no doubt, from the sentiment of love with which I was imbued; but chiefly from my conviction of the extreme sensibility of the singer. It is beyond the reach of art to endow either air or recitative with more impassioned expression than was hers. Her utterance of the romance in *Otello* – the tone with which she gave the words '*Sul mio sasso*', in the Capuletti – is ringing in my memory yet. Her lower tones were absolutely miraculous. Her voice embraced three complete octaves, extending from the contralto D to the D upper soprano, and, though sufficiently powerful to have filled the San Carlos, executed, with the minutest precision, every difficulty of vocal composition – ascending and descending scales, cadences, or *fiorituri*. In the final of the *somnambula*, she brought about a most remarkable effect at the words:

> *Ah! non guinge uman pensiero*
> *Al contento ond 'io son piena.*

Here, in imitation of Malibran, she modified the original phrase of Bellini, so as to let her voice descend to the tenor G, when, by a rapid transition, she struck the G above the treble stave, springing over an interval of two octaves.

Upon rising from the piano after these miracles of vocal execution, she resumed her seat by my side; when I expressed to her, in terms of the deepest enthusiasm, my delight at her performance. Of my surprise I said nothing, and yet was I most unfeignedly surprised; for a certain feebleness, or rather a certain tremulous indecision of voice in ordinary conversation, had prepared me to anticipate that, in singing, she would not acquit herself with any remarkable ability.

Our conversation was now long, earnest, uninterrupted, and totally unreserved. She made me relate many of the earlier passages of my life, and listened with breathless attention to every word of the narrative. I concealed nothing – felt that I had a right to conceal nothing – from her confiding affection. Encouraged by her candour upon the delicate point of her age, I entered, with perfect frankness, not only into a detail of my many minor vices, but made full confession of those moral and even of those physical infirmities, the disclosure of which, in demanding so much higher a degree of courage, is so much surer an evidence of love. I touched upon my college indiscretions – upon my extravagances – upon my carousals – upon my debts – upon my flirtations. I even went so far as to speak of a slightly hectic cough with which, at one time, I had been troubled – of a chronic rheumatism – of a twinge of hereditary gout – and, in conclusion, of the disagreeable and inconvenient, but hitherto carefully concealed, weakness of my eyes.

'Upon this latter point,' said Mme Lalande, laughingly, 'you have been surely injudicious in coming to confession; for, without the confession, I take it for granted that no one would have accused you of the crime. By the by,' she continued, 'have you any recollection – ' and here I fancied that a blush, even through the gloom of the apartment, became distinctly visible upon her cheek – 'have you any recollection, *mon cher ami*, of this little ocular assistant, which now depends from my neck?'

As she spoke she twirled in her fingers the identical double eyeglass which had so overwhelmed me with confusion at the opera.

'Full well – alas! do I remember it,' I exclaimed, pressing passionately the delicate hand which offered the glasses for my inspection. They formed a complex and magnificent toy, richly chased and filigreed, and gleaming with jewels, which, even in the deficient light, I could not help perceiving were of high value.

'*Eh bien! mon ami*,' she resumed with a certain *empressement* of manner that rather surprised me – '*Eh bien! mon ami*, you have earnestly besought of me a favour which you have been pleased to denominate priceless. You have demanded of me my hand upon the morrow. Should I yield to your entreaties – and, I may add, to the pleadings of my own bosom – would

I not be entitled to demand of you a very – a very little boon in return?'

'Name it!' I exclaimed with an energy that had nearly drawn upon us the observation of the company, and restrained by their presence alone from throwing myself impetuously at her feet. 'Name it, my beloved, my Eugénie, my own! – name it! – but, alas! it is already yielded ere named.'

'You shall conquer, then, *mon ami*,' said she, 'for the sake of the Eugénie whom you love, this little weakness which you have at last confessed – this weakness more moral than physical – and which, let me assure you, is so unbecoming the nobility of your real nature – so inconsistent with the candour of your usual character – and which, if permitted further control, will assuredly involve you, sooner or later, in some very disagreeable scrape. You shall conquer, for my sake, this affectation which leads you, as you yourself acknowledge, to the tacit or implied denial of your infirmity of vision. For, this infirmity you virtually deny, in refusing to employ the customary means for its relief. You will understand me to say, then, that I wish you to wear spectacles – ah, hush! – you have already consented to wear them, for my sake. You shall accept the little toy which I now hold in my hand, and which, though admirable as an aid to vision, is really of no very immense value as a gem. You perceive that, by a trifling modification thus – or thus – it can be adapted to the eyes in the form of spectacles, or worn in the waistcoat pocket as an eyeglass. It is in the former mode, however, and habitually, that you have already consented to wear it for my sake.'

This request – must I confess it? – confused me in no little degree. But the condition with which it was coupled rendered hesitation, of course, a matter altogether out of the question.

'It is done!' I cried, with all the enthusiasm that I could muster at the moment. 'It is done – it is most cheerfully agreed. I sacrifice every feeling for your sake. Tonight I wear this dear eyeglass, as an eyeglass, and upon my heart; but with the earliest dawn of that morning which gives me the pleasure of calling you wife, I will place it upon my – upon my nose – and there wear it ever afterwards, in the less romantic, and less fashionable, but certainly in the more serviceable, form which you desire.'

Our conversation now turned upon the details of our arrangements for the morrow. Talbot, I learned from my betrothed, had just arrived in town. I was to see him at once, and procure a carriage. The *soirée* would scarcely break up before two; and by this hour the vehicle was to be at the door, when, in the confusion occasioned by the departure of the company, Mme L— could easily enter it unobserved. We were then to call at the house of a clergyman who would be in waiting; there be married, drop Talbot, and proceed on a short tour to the East, leaving the fashionable world at home to make whatever comments upon the matter it thought best.

Having planned all this, I immediately took leave, and went in search of Talbot, but, on the way, I could not refrain from stepping into a hotel, for the purpose of inspecting the miniature; and this I did by the powerful aid of the glasses. The countenance was a surpassingly beautiful one! Those large luminous eyes! – that proud Grecian nose! – those dark luxuriant curls! – 'Ah!' said I, exultingly to myself, 'this is indeed the speaking image of my beloved!' I turned the reverse, and discovered the words – 'Eugénie Lalande – aged twenty-seven years and seven months.'

I found Talbot at home, and proceeded at once to acquaint him with my good fortune. He professed excessive astonishment, of course, but congratulated me most cordially, and proffered every assistance in his power. In a word, we carried out our arrangement to the letter, and, at two in the morning, just ten minutes after the ceremony, I found myself in a close carriage with Mme Lalande – with Mrs Simpson, I should say – and driving at a great rate out of town, in a direction nor'east by north, half-north.

It had been determined for us by Talbot, that, as we were to be up all night, we should make our first stop at C—, a village about twenty miles from the city, and there get an early breakfast and some repose, before proceeding upon our route. At four precisely, therefore, the carriage drew up at the door of the principal inn. I handed my adored wife out, and ordered breakfast forthwith. In the meantime we were shown into a small parlour, and sat down.

It was now nearly if not altogether daylight; and, as I gazed, enraptured, at the angel by my side, the singular idea came, all at once, into my head, that this was really the very first moment since my acquaintance with the celebrated loveliness of Mme Lalande that I had enjoyed a near inspection of that loveliness by daylight at all.

'And now, *mon ami*,' said she, taking my hand, and so interrupting this train of reflection, 'and now, *mon cher ami*, since we are indissolubly one – since I have yielded to your passionate entreaties, and performed my portion of our agreement – I presume you have not forgotten that you also have a little favour to bestow – a little promise which it is your intention to keep. Ah! let me see! Let me remember! Yes; full easily do I call to mind the precise words of the dear promise you made to Eugénie last night. Listen! You spoke thus: "It is done! – it is most cheerfully agreed! I sacrifice every feeling for your sake. Tonight I wear this dear eyeglass as an eyeglass, and upon my heart; but with the earliest dawn of that morning which gives me the privilege of calling you wife, I will place it upon my – upon my nose – and there wear it ever afterwards, in the less romantic, and less fashionable, but certainly in the more serviceable, form which you desire." These were the exact words, my beloved husband, were they not?'

'They were,' I said; 'you have an excellent memory; and assuredly, my beautiful Eugénie, there is no disposition on my part to evade the performance of the trivial promise they imply. See! Behold! they are becoming – rather – are they not?' And here, having arranged the glasses in the ordinary form of spectacles, I applied them gingerly in their proper position; while Mme Simpson, adjusting her cap, and folding her arms, sat bolt upright in her chair, in a somewhat stiff and prim, and indeed, in a somewhat undignified position.

'Goodness gracious me!' I exclaimed, almost at the very instant that the rim of the spectacles had settled upon my nose – 'My goodness gracious me! – why, what can be the matter with these glasses?' and taking them quickly off, I wiped them carefully with a silk handkerchief, and adjusted them again.

But if, in the first instance, there had occurred something which occasioned me surprise, in the second, this surprise became elevated into astonishment; and this astonishment was profound – was extreme –

indeed I may say it was horrific. What, in the name of everything hideous, did this mean? Could I believe my eyes? – could I? – that was the question. Was that – was that – was that rouge? And were those – and were those – were those wrinkles, upon the visage of Eugénie Lalande? And oh! Jupiter, and every one of the gods and goddesses, little and big! what – what – what – what had become of her teeth? I dashed the spectacles violently to the ground, and, leaping to my feet, stood erect in the middle of the floor, confronting Mrs Simpson, with my arms set akimbo, and grinning and foaming, but, at the same time, utterly speechless with terror and with rage.

Now I have already said that Mme Eugénie Lalande – that is to say, Simpson – spoke the English language but very little better than she wrote it, and for this reason she very properly never attempted to speak it upon ordinary occasions. But rage will carry a lady to any extreme; and in the present case it carried Mrs Simpson to the very extraordinary extreme of attempting to hold a conversation in a tongue that she did not altogether understand.

'Vell, *monsieur*,' said she, after surveying me, in great apparent astonishment, for some moments – 'Vell, *monsieur*? – and vat den? – vat de matter now? Is it de dance of de St Vitusse dat you ave? If not like me, vat for vy buy de pig in the poke?'

'You wretch!' said I, catching my breath – 'you – you – you villainous old hag!'

'Ag? – ole? – me not so ver ole, after all! Me not one single day more dan de eighty-doo.'

'Eighty-two!' I ejaculated, staggering to the wall – 'eighty-two hundred thousand baboons! The miniature said twenty-seven years and seven months!'

'To be sure! – dat is so! – ver true! but den de portraite has been take for dese fifty-five year. Ven I go marry my segonde usbande, M. Lalande, at dat time I had de portraite take for my daughter by my first usbande, M. Moissart!'

'Moissart!' said I.

'Yes, Moissart,' said she, mimicking my pronunciation, which, to speak the truth, was none of the best, 'and vat den? Vat you know about de Moissart?'

'Nothing, you old fright! – I know nothing about him at all; only I had an ancestor of that name, once upon a time.'

'Dat name! and vat you ave for say to dat name? 'Tis ver goot name; and so is Voissart – dat is ver goot name too. My daughter, Mlle Moissart, she marry von M. Voissart – and de name is both *ver* respectaable name.'

'Moissart?' I exclaimed, 'and Voissart! Why, what is it you mean?'

'Vat I mean? – I mean Moissart and Voissart; and for de matter of dat, I mean Croissart and Froissart, too, if I only tink proper to mean it. My daughter's daughter, Mlle Voissart, she marry von M. Croissart, and den again, my daughter's granddaughter, Mlle Croissart, she marry von M. Froissart; and I suppose you say dat *dat* is not von *ver* respectaable name.'

'Froissart!' said I, beginning to faint, 'why, surely you don't say Moissart, and Voissart, and Croissart, and Froissart?'

'Yes,' she replied, leaning fully back in her chair, and stretching out her lower limbs at great length; 'yes, Moissart, and Voissart, and Croissart, and Froissart. But M. Froissart, he vas von ver big vat you call fool – he vas von ver great big donce like yourself –

335

for he lef *la belle France* for come to dis stupide Amérique – and ven he get here he went and ave von *ver* stupide, von *ver, ver* stupide sonn, so I hear, dough I not yet av ad de plaisir to meet vid him – neither me nor my companion, de Mme Stephanie Lalande. He is name de Napoleon Bonaparte Froissart, and I suppose you say dat *dat*, too, is not von *ver* respectable name.'

Either the length or the nature of this speech had the effect of working up Mrs Simpson into a very extra-ordinary passion indeed; and as she made an end of it, with great labour, she jumped up from her chair like somebody bewitched, dropping upon the floor an entire universe of bustle as she jumped. Once upon her feet, she gnashed her gums, brandished her arms, rolled up her sleeves, shook her fist in my face, and concluded the performance by tearing the cap from her head, and with it an immense wig of the most valuable and beautiful black hair, the whole of which she dashed upon the ground with a yell, and there trampled and danced a fandango upon it, in an absolute ecstasy and agony of rage.

Meantime I sank aghast into the chair which she had vacated. 'Moissart and Voissart!' I repeated, thoughtfully, as she cut one of her pigeon-wings, and, 'Croissart and Froissart!' as she completed another – 'Moissart and Voissart and Croissart and Napoleon Bonaparte Froissart! – why, you ineffable old serpent, that's me – that's me – d'ye hear? that's me' – here I screamed at the top of my voice – 'that's me–e–e! I am Napoleon Bonaparte Froissart! and if I haven't married my great-great-grandmother, I wish I may be everlastingly confounded!'

Mme Eugénie Lalande, quasi Simpson – formerly

Moissart – was, in sober fact, my great-great-grand-mother. In her youth she had been beautiful, and even at eighty-two, retained the majestic height, the sculptural contour of head, the fine eyes and the Grecian nose of her girlhood. By the aid of these, of pearl-powder, of rouge, of false hair, false teeth, and false *tournure*, as well as of the most skilful modistes of Paris, she contrived to hold a respectable footing among the beauties *en peu pàssées* of the French metropolis. In this respect, indeed, she might have been regarded as little less than the equal of the celebrated Ninon de L'Enclos.

She was immensely wealthy, and being left, for the second time, a widow without children, she bethought herself of my existence in America, and for the purpose of making me her heir, paid a visit to the United States, in company with a distant and exceedingly lovely relative of her second husband's – a Mme Stephanie Lalande.

At the opera, my great-great-grandmother's attention was arrested by my notice; and, upon surveying me through her eyeglass, she was struck with a certain family resemblance to herself. Thus interested, and knowing that the heir she sought was actually in the city, she made enquiries of her party respecting me. The gentleman who attended her knew my person, and told her who I was. The information thus obtained induced her to renew her scrutiny; and this scrutiny it was which so emboldened me that I behaved in the absurd manner already detailed. She returned my bow, however, under the impression that, by some odd accident, I had discovered her identity. When, deceived by my weakness of vision, and the arts of the toilet, in respect to the age and charms of the strange lady, I demanded so enthusiastically of Talbot who she was, he concluded that I meant the younger beauty, as a matter of course, and so informed me, with perfect truth, that she was 'the celebrated widow, Mme Lalande'.

In the street, next morning, my great-great-grandmother encountered Talbot, an old Parisian acquaintance; and the conversation, very naturally, turned upon myself. My deficiencies of vision were then explained; for these were notorious, although I was entirely ignorant of their notoriety, and my good old relative discovered, much to her chagrin, that she had been deceived in supposing me aware of her identity, and that I had been merely making a fool of myself in making open love, in a theatre, to an old woman unknown. By way of punishing me for this imprudence, she concocted with Talbot a plot. He purposely kept out of my way to avoid giving me the introduction. My street enquiries about 'the lovely widow, Mme Lalande', were supposed to refer to the younger lady, of course, and thus the conversation with the three gentlemen whom I encountered shortly after leaving Talbot's hotel will be easily explained, as also their allusion to Ninon de L'Enclos. I had no opportunity of seeing Mme Lalande closely during daylight; and, at her musical *soirée*, my silly weakness in refusing the aid of glasses effectually prevented me from making a discovery of her age. When 'Mme Lalande' was called upon to sing, the younger lady was intended; and it was she who arose to obey the call; my great-great-grandmother, to further the deception, arising at the same moment and accompanying her to the piano in the main drawing room. Had I decided upon escorting her thither, it had been her design to suggest the propriety of my remaining where I was; but my own prudential views rendered this unnecessary. The songs which I so much admired, and which so confirmed my impression of the youth of my mistress, were executed by Mme Stephanie Lalande. The eyeglass was presented by way of adding a reproof to the hoax – a sting to the epigram of the deception. Its presentation afforded an opportunity for the lecture upon affectation with which I was so especially edified. It is almost superfluous to add that the glasses of the instrument, as worn by the old lady, had been exchanged by her for a pair better adapted to my years. They suited me, in fact, to a T.

The clergyman, who merely pretended to tie the fatal knot, was a boon companion of Talbot's, and no priest. He was an excellent 'whip', however; and having doffed his cassock to put on a greatcoat, he drove the hack which conveyed the 'happy couple' out of town. Talbot took a seat at his side. The two scoundrels were thus 'in at the death', and through a half-open window of the back parlour of the inn, amused themselves in grinning at the denouement of the drama. I believe I shall be forced to call them both out.

Nevertheless, I am not the husband of my great-great-grandmother; and this is a reflection which affords me infinite relief – but I am the husband of Mme Lalande – of Mme Stephanie Lalande – with whom my good old relative, besides making me her sole heir when she dies – if she ever does – has been at the trouble of concocting me a match. In conclusion: I am done for ever with *billets doux* and am never to be met without SPECTACLES.

The Imp of the Perverse

In the consideration of the faculties and impulses – of the *prima mobilia* of the human soul, the phrenologists have failed to make room for a propensity which, although obviously existing as a radical, primitive, irreducible sentiment, has been equally overlooked by all the moralists who have preceded them. In the pure arrogance of the reason, we have all overlooked it. We have suffered its existence to escape our senses, solely through want of belief – of faith – whether it be faith in Revelation, or faith in the Kabbala. The idea of it has never occurred to us, simply because of its super-erogation. We saw no need of the impulse – for the propensity. We could not perceive its necessity. We could not understand, that is to say, we could not have understood, had the notion of this *primum mobile* ever obtruded itself – we could not have understood in what manner it might be made to further the objects of humanity, either temporal or eternal. It cannot be denied that phrenology and, in great measure, all metaphysicianism have been concocted *a priori*. The intellectual or logical man, rather than the under-standing or observant man, set himself to imagine designs – to dictate purposes to God. Having thus fathomed, to his satisfaction, the intentions of Jehovah, out of these intentions he built his innumerable systems of mind. In the matter of phrenology, for example, we first determined, naturally enough, that it was the design of the deity that man should eat. We then assigned to man an organ of alimentiveness, and this organ is the scourge with which the deity compels man, willy-nilly, into eating. Secondly, having settled it to be God's will that man should continue his species, we discovered an organ of amativeness, forthwith. And so with combativeness, with ideality, with causality, with constructiveness – so, in short, with every organ, whether representing a propensity, a moral sentiment, or a faculty of the pure intellect. And in these arrangements of the *principia* of human action, the Spurzheimites, whether right or wrong, in part, or upon the whole, have but followed, in principle, the footsteps of their predecessors: deducing and establishing everything from the preconceived destiny of man, and upon the ground of the objects of his creator.

It would have been wiser, it would have been safer, to classify (if classify we must) upon the basis of what man usually or occasionally did, and was always occasionally doing, rather than upon the basis of what we took it for granted the deity intended him to do. If we cannot comprehend God in his visible works, how then in his inconceivable thoughts, that call the works into being? If we cannot understand him in his objective creatures, how then in his substantive moods and phases of creation?

Induction, *a posteriori*, would have brought phrenology to admit, as an innate and primitive principle of human action, a paradoxical something, which we may call perverseness, for want of a more characteristic term. In the sense I intend, it is, in fact, a *mobile* without motive, a motive not *motivert*. Through its promptings we act without comprehensible object; or, if this shall be understood as a contradiction in terms, we may so far modify the proposition as to say, that through its promptings we act, for the reason that we should *not*. In theory, no reason can be more unreasonable, but, in fact, there is none more strong. With certain minds, under certain conditions, it becomes absolutely irresistible. I am not more certain that I breathe, than that the assurance of the wrong or error of any action is often the one unconquerable force which impels us, and alone impels us to its prosecution. Nor will this overwhelming tendency to do wrong for the wrong's sake, admit of analysis, or resolution into ulterior elements. It is a radical, a primitive impulse – elementary. It will be said, I am aware, that when we persist in acts because we feel we should not persist in them, our conduct is but a modification of that which ordinarily springs from the combativeness of phrenology. But a glance will show the fallacy of this idea. The phrenological combativeness has for its essence, the necessity of self-defence. It is our safeguard against injury. Its principle regards our well-being; and thus the desire to be well is excited simultaneously with its development. It follows, that the desire to be well must be excited simultaneously with any principle which shall be merely a modification of combativeness, but in the case of that something which I term perverseness, the desire to be well is not only not aroused, but a strongly antagonistical sentiment exists.

An appeal to one's own heart is, after all, the best reply to the sophistry just noticed. No one who trustingly consults and thoroughly questions his own soul, will be disposed to deny the entire radicalness of the propensity in question. It is not more incomprehensible than distinctive. There lives no man who at some period has not been tormented, for example, by an earnest desire to tantalise a listener by circumlocution. The speaker is aware that he displeases; he has every intention to please, he is usually curt, precise, and clear, the most laconic and luminous language is struggling for utterance upon his tongue, it is only with difficulty that he restrains himself from giving it flow; he dreads and deprecates the anger of him whom he addresses; yet, the thought strikes him, that by certain involutions and parentheses this anger may be engendered. That single thought is enough. The impulse increases to a wish, the wish to a desire, the desire to an uncontrollable longing, and the longing (to the deep regret and mortification of the speaker, and in defiance of all consequences) is indulged.

We have a task before us which must be speedily performed. We know that it will be ruinous to make delay. The most important crisis of our life calls, trumpet-tongued, for immediate energy and action. We glow, we are consumed with eagerness to commence the work, with the anticipation of whose glorious result our whole souls are on fire. It must, it shall be undertaken today, and yet we put it off until tomorrow, and why? There is no answer, except that we feel perverse, using the word with no comprehension of the principle. Tomorrow arrives, and with it a more impatient anxiety to do our duty, but with this very increase of anxiety arrives, also, a nameless, a positively fearful, because unfathomable, craving for delay. This craving gathers strength as the moments fly. The last hour for action is at hand. We tremble with the violence of the conflict within us – of the definite with the indefinite – of the substance with the shadow. But, if the contest have proceeded thus far, it is the shadow which prevails – we struggle in vain. The clock strikes, and is the knell of our welfare. At the same time, it is the chanticleer-note to the ghost that has so long overawed us. It flies – it disappears – we are free. The old energy returns. We will labour now. Alas, it is too late!

We stand upon the brink of a precipice. We peer into the abyss – we grow sick and dizzy. Our first impulse is to shrink from the danger. Unaccountably we remain. By slow degrees our sickness and dizziness and horror become merged in a cloud of nameable feeling. By gradations, still more imperceptible, this cloud assumes shape, as did the vapour from the bottle out of which arose the genius in the Arabian Nights. But out of this our cloud upon the precipice's edge, there grows into palpability, a shape, far more terrible than any genius or any demon of a tale, and yet it is but a thought, although a fearful one, and one which chills the very marrow of our bones with the fierceness of the delight of its horror. It is merely the idea of what would be our sensations during the sweeping precipitancy of a fall from such a height. And this fall – this rushing annihilation – for the very reason that it involves that one most ghastly and loathsome of all the most ghastly and loathsome images of death and suffering which have ever presented themselves to our imagination – for this very cause do we now the most vividly desire it. And because our reason violently deters us from the brink, therefore do we the most impetuously approach it. There is no passion in nature so demoniacally impatient, as that of him who, shuddering upon the edge of a precipice, thus meditates a plunge. To indulge, for a moment, in any attempt at thought, is to be inevitably lost; for reflection but urges us to forbear, and therefore it is, I say, that we cannot. If there be no friendly arm to check us, or if we fail in a sudden effort to prostrate ourselves backwards from the abyss, we plunge, and are destroyed.

Examine these similar actions as we will, we shall find them resulting solely from the spirit of the perverse. We perpetrate them because we feel that we should not. Beyond or behind this there is no intelligible principle; and we might, indeed, deem this perverseness a direct instigation of the arch-fiend, were it not occasionally known to operate in furtherance of good.

I have said thus much, that in some measure I may answer your question, that I may explain to you why I am here, that I may assign to you something that shall have at least the faint aspect of a cause for my wearing these fetters, and for my tenanting this cell of the condemned. Had I not been thus prolix, you might either have misunderstood me altogether, or, with the rabble, have fancied me mad. As it is, you will easily perceive that I am one of the many uncounted victims of the Imp of the Perverse.

It is impossible that any deed could have been wrought with a more thorough deliberation. For weeks, for months, I pondered upon the means of the murder. I rejected a thousand schemes, because their accomplishment involved a chance of detection. At length, in reading some French memoirs, I found an account of a nearly fatal illness that occurred to Mme Pilau, through the agency of a candle accidentally poisoned. The idea struck my fancy at once. I knew my victim's habit of reading in bed. I knew, too, that his apartment was narrow and ill-ventilated. But I need not vex you with impertinent details. I need not describe the easy artifices by which I substituted, in his bedroom candle-stand, a wax-light of my own making for the one which I there found. The next morning he was discovered dead in his bed, and the coroner's verdict was – 'Death by the visitation of God'.

Having inherited his estate, all went well with me for years. The idea of detection never once entered my brain. Of the remains of the fatal taper I had myself carefully disposed. I had left no shadow of a clue by which it would be possible to convict, or even to suspect me of the crime. It is inconceivable how rich a sentiment of satisfaction arose in my bosom as I reflected upon my absolute security. For a very long period of time I was accustomed to revel in this sentiment. It afforded me more real delight than all the mere worldly advantages accruing from my sin. But there arrived at length an epoch, from which the pleasurable feeling grew, by scarcely perceptible gradations, into a haunting and harassing thought. It harassed because it haunted. I could scarcely get rid of it for an instant. It is quite a common thing to be thus annoyed with the ringing in our ears, or rather in our memories, of the burthen of some ordinary song, or some unimpressive snatches from an opera. Nor will we be the less tormented if the song in itself be good, or the opera air meritorious. In this manner, at last, I would perpetually catch myself pondering upon my security, and repeating, in a low undertone, the phrase, 'I am safe.'

One day, whilst sauntering along the streets, I arrested myself in the act of murmuring, half aloud, these customary syllables. In a fit of petulance, I remodelled them thus: 'I am safe – I am safe – yes – if I be not fool enough to make open confession!'

No sooner had I spoken these words, than I felt an icy chill creep to my heart. I had had some experience in these fits of perversity (whose nature I have been at some trouble to explain), and I remembered well that in no instance had I successfully resisted their attacks. And now my own casual self-suggestion that I might possibly be fool enough to confess the murder of which I had been guilty, confronted me, as if the very ghost of him whom I had murdered – and beckoned me on to death.

At first, I made an effort to shake off this nightmare of the soul. I walked vigorously – faster – still faster – at length I ran. I felt a maddening desire to shriek aloud. Every succeeding wave of thought overwhelmed me with new terror, for, alas! I well, too well, understood that to think, in my situation, was to be lost. I still quickened my pace. I bounded like a madman through the crowded thoroughfares. At length, the populace took the alarm, and pursued me. I felt then the consummation of my fate. Could I have torn out my tongue, I would have done it, but a rough voice resounded in my ears – a rougher grasp seized me by the shoulder. I turned – I gasped for breath. For a moment I experienced all the pangs of suffocation; I became blind, and deaf, and giddy; and then some invisible fiend, I thought, struck me with his broad palm upon the back. The long imprisoned secret burst forth from my soul.

They say that I spoke with a distinct enunciation, but with marked emphasis and passionate hurry, as if in dread of interruption before concluding the brief but pregnant sentences that consigned me to the hangman and to hell.

Having related all that was necessary for the fullest judicial conviction, I fell prostrate in a swoon.

But why shall I say more? Today I wear these chains, and am here! Tomorrow I shall be fetterless! – *but where?*

The Sphinx

During the dread reign of cholera in New York, I had accepted the invitation of a relative to spend a fortnight with him in the retirement of his *cottage ornée* on the banks of the Hudson. We had here around us all the ordinary means of summer amusement; and what with rambling in the woods, sketching, boating, fishing, bathing, music, and books, we should have passed the time pleasantly enough, but for the fearful intelligence which reached us every morning from the populous city. Not a day elapsed which did not bring us news of the decease of some acquaintance. Then as the fatality increased, we learned to expect daily the loss of some friend. At length we trembled at the approach of every messenger. The very air from the South seemed to us redolent with death. That palsying thought, indeed, took entire possession of my soul. I could neither speak, think, nor dream of anything else. My host was of a less excitable temperament, and, although greatly depressed in spirits, exerted himself to sustain my own. His richly philosophical intellect was not at any time affected by unrealities. To the substances of terror he was sufficiently alive, but of its shadows he had no apprehension.

His endeavours to arouse me from the condition of abnormal gloom into which I had fallen, were frustrated, in great measure, by certain volumes which I had found in his library. These were of a character to force into germination whatever seeds of hereditary superstition lay latent in my bosom. I had been reading these books without his knowledge, and thus he was often at a loss to account for the forcible impressions which had been made upon my fancy.

A favourite topic with me was the popular belief in omens – a belief which, at this one epoch of my life, I was almost seriously disposed to defend. On this subject we had long and animated discussions – he maintaining the utter groundlessness of faith in such matters – I contending that a popular sentiment arising with absolute spontaneity – that is to say, without apparent traces of suggestion – had in itself the unmistakable elements of truth, and was entitled to as much respect as that intuition which is the idiosyncrasy of the individual man of genius.

The fact is, that soon after my arrival at the cottage there had occurred to myself an incident so entirely inexplicable, and which had in it so much of the portentous character, that I might well have been excused for regarding it as an omen. It appalled, and at the same time so confounded and bewildered me, that many days elapsed before I could make up my mind to communicate the circumstances to my friend.

Near the close of exceedingly warm day, I was sitting, book in hand, at an open window, commanding, through a long vista of the river banks, a view of a distant hill, the face of which nearest my position had been denuded by what is termed a landslide, of the principal portion of its trees. My thoughts had been long wandering from the volume before me to the gloom and desolation of the neighbouring city. Uplifting my eyes from the page, they fell upon the naked face of the hill, and upon an object – upon some living monster of hideous conformation, which very rapidly made its way from the summit to the bottom, disappearing finally in the dense forest below. As this creature first came in sight, I doubted my own sanity – or at least the evidence of my own eyes; and many minutes passed before I succeeded in convincing myself that I was neither mad nor in a dream. Yet when I described the monster (which I distinctly saw, and calmly surveyed through the whole period of its progress), my readers, I fear, will feel more difficulty in being convinced of these points than even I did myself.

Estimating the size of the creature by comparison with the diameter of the large trees near which it passed – the few giants of the forest which had escaped the fury of the landslide – I concluded it to be far larger than any ship of the line in existence. I say ship of the line, because the shape of the monster suggested the idea – the hull of one of our seventy-fours might convey a very tolerable conception of the general outline. The mouth of the animal was situated at the extremity of a proboscis some sixty or seventy feet in length, and about as thick as the body of an ordinary elephant. Near the root of this trunk was an immense quantity of black shaggy hair – more than could have been supplied by the coats of a score of buffaloes; and projecting from this hair downwardly and laterally, sprang two gleaming tusks not unlike those of the wild boar, but of infinitely greater dimensions. Extending forward, parallel with the proboscis, and on each side of it, was a gigantic staff, thirty or forty feet in length, formed seemingly of pure crystal and in shape a perfect prism – it reflected in the most gorgeous manner the rays of the declining sun. The trunk was fashioned like a wedge with the apex to the earth.

From it there were outspread two pairs of wings – each wing nearly one hundred yards in length – one pair being placed above the other, and all thickly covered with metal scales; each scale apparently some ten or twelve feet in diameter. I observed that the upper and lower tiers of wings were connected by a strong chain. But the chief peculiarity of this horrible thing was the representation of a Death's Head, which covered nearly the whole surface of its breast, and which was as accurately traced in glaring white, upon the dark ground of the body, as if it had been there carefully designed by an artist. While I regarded the terrific animal, and more especially the appearance on its breast, with a feeling or horror and awe – with a sentiment of forthcoming evil, which I found it impossible to quell by any effort of the reason, I perceived the huge jaws at the extremity of the proboscis suddenly expand themselves, and from them there proceeded a sound so loud and so expressive of woe, that it struck upon my nerves like a knell, and as the monster disappeared at the foot of the hill, I fell at once, fainting, to the floor.

Upon recovering, my first impulse, of course, was to inform my friend of what I had seen and heard – and I can scarcely explain what feeling of repugnance it was which, in the end, operated to prevent me.

At length, one evening, some three or four days after the occurrence, we were sitting together in the room in which I had seen the apparition – I occupying the same seat at the same window, and he lounging on a sofa near at hand. The association of the place and time impelled me to give him an account of the phenomenon. He heard me to the end – at first laughed heartily – and then lapsed into an excessively grave demeanour, as if my insanity was a thing beyond suspicion. At this instant I again had a distinct view of the monster – to which, with a shout of absolute terror, I now directed his attention. He looked eagerly – but maintained that he saw nothing – although I designated minutely the course of the creature, as it made its way down the naked face of the hill.

I was now immeasurably alarmed, for I considered the vision either as an omen of my death, or, worse, as the forerunner of an attack of mania. I threw myself passionately back in my chair, and for some moments buried my face in my hands. When I uncovered my eyes, the apparition was no longer visible.

My host, however, had in some degree resumed the calmness of his demeanour, and questioned me very rigorously in respect to the conformation of the visionary creature. When I had fully satisfied him on this head, he sighed deeply, as if relieved of some intolerable burden, and went on to talk, with what I thought a cruel calmness, of various points of speculative philosophy, which had heretofore formed subject of discussion between us. I remember his insisting very especially (among other things) upon the idea that the principal source of error in all human investigations lay in the liability of the understanding to underrate or to overvalue the importance of an object, through mere mis-admeasurement of its propinquity. 'To estimate properly, for example,' he said, 'the influence to be exercised on mankind at large by the thorough diffusion of Democracy, the distance of the epoch at which such diffusion may possibly be accomplished should not fail to form an item in the estimate. Yet can you tell me one writer on the subject of government who has ever thought this particular branch of the subject worthy of discussion at all?'

He here paused for a moment, stepped to a book-case, and brought forth one of the ordinary synopses of Natural History. Requesting me then to exchange seats with him, that he might the better distinguish the fine print of the volume, he took my armchair at the window, and, opening the book, resumed his discourse very much in the same tone as before.

'But for your exceeding minuteness,' he said, 'in describing the monster, I might never have had it in my power to demonstrate to you what it was. In the first place, let me read to you a schoolboy account of the genus Sphinx, of the family *Crepuscularia*, of the order *Lepidoptera*, of the class of *Insecta* – or insects. The account runs thus:

'Four membranous wings covered with little coloured scales of metallic appearance; mouth forming a rolled proboscis, produced by an elongation of the jaws, upon the sides of which are found the rudiments of mandibles and downy palpi; the inferior wings retained to the superior by a stiff hair; antennae in the form of an elongated club, prismatic; abdomen pointed. The Death's-headed Sphinx has occasioned much terror among the vulgar, at times, by the melancholy kind of cry which it utters, and the insignia of death which it wears upon its corslet.'

He here closed the book and leaned forward in the chair, placing himself accurately in the position which I had occupied at the moment of beholding 'the monster'.

'Ah, here it is,' he presently exclaimed – 'it is reascending the face of the hill, and a very remarkable-looking creature I admit it to be. Still, it is by no means so large or so distant as you imagined it, for the fact is that, as it wriggles its way up this thread, which some spider has wrought along the window-sash, I find it to be about the sixteenth of an inch in its extreme length, and also about the sixteenth of an inch distant from the pupil of my eye.'

The Domain of Arnheim
or The Landscape Garden

The garden like a lady fair was cut,
That lay as if she slumbered in delight,
And to the open skies her eyes did shut.
The azure fields of Heaven were 'sembled right
 In a large round, set with the flowers of light.
The flowers *de luce*, and the round sparks of dew
That hung upon their azure leaves did shew
Like twinkling stars that sparkle in the evening blue.

GILES FLETCHER

From his cradle to his grave a gale of prosperity bore my friend Ellison along. Nor do I use the word prosperity in its mere worldly sense. I mean it as synonymous with happiness. The person of whom I speak seemed born for the purpose of foreshadowing the doctrines of Turgot, Price, Priestley, and Condorcet – of exemplifying by individual instance what has been deemed the chimera of the perfectionists. In the brief existence of Ellison I fancy that I have seen refuted the dogma, that in man's very nature lies some hidden principle, the antagonist of bliss. An anxious examination of his career has given me to understand that, in general, from the violation of a few simple laws of humanity arises the wretchedness of mankind – that as a species we have in our possession the as yet unwrought elements of content – and that, even now, in the present darkness and madness of all thought on the great question of the social condition, it is not impossible that man, the individual, under certain unusual and highly fortuitous conditions, may be happy.

With opinions such as these my young friend, too, was fully imbued, and thus it is worthy of observation that the uninterrupted enjoyment which distinguished his life was, in great measure, the result of preconcert. It is indeed evident that with less of the instinctive philosophy which, now and then, stands so well in the stead of experience, Mr Ellison would have found himself precipitated, by the very extraordinary success of his life, into the common vortex of unhappiness which yawns for those of pre-eminent endowments. But it is by no means my object to pen an essay on happiness. The ideas of my friend may be summed up in a few words. He admitted but four elementary principles, or more strictly, conditions of bliss. That which he considered chief was (strange to say!) the simple and purely physical one of free exercise in the open air. 'The health,' he said, 'attainable by other means is scarcely worth the name.' He instanced the ecstasies of the fox-hunter, and pointed to the tillers of the earth, the only people who, as a class, can be fairly considered happier than others. His second condition was the love of woman. His third, and most difficult of realisation, was the contempt of ambition. His fourth was an object of unceasing pursuit; and he held that, other things being equal, the extent of attainable happiness was in proportion to the spirituality of this object.

Ellison was remarkable in the continuous profusion of good gifts lavished upon him by fortune. In personal grace and beauty he exceeded all men. His intellect was of that order to which the acquisition of knowledge is less a labour than an intuition and a necessity. His family was one of the most illustrious of the empire. His bride was the loveliest and most devoted of women. His possessions had been always ample; but on the attainment of his majority, it was discovered that one of those extraordinary freaks of fate had been played in his behalf which startle the whole social world amid which they occur, and seldom fail radically to alter the moral constitution of those who are their objects.

It appears that about a hundred years before Mr Ellison's coming of age, there had died, in a remote province, one Mr Seabright Ellison. This gentleman had amassed a princely fortune, and, having no immediate connections, conceived the whim of suffering his wealth to accumulate for a century after his decease. Minutely and sagaciously directing the various modes of investment, he bequeathed the aggregate amount to the nearest of blood, bearing the name of Ellison, who should be alive at the end of the hundred years. Many attempts had been made to set aside this singular bequest; their *ex post facto* character rendered them abortive; but the attention of a jealous government was aroused, and a legislative act finally obtained, forbidding all similar accumulations. This act, however, did not prevent young Ellison from entering into possession, on his twenty-first birthday, as the heir of his ancestor Seabright, of a fortune of $450,000,000.*

---

* An incident, similar in outline to the one here imagined, occurred, not very long ago, in England. The name of the fortunate heir was Thelluson. I first saw an account of this matter in the *Tour* of Prince Puckler Muskau, who makes the sum inherited £90,000,000, and justly observes that 'in the contemplation of so vast a sum, and of the services to which it might be applied, there is something even of

When it had become known that such was the enormous wealth inherited, there were, of course, many speculations as to the mode of its disposal. The magnitude and the immediate availability of the sum bewildered all who thought on the topic. The possessor of any appreciable amount of money might have been imagined to perform any one of a thousand things. With riches merely surpassing those of any citizen, it would have been easy to suppose him engaging to supreme excess in the fashionable extravagances of his time – or busying himself with political intrigue – or aiming at ministerial power – or purchasing increase of nobility – or collecting large museums of virtu – or playing the munificent patron of letters, of science, of art – or endowing, and bestowing his name upon extensive institutions of charity. But for the inconceivable wealth in the actual possession of the heir, these objects and all ordinary objects were felt to afford too limited a field. Recourse was had to figures, and these but sufficed to confound. It was seen that, even at three per cent, the annual income of the inheritance amounted to no less than $13,500,000; which was $1,125,000 per month; or $36,986 per day; or $1,541 per hour; or $26 every minute that flew. Thus the usual track of supposition was thoroughly broken up. Men knew not what to imagine. There were some who even conceived that

---

the sublime'. To suit the views of this article I have followed the prince's statement, although a grossly exaggerated one. The germ, and in fact, the commencement of the present paper was published many years ago – previous to the issue of the first number of Sue's admirable account *Juif Errant*, which may possibly have been suggested to him by Muskau's account.

Mr Ellison would divest himself of at least one-half of his fortune, as of utterly superfluous opulence – enriching whole troops of his relatives by division of his superabundance. To the nearest of these he did, in fact, abandon the very unusual wealth which was his own before the inheritance.

I was not surprised, however, to perceive that he had long made up his mind on a point which had occasioned so much discussion to his friends. Nor was I greatly astonished at the nature of his decision. In regard to individual charities he had satisfied his conscience. In the possibility of any improvement, properly so called, being effected by man himself in the general condition of man, he had (I am sorry to confess it) little faith. Upon the whole, whether happily or unhappily, he was thrown back, in very great measure, upon self.

In the widest and noblest sense he was a poet. He comprehended, moreover, the true character, the august aims, the supreme majesty and dignity of the poetic sentiment. The fullest, if not the sole proper satisfaction of this sentiment he instinctively felt to lie in the creation of novel forms of beauty. Some peculiarities, either in his early education, or in the nature of his intellect, had tinged with what is termed materialism all his ethical speculations; and it was this bias, perhaps, which led him to believe that the most advantageous at least, if not the sole legitimate field for the poetic exercise, lies in the creation of novel moods of purely physical loveliness. Thus it happened he became neither musician nor poet – if we use this latter term in its everyday acceptation. Or it might have been that he neglected to become either, merely in pursuance of his idea that in contempt of ambition is to be found one of the essential principles of happiness on earth. Is it not, indeed, possible that, while a high order of genius is necessarily ambitious, the highest is above that which is termed ambition? And may it not thus happen that many far greater than Milton have contentedly remained 'mute and inglorious'? I believe that the world has never seen – and that, unless through some series of accidents goading the noblest order of mind into distasteful exertion, the world will never see – that full extent of triumphant execution, in the richer domains of art, of which the human nature is absolutely capable.

Ellison became neither musician nor poet; although no man lived more profoundly enamoured of music and poetry. Under other circumstances than those which invested him, it is not impossible that he would have become a painter. Sculpture, although in its nature rigorously poetical, was too limited in its extent and consequences to have occupied, at any time, much of his attention. And I have now mentioned all the provinces in which the common understanding of the poetic sentiment has declared it capable of expatiating. But Ellison maintained that the richest, the truest, and most natural, if not altogether the most extensive province, had been unaccountably neglected. No definition had spoken of the landscape-gardener as of the poet; yet it seemed to my friend that the creation of the landscape-garden offered to the proper Muse the most magnificent of opportunities. Here, indeed, was the fairest field for the display of imagination in the endless combining of forms of novel beauty; the elements to enter into combination being, by a vast superiority, the most glorious which the earth could afford. In the multiform and multicolour of the flowers and the trees, he recognised the most direct and energetic efforts of Nature at physical loveliness. And in the direction or concentration of this effort – or, more properly, in its adaptation to the eyes which were to behold it on earth – he perceived that he should be employing the best means – labouring to the greatest advantage – in the fulfilment, not only of his own destiny as poet, but of the august purposes for which the deity had implanted the poetic sentiment in man.

'Its adaptation to the eyes which were to behold it on earth.' In his explanation of this phraseology, Mr Ellison did much towards solving what has always seemed to me an enigma – I mean the fact (which none but the ignorant dispute) that no such combination of scenery exists in nature as the painter of genius may produce. No such paradises are to be found in reality as have glowed on the canvas of Claude. In the most enchanting of natural landscapes, there will always be found a defect or an excess – many excesses and defects. While the component parts may defy, individually, the highest skill of the artist, the arrangement of these parts will always be susceptible of improvement. In short, no position can be attained on the wide surface of the natural earth, from which an artistical eye, looking steadily, will not find matter of offence in what is termed the 'composition' of the landscape. And yet how unintelligible is this! In all other matters we are justly instructed to regard nature as supreme. With her details we shrink from competition. Who shall presume to imitate the colours of the tulip, or to improve the proportions of the lily of the valley? The criticism which says, of sculpture or portraiture, that here nature is to be exalted or idealised rather than imitated, is in error. No pictorial or sculptural combinations of points of human liveliness do more than approach the living and breathing beauty. In landscape alone is the principle of the critic true; and, having felt its truth here, it is but the headlong spirit of generalisation which has led him to pronounce it true throughout all the domains of art. Having, I say, felt its truth here; for the feeling is no affectation or chimera. The mathematics afford no more absolute demonstrations than the sentiments of his art yields the artist. He not only believes, but positively knows, that such and such apparently arbitrary arrangements of matter constitute and alone constitute the true beauty. His reasons, however, have not yet been matured into expression. It remains for a more profound analysis than the world has yet seen, fully to investigate and express them. Nevertheless he is confirmed in his instinctive opinions by the voice of all his brethren. Let a 'composition' be defective; let an emendation be wrought in its mere arrangement of form; let this emendation be submitted to every artist in the world; by each will its necessity be admitted. And even far more than this – in remedy of the defective composition, each insulated member of the fraternity would have suggested the identical emendation.

I repeat that in landscape arrangements alone is the physical nature susceptible of exaltation, and that, therefore, her susceptibility of improvement at this one point, was a mystery I had been unable to solve. My own thoughts on the subject had rested in the idea that the primitive intention of nature would have so arranged the earth's surface as to have fulfilled at all points man's sense of perfection in the beautiful, the sublime, or the picturesque; but that this primitive intention had been frustrated by the known geological disturbances – disturbances of form and colour-grouping, in the correction or allaying of which lies the soul of art. The force of this idea was much weakened, however, by the necessity which it involved of considering the disturbances abnormal and unadapted to any purpose. It was Ellison who suggested that they were prognostic of death. He thus explained: Admit the earthly immortality of man to have been the first intention. We have then the primitive arrangement of the earth's surface adapted to his blissful estate, as not existent but designed. The disturbances were the preparations for his subsequently conceived deathful condition.

'Now,' said my friend, 'what we regard as exaltation of the landscape may be really such as respects only the moral or human point of view. Each alteration of the natural scenery may possibly effect a blemish in the picture, if we can suppose this picture viewed at large – in mass – from some point distant from the earth's surface, although not beyond the limits of its atmosphere. It is easily understood that what might improve a closely scrutinised detail, may at the same time injure a general or more distantly observed effect. There may be a class of beings, human once, but now invisible to humanity, to whom, from afar, our disorder may seem order – our unpicturesqueness picturesque; in a word, the earth-angels, for whose scrutiny more especially than our own, and for whose death-refined appreciation of the beautiful, may have been set in array by God the wide landscape-gardens of the hemispheres.'

In the course of discussion, my friend quoted some

passages from a writer on landscape-gardening who has been supposed to have well treated his theme:

There are properly but two styles of landscape-gardening, the natural and the artificial. One seeks to recall the original beauty of the country, by adapting its means to the surrounding scenery, cultivating trees in harmony with the hills or plains of the neighbouring land; detecting and bringing into practice those nice relations of size, proportion, and colour which, hid from the common observer, are revealed everywhere to the experienced student of nature. The result of the natural style of gardening, is seen rather in the absence of all defects and incongruities – in the prevalence of a healthy harmony and order – than in the creation of any special wonders or miracles. The artificial style has as many varieties as there are different tastes to gratify. It has a certain general relation to the various styles of building. There are the stately avenues and retirements of Versailles; Italian terraces; and a various mixed old English style, which bears some relation to the domestic Gothic or English Elizabethan architecture. Whatever may be said against the abuses of the artificial landscape-gardening, a mixture of pure art in a garden scene adds to it a great beauty. This is partly pleasing to the eye, by the show of order and design, and partly moral. A terrace, with an old moss-covered balustrade, calls up at once to the eye the fair forms that have passed there in other days. The slightest exhibition of art is an evidence of care and human interest.

'From what I have already observed,' said Ellison, 'you will understand that I reject the idea, here expressed, of recalling the original beauty of the country. The original beauty is never so great as that which may be introduced. Of course, everything depends on the selection of a spot with capabilities. What is said about detecting and bringing into practice nice relations of size, proportion, and colour, is one of those mere vaguenesses of speech which serve to veil inaccuracy of thought. The phrase quoted may mean anything, or nothing, and guides in no degree. That the true result of the natural style of gardening is seen rather in the absence of all defects and incongruities than in the creation of any special wonders or miracles, is a proposition better suited to the grovelling apprehension of the herd than to the fervid dreams of the man of genius. The negative merit suggested appertains to that hobbling criticism which, in letters, would elevate Addison into apotheosis. In truth, while that virtue which consists in the mere avoidance of vice appeals directly to the understanding, and can thus be circumscribed in rule, the loftier virtue, which flames in creation, can be apprehended in its results alone. Rule applies but to the merits of denial – to the excellencies which refrain. Beyond these, the critical art can but suggest. We may be instructed to build a "Cato", but we are in vain told how to conceive a Parthenon or an "Inferno". The thing done, however; the wonder accomplished; and the capacity for apprehension becomes universal. The sophists of the negative school who, through inability to create, have scoffed at creation, are now found the loudest in applause. What, in its chrysalis condition of principle, affronted their demure reason, never fails, in its maturity of accomplishment, to extort admiration from their instinct of beauty.

'The author's observations on the artificial style,' continued Ellison, 'are less objectionable. A mixture of pure art in a garden scene adds to it a great beauty. This is just; as also is the reference to the sense of human interest. The principle expressed is incontrovertible – but there may be something beyond it. There may be an object in keeping with the principle – an object unattainable by the means ordinarily possessed by individuals, yet which, if attained, would lend a charm to the landscape-garden far surpassing that which a sense of merely human interest could bestow. A poet, having very unusual pecuniary resources, might, while retaining the necessary idea of art or culture, or, as our author expresses it, of interest, so imbue his designs at once with extent and novelty of beauty, as to convey the sentiment of spiritual interference. It will be seen that, in bringing about such result, he secures all the advantages of interest or design, while relieving his work of the harshness or technicality of the worldly art. In the most rugged of wildernesses – in the most savage of the scenes of pure nature – there is apparent the art of a creator; yet this art is apparent to reflection only; in no respect has it the obvious force of a feeling. Now let us suppose this sense of the Almighty design to be one step depressed – to be brought into something like harmony or consistency with the sense of human art – to form an intermedium between the two – let us imagine, for example, a landscape whose combined vastness and definitiveness – whose united beauty, magnificence, and strangeness, shall convey the idea of care, or culture, or superintendence, on the part of beings superior, yet akin to humanity – then the

sentiment of interest is preserved, while the art inter-
volved is made to assume the air of an intermediate
or secondary nature – a nature which is not God, nor
an emanation from God, but which still is nature in
the sense of the handiwork of the angels that hover
between man and God.'

It was in devoting his enormous wealth to the
embodiment of a vision such as this – in the free
exercise in the open air ensured by the personal
superintendence of his plans – in the unceasing object
which these plans afforded – in the high spirituality of
the object – in the contempt of ambition which it
enabled him truly to feel – in the perennial springs
with which it gratified, without possibility of satiating,
that one master passion of his soul, the thirst for
beauty; above all, it was in the sympathy of a woman,
not unwomanly, whose loveliness and love enveloped
his existence in the purple atmosphere of Paradise,
that Ellison thought to find, and found, exemption
from the ordinary cares of humanity, with a far greater
amount of positive happiness than ever glowed in the
rapt daydreams of De Staël.

I despair of conveying to the reader any distinct
conception of the marvels which my friend did
actually accomplish. I wish to describe, but am
disheartened by the difficulty of description, and
hesitate between detail and generality. Perhaps the
better course will be to unite the two in their
extremes.

Mr Ellison's first step regarded, of course, the
choice of a locality, and scarcely had he commenced
thinking on this point, when the luxuriant nature of
the Pacific Islands arrested his attention. In fact, he
had made up his mind for a voyage to the South Seas,

when a night's reflection induced him to abandon the idea. 'Were I misanthropic,' he said, 'such a locale would suit me. The thoroughness of its insulation and seclusion, and the difficulty of ingress and egress, would in such case be the charm of charms; but as yet I am not Timon. I wish the composure but not the depression of solitude. There must remain with me a certain control over the extent and duration of my repose. There will be frequent hours in which I shall need, too, the sympathy of the poetic in what I have done. Let me seek, then, a spot not far from a populous city – whose vicinity, also, will best enable me to execute my plans.'

In search of a suitable place so situated, Ellison travelled for several years, and I was permitted to accompany him. A thousand spots with which I was enraptured he rejected without hesitation, for reasons which satisfied me, in the end, that he was right. We came at length to an elevated tableland of wonderful fertility and beauty, affording a panoramic prospect very little less in extent than that of Etna, and, in Ellison's opinion as well as my own, surpassing the far-famed view from that mountain in all the true elements of the picturesque.

'I am aware,' said the traveller, as he drew a sigh of deep delight after gazing on this scene, entranced, for nearly an hour, 'I know that here, in my circumstances, nine-tenths of the most fastidious of men would rest content. This panorama is indeed glorious, and I should rejoice in it but for the excess of its glory. The taste of all the architects I have ever known leads them, for the sake of "prospect", to put up buildings on hilltops. The error is obvious. Grandeur in any of its moods, but especially in that of extent, startles, excites – and then fatigues, depresses. For the occasional scene nothing can be better – for the constant view nothing worse. And, in the constant view, the most objectionable phase of grandeur is that of extent; the worst phase of extent, that of distance. It is at war with the sentiment and with the sense of seclusion – the sentiment and sense which we seek to humour in "retiring to the country". In looking from the summit of a mountain we cannot help feeling abroad in the world. The heartsick avoid distant prospects as a pestilence.'

It was not until towards the close of the fourth year of our search that we found a locality with which Ellison professed himself satisfied. It is, of course, needless to say where was the locality. The late death of my friend, in causing his domain to be thrown open to certain classes of visitors, has given to Arnheim a species of secret and subdued if not solemn celebrity, similar in kind, although infinitely superior in degree, to that which so long distinguished Fonthill.

The usual approach to Arnheim was by the river. The visitor left the city in the early morning. During the forenoon he passed between shores of a tranquil and domestic beauty, on which grazed innumerable sheep, their white fleeces spotting the vivid green of rolling meadows. By degrees the idea of cultivation subsided into that of merely pastoral care. This slowly became merged in a sense of retirement – this again in a consciousness of solitude. As the evening approached, the channel grew more narrow, the banks more and more precipitous; and these latter were clothed in rich, more profuse, and more sombre foliage. The water increased in transparency. The stream took a thousand turns, so that at no moment could its gleaming surface be seen for a greater distance than a furlong. At every instant the vessel seemed imprisoned within an enchanted circle, having insuperable and impenetrable walls of foliage, a roof of ultramarine satin, and no floor – the keel balancing itself with admirable nicety on that of a phantom bark which, by some accident having been turned upside down, floated in constant company with the substantial one, for the purpose of sustaining it. The channel now became a gorge – although the term is somewhat inapplicable, and I employ it merely because the language has no word which better represents the most striking – not the most distinctive – feature of the scene. The character of gorge was maintained only in the height and parallelism of the shores; it was lost altogether in their other traits. The walls of the ravine (through which the clear water still tranquilly flowed) arose to an elevation of a hundred and occasionally of a hundred and fifty feet, and inclined so much towards each other as, in a great measure, to shut out the light of day; while the long plume-like moss which depended densely from the intertwining shrubberies overhead, gave the whole chasm an air of funereal gloom. The windings became more frequent and intricate, and seemed often as if returning in upon themselves, so that the voyager had long lost all idea of direction. He was, moreover, enwrapt in an exquisite sense of the strange. The thought of nature still remained, but her character seemed to have undergone modification, there was a weird symmetry, a thrilling uniformity, a wizard propriety in these her works. Not a dead branch – not a withered leaf – not a stray pebble – not a patch of the brown earth was anywhere visible. The crystal water welled up against the clean granite, or the unblemished moss, with a sharpness of outline that delighted while it bewildered the eye.

Having threaded the mazes of this channel for some hours, the gloom deepening every moment, a sharp and unexpected turn of the vessel brought it suddenly, as if dropped from heaven, into a circular basin of very considerable extent when compared with the width of the gorge. It was about two hundred yards in diameter, and girt in at all points but one – that immediately fronting the vessel as it entered – by hills equal in general height to the walls of the chasm, although of a thoroughly different character. Their sides sloped from the water's edge at an angle of some forty-five degrees, and they were clothed from base to summit – not a perceptible point escaping – in a drapery of the most gorgeous flower-blossoms; scarcely a green leaf being visible among the sea of odorous and fluctuating colour. This basin was of great depth, but so transparent was the water that the bottom, which seemed to consist of a thick mass of small round alabaster pebbles, was distinctly visible by glimpses – that is to say, whenever the eye could permit itself not to see, far down in the inverted heaven, the duplicate blooming of the hills. On these latter there were no trees, nor even shrubs of any size. The impressions wrought on the observer were those of richness, warmth, colour, quietude, uniformity, softness, delicacy, daintiness, voluptuousness, and a miraculous extremeness of culture that suggested dreams of a new race of fairies, laborious, tasteful, magnificent, and fastidious; but as the eye traced upwards the myriad-tinted slope, from its sharp junction with the water to its vague termination amid the folds of overhanging cloud, it became, indeed, difficult not to fancy a panoramic cataract of rubies, sapphires, opals, and golden onyxes, rolling silently out of the sky.

The visitor, shooting suddenly into this bay from out the gloom of the ravine, is delighted but astounded by the full orb of the declining sun, which he had supposed to be already far below the horizon, but which now confronts him, and forms the sole termination of an otherwise limitless vista seen through another chasm-like rift in the hills.

But here the voyager quits the vessel which has borne him so far, and descends into a light canoe of ivory, stained with arabesque devices in vivid scarlet, both within and without. The poop and beak of this boat arise high above the water, with sharp points, so that the general form is that of an irregular crescent. It lies on the surface of the bay with the proud grace of a swan. On its ermined floor reposes a single feathery paddle of satinwood; but no oarsmen or attendant is to be seen. The guest is bidden to be of good cheer – that the fates will take care of him. The larger vessel disappears, and he is left alone in the canoe, which lies apparently motionless in the middle of the lake. While he considers what course to pursue, however, he becomes aware of a gentle movement in the fairy bark. It slowly swings itself around until its prow points towards the sun. It advances with a gentle but gradually accelerated velocity, while the slight ripples it creates seem to break about the ivory side in divinest melody – seem to offer the only possible explanation of the soothing yet melancholy music for whose unseen origin the bewildered voyager looks around him in vain.

The canoe steadily proceeds, and the rocky gate of the vista is approached, so that its depths can be more distinctly seen. To the right arise a chain of lofty hills rudely and luxuriantly wooded. It is observed, however, that the trait of exquisite cleanness where the bank dips into the water, still prevails. There is not one token of the usual river debris. To the left the character of the scene is softer and more obviously artificial. Here the bank slopes upwards from the stream in a very gentle ascent, forming a broad sward of grass of a texture resembling nothing so much as velvet, and of a brilliancy of green which would bear comparison with the tint of the purest emerald. This plateau varies in width from ten to three hundred yards; reaching from the river-bank to a wall, fifty feet high, which extends, in an infinity of curves, but following the general direction of the river, until lost in the distance to the westward. This wall is of one continuous rock, and has been formed by cutting perpendicularly the once rugged precipice of the stream's southern bank, but no trace of the labour has been suffered to remain. The chiselled stone has the hue of ages, and is profusely overhung and overspread with the ivy, the coral honey-suckle, the eglantine, and the clematis. The uniformity of the top and bottom lines of the wall is fully relieved by occasional trees of gigantic height, growing singly or in small groups, both along the plateau and in the domain behind the wall, but in close proximity to it; so that frequent limbs (of the black walnut especially) reach over and dip their pendent extremities into the water. Farther back within the domain, the vision is impeded by an impenetrable screen of foliage.

These things are observed during the canoe's gradual approach to what I have called the gate of the vista. On drawing nearer to this, however, its chasm-like appearance vanishes; a new outlet from the bay is discovered to the left – in which direction the wall is also seen to sweep, still following the general course of the stream. Down this new opening the eye cannot penetrate very far; for the stream, accompanied by the wall, still bends to the left, until both are swallowed up by the leaves.

The boat, nevertheless, glides magically into the winding channel; and here the shore opposite the wall is found to resemble that opposite the wall in the straight vista. Lofty hills, rising occasionally into mountains, and covered with vegetation in wild luxuriance, still shut in the scene.

Floating gently onwards, but with a velocity slightly augmented, the voyager, after many short turns, finds his progress apparently barred by a gigantic gate or rather door of burnished gold, elaborately carved and fretted, and reflecting the direct rays of the now fast-sinking sun with an effulgence that seems to wreathe the whole surrounding forest in flames. This gate is inserted in the lofty wall; which here appears to cross the river at right angles. In a few moments, however, it is seen that the main body of the water still sweeps in a gentle and extensive curve to the left, the wall following it as before, while a stream of considerable volume, diverging from the principal one, makes its way, with a slight ripple, under the door, and is thus hidden from sight. The canoe falls into the lesser channel and approaches the gate. Its ponderous wings are slowly and musically expanded. The boat glides between them, and commences a rapid descent into a vast amphitheatre entirely begirt with purple mountains, whose bases are laved by a gleaming river throughout the full extent of their circuit. Meantime the whole Paradise of Arnheim bursts upon the view.

There is a gush of entrancing melody; there is an oppressive sense of strange sweet odour – there is a dream-like intermingling to the eye of tall slender Eastern trees – bosky shrubberies – flocks of golden and crimson birds – lily-fringed lakes – meadows of violets, tulips, poppies, hyacinths, and tuberoses – long intertangled lines of silver streamlets – and, upspringing confusedly from amid all, a mass of semi-Gothic, semi-Saracenic architecture sustaining itself by miracle in mid-air, glittering in the red sunlight with a hundred oriels, minarets, and pinnacles; and seeming the phantom handiwork, conjointly, of the sylphs, of the fairies, of the genii and of the gnomes.

Von Kempelen and His Discovery

After the very minute and elaborate paper by Arago, to say nothing of the summary in *Silliman's Journal*, with the detailed statement just published by Lieutenant Maury, it will not be supposed, of course, that in offering a few hurried remarks in reference to Von Kempelen's discovery, I have any design to look at the subject in a scientific point of view. My object is simply, in the first place, to say a few words of Von Kempelen himself (with whom, some years ago, I had the honour of a slight personal acquaintance), since everything which concerns him must necessarily, at this moment, be of interest; and, in the second place, to look in a general way, and speculatively, at the results of the discovery.

It may be as well, however, to premise the cursory observations which I have to offer, by denying, very decidedly, what seems to be a general impression (gleaned, as usual in a case of this kind, from the newspapers), viz.: that this discovery, astounding as it unquestionably is, is unanticipated.

By reference to the *Diary of Sir Humphrey Davy* (Cottle and Munroe, London, pp. 150), it will be seen at pp. 53 and 82, that this illustrious chemist had not only conceived the idea now in question, but had actually made no inconsiderable progress, experimentally, in the very identical analysis now so triumphantly brought to an issue by Von Kempelen, who although he makes not the slightest allusion to it, is, without doubt (I say it unhesitatingly, and can prove it, if required), indebted to the *Diary* for at least the first hint of his own undertaking.

The paragraph from the *Courier and Enquirer*, which is now going the rounds of the press, and which purports to claim the invention for a Mr Kissam, of Brunswick, Maine, appears to me, I confess, a little apocryphal, for several reasons; although there is nothing either impossible or very improbable in the statement made. I need not go into details. My opinion of the paragraph is founded principally upon its manner. It does not look true. Persons who are narrating facts are seldom so particular as Mr Kissam seems to be, about day and date and precise location. Besides, if Mr Kissam actually did come upon the discovery he says he did, at the period designated – nearly eight years ago – how happens it that he took no steps, on the instant, to reap the immense benefits which the merest bumpkin must have known would have resulted to him individually, if not to the world at large, from the discovery? It seems to me quite incredible that any man of common understanding could have discovered what Mr Kissam says he did, and yet have subsequently acted so like a baby – so like an owl – as Mr Kissam admits that he did. By the way, who *is* Mr Kissam? and is not the whole paragraph in the *Courier and Enquirer* a fabrication got up to 'make a talk'? It must be confessed that it has an amazingly moon-hoaxy-air. Very little dependence is to be placed upon it, in my humble opinion; and if I were not well aware, from experience, how very easily men of science are mystified, on points out of their usual range of enquiry, I should be profoundly astonished at finding so eminent a chemist as Professor Draper, discussing Mr Kissam's (or is it

Mr Quizzem's?) pretensions to the discovery, in so serious a tone.

But to return to the *Diary* of Sir Humphrey Davy. This pamphlet was not designed for the public eye, even upon the decease of the writer, as any person at all conversant with authorship may satisfy himself at once by the slightest inspection of the style. At page 13, for example, near the middle, we read, in reference to his researches about the protoxide of azote: 'In less than half a minute the respiration being continued, diminished gradually and were succeeded by analogous to gentle pressure on all the muscles.' That the respiration was not 'diminished', is not only clear by the subsequent context, but by the use of the plural, 'were'. The sentence, no doubt, was thus intended: 'In less than half a minute, the respiration being continued, [these feelings] diminished gradually, and were succeeded by [a sensation] analogous to gentle pressure on all the muscles.' A hundred similar instances go to show that the manuscript so inconsiderately published, was merely a rough notebook, meant only for the writer's own eye, but an inspection of the pamphlet will convince almost any thinking person of the truth of my suggestion. The fact is, Sir Humphrey Davy was about the last man in the world to commit himself on scientific topics. Not only had he a more than ordinary dislike to quackery, but he was morbidly afraid of appearing empirical; so that, however fully he might have been convinced that he was on the right track in the matter now in question, he would never have spoken out, until he had everything ready for the most practical demonstration. I verily believe that his last moments would have been rendered wretched, could he have suspected that his wishes in regard to burning this *Diary* (full of crude speculations) would have been unattended to; as, it seems, they were. I say 'his wishes', for that he meant to include this notebook among the miscellaneous papers directed 'to be burnt', I think there can be no manner of doubt. Whether it escaped the flames by good fortune or by bad, yet remains to be seen. That the passages quoted above, with the other similar ones referred to, gave Von Kempelen the hint, I do not in the slightest degree question; but I repeat, it yet remains to be seen whether this momentous discovery itself (momentous under any circumstances) will be of service or disservice to mankind at large. That Von Kempelen and his immediate friends will reap a rich harvest, it would be folly to doubt for a moment. They will scarcely be so weak as not to 'realise', in time, by large purchases of houses and land, with other property of intrinsic value.

In the brief account of Von Kempelen which appeared in the *Home Journal*, and has since been extensively copied, several misapprehensions of the German original seem to have been made by the translator, who professes to have taken the passage from a late number of the Presburg *Schnellpost*. '*Viele*' has evidently been misconceived (as it often is), and what the translator renders by 'sorrows', is probably '*lieden*', which, in its true version, 'sufferings', would give a totally different complexion to the whole account; but, of course, much of this is merely guess, on my part.

Von Kempelen, however, is by no means a 'misanthrope', in appearance at least, whatever he may be in fact. My acquaintance with him was casual altogether; and I am scarcely warranted in saying that

I know him at all; but to have seen and conversed with a man of so prodigious a notoriety as he has attained, or will attain in a few days, is not a small matter, as times go.

The *Literary World* speaks of him, confidently, as a native of Presburg (misled, perhaps, by the account in the *Home Journal*), but I am pleased in being able to state positively, since I have it from his own lips, that he was born in Utica, in the State of New York, although both his parents, I believe, are of Presburg descent. The family is connected, in some way, with Maelzel, of automaton-chess-player memory. In person, he is short and stout, with large, fat, blue eyes, sandy hair and whiskers, a wide but pleasing mouth, fine teeth, and I think a Roman nose. There is some defect in one of his feet. His address is frank, and his whole manner noticeable for *bonhomie*. Altogether, he looks, speaks, and acts as little like 'a misanthrope' as any man I ever saw. We were fellow-sojourners for a week about six years ago, at Earl's Hotel, in Providence, Rhode Island; and I presume that I conversed with him, at various times, for some three or four hours altogether. His principal topics were those of the day, and nothing that fell from him led me to suspect his scientific attainments. He left the hotel before me, intending to go to New York, and thence to Bremen; it was in the latter city that his great discovery was first made public; or, rather, it was there that he was first suspected of having made it. This is about all that I personally know of the now immortal Von Kempelen; but I have thought that even these few details would have interest for the public.

There can be little question that most of the marvellous rumours afloat about this affair are pure inventions, entitled to about as much credit as the story of Aladdin's lamp; and yet, in a case of this kind, as in the case of the discoveries in California, it is clear that the truth may be stranger than fiction. The following anecdote, at least, is so well authenticated, that we may receive it implicitly.

Von Kempelen had never been even tolerably well off during his residence at Bremen; and often, it was well known, he had been put to extreme shifts in order to raise trifling sums. When the great excitement occurred about the forgery on the house of Gutsmuth & Co., suspicion was directed towards Von Kempelen, on account of his having purchased a considerable property in Gasperitch Lane, and his refusing, when questioned, to explain how he became possessed of the purchase money. He was at length arrested, but nothing decisive appearing against him, was in the end set at liberty. The police, however, kept a strict watch upon his movements, and thus discovered that he left home frequently, taking always the same road, and invariably giving his watchers the slip in the neighbourhood of that labyrinth of narrow and crooked passages known by the flash name of the 'Dondergat'. Finally, by dint of great perseverance, they traced him to a garret in an old house of seven storeys, in an alley called Flatzplatz – and, coming upon him suddenly, found him, as they imagined, in the midst of his counterfeiting operations. His agitation is represented as so excessive that the officers had not the slightest doubt of his guilt. After handcuffing him, they searched his room, or rather rooms, for it appears he occupied all the mansard.

Opening into the garret where they caught him, was a closet, ten feet by eight, fitted up with some chemical apparatus, of which the object has not yet been ascertained. In one corner of the closet was a very small furnace, with a glowing fire in it, and on the fire a kind of duplicate crucible – two crucibles connected by a tube. One of these crucibles was nearly full of lead in a state of fusion, but not reaching up to the aperture of the tube, which was close to the brim. The other crucible had some liquid in it, which, as the officers entered, seemed to be furiously dissipating in vapour. They relate that, on finding himself taken, Kempelen seized the crucibles with both hands (which were encased in gloves that afterwards turned out to be asbestic), and threw the contents on the tiled floor. It was now that they handcuffed him; and before proceeding to ransack the premises they searched his person, but nothing unusual was found about him, excepting a paper parcel, in his coat-pocket, containing what was afterwards ascertained to be a mixture of antimony and some unknown substance, in nearly, but not quite, equal proportions. All attempts at analysing the unknown substance have, so far, failed, but that it will ultimately be analysed, is not to be doubted.

Passing out of the closet with their prisoner, the officers went through a sort of antechamber, in which nothing material was found, to the chemist's sleeping room. They here rummaged some drawers and boxes, but discovered only a few papers, of no importance, and some good coin, silver and gold. At length, looking under the bed, they saw a large, common hair trunk, without hinges, hasp, or lock, and with the top lying carelessly across the bottom portion. Upon attempting to draw this trunk out from under the bed, they found that, with their united strength (there were three of them, all powerful men), they 'could not stir it one inch'. Much astonished at this, one of them crawled under the bed, and looking into the trunk, said: 'No wonder we couldn't move it – why it's full to the brim of old bits of brass!'

Putting his feet, now, against the wall, so as to get a good purchase, and pushing with all his force, while his companions pulled with all theirs, the trunk, with much difficulty, was slid out from under the bed, and its contents examined. The supposed brass with which it was filled was all in small, smooth pieces, varying from the size of a pea to that of a dollar; but the pieces were irregular in shape, although more or less flat-looking, upon the whole, 'very much as lead looks when thrown upon the ground in a molten state, and there suffered to grow cool'. Now, not one of these officers for a moment suspected this metal to be anything but brass. The idea of its being gold never entered their brains, of course; how could such a wild fancy have entered it? And their astonishment may be well conceived, when the next day it became known, all over Bremen, that the 'lot of brass' which they had carted so contemptuously to the police office, without putting themselves to the trouble of pocketing the smallest scrap, was not only gold – real gold – but gold far finer than any employed in coinage – gold, in fact, absolutely pure, virgin, without the slightest appreciable alloy!

I need not go over the details of Von Kempelen's confession (as far as it went) and release, for these are familiar to the public. That he has actually realised, in spirit and in effect, if not to the letter, the old chimaera of the philosopher's stone, no sane person is at liberty to doubt. The opinions of Arago are, of course, entitled to the greatest consideration; but he is by no means infallible; and what he says of bismuth, in his report to the Academy, must be taken *cum grano salis*. The simple truth is, that up to this period all analysis has failed; and until Von Kempelen chooses to let us have the key to his own published enigma, it is more than probable that the matter will remain, for years, *in statu quo*. All that as yet can fairly be said to be known is, that 'pure gold can be made at will, and very readily from lead in connection with certain other substances, in kind and in proportions, unknown'.

Speculation, of course, is busy as to the immediate and ultimate results of this discovery – a discovery which few thinking persons will hesitate in referring to an increased interest in the matter of gold generally, by the late developments in California; and this reflection brings us inevitably to another – the exceeding inopportuneness of Von Kempelen's analysis. If many were prevented from adventuring to California, by the mere apprehension that gold would so materially diminish in value, on account of its plentifulness in the mines there, as to render the speculation of going so far in search of it a doubtful one – what impression will be wrought now, upon the minds of those about to emigrate, and especially upon the minds of those actually in the mineral region, by the announcement of this astounding discovery of Von Kempelen? a discovery which declares, in so many words, that beyond its intrinsic worth for manufacturing purposes (whatever that worth may be), gold now is, or at least soon will be (for it cannot be supposed that Von Kempelen can long retain his secret), of no greater value than lead, and of far inferior value to silver. It is, indeed, exceedingly difficult to speculate prospectively upon the consequences of the discovery, but one thing may be positively maintained – that the announcement of the discovery six months ago would have had material influence in regard to the settlement of California.

In Europe, as yet, the most noticeable results have been a rise of two hundred per cent in the price of lead, and nearly twenty-five per cent in that of silver.

X-ing a Paragrab

As it is well known that the 'wise men' came 'from the East', and as Mr Touch-and-go Bullet-head came from the East, it follows that Mr Bullet-head was a wise man; and if collateral proof of the matter be needed, here we have it – Mr B— was an editor. Irascibility was his sole foible, for in fact the obstinacy of which men accused him was anything but his foible, since he justly considered it his forte. It was his strong point – his virtue; and it would have required all the logic of a Brownson to convince him that it was 'anything else'.

I have shown that Touch-and-go Bullet-head was a wise man; and the only occasion on which he did not prove infallible, was when, abandoning that legitimate home for all wise men, the East, he migrated to the city of Alexander-the-Great-o-nopolis, or some place of a similar title, out West.

I must do him the justice to say, however, that when he made up his mind finally to settle in that town, it was under the impression that no newspaper, and consequently no editor, existed in that particular section of the country. In establishing *The Teapot* he expected to have the field all to himself. I feel confident he never would have dreamed of taking up his residence in Alexander-the-Great-o-nopolis had he been aware that, in Alexander-the-Great-o-nopolis, there lived a gentleman named John Smith (if I rightly remember), who for many years had there quietly grown fat in editing and publishing *The Alexander-the-*

Great-o-nopolis Gazette. It was solely, therefore, on account of having been misinformed, that Mr Bullet-head found himself in Alex— suppose we call it Nopolis, 'for short' – but, as he *did* find himself there, he determined to keep up his character for obst— for firmness, and remain. So remain he did; and he did more; he unpacked his press, type, etc., etc., rented an office exactly opposite to that of *The Gazette*, and, on the third morning after his arrival, issued the first number of *The Alexan*— that is to say, of *The Nopolis Teapot* – as nearly as I can recollect, this was the name of the new paper.

The leading article, I must admit, was brilliant – not to say severe. It was especially bitter about things in general – and as for the editor of *The Gazette*, he was torn all to pieces in particular. Some of Bullet-head's remarks were really so fiery that I have always, since that time, been forced to look upon John Smith, who is still alive, in the light of a salamander. I cannot pretend to give all *The Teapot*'s paragraphs verbatim, but one of them runs thus: 'Oh, yes! – Oh, we perceive! Oh, no doubt! The editor over the way is a genius – Oh, my! Oh, goodness, gracious! – what is this world coming to? Oh, *tempora*! Oh, Moses!'

A philippic at once so caustic and so classical, alighted like a bombshell among the hitherto peaceful citizens of Nopolis. Groups of excited individuals gathered at the corners of the streets. Everyone awaited, with heartfelt anxiety, the reply of the dignified Smith. Next morning it appeared as follows:

We quote from *The Teapot* of yesterday the sub-joined paragraph: 'Oh, yes! Oh, we perceive! Oh, no doubt! Oh, my! Oh, goodness! Oh, *tempora*! Oh,

Moses!' Why, the fellow is all O! That accounts for his reasoning in a circle, and explains why there is neither beginning nor end to him, nor to anything he says. We really do not believe the vagabond can write a word that hasn't an O in it. Wonder if this O-ing is a habit of his? By the by, he came away from down-east in a great hurry. Wonder if he O's as much there as he does here? 'O! it is pitiful.'

The indignation of Mr Bullet-head at these scandalous insinuations, I shall not attempt to describe. On the eel-skinning principle, however, he did not seem to be so much incensed at the attack upon his integrity as one might have imagined. It was the sneer at his style that drove him to desperation. What! – *he*, Touch-and-go Bullet-head! – not able to write a word without an O in it! He would soon let the jackanapes see that he was mistaken. Yes! he would let him see how much he was mistaken, the puppy! He, Touch-and-go Bullet-head, of Frogpondium, would let Mr John Smith perceive that he, Bullet-head, could indict, if it so pleased him, a whole paragraph – aye! a whole article – in which that contemptible vowel should not once – not even once – make its appearance. But no – that would be yielding a point to the said John Smith. He, Bullet-head, would make no alteration in his style, to suit the caprices of any Mr Smith in Christendom. Perish so vile a thought! The O for ever! He would persist in the O. He would be as O-wy as O-wy could be.

Burning with the chivalry of this determination, the great Touch-and-go, in the next *Teapot*, came out merely with this simple but resolute paragraph, in reference to this unhappy affair:

The editor of *The Teapot* has the honour of advising
the editor of *The Gazette* that he (*The Teapot*) will
take an opportunity in tomorrow morning's paper,
of convincing him (*The Gazette*) that he (*The
Teapot*) both can and will be his own master, as
regards style; he (*The Teapot*) intending to show
him (the *Gazette*) the supreme, and indeed the
withering contempt with which the criticism of
him (*The Gazette*) inspires the independent bosom
of him (*The Teapot*) by composing for the especial
gratification (?) of him (*The Gazette*) a leading
article, of some extent, in which the beautiful
vowel – the emblem of eternity – yet so offensive to
the hyper-exquisite delicacy of him (*The Gazette*)
shall most certainly not be avoided by his (*The
Gazette*'s) most obedient, humble servant, *The
Teapot*. 'So much for Buckingham!'

In fulfilment of the awful threat thus darkly inti-
mated rather than decidedly enunciated, the great
Bullet-head, turning a deaf ear to all entreaties for
'copy', and simply requesting his foreman to 'go to the
d—l', when he (the foreman) assured him (*The Teapot!*) that it was high time to 'go to press': turning a
deaf ear to everything, I say, the great Bullet-head sat
up until daybreak, consuming the midnight oil, and
absorbed in the composition of the really unparalleled
paragraph, which follows:

So ho, John! how now? Told you so, you know. Don't
crow, another time, before you're out of the woods!
Does your mother know you're out? Oh, no, no! – so
go home at once, now, John, to your odious old
woods of Concord! Go home to your woods, old
owl – go! You won't? Oh, poh, poh, John don't do so!

You've *got* to go, you know! So go at once, and don't go slow, for nobody owns you here, you know! Oh! John, John, if you *don't* go you're no *homo* – no! You're only a fowl, an owl, a cow, a sow – a doll, a poll; a poor, old, good-for-nothing-to-nobody, log, dog, hog, or frog, come out of a Concord bog. Cool, now – cool! *Do* be cool, you fool! None of your crowing, old cock! Don't frown so – don't! Don't hollo, nor howl nor growl, nor bow-wow-wow! Good Lord, John, how you do look! Told you so, you know – but stop rolling your goose of an old poll about so, and go and drown your sorrows in a bowl!

Exhausted, very naturally, by so stupendous an effort, the great Touch-and-go could attend to nothing farther that night. Firmly, composedly, yet with an air of conscious power, he handed his manuscript to the devil in waiting, and then, walking leisurely home, retired, with ineffable dignity, to bed.

Meantime the devil, to whom the copy was entrusted, ran upstairs to his case, in an unutterable hurry, and forthwith made a commencement at setting the manuscript up.

In the first place, of course – as the opening word was 'So', he made a plunge into the capital S hole and came out in triumph with a capital S. Elated by this success, he immediately threw himself upon the little-o box with a blindfold impetuosity – but who shall describe his horror when his fingers came up without the anticipated letter in their clutch? who shall paint his astonishment and rage at perceiving, as he rubbed his knuckles, that he had been only thumping them to no purpose, against the bottom of an empty box. Not a single little-o was in the little-o hole; and, glancing fearfully at the capital-O partition, he found *that*, to his extreme terror, in a precisely similar predicament. Awe-stricken, his first impulse was to rush to the foreman.

'Sir!' said he, gasping for breath, 'I can't never set up nothing without no o's.'

'What do you mean by that?' growled the foreman, who was in a very ill humour at being kept so late.

'Why, sir, there beant an o in the office, neither a big un nor a little un!'

'What – what the d—l has become of all that were in the case?'

'I don't know, sir,' said the boy, 'but one of them ere *G'zette* devils is bin prowling 'bout here all night, and I spect he's gone and cabbaged 'em every one.'

'Dod rot him! I haven't a doubt of it,' replied the foreman, getting purple with rage – 'but I tell you what you do, Bob, that's a good boy – you go over the first chance you get and hook every one of their i's and (d—n them!) their izzards.'

'Jist so,' replied Bob, with a wink and a frown – 'I'll be into 'em, I'll let 'em know a thing or two; but in de meantime, that ere paragrab? Mus go in tonight, you know – else there'll be the d—l to pay, and – '

'And not a *bit* of pitch hot,' interrupted the foreman, with a deep sigh, and an emphasis on the 'bit'. 'Is it a *very* long paragraph, Bob?'

'Shouldn't call it a *wery* long paragrab,' said Bob.

'Ah, well, then! do the best you can with it! We must get to press,' said the foreman, who was over head and ears in work; 'just stick in some other letter for o; nobody's going to read the fellow's trash anyhow.'

'Wery well,' replied Bob, 'here goes it!' and off he

392

hurried to his case, muttering as he went: 'Considdeble vell, them ere expressions, perticcler for a man as doesn't swar. So I's to gouge out all their eyes, eh? and d—n all their gizzards! Vell! this here's the chap as is just able for to do it.' The fact is that although Bob was but twelve years old and four feet high, he was equal to any amount of fight, in a small way.

The exigency here described is by no means of rare occurrence in printing offices; and I cannot tell how to account for it, but the fact is indisputable, that when the exigency does occur, it almost always happens that x is adopted as a substitute for the letter deficient. The true reason, perhaps, is that x is rather the most superabundant letter in the cases, or at least was so in the old times – long enough to render the substitution in question an habitual thing with printers. As for Bob, he would have considered it heretical to employ any other character, in a case of this kind, than the x to which he had been accustomed.

'I shell have to x this ere paragrab,' said he to himself, as he read it over in astonishment, 'but it's jest about the awfulest o-wy paragrab I ever did see': so x it he did, unflinchingly, and to press it went x-ed.

Next morning the population of Nopolis were taken all aback by reading in *The Teapot*, the following extraordinary leader:

Sx hx, Jxhn! hxw nxw? Txld yxu sx, yxu knxw. Dxn't crxw, anxther time, befxre yxu're xut xf the wxxds! Dxes yxur mxther knxw yxu're xut? Xh, nx, nx! – sx gx hxme at xnce, nxw, Jxhn, tx yxur xdixus xld wxxds xf Cxncxrd! Gx hxme tx yxur wxxds, xld xwl – gx! Yxu wxn't? Xh, pxh, pxh, Jxhn, dxn't dx sx! Yxu've *gxt* tx gx, yxu knxw! Sx gx at xnce, and dxn't gx slxw; fxr nxbxdy xwns yxu here, yxu knxw! Xh! Jxhn, Jxhn, if yxu dxn't gx yxu're nx *hxmx* – nx! Yxu're xnly a fxwl, an xwl, a cxw, a sxw – a dxll, a pxll; a pxxr, xld, gxxd-fxr-nxthing-tx-nxbxdy, lxg, dxg, hxg, xr frxg, cxme xut xf a Cxncxrd bxg. Cxxl, nxw – cxxl! Dx be cxxl, yxu fxxl! Nxne xf yxur crxwing, xld cxck! Dxn't frxwn sx – dxn't! Dxn't hxllx, nxr hxwl, nxr grxwl, nxr bxw-wxw-wxw! Gxxd Lxrd, Jxhn, hxw yxu dx lxxk! Txld yxu sx, yxu knxw – but stxp rxlling yxur gxxse xf an xld pxll abxut sx, and gx and drxwn yxur sxrrxws in a bxwl!

The uproar occasioned by this mystical and cabbalistical article, is not to be conceived. The first definite idea entertained by the populace was, that some diabolical treason lay concealed in the hiero-glyphics; and there was a general rush to Bullet-head's residence, for the purpose of riding him on a rail; but that gentleman was nowhere to be found. He had vanished, no one could tell how; and not even the ghost of him has ever been seen since.

Unable to discover its legitimate object, the popular fury at length subsided; leaving behind it, by way of sediment, quite a medley of opinion about this unhappy affair.

One gentleman thought the whole an x-ellent joke.

Another said that, indeed, Bullet-head had shown much x-uberance of fancy.

A third admitted him x-entric, but no more.

A fourth could only suppose it the Yankee's design to x-press, in a general way, his x-asperation.

'Say, rather, to set an x-ample to posterity,' suggested a fifth.

That Bullet-head had been driven to an extremity,

was clear to all; and in fact, since *that* editor could not be found, there was some talk about lynching the other one.

The more common conclusion, however, was that the affair was, simply, x-traordinary and in-x-plicable. Even the town mathematician confessed that he could make nothing of so dark a problem. X, everybody knew, was an unknown quantity; but in this case (as he properly observed), there was an unknown quantity of x.

The opinion of Bob, the devil (who kept dark about his having 'x-ed the paragrab'), did not meet with so much attention as I think it deserved, although it was very openly and very fearlessly expressed. He said that, for his part, he had no doubt about the matter at all, that it was a clear case, that Mr Bullet-head 'never could be persuaded fur to drink like other folks, but vas continually a-svigging o' that ere blessed XXX ale, and as a naiteral consekvence, it just puffed him up savage, and made him x (cross) in the x-treme.'

Hop-Frog

I never knew anyone so keenly alive to a joke as the king was. He seemed to live only for joking. To tell a good story of the joke kind, and to tell it well, was the surest road to his favour. Thus it happened that his seven ministers were all noted for their accomplishments as jokers. They all took after the king, too, in being large, corpulent, oily men, as well as inimitable jokers. Whether people grow fat by joking, or whether there is something in fat itself which predisposes to a joke, I have never been quite able to determine; but certain it is that a lean joker is a *rara avis in terris*.

About the refinements, or, as he called them, the 'ghost' of wit, the king troubled himself very little. He had an especial admiration for breadth in a jest, and would often put up with length, for the sake of it. Over-niceties wearied him. He would have preferred Rabelais' *Gargantua* to the *Zadig* of Voltaire: and, upon the whole, practical jokes suited his taste far better than verbal ones.

At the date of my narrative, professing jesters had not altogether gone out of fashion at court. Several of the great continental 'powers' still retained their 'fools', who wore motley, with caps and bells, and who were expected to be always ready with sharp witticisms, at a moment's notice, in consideration of the crumbs that fell from the royal table.

Our king, as a matter of course, retained his 'fool'. The fact is, he required something in the way of folly – if only to counterbalance the heavy wisdom of the seven wise men who were his ministers – not to mention himself.

His fool, or professional jester, was not *only* a fool, however. His value was trebled in the eyes of the king, by the fact of his being also a dwarf and a cripple. Dwarfs were as common at court, in those days, as fools; and many monarchs would have found it difficult to get through their days (days are rather longer at court than elsewhere) without both a jester to laugh with, and a dwarf to laugh at. But, as I have already observed, your jesters, in ninety-nine cases out of a hundred, are fat, round, and unwieldy – so that it was no small source of self-gratulation with our king that, in Hop-Frog (this was the fool's name), he possessed a triplicate treasure in one person.

I believe the name 'Hop-Frog' was not that given to the dwarf by his sponsors at baptism, but it was conferred upon him, by general consent of the several ministers, on account of his inability to walk as other men do. In fact, Hop-Frog could only get along by a sort of interjectional gait – something between a leap and a wriggle – a movement that afforded illimitable amusement, and of course consolation, to the king, for (notwithstanding the protuberance of his stomach and a constitutional swelling of the head) the king, by his whole court, was accounted a capital figure.

But although Hop-Frog, through the distortion of his legs, could move only with great pain and difficulty along a road or floor, the prodigious muscular power which nature seemed to have bestowed upon his arms, by way of compensation for deficiency in the lower limbs, enabled him to perform many feats of wonderful dexterity, where trees or ropes were in question, or anything else to climb. At such exercises he certainly much more resembled a squirrel, or a small monkey, than a frog.

I am not able to say, with precision, from what country Hop-Frog originally came. It was from some barbarous region, however, that no person ever heard of – a vast distance from the court of our king. Hop-Frog, and a young girl very little less dwarfish than himself (although of exquisite proportions, and a marvellous dancer), had been forcibly carried off from their respective homes in adjoining provinces, and sent as presents to the king, by one of his ever-victorious generals.

Under these circumstances, it is not to be wondered at that a close intimacy arose between the two little captives. Indeed, they soon became sworn friends. Hop-Frog, who, although he made a great deal of sport, was by no means popular, had it not in his power to render Trippetta many services; but she, on account of her grace and exquisite beauty (although a dwarf), was universally admired and petted; so she possessed much influence; and never failed to use it, whenever she could, for the benefit of Hop-Frog.

On some grand state occasion – I forgot what – the king determined to have a masquerade, and whenever a masquerade, or anything of that kind, occurred at our court, then the talents both of Hop-Frog and Trippetta were sure to be called into play. Hop-Frog, in especial, was so inventive in the way of getting up pageants, suggesting novel characters, and arranging costumes for masked balls, that nothing could be done, it seems, without his assistance.

The night appointed for the fete had arrived. A gorgeous hall had been fitted up, under Trippetta's eye, with every kind of device which could possibly give *éclat* to a masquerade. The whole court was in a fever of expectation. As for costumes and characters, it might well be supposed that everybody had come to a decision on such points. Many had made up their minds (as to what roles they should assume) a week, or even a month, in advance; and, in fact, there was not a particle of indecision anywhere – except in the case of the king and his seven ministers. Why they hesitated I never could tell, unless they did it by way of a joke. More probably, they found it difficult, on account of being so fat, to make up their minds. At all events, time flew; and, as a last resort they sent for Trippetta and Hop-Frog.

When the two little friends obeyed the summons of the king they found him sitting at his wine with the seven members of his cabinet council; but the monarch appeared to be in a very ill humour. He knew that Hop-Frog was not fond of wine, for it excited the poor cripple almost to madness; and madness is no comfortable feeling. But the king loved his practical jokes, and took pleasure in forcing Hop-Frog to drink and (as the king called it) 'to be merry'.

'Come here, Hop-Frog,' said he, as the jester and his friend entered the room; 'swallow this bumper to the health of your absent friends [here Hop-Frog sighed], and then let us have the benefit of your invention. We want characters – characters, man – something novel – out of the way. We are wearied with this everlasting sameness. Come, drink! the wine will brighten your wits.'

Hop-Frog endeavoured, as usual, to get up a jest in reply to these advances from the king; but the effort was too much. It happened to be the poor dwarf's birthday, and the command to drink to his 'absent friends' forced the tears to his eyes. Many large, bitter drops fell into the goblet as he took it, humbly, from the hand of the tyrant.

'Ah! ha! ha!' roared the latter, as the dwarf reluctantly drained the beaker, 'See what a glass of good wine can do! Why, your eyes are shining already!'

Poor fellow! his large eyes gleamed, rather than shone; for the effect of wine on his excitable brain was not more powerful than instantaneous. He placed the goblet nervously on the table, and looked round upon the company with a half-insane stare. They all seemed highly amused at the success of the king's 'joke'.

'And now to business,' said the prime minister, a very fat man.

'Yes,' said the king. 'Come lend us your assistance. Characters, my fine fellow; we stand in need of characters – all of us – ha! ha! ha!' and as this was seriously meant for a joke, his laugh was chorused by the seven.

Hop-Frog also laughed, although feebly and somewhat vacantly.

'Come, come,' said the king, impatiently, 'have you nothing to suggest?'

'I am endeavouring to think of something novel,' replied the dwarf, abstractedly, for he was quite bewildered by the wine.

'Endeavouring!' cried the tyrant, fiercely; 'what do you mean by that? Ah, I perceive. You are sulky, and want more wine. Here, drink this!' and he poured out another goblet full and offered it to the cripple, who merely gazed at it, gasping for breath.

'Drink, I say!' shouted the monster, 'or by the fiends – '

The dwarf hesitated. The king grew purple with

rage. The courtiers smirked. Trippetta, pale as a corpse, advanced to the monarch's seat, and, falling on her knees before him, implored him to spare her friend.

The tyrant regarded her, for some moments, in evident wonder at her audacity. He seemed quite at a loss what to do or say – how most becomingly to express his indignation. At last, without uttering a syllable, he pushed her violently from him, and threw the contents of the brimming goblet in her face.

The poor girl got up as best she could, and, not daring even to sigh, resumed her position at the foot of the table.

There was a dead silence for about half a minute, during which the falling of a leaf, or of a feather, might have been heard. It was interrupted by a low, but harsh and protracted grating sound which seemed to come at once from every corner of the room.

'What – what – what are you making that noise for?' demanded the king, turning furiously to the dwarf.

The latter seemed to have recovered, in great measure, from his intoxication, and looking fixedly but quietly into the tyrant's face, merely ejaculated: 'I – I? How could it have been me?'

'The sound appeared to come from without,' observed one of the courtiers. 'I fancy it was the parrot at the window, whetting his bill upon his cage-wires.'

'True,' replied the monarch, as if much relieved by the suggestion; 'but, on the honour of a knight, I could have sworn that it was the gritting of this vagabond's teeth.'

Hereupon the dwarf laughed (the king was too confirmed a joker to object to anyone's laughing), and displayed a set of large, powerful, and very repulsive teeth. Moreover, he avowed his perfect willingness to swallow as much wine as desired. The monarch was pacified; and having drained another bumper with no very perceptible ill effect, Hop-Frog entered at once, and with spirit, into the plans for the masquerade.

'I cannot tell what was the association of idea,' observed he, very tranquilly, and as if he had never tasted wine in his life, 'but just after your majesty had struck the girl and thrown the wine in her face – just after your majesty had done this, and while the parrot was making that odd noise outside the window, there came into my mind a capital diversion – one of my own country frolics – often enacted among us, at our masquerades: but here it will be new altogether. Unfortunately, however, it requires a company of eight persons and –'

'Here we are!' cried the king, laughing at his acute discovery of the coincidence; 'eight to a fraction – I and my seven ministers. Come! what is the diversion?'

'We call it,' replied the cripple, 'the Eight Chained Orang-utans, and it really is excellent sport if well enacted.'

'We will enact it,' remarked the king, drawing himself up, and lowering his eyelids.

'The beauty of the game,' continued Hop-Frog, 'lies in the fright it occasions among the women.'

'Capital!' roared in chorus the monarch and his ministry.

'I will equip you as orang-utans,' proceeded the dwarf; 'leave all that to me. The resemblance shall be so striking, that the company of masqueraders will take you for real beasts – and of course, they will be as much terrified as astonished.'

'Oh, this is exquisite!' exclaimed the king.

'Hop-Frog! I will make a man of you.'

'The chains are for the purpose of increasing the confusion by their jangling. You are supposed to have escaped, *en masse*, from your keepers. Your majesty cannot conceive the effect produced, at a masquerade, by eight chained orang-utans, imagined to be real ones by most of the company; and rushing in with savage cries, among the crowd of delicately and gorgeously habited men and women. The contrast is inimitable!'

'It must be,' said the king: and the council arose hurriedly (as it was growing late), to put in execution the scheme of Hop-Frog.

His mode of equipping the party as orang-utans was very simple, but effective enough for his purposes. The animals in question had, at the epoch of my story, very rarely been seen in any part of the civilised world; and as the imitations made by the dwarf were sufficiently beast-like and more than sufficiently hideous, their truthfulness to nature was thus thought to be secured.

The king and his ministers were first encased in tight-fitting stockinet shirts and drawers. They were then saturated with tar. At this stage of the process, someone of the party suggested feathers; but the suggestion was at once overruled by the dwarf, who soon convinced the eight, by ocular demonstration, that the hair of such a brute as the orang-utan was much more efficiently represented by flax. A thick coating of the latter was accordingly plastered upon the coating of tar. A long chain was now procured. First, it was passed about the waist of the king, and tied, then about another of the party, and also tied; then about all successively, in the same manner. When this chaining arrangement was complete, and the party stood as far apart from each other as possible, they formed a circle; and to make all things appear natural, Hop-Frog passed the residue of the chain in two diameters, at right angles, across the circle, after the fashion adopted, at the present day, by those who capture chimpanzees, or other large apes, in Borneo.

The grand saloon in which the masquerade was to take place was a circular room, very lofty, and receiving the light of the sun only through a single window at the top. At night (the season for which the apartment was especially designed) it was illuminated principally by a large chandelier, depending by a chain from the centre of the skylight, and lowered, or elevated, by means of a counterbalance as usual; but (in order not to look unsightly) this latter passed outside the cupola and over the roof.

The arrangements of the room had been left to Trippetta's superintendence; but, in some particulars, it seems, she had been guided by the calmer judgement of her friend the dwarf. At his suggestion it was that, on this occasion, the chandelier was removed. Its waxen drippings (which, in weather so warm, it was quite impossible to prevent) would have been seriously detrimental to the rich dresses of the guests, who, on account of the crowded state of the saloon, could not all be expected to keep from out its centre; that is to say, from under the chandelier. Additional sconces were set in various parts of the hall, out of the way, and a flambeau, emitting sweet odour, was placed in the right hand of each of the caryatides that stood against the wall – some fifty or sixty altogether.

The eight orang-utans, taking Hop-Frog's advice, waited patiently until midnight (when the room was thoroughly filled with masqueraders) before making their appearance. No sooner had the clock ceased striking, however, than they rushed, or rather rolled in, all together – for the impediments of their chains caused most of the party to fall, and all to stumble as they entered.

The excitement among the masqueraders was prodigious, and filled the heart of the king with glee. As had been anticipated, there were not a few of the guests who supposed the ferocious-looking creatures to be beasts of some kind in reality, if not precisely orang-utans. Many of the women swooned with affright; and had not the king taken the precaution to exclude all weapons from the saloon, his party might soon have expiated their frolic in their blood. As it was, a general rush was made for the doors; but the king had ordered them to be locked immediately upon his entrance; and, at the dwarf's suggestion, the keys had been deposited with him.

While the tumult was at its height, and each masquerader attentive only to his own safety (for, in fact, there was much real danger from the pressure of the excited crowd), the chain by which the chandelier ordinarily hung, and which had been drawn up on its removal, might have been seen very gradually to descend, until its hooked extremity came within three feet of the floor.

Soon after this, the king and his seven friends having reeled about the hall in all directions, found themselves, at length, in its centre, and, of course, in immediate contact with the chain. While they were thus situated, the dwarf, who had followed noiselessly at their heels, inciting them to keep up the commotion, took hold of their own chain at the intersection of the two portions which crossed the circle diametrically and at right angles. Here, with the rapidity of thought, he inserted the hook from which the chandelier had been wont to depend; and, in an instant, by some unseen agency, the chandelier-chain was drawn so far upwards as to take the hook out of reach, and, as an inevitable consequence, to drag the orang-utans together in close connection, and face to face.

The masqueraders, by this time, had recovered, in some measure, from their alarm; and, beginning to regard the whole matter as a well-contrived pleasantry, set up a loud shout of laughter at the predicament of the apes.

'Leave them to me!' now screamed Hop-Frog, his shrill voice making itself easily heard through all the din. 'Leave them to me. I fancy I know them. If I can only get a good look at them, I can soon tell who they are.'

Here, scrambling over the heads of the crowd, he managed to get to the wall; when, seizing a flambeau from one of the caryatides, he returned, as he went, to the centre of the room – leaping, with the agility of a monkey, upon the king's head, and thence clambered a few feet up the chain; holding down the torch to examine the group of orang-utans, and still screaming: 'I shall soon find out who they are!'

And now, while the whole assembly (the apes included) were convulsed with laughter, the jester suddenly uttered a shrill whistle; when the chain flew violently up for about thirty feet – dragging with it the dismayed and struggling orang-utans, and leaving them suspended in mid-air between the skylight and the floor. Hop-Frog, clinging to the chain as it rose, still maintained his relative position in respect to the eight maskers, and still (as if nothing were the matter) continued to thrust his torch down towards them, as though endeavouring to discover who they were.

So thoroughly astonished was the whole company at this ascent, that a dead silence, of about a minute's duration, ensued. It was broken by just such a low, harsh, grating sound, as had before attracted the attention of the king and his councillors when the former threw the wine in the face of Trippetta. But, on the present occasion, there could be no question as to whence the sound issued. It came from the fang-like teeth of the dwarf, who ground them and gnashed them as he foamed at the mouth, and glared, with an expression of maniacal rage, into the upturned countenances of the king and his seven companions.

'Ah, ha!' said at length the infuriated jester. 'Ah, ha! I begin to see who these people are now!' Here, pretending to scrutinise the king more closely, he held the flambeau to the flaxen coat which enveloped him, and which instantly burst into a sheet of vivid flame. In less than half a minute the whole eight orang-utans were blazing fiercely, amid the shrieks of the multitude who gazed at them from below, horror-stricken, and without the power to render them the slightest assistance.

At length the flames, suddenly increasing in virulence, forced the jester to climb higher up the chain, to be out of their reach; and, as he made this movement, the crowd again sank, for a brief instant, into silence. The dwarf seized his opportunity, and once more spoke: 'I now see distinctly,' he said, 'what manner of people these maskers are. They are a great king and his seven privy-councillors – a king who does not scruple to strike a defenceless girl and his seven councillors who abet him in the outrage. As for myself, I am simply Hop-Frog, the jester – and this is my last jest.'

Owing to the high combustibility of both the flax and the tar to which it adhered, the dwarf had scarcely made an end of his brief speech before the work of vengeance was complete. The eight corpses swung in their chains, a fetid, blackened, hideous, and indistinguishable mass. The cripple hurled his torch at them, clambered leisurely to the ceiling, and disappeared through the skylight.

It is supposed that Trippetta, stationed on the roof of the saloon, had been the accomplice of her friend in his fiery revenge, and that, together, they effected their escape to their own country: for neither was seen again.

THE POEMS

The Raven

Once upon a midnight dreary, while I pondered,
    weak and weary,
Over many a quaint and curious volume of forgotten
    lore –
While I nodded, nearly napping, suddenly there
    came a tapping,
As of someone gently rapping, rapping at my
    chamber door.
' 'Tis some visitor,' I muttered, 'tapping at my
    chamber door –

> Only this, and nothing more.'

Ah, distinctly I remember it was in the bleak
    December,
And each separate dying ember wrought its ghost
    upon the floor.
Eagerly I wished the morrow – vainly I had sought to
    borrow
From my books surcease of sorrow – sorrow for the
    lost Lenore –
For the rare and radiant maiden whom the angels
    name Lenore –

> Nameless here for evermore.

And the silken sad uncertain rustling of each purple
    curtain
Thrilled me – filled me with fantastic terrors never
    felt before;
So that now, to still the beating of my heart, I stood
    repeating:
' 'Tis some visitor entreating entrance at my
    chamber door –

Some late visitor entreating entrance at my chamber
    door;
                 This it is and nothing more.'

Presently my soul grew stronger; hesitating then no
    longer,
'Sir,' said I, 'or Madam, truly your forgiveness I
    implore;
But the fact is I was napping, and so gently you
    came rapping,
And so faintly you came tapping, tapping at my
    chamber door,
That I scarce was sure I heard you' – here I opened
    wide the door;
                 Darkness there and nothing more.

Deep into that darkness peering, long I stood there
    wondering, fearing,
Doubting, dreaming dreams no mortal ever dared to
    dream before;
But the silence was unbroken, and the darkness gave
    no token,
And the only word there spoken was the whispered
    word, 'Lenore!'
This I whispered, and an echo murmured back the
    word, 'Lenore!' –
                 Merely this and nothing more.

Back into the chamber turning, all my soul within
    me burning,
Soon I heard again a tapping something louder than
    before.
'Surely,' said I, 'surely that is something at my
    window lattice;

Let me see, then, what thereat is, and this mystery
    explore –
Let my heart be still a moment, and this mystery
    explore;
                'Tis the wind and nothing more!'

Open here I flung the shutter, when, with many a
    flirt and flutter,
In there stepped a stately raven of the saintly days of
    yore.
Not the least obeisance made he; not an instant
    stopped or stayed he;
But, with mien of lord or lady, perched above my
    chamber door –
Perched upon a bust of Pallas just above my
    chamber door –
                Perched, and sat, and nothing more.

Then this ebony bird beguiling my sad fancy into
    smiling,
By the grave and stern decorum of the countenance
    it wore,
'Though thy crest be shorn and shaven, thou,' I
    said, 'art sure no craven,
Ghastly grim and ancient raven wandering from the
    Nightly shore –
Tell me what thy lordly name is on the Night's
    Plutonian shore!'
                Quoth the raven, 'Nevermore.'

Much I marvelled this ungainly fowl to hear
    discourse so plainly,
Though its answer little meaning – little relevancy
    bore;

For we cannot help agreeing that no living human
being
Ever yet was blessed with seeing bird above his
chamber door –
Bird or beast upon the sculptured bust above his
chamber door,
>> With such name as 'Nevermore'.

But the raven, sitting lonely on that placid bust,
spoke only
That one word, as if his soul in that one word he did
outpour.
Nothing farther then he uttered – not a feather then
he fluttered –
Till I scarcely more than muttered: 'Other friends
have flown before –
On the morrow *he* will leave me, as my Hopes have
flown before.'
>> Then the bird said, 'Nevermore.'

Startled at the stillness broken by reply so aptly
spoken,
'Doubtless,' said I, 'what it utters is its only stock
and store,
Caught from some unhappy master whom
unmerciful Disaster
Followed fast and followed faster till his songs one
burden bore –
Till the dirges of his Hope that melancholy burden
bore
>> Of 'Never – nevermore'.

But the raven still beguiling all my sad soul into
smiling,

Straight I wheeled a cushioned seat in front of bird
    and bust and door;
Then, upon the velvet sinking, I betook myself to
    linking
Fancy unto fancy, thinking what this ominous bird
    of yore –
What this grim, ungainly, ghastly, gaunt and
    ominous bird of yore
              Meant in croaking 'Nevermore.'

This I sat engaged in guessing, but no syllable
    expressing
To the fowl whose fiery eyes now burned into my
    bosom's core;
This and more I sat divining, with my head at ease
    reclining
On the cushion's velvet lining that the lamplight
    gloated o'er,
But whose velvet violet lining with the lamplight
    gloating o'er,
              She shall press, ah, nevermore!

Then, methought, the air grew denser, perfumed
    from an unseen censer
Swung by Angels whose faint footfalls tinkled on the
    tufted floor.
'Wretch,' I cried, 'thy God hath lent thee – by these
    angels he hath sent thee
Respite – respite and nepenthe from thy memories
    of Lenore!
Quaff, oh quaff this kind nepenthe and forget this
    lost Lenore!'
              Quoth the raven, 'Nevermore.'

'Prophet!' said I, 'thing of evil! – prophet still, if bird
    or devil! –

Whether Tempter sent, or whether tempest tossed
    thee here ashore,

Desolate, yet all undaunted, on this desert land
    enchanted –

On this home by Horror haunted – tell me truly, I
    implore –

Is there – *is* there balm in Gilead? – tell me – tell me,
    I implore!'

                      Quoth the raven, 'Nevermore.'

'Prophet!' said I, 'thing of evil! – prophet still, if bird
    or devil!

By that Heaven that bends above us – by that God
    we both adore –

Tell this soul with sorrow laden if, within the distant
    Aidenn,

It shall clasp a sainted maiden whom the angels
    name Lenore –

Clasp a rare and radiant maiden whom the angels
    name Lenore.'

                      Quoth the raven, 'Nevermore.'

'Be that word our sign of parting, bird or fiend!' I
    shrieked, upstarting –

'Get thee back into the tempest and the Night's
    Plutonian shore!

Leave no black plume as a token of that lie thy soul
    hath spoken!

Leave my loneliness unbroken! – quit the bust above
    my door!

Take thy beak from out my heart, and take thy form
    from off my door!'

                      Quoth the raven, 'Nevermore.'

And the raven, never flitting, still is sitting, still is
    sitting
On the pallid bust of Pallas just above my chamber
    door;
And his eyes have all the seeming of a demon's that
    is dreaming,
And the lamplight o'er him streaming throws his
    shadow on the floor;
And my soul from out that shadow that lies floating
    on the floor

               Shall be lifted – nevermore!

Lenore

Ah, broken is the golden bowl! the spirit flown
 forever!
Let the bell toll! – a saintly soul floats on the Stygian
 river;
And, Guy De Vere, hast *thou* no tear? – weep now or
 never more!
See on yon drear and rigid bier low lies thy love,
 Lenore!
Come! let the burial rite be read – the funeral song
 be sung! –
An anthem for the queenliest dead that ever died so
 young –
A dirge for her the doubly dead in that she died so
 young.

'Wretches! ye loved her for her wealth and hated her
 for her pride,
And when she fell in feeble health, ye blessed her –
 that she died!
How *shall* the ritual, then, be read? – the requiem
 how be sung
By you – by yours, the evil eye – by yours, the
 slanderous tongue
That did to death the innocence that died, and died
 so young?'

Peccavimus; but rave not thus! and let a Sabbath song
Go up to God so solemnly the dead may feel no
 wrong!
The sweet Lenore hath 'gone before', with Hope,
 that flew beside,

Leaving thee wild for the dear child that should have
      been thy bride –
For her, the fair and debonair, that now so lowly
      lies,
The life upon her yellow hair but not within her eyes –
The life still there, upon her hair – the death upon
      her eyes.

'Avaunt! tonight my heart is light. No dirge will I
      upraise,
But waft the angel on her flight with a Paean of old
      days!
Let *no* bell toll! – lest her sweet soul, amid its
      hallowed mirth,
Should catch the note, as it doth float up from the
      damnèd Earth.
To friends above, from fiends below, the indignant
      ghost is riven –
From Hell unto a high estate far up within the
      Heaven –
From grief and groan, to a golden throne, beside the
      King of Heaven.'

Hymn

At morn – at noon – at twilight dim –
Maria! thou hast heard my hymn!
In joy and woe – in good and ill –
Mother of God, be with me still!
When the Hours flew brightly by,
And not a cloud obscured the sky,
My soul, lest it should truant be,
Thy grace did guide to thine and thee;
Now, when storms of Fate o'ercast
Darkly my Present and my Past,
Let my Future radiant shine
With sweet hopes of thee and thine!

A Valentine

For her this rhyme is penned, whose luminous eyes,
   Brightly expressive as the twins of Loeda,
Shall find her own sweet name, that, nestling lies
   Upon the page, enwrapped from every reader.
Search narrowly the lines! – they hold a treasure
   Divine – a talisman – an amulet
That must be worn *at heart*. Search well the measure –
   The words – the syllables! Do not forget
The trivialest point, or you may lose your labour!
   And yet there is in this no Gordian knot
Which one might not undo without a sabre,
   If one could merely comprehend the plot.
Enwritten upon the leaf where now are peering
   Eyes' scintillating soul, there lie *perdus*
Three eloquent words oft uttered in the hearing
   Of poets, by poets – as the name is a poet's too.
Its letters, although naturally lying
   Like the knight Pinto – Mendez Ferdinando –
Still form a synonym for Truth. – Cease trying!
   You will not read the riddle, though you do the
                     best you *can* do.

[To discover the names in this and the following poem read
the first letter of the first line in connection with the second
letter of the second line, the third letter of the third line, the
fourth of the fourth and so on to the end.]

The Coliseum

Type of the antique Rome! Rich reliquary
Of lofty contemplation left to Time
By buried centuries of pomp and power!
At length – at length – after so many days
Of weary pilgrimage and burning thirst
(Thirst for the springs of lore that in thee lie),
I kneel, an altered and an humble man,
Amid thy shadows, and so drink within
My very soul thy grandeur, gloom, and glory!

Vastness! and Age! and Memories of Eld!
Silence! and Desolation! and dim Night!
I feel ye now – I feel ye in your strength –
O spells more sure than e'er Judaean king
Taught in the gardens of Gethsemane!
O charms more potent than the rapt Chaldee
Ever drew down from out the quiet stars!

Here, where a hero fell, a column falls!
Here, where the mimic eagle glared in gold,
A midnight vigil holds the swarthy bat!
Here, where the dames of Rome their gilded hair
Waved to the wind, now wave the reed and thistle!
Here, where on golden throne the monarch lolled,
Glides, spectre-like, unto his marble home,
Lit by the wan light of the hornèd moon,
The swift and silent lizard of the stones!

But stay! these walls – these ivy-clad arcades –
These mouldering plinths – these sad and
                                    blackened shafts –
These vague entablatures – this crumbling frieze –

These shattered cornices – this wreck – this ruin –
These stones – alas! these grey stones – are they all –
All of the famed, and the colossal left
By the corrosive Hours to Fate and me?

'Not all' – the Echoes answer me – 'not all!
Prophetic sounds and loud arise for ever
From us, and from all Ruin, unto the wise,
As melody from Memnon to the Sun.
We rule the hearts of mightiest men – we rule
With a despotic sway all giant minds.
We are not impotent – we pallid stones.
Not all our power is gone – not all our fame –
Not all the magic of our high renown –
Not all the wonder that encircles us –
Not all the mysteries that in us lie –
Not all the memories that hang upon
And cling around about us as a garment,
Clothing us in a robe of more than glory.'

To Helen

I saw thee once – once only – years ago;
I must not say *how* many – but *not* many.
It was a July midnight; and from out
A full-orbed moon, that, like thine own soul,
    soaring,
Sought a precipitate pathway up through heaven,
There fell a silvery-silken veil of light,
With quietude, and sultriness, and slumber,
Upon the upturn'd faces of a thousand
Roses that grew in an enchanted garden,
Where no wind dared to stir, unless on tiptoe –
Fell on the upturn'd faces of these roses
That gave out, in return for the love-light,
Their odorous souls in an ecstatic death –
Fell on the upturn'd faces of these roses
That smiled and died in this parterre, enchanted
By thee, and by the poetry of thy presence.

Clad all in white, upon a violet bank
I saw thee half reclining; while the moon
Fell on the upturn'd faces of the roses,
And on thine own, upturn'd – alas, in sorrow!

Was it not Fate that, on this July midnight –
Was it not Fate (whose name is also Sorrow),
That bade me pause before that garden-gate,
To breathe the incense of those slumbering roses?
No footsteps stirred; the hated world all slept,
Save only thee and me. (Oh, Heaven! – oh, God!
How my heart beats in coupling those two words!)
Save only thee and me. I paused – I looked –

And in an instant all things disappeared.
(Ah, bear in mind this garden was enchanted!)

The pearly lustre of the moon went out;
The mossy banks and the meandering paths,
The happy flowers and the repining trees,
Were seen no more: the very roses' odours
Died in the arms of the adoring airs.
All – all expired save thee – save less than thou:
Save only the divine light in thine eyes –
Save but the soul in thine uplifted eyes.
I saw but them – they were the world to me.
I saw but them – saw only them for hours –
Saw only them until the moon went down.
What wild heart-histories seemed to lie enwritten
Upon those crystalline, celestial spheres!
How dark a woe, yet how sublime a hope!
How silently serene a sea of pride!
How daring an ambition; yet how deep –
How fathomless a capacity for love!

But now, at length, dear Dian sank from sight,
Into a western couch of thunder-cloud;
And thou, a ghost, amid the entombing trees
Didst glide away. *Only thine eyes remained.*
They *would not* go – they never yet have gone.
Lighting my lonely pathway home that night,
They have not left me (as my hopes have) since;
They follow me – they lead me through the years.
They are my ministers – yet I their slave.
Their office is to illumine and enkindle –
My duty, *to be saved* by their bright light,
And purified in their electric fire,
And sanctified in their Elysian fire.

They fill my soul with Beauty (which is Hope),
And are far up in Heaven – the stars I kneel to
In the sad, silent watches of my night;
While even in the meridian glare of day
I see them still – two sweetly scintillant
Venuses, unextinguished by the sun!

To —

Not long ago, the writer of these lines,
In the mad pride of intellectuality,
Maintained 'the power of words' – denied that ever
A thought arose within the human brain
Beyond the utterance of the human tongue:
And now, as if in mockery of that boast,
Two words – two foreign soft dissyllables –
Italian tones, made only to be murmured
By angels dreaming in the moonlit 'dew
That hangs like chains of pearl on Hermon hill' –
Have stirred from out the abysses of his heart,
Unthought-like thoughts that are the souls of thought,
Richer, far wilder, far diviner visions
Than even the seraph harper, Israfel
(Who has 'the sweetest voice of all God's creatures'),
Could hope to utter. And I! my spells are broken.
The pen falls powerless from my shivering hand.
With thy dear name as text, though bidden by thee,
I cannot write – I cannot speak or think –
Alas, I cannot feel; for 'tis not feeling,
This standing motionless upon the golden
Threshold of the wide-open gate of dreams,
Gazing, entranced, adown the gorgeous vista,
And thrilling as I see, upon the right,
Upon the left, and all the way along,
Amid unpurpled vapours, far away
To where the prospect terminates – *thee only.*

Ulalume

The skies they were ashen and sober;
    The leaves they were crisped and sere –
    The leaves they were withering and sere;
It was night in the lonesome October
    Of my most immemorial year;
It was hard by the dim lake of Auber,
    In the misty mid region of Weir –
It was down by the dank tarn of Auber,
    In the ghoul-haunted woodland of Weir.

Here once, through an alley Titanic,
    Of cypress, I roamed with my Soul –
    Of cypress, with Psyche, my Soul.
There were days when my heart was volcanic
    As the scoriac rivers that roll –
    As the lavas that restlessly roll
Their sulphurous currents down Yaanek,
    In the ultimate climes of the Pole –
That groan as they roll down Mount Yaanek
    In the realms of the Boreal Pole.

Our talk had been serious and sober,
    But our thoughts they were palsied and sere –
    Our memories were treacherous and sere;
For we knew not the month was October,
    And we marked not the night of the year
    (Ah, night of all nights in the year!)
We noted not the dim lake of Auber
(Though once we had journeyed down here) –
Remembered not the dank tarn of Auber,
    Nor the ghoul-haunted woodland of Weir.

And now, as the night was senescent,
    And star-dials pointed to morn –
    As the star-dials hinted of morn –
At the end of our path a liquescent
    And nebulous lustre was born,
Out of which a miraculous crescent
    Arose with a duplicate horn –
Astarte's be-diamonded crescent,
    Distinct with its duplicate horn.
And I said: 'She is warmer than Dian:
    She rolls through an ether of sighs –
    She revels in a region of sighs.

She has seen that the tears are not dry on
    These cheeks, where the worm never dies,
And has come past the stars of the Lion,
    To point us the path to the skies –
    To the Lethean peace of the skies –
Come up, in despite of the Lion,
    To shine on us with her bright eyes –
Come up, through the lair of the Lion,
    With love in her luminous eyes.'

But Psyche, uplifting her finger,
    Said: 'Sadly this star I mistrust –
    Her pallor I strangely mistrust –
Oh, hasten! – oh, let us not linger!
    Oh, fly! – let us fly! – for we must.'
In terror she spoke, letting sink her
    Wings till they trailed in the dust –
In agony sobbed, letting sink her
    Plumes till they trailed in the dust –
    Till they sorrowfully trailed in the dust.

I replied: 'This is nothing but dreaming.
   Let us on, by this tremulous light!
   Let us bathe in this crystalline light!
Its Sybillic splendour is beaming
   With Hope and in Beauty tonight –
   See! – it flickers up the sky through the night!
Ah, we safely may trust to its gleaming,
   And be sure it will lead us aright –
We safely may trust to a gleaming
   That cannot but guide us aright,
   Since it flickers up to Heaven through the night.'

Thus I pacified Psyche and kissed her,
   And tempted her out of her gloom –
   And conquered her scruples and gloom;
And we passed to the end of the vista,
   But were stopped by the door of a tomb –
   By the door of a legended tomb;
And I said: 'What is written, sweet sister,
   On the door of this legended tomb?'
   She replied: 'Ulalume – Ulalume –
   'Tis the vault of thy lost Ulalume!'

Then my heart it grew ashen and sober
   As the leaves that were crisped and sere –
   As the leaves that were withering and sere –
And I cried: 'It was surely October
   On *this* very night of last year,
   That I journeyed – I journeyed down here! –
   That I brought a dread burden down here –
   On this night of all nights in the year,
   Ah, what demon has tempted me here?
Well I know, now, this dim lake of Auber –
   This misty mid region of Weir –
Well I know, now, this dank tarn of Auber,
   This ghoul-haunted woodland of Weir.'

The Bells

1

Hear the sledges with the bells –
                Silver bells!
What a world of merriment their melody foretells!
        How they tinkle, tinkle, tinkle,
                In the icy air of night!
        While the stars that oversprinkle
        All the heavens seem to twinkle
                With a crystalline delight;
                Keeping time, time, time,
                In a sort of Runic rhyme,
To the tintinnabulation that so musically wells
        From the bells, bells, bells, bells,
                Bells, bells, bells –
From the jingling and the tinkling of the bells.

2

        Hear the mellow wedding bells
                Golden bells!
What a world of happiness their harmony foretells!
        Through the balmy air of night
        How they ring out their delight!
                From the molten-golden notes,
                        And all in tune,
                What a liquid ditty floats
To the turtledove that listens, while she gloats
                        On the moon!
                Oh, from out the sounding cells,
What a gush of euphony voluminously wells!
                How it swells!

How it dwells
On the Future! – how it tells
Of the rapture that impels
To the swinging and the ringing
Of the bells, bells, bells,
Of the bells, bells, bells, bells,
Bells, bells, bells –
To the rhyming and the chiming of the bells!

3

Hear the loud alarum bells –
Brazen bells!
What tale of terror, now, their turbulency tells!
In the startled ear of night
How they scream out their affright!
Too much horrified to speak,
They can only shriek, shriek,
Out of tune,
In a clamorous appealing to the mercy of the fire,
In a mad expostulation with the deaf and frantic fire,
Leaping higher, higher, higher,
With a desperate desire,
And a resolute endeavour
Now – now to sit, or never,
By the side of the pale-faced moon.
Oh, the bells, bells, bells!
What a tale their terror tells
Of Despair!
How they clang, and clash, and roar!
What a horror they outpour
On the bosom of the palpitating air!
Yet the ear it fully knows,
By the twanging,

And the clanging,
How the danger ebbs and flows;
Yet the ear distinctly tells,
In the jangling
And the wrangling,
How the danger sinks and swells,
By the sinking or the swelling in the anger of the bells –
Of the bells –
Of the bells, bells, bells, bells,
Bells, bells, bells –
In the clamour and the clangour of the bells!

4

Hear the tolling of the bells –
Iron bells!
What a world of solemn thought their melody compels!
In the silence of the night,
How we shiver with affright
At the melancholy meaning of their tone!
For every sound that floats
From the rust within their throats
Is a groan.
And the people – ah, the people –
They that dwell up in the steeple,
All alone,
And who, tolling, tolling, tolling,
In that muffled monotone,
Feel a glory in so rolling
On the human heart a stone –
They are neither man nor woman –
They are neither brute nor human –
They are Ghouls:
And their king it is who tolls;

And he rolls, rolls, rolls,
 Rolls
  A paean from the bells!
And his merry bosom swells
 With the paean of the bells!
And he dances, and he yells;
Keeping time, time, time,
In a sort of Runic rhyme,
 To the paean of the bells –
  Of the bells:
Keeping time, time, time,
In a sort of Runic rhyme,
 To the throbbing of the bells –
 Of the bells, bells, bells –
  To the sobbing of the bells;
Keeping time, time, time,
 As he knells, knells, knells,
In a happy Runic rhyme,
 To the rolling of the bells –
 Of the bells, bells, bells –
  To the tolling of the bells,
Of the bells, bells, bells, bells –
  Bells, bells, bells –
To the moaning and the groaning of the bells.

An Enigma

'Seldom we find,' says Solomon Don Dunce,
    'Half an idea in the profoundest sonnet.
Through all the flimsy things we see at once
    As easily as through a Naples bonnet –
    Trash of all trash! – how *can* a lady don it?
Yet heavier far than your Petrarchan stuff–
Owl-downy nonsense that the faintest puff
    Twirls into trunk-paper the while you con it.'
And, veritably, Sol is right enough.
The general tuckermanities are arrant
Bubbles – ephemeral and *so* transparent –
    But *this* is, now – you may depend upon it –
Stable, opaque, immortal – all by dint
Of the dear names that lie concealed within 't.

Annabel Lee

It was many and many a year ago,
    In a kingdom by the sea,
That a maiden lived whom you may know
    By the name of ANNABEL LEE;
And this maiden she lived with no other thought
    Than to love and be lovèd by me.

I was a child and *she* was a child,
    In this kingdom by the sea,
But we loved with a love that was more than love –
    I and my ANNABEL LEE;
With a love that the wingèd seraphs of Heaven
    Coveted her and me.

And this was the reason that, long ago,
    In this kingdom by the sea,
A wind blew out of a cloud, chilling
    My beautiful ANNABEL LEE;
So that her high-born kinsman came
    And bore her away from me,
To shut her up in a sepulchre
    In this kingdom by the sea.

The angels, not half so happy in Heaven,
    Went envying her and me;
Yes! that was the reason (as all men know,
    In this kingdom by the sea)
That the wind came out of the cloud by night,
    Chilling and killing my ANNABEL LEE.

But our love it was stronger by far than the love
    Of those who were older than we –
    Of many far wiser than we –
And neither the angels in Heaven above,
    Nor the demons down under the sea,
Can ever dissever my soul from the soul
    Of the beautiful ANNABEL LEE:

For the moon never beams without bringing me dreams
    Of the beautiful ANNABEL LEE;
And the stars never rise but I see the bright eyes
    Of the beautiful ANNABEL LEE;
And so, all the night-tide, I lie down by the side
Of my darling, my darling, my life and my bride,
    In her sepulchre there by the sea –
    In her tomb by the sounding sea.

To My Mother

Because I feel that, in the Heavens above,
    The angels, whispering to one another,
Can find, among their burning terms of love,
    None so devotional as that of 'Mother',
Therefore by that dear name I long have called you –
    You who are more than mother unto me,
And fill my heart of hearts, where Death installed you,
    In setting my Virginia's spirit free.
My mother – my own mother, who died early,
    Was but the mother of myself; but you
Are mother to the one I loved so dearly,
    And thus are dearer than the mother I knew
By that infinity with which my wife
Was dearer to my soul than its soul-life.

The Haunted Palace

In the greenest of our valleys
   By good angels tenanted,
Once a fair and stately palace –
   Radiant palace – reared its head.
In the monarch Thought's dominion –
   It stood there!
Never seraph spread a pinion
   Over fabric half so fair.

Banners yellow, glorious, golden,
   On its roof did float and flow,
(This – all this – was in the olden
   Time long ago),
And every gentle air that dallied,
   In that sweet day,
Along the ramparts plumed and pallid,
   A wingèd odour went away.

Wanderers in that happy valley,
   Through two luminous windows, saw
Spirits moving musically,
   To a lute's well-tunèd law,
Round about a throne where, sitting
   (Porphyrogene!)
In state his glory well befitting,
   The ruler of the realm was seen.

And all with pearl and ruby glowing
   Was the fair palace door,
Through which came flowing, flowing, flowing,
   And sparkling evermore,
A troop of Echoes, whose sweet duty

Was but to sing,
In voices of surpassing beauty,
    The wit and wisdom of their king.

But evil things, in robes of sorrow,
    Assailed the monarch's high estate.
(Ah, let us mourn! – for never morrow
    Shall dawn upon him desolate!)
And round about his home, the glory
    That blushed and bloomed
Is but a dim-remembered story
    Of the old time entombed.

And travellers, now, within that valley,
    Through the red-litten windows see
Vast forms, that move fantastically
    To a discordant melody,
While, lie a ghastly rapid river,
    Through the pale door
A hideous throng rush out for ever
    And laugh – but smile no more.

The Conqueror Worm

Lo! 'tis a gala night
   Within the lonesome latter years!
An angel throng, bewinged, bedight
   In veils, and drowned in tears,
Sit in a theatre, to see
   A play of hopes and fears,
While the orchestra breathes fitfully
   The music of the spheres.

Mimes, in the form of God on high,
   Mutter and mumble low,
And hither and thither fly –
   Mere puppets they, who come and go
At bidding of vast formless things
   That shift the scenery to and fro,
Flapping from out their Condor wings
   Invisible Woe!

That motley drama – oh, be sure
   It shall not be forgot!
With its Phantom chased for evermore,
   By a crowd that seize it not,
Through a circle that ever returneth in
   To the selfsame spot,
And much of Madness, and more of Sin,
   And Horror the soul of the plot.

But see, amid the mimic rout
   A crawling shape intrude!
A blood-red thing that writhes from out
   The scenic solitude!
It writhes! – it writhes! – with mortal pangs

The mimes become its food,
And the angels sob at vermin fangs
In human gore imbued.

Out – out are the lights – out all!
And, over each quivering form,
The curtain, a funeral pall,
Comes down with the rush of a storm,
And the angels, all pallid and wan,
Uprising, unveiling, affirm
That the play is the tragedy 'Man',
And its hero the Conqueror Worm.

To Frances S. Osgood

Thou wouldst be loved – then let thy heart
From its present pathway part not!
Being everything which now thou art,
Be nothing which thou art not.
So with the world thy gentle ways,
Thy grace, thy more than beauty,
Shall be an endless theme of praise,
And love – a simple duty.

To One in Paradise

Thou wast all that to me, love,
  For which my soul did pine –
A green isle in the sea, love,
  A fountain and a shrine,
All wreathed with fairy fruits and flowers,
  And all the flowers were mine.

Ah, dream too bright to last!
  Ah, starry Hope! that didst arise
But to be overcast!
  A voice from out the Future cries,
'On! on!' – but o'er the Past
  (Dim gulf!) my spirit hovering lies
Mute, motionless, aghast!

For, alas! alas! with me
  The light of Life is o'er!
  'No more – no more – no more –'
(Such language holds the solemn sea
  To the sands upon the shore)
Shall bloom the thunder-blasted tree,
  Or the stricken eagle soar!

And all my days are trances,
  And all my nightly dreams
Are where thy dark eye glances,
  And where thy footstep gleams –
In what ethereal dances,
  By what eternal streams.

The Valley of Unrest

Once it smiled a silent dell
Where the people did not dwell;
They had gone unto the wars,
Trusting to the mild-eyed stars,
Nightly, from their azure towers,
To keep watch above the flowers,
In the midst of which all day
The red sunlight lazily lay.
Now each visitor shall confess
The sad valley's restlessness.
Nothing there is motionless –
Nothing save the airs that brood
Over the magic solitude.
Ah, by no wind are stirred those trees
That palpitate like the chill seas
Around the misty Hebrides!
Ah, by no wind those clouds are driven
That rustle through the unquiet Heaven
Uneasily, from morn till even,
Over the violets there that lie
In myriad types of the human eye –
Over the lilies there that wave
And weep above a nameless grave!
They wave: from out their fragrant tops
Eternal dews come down in drops.
They weep: from off their delicate stems
Perennial tears descend in gems.

The City in the Sea

Lo! Death has reared himself a throne
In a strange city lying alone
Far down within the dim West,
Where the good and the bad and the worst
   and the best
Have gone to their eternal rest.
There shrines and palaces and towers
(Time-eaten towers that tremble not!)
Resemble nothing that is ours.
Around, by lifting winds forgot,
Resignedly beneath the sky
The melancholy waters lie.

No rays from the holy heaven come down
On the long night-time of that town;
But light from out the lurid sea
Streams up the turrets silently –
Gleams up the pinnacles far and free –
Up domes – up spires – up kingly halls –
Up fanes – up Babylon-like walls –
Up shadowy long-forgotten bowers
Of sculptured ivy and stone flowers –
Up many and many a marvellous shrine
Whose wreathèd friezes intertwine
The viol, the violet, and the vine.
Resignedly beneath the sky
The melancholy waters lie.
So blend the turrets and shadows there
That all seem pendulous in air,
While from a proud tower in the town
Death looks gigantically down.

There open fanes and gaping graves
Yawn level with the luminous waves;
But not the riches there that lie
In each idol's diamond eye –
Not the gaily-jewelled dead
Tempt the waters from their bed;
For no ripples curl, alas!
Along that wilderness of glass –
No swellings tell that winds may be
Upon some far-off happier sea –
No heavings hint that winds have been
On seas less hideously serene.

But lo, a stir is in the air!
The wave – there is a movement there!
As if the towers had thrown aside,
In slightly sinking, the dull tide –
As if their tops had feebly given
A void within the filmy Heaven.
The waves have now a redder glow –
The hours are breathing faint and low –
And when, amid no earthly moans,
Down, down that town shall settle hence,
Hell, rising from a thousand thrones,
Shall do it reverence.

The Sleeper

At midnight, in the month of June,
I stand beneath the mystic moon.
An opiate vapour, dewy, dim,
Exhales from out her golden rim,
And, softly dripping, drop by drop,
Upon the quiet mountain top,
Steals drowsily and musically
Into the universal valley.
The rosemary nods upon the grave;
The lily lolls upon the wave;
Wrapping the fog about its breast,
The ruin moulders into rest;
Looking like Lethe, see! the lake
A conscious slumber seems to take,
And would not, for the world, awake.
All Beauty sleeps! – and lo! where lies
(Her casement open to the skies)
Irene, with her Destinies!

Oh, lady bright! can it be right –
This window open to the night?
The wanton airs, from the treetop,
Laughingly through the lattice drop –
The bodiless airs, a wizard rout,
Flit through thy chamber in and out,
And wave the curtain canopy
So fitfully – so fearfully –
Above the closed and fringèd lid
'Neath which thy slumb'ring soul lies hid,
That o'er the floor and down the wall,
Like ghosts the shadows rise and fall!

Oh, lady dear, hast thou no fear?
Why and what art thou dreaming here?
Sure thou art come o'er far-off seas,
A wonder to these garden trees!
Strange is thy pallor! strange thy dress!
Strange, above all, thy length of tress,
And this all solemn silentness!

The lady sleeps! Oh, may her sleep,
Which is enduring, so be deep!
Heaven have her in its sacred keep!
This chamber changed for one more holy,
This bed for one more melancholy,
I pray to God that she may lie
For ever with unopened eye,
While the dim sheeted ghosts go by!

My love, she sleeps! Oh, may her sleep,
As it is lasting, so be deep!
Soft may the worms about her creep!
Far in the forest, dim and old,
For her may some tall vault unfold –
Some vault that oft hath flung its black
And wingèd panels fluttering back,
Triumphant, o'er the crested palls,
Of her grand family funerals –
Some sepulchre, remote, alone,
Against whose portal she hath thrown,
In childhood, many an idle stone –
Some tomb from out whose sounding door
She ne'er shall force an echo more,
Thrilling to think, poor child of sin!
It was the dead who groaned within.

Silence

There are some qualities – some incorporate things,
    That have a double life, which thus is made
A type of that twin entity which springs
    From matter and light, evinced in solid and shade.
There is a twofold *Silence* – sea and shore –
    Body and soul. One dwells in lonely places,
    Newly with grass o'ergrown; some solemn graces,
Some human memories and tearful lore,
Render him terrorless: his name's 'No More'.
He is the corporate Silence: dread him not!
    No power hath he of evil in himself;
But should some urgent fate (untimely lot!)
    Bring thee to meet his shadow (nameless elf,
That haunteth the lone regions where hath trod
No foot of man), commend thyself to God!

A Dream within a Dream

Take this kiss upon the brow!
And, in parting from you now,
Thus much let me avow –
You are not wrong, who deem
That my days have been a dream;
Yet if hope has flown away
In a night, or in a day,
In a vision, or in none,
Is it therefore the less *gone*?
All that we see or seem
Is but a dream within a dream.

I stand amid the roar
Of a surf-tormented shore,
And I hold within my hand
Grains of the golden sand –
How few! yet how they creep
Through my fingers to the deep,
While I weep – while I weep!
O God! can I not grasp
Them with a tighter clasp?
O God! can I not save
One from the pitiless wave?
Is *all* that we see or seem
But a dream within a dream?

Dream-Land

By a route obscure and lonely,
Haunted by ill angels only,
Where an Eidolon, named NIGHT,
On a black throne reigns upright,
I have reached these lands but newly
From an ultimate dim Thule –
From a wild weird clime that lieth, sublime,
　　Out of SPACE – out of TIME.

Bottomless vales and boundless floods,
And chasms, and caves, and Titian woods,
With forms that no man can discover
For the dews that drip all over;
Mountains toppling evermore
Into seas without a shore;
Seas that restlessly aspire,
Surging, unto skies of fire;
Lakes that endlessly outspread
Their lone waters – lone and dead –
Their still waters – still and chilly
With the snows of the lolling lily.

By the lakes that thus outspread
Their lone waters, lone and dead –
Their sad waters, sad and chilly
With the snows of the lolling lily –
By the mountains – near the river
Murmuring lowly, murmuring ever –
By the grey woods – by the swamp
Where the toad and the newt encamp –
By the dismal tarns and pools

Where dwell the Ghouls –
By each spot the most unholy –
In each nook most melancholy –
There the traveller meets aghast
Sheeted Memories of the Past –
Shrouded forms that start and sigh
As they pass the wanderer by –
White-robed forms of friends long given,
In agony, to the Earth – and Heaven.

For the heart whose woes are legion
'Tis a peaceful, soothing region –
For the spirit that walks in shadow
'Tis – oh 'tis an Eldorado!
But the traveller, travelling through it,
May not – dare not openly view it;
Never its mysteries are exposed
To the weak human eye unclosed;
So wills its King, who hath forbid
The uplifting of the fringèd lid;
And thus the sad Soul that here passes
Beholds it but through darkened glasses.

By a route obscure and lonely,
Haunted by ill angels only,
Where an Eidolon, named NIGHT,
On a black throne reigns upright,
I have wandered home but newly
From this ultimate dim Thule.

To Zante

Fair isle, that from the fairest of all flowers,
  Thy gentlest of all gentle names dost take!
How many memories of what radiant hours
  At sight of thee and thine at once awake!
How many scenes of what departed bliss!
  How many thoughts of what entombèd hopes!
How many visions of a maiden that is
  No more – no more upon thy verdant slopes!
No more! alas, that magical sad sound
  Transforming all! Thy charms shall please *no more!*
Thy memory *no more!* Accursèd ground
  Henceforth I hold thy flower-enamelled shore,
O hyacinthine isle! O purple Zante!
  'Isola d'oro! Fior di Levante!'

Eulalie

I dwelt alone
In a world of moan,
And my soul was a stagnant tide,
Till the fair and gentle Eulalie became my blushing
bride –
Till the yellow-haired young Eulalie became my
smiling bride.

Ah, less – less bright
The stars of the night
Than the eyes of the radiant girl!
And never a flake
That the vapour can make
With the moon-tints of purple and pearl,
Can vie with the modest Eulalie's most unregarded
curl –
Can compare with the bright-eyed Eulalie's most
humble and careless curl.

Now Doubt – now Pain
Come never again,
For her soul gives me sigh for sigh,
And all day long
Shines, bright and strong,
Astarté within the sky,
While ever to her dear Eulalie upturns her matron
eye –
While ever to her young Eulalie upturns her violet eye.

Eldorado

Gaily bedight,
A gallant knight,
In sunshine and in shadow,
Had journeyed long,
Singing a song,
In search of Eldorado.

But he grew old –
This knight so bold –
And o'er his heart a shadow
Fell, as he found
No spot of ground
That looked like Eldorado.

And, as his strength
Failed him at length,
He met a pilgrim shadow –
'Shadow,' said he,
'Where can it be –
This land of Eldorado?'

'Over the Mountains
Of the Moon,
Down the Valley of the Shadow,
Ride, boldly ride,'
The shade replied –
'If you seek for Eldorado!'

Israfel

In Heaven a spirit doth dwell
'Whose heart-strings are a lute';
None sing so wildly well
As the angel Israfel,
And the giddy stars (so legends tell)
Ceasing their hymns, attend the spell
    Of his voice, all mute.

Tottering above
    In her highest noon
    The enamoured moon
Blushes with love,
    While, to listen, the red levin
    (With the rapid Pleiads, even,
    Which were seven),
    Pauses in Heaven.

And they say (the starry choir
    And the other listening things)
That Israfeli's fire
Is owing to that lyre
    By which he sits and sings –
The trembling living wire
    Of those unusual strings.

But the skies that angel trod,
    Where deep thoughts are a duty –
Where Love's a grown-up God –
    Where the houri glances are
Imbued with all the beauty
    Which we worship in a star.

Therefore, thou art not wrong,
  Israfeli, who despisest
An unimpassion'd song;
To thee the laurels belong
  Best bard, because the wisest!
Merrily live, and long!

The ecstasies above
  With thy burning measures suit –
Thy grief, thy joy, thy hate, thy love,
  With the fervour of thy lute –
  Well may the stars be mute!

Yes, Heaven is thine; but this
  Is a world of sweets and sours;
  Our flowers are merely – flowers,
And the shadow of thy perfect bliss
  Is the sunshine of ours.

If I could dwell
Where Israfel
  Hath dwelt, and he where I,
He might not sing so wildly well
  A mortal melody,
While a bolder note than this might swell
  From my lyre within the sky.

For Annie

Thank Heaven! the crisis –
    The danger is past,
And the lingering illness
    Is over at last –
And the fever called 'Living'
    Is conquered at last.
Sadly, I know
    I am shorn of my strength,
And no muscle I move
    As I lie at full length –
But no matter! – I feel
    I am better at length.

And I rest so composed,
    Now, in my bed,
That any beholder
    Might fancy me dead –
Might start at beholding me,
    Thinking me dead.
The moaning and groaning,
    The sighing and sobbing,
Are quieted now,
    With that horrible throbbing
At heart: ah, that horrible,
    Horrible throbbing!
The sickness – the nausea –
    The pitiless pain –
Have ceased, with the fever
    That maddened my brain –
With the fever called 'Living'
    That burned in my brain.

And oh! of all tortures
   That torture the worst
Has abated – the terrible
   Torture of thirst
For the naphthaline river
   Of Passion accurst:
I have drank of a water
   That quenches all thirst:

Of a water that flows,
   With a lullaby sound,
From a spring but a very few
   Feet under ground –
From a cavern not very far
   Down under ground.

And ah! let it never
   Be foolishly said
That my room it is gloomy
   And narrow my bed;
For man never slept
   In a different bed –
And, to *sleep*, you must slumber
   In just such a bed.

My tantalised spirit
   Here blandly reposes,
Forgetting, or never
   Regretting its roses –
Its old agitations
   Of myrtles and roses:

For now, while so quietly
   Lying, it fancies

A holier odour
  About it, of pansies –
A rosemary odour,
  Commingled with pansies –
With rue and the beautiful
  Puritan pansies.

And so it lies happily,
  Bathing in many
A dream of the truth
  And the beauty of Annie –
Drowned in a bath
  Of the tresses of Annie.

She tenderly kissed me,
  She fondly caressed,
And then I fell gently
  To sleep on her breast –
Deeply to sleep
  From the heaven of her breast.

When the light was extinguished,
  She covered me warm,
And she prayed to the angels
  To keep me from harm –
To the queen of the angels
  To shield me from harm.

And I lie so composedly,
  Now in my bed,
(Knowing her love),
  That you fancy me dead –
And I rest so contentedly,
  Now in my bed,
(With her love at my breast),

That you fancy me dead –
 That you shudder to look at me,
  Thinking me dead:

But my heart it is brighter
 Than all of the many
Stars in the sky,
 For it sparkles with Annie –
It glows with the light
 Of the love of my Annie –
With the thought of the light
 Of the eyes of my Annie.

To —

I heed not that my earthly lot
 Hath little of Earth in it –
That years of love have been forgot
 In the hatred of a minute:
I mourn not that the desolate
 Are happier, sweet, than I,
But that *you* sorrow for *my* fate
 Who am a passer-by.

Bridal Ballad

The ring is on my hand,
  And the wreath is on my brow;
Satins and jewels grand
Are all at my command,
  And I am happy now.

And my lord he loves me well;
  But when first he breathed his vow
I felt my bosom swell –
For the words rang as a knell,
And the voice seemed *his* who fell
In the battle down the dell,
  And who is happy now.

But he spoke to reassure me,
  And he kissed my pallid brow,
While a reverie came o'er me,
And to the churchyard bore me,
And I sighed to him before me,
Thinking him dead D'Elormie,
  'Oh, I am happy now!'

And thus the words were spoken,
  And this the plighted vow,
And, though my faith be broken,
And, though my heart be broken,
Behold the golden token
  That *proves* me happy now!

Would God I could awaken!
  For I dream I know not how,

And my soul is sorely shaken
Lest an evil step be taken –
Lest the dead who is forsaken
  May not be happy now.

To F—

Beloved! amid the earnest woes
  That crowd around my earthly path –
(Drear path, alas! where grows
Not even one lonely rose) –
  My soul at least a solace hath
In dreams of thee, and therein knows
An Eden of bland repose.

And thus thy memory is to me
  Like some enchanted far-off isle
In some tumultuous sea –
Some ocean throbbing far and free
  With storms – but where meanwhile
Serenest skies continually
  Just o'er that one bright island smile.

Afterword

> The nose of a mob is its imagination.
> By this, at any time, it can be quietly led.
>
> 'Marginalia', 1849

Appropriately, since he is so associated with literary mysteries, Edgar Allan Poe remains an unknown quantity to most people. Despite this, his works have been highly influential: he created the first modern detective in Auguste Dupin; he developed an early form of what we would now call science fiction (often convincing enough to hoax thousands of readers); he was an inventive comic and satirical author and journalist; and he wrote some of the most famous poems in the American literary canon. Yet somehow he has been reduced by legend to a crazed alcoholic whose tales are all of one kind. Thankfully, that view of Poe is not one that could be sustained by readers of this selection of his best tales and poems, a companion volume to the *Tales of Mystery and Imagination*.

Poe's talents in many different fields are demonstrated here, from the thrill of the mysterious and macabre short stories for which he is best remembered through the sheer comic delight of his best humorous pieces to intricately beautiful descriptions in his works of fantasy. Poe is a hard author for readers and critics to pin down since he seems determined to be sincere while ridiculing his audience's taste for the sensational and simultaneously to make salient points about the nature of contemporary scientific achievement. What line can the reader take when it is not even clear which one the author follows? Marketing such a willful author has also presented problems. Of course, the journey to any bookshop will show you what choice tends to be made by publishers; from every edition of Poe stares a disturbing image of blood, skeletons or shadowy rooms. While not an inaccurate summation of the themes of "The Fall of the House of Usher," "The Cask of Amontillado" and other stories of the 'Germanic' type, it does not reflect the range of Poe's writing. In 1845, Poe summarized this in a letter to his friend Philip P. Cooke: "Were all my Tales now before me in a large volume . . . the merit which would principally arrest my attention would be the wide diversity and variety . . . There is a vast variety of kinds and, in degree of value, these kinds vary – but each tale is equally good of its kind."

It is often hard to imagine these tales and poems coming from the same pen. Compare the tendencies toward outrageous horror in "Berenice," idyllic fantasy in "The Domain of Arnheim," black comedy in "The Man Who Was Used Up," and devoted love in "To Helen." Even those examples hint at just a fraction of the author's considerable scope. Poe published journalism, philosophical works, apocalyptic dialogues, and two pieces of longer fiction. At every point of his career Poe varied his approach. This tendency is explained vividly in a letter to James Lowell of 1844:

"I have been too deeply conscious of the mutability and evanescence of temporal things, to give any continuous effort to anything – to be consistent in anything. My life has been whim – impulse – passion – a longing for solitude – a scorn of all things present, in an earnest desire for the future." Behind the façade of self-deprecation inherent in these lines lies a truthful description of his inspiration: a restless wish to investigate all things, all sensations, every component of Man, and so to discover the secrets of extreme action and violent emotion.

Unavoidably, Poe was sometimes too ambitiously adaptable for his own good. Much of his poetry falls rather flat (though it should be remembered that most of it was written by the age of 22) and tales like "Lionizing" have not stood the test of time. The hoax "Von Kempelen and His Discovery," with its faux-reportage analysis of a devaluation of gold following the success of alchemy did not fool readers in its time; Poe had been too ambitious. However, Poe's science fiction piece "Mesmeric Revelation" was read even by some experts in the field as documentary fact. In Poe's tales there is almost always enough vitality to ensure interest in what he is saying, if not always faith in his 'facts.'

In spite of the occasional misfire, Poe's sheer invention occupies the reader regardless of how seriously the subject matter may be taken. This is partly because we are never faced with realism in Poe but rather a carefully staged depiction of the bizarre. His is an intellectual deception. He describes the extraordinary in a matter-of-fact manner like a portrait artist viewing his subject in a hall of mirrors. We are either tricked in to taking low-art themes seriously, or underestimating serious philosophy or psychology because of their bloodied attire. Sometimes Poe would simply lift passages from other works to add a level of verisimilitude. "Hans Pfaall" borrows much from Sir John Herschel's A *Treatise on Astronomy* while his "Balloon Hoax" repeats passages of Monck Mason's *Remarks on the Ellipsoidal Balloon* almost word for word.

Yet this sham authenticity has not devalued his work. Poe was able to use such effects to his advantage. When he draws his comedy from the same murky depths as his more intense stories, he has the ability to shock and amuse at the same time. So, in "The System of Dr Tarr and Professor Fether" lunatics literally take over the asylum in a manner that is both amusing and unnerving. At his most shocking, it is not uncommon for Poe to let anarchy reign temporarily. The eponymous midget fool in "Hop-Frog," for example, wrestles power from a foolish king in one final and fatal jest with an act of great cunning. Poe succeeds in making risible the horrific flaming demise of the unpleasant monarch and his counselors. The origin of such demented violence is, by no means for the only time in Poe, a relationship with a beloved female.

In fact, murder committed by a story's narrator because of an idolized female occurs unnervingly often in these stories. In 1835, Poe published "Morella" and "Berenice," both showing a morbid interest in the demise of a loved one, although in both cases the men who have survived their wives distance them completely. The narrator of "Morella" calls her "my friend" while in "Berenice" Egaeus tells us, "most surely I had never loved her . . . my passions *always were* of the mind. " Egaeus articulates the problem expressed in these tales as follows: "How is it that from beauty I have derived a type of unloveliness – from the covenant of peace, a simile of sorrow?" The subjects of the narrators' unusual affections are reduced to a single quality: in Morella's case to her remarkable intelligence and in Berenice's to her teeth. The fate of these men is, however, very different. The spirit of Morella returns ominously in the child given her name. By contrast, Egaeus hacks out the teeth of the innocent Berenice in a state of confusion or somnambulant mania. In both cases, their relationships have been transformed from affection to horror by a disturbance of the mind: to the "unearthly" and a "train of maladies" respectively. Such was the significance of devotion to Poe that he would return to the themes of death in the context of lost love in both "Ligeia" and "Eleonora." In each case, he blurs the boundaries between the real and the supernatural so his readers must question where truth ends and his narrator's delusions begin.

In "Morella" the tale is taken up entirely with the details of painful memory. It is this sense of the narrative as confession that has encouraged readers of Poe to equate the author with his characters. Berenice is the cousin of Egaeus, reminding us of Poe and his young bride Virginia. Poe seems almost to have encouraged this confusion at times. In "William Wilson," his great tale of the double selves of conscience and action, the narrator has the same birthday (January 19) as the author. In the ineffective dialect sketch "Why the Little Frenchman Wears His Hand in a Sling" the narrator even has Poe's real London address of 39, Southampton Row. Strangest of all, "The Imp of the Perverse" begins as an essay about what causes people to act against reason (in a voice we might assume is Poe's) before transforming itself into a confession by a murderer. The 'essay' becomes a psychological profile, a prelude to the declaration of guilt. Here, and in his hoaxes, the blending of the real and the make-believe tempt us to imply that Poe and his narrators are one and the same, and that the fiction must be based in truth. Yet it would be a mistake to suggest that Poe felt such sinister desires or fought schizophrenia any more than we should imply that he really caught a lethal ape in France or conducted lunar explorations in a balloon. It is enough to note how frequently he returns to bleak or unhappy subjects, especially those of great loss and madness.

However as this selection establishes beyond doubt, Poe's best lesser-known stories confound his reputation for humorless morbidity. He entertains to this day with his insightful depiction of the deluded writer Signora Zenobia. The joke at the expense of the sensationalist *Blackwood's Magazine* in "How to Write A Blackwood Article" sets up Zenobia's story "A Predicament." Sourced from the likes of the thriller "The Man in the Bell," this mock-sensational tale (like its narrator) is hilariously executed. Zenobia takes us through events that leave her stuck improbably and fatally under the enormous hand of a steeple clock. She misquotes, makes irrelevant statements and flounders in non-sequiturs to uproarious effect. Even in this burlesque, Poe's writing is vivid but to a comic end. He has great fun making his narrator dither trying to explain how it feels to be decapitated by a giant timepiece. The dark comedy of the tale is akin to P. G. Wodehouse. Upon losing one eyeball from its socket, the aspiring hack chastises it for "the insolent air of independence and contempt with which it regarded me after it was out." This ghastly image is cut from the same cloth as the likes of "King Pest" but the manner is successfully comic. The addition of a meta-narrative and self-referential subject matter show the degree to which Poe could laugh even at his own excesses.

Elsewhere, Poe shows an enthusiasm for altering scale and perspective. This is seen in the large age difference between lover and beloved in "The Spectacles" and in the seeming monster of "The Sphinx" which is both enormous and tiny. In "The Domain of Arnheim," an impossibly large fortune is amassed by an artistic man with Poe-like passions for music and poetry. Using this extreme of wealth and artistic intent as a starting point he describes a wonderland of rivers, valleys and perfected "supernal" beauty. His descriptions here are as lavish as those of the decaying abode of Roderick Usher but to the end of beauty not of terror. Here and in "The Island of the Fay" Poe expresses the "death-refined appreciation of the beautiful" that is distant from the gloom with which he is associated.

The myths that have grown up around Poe seem a little too convenient, and too much like his art and life have been combined for the benefit of intrigued readers. Nonetheless, he certainly suffered in various ways over the years. He was orphaned and subsequently angered his adoptive father so much through gambling that he was struck out of his will. Poe failed in his many attempts to begin his projected intellectual magazine, *The Stylus*, and caused much bitterness with his scathing reviews and occasional obstinacy. Most significantly, he watched his wife suffer and deteriorate for years before she finally died of tuberculosis in January 1847. Depending on whose account you believe he was also an alcoholic and a drug addict: a hopeless case.

Yet of his biography it is safest to say the following: much of what has been stated as fact is conjecture and is likely to mislead. Layers of falsehood and guesswork began to build up from the first biography – that of his self-elected literary executor and enemy Rufus Griswold. Griswold decided out of a long-established dislike for Poe to defame his subject by fabricating letters and events in the author's life. It is not in doubt that Poe could be a heavy drinker, but not on the scale Griswold claimed. Indeed, he was often temperate for years at a time. As for his apparent opium misuse, Dr John Carter who examined him stated that "Poe never used opium in any instance I am aware of." Even his enemy Dr Thomas Dunn English stated that he "saw no signs" of a drug habit. The other "shocking" matter of Poe's marriage to Virginia, his 14-year-old cousin, much frowned upon by critics, seems to have passed without comment among his contemporaries.

A situation emerged where no less than the President of Yale University, Arthur Twining Hadley, felt confident in pronouncing in 1909 that "Poe wrote like a drunkard and a man who is not accustomed to pay his debts." That such utterly wrong-headed comments have long been accepted is directly attributable to the conflation of art and life that disguises Poe's most singular talent: his adaptability. As Poe himself commented in a 1845 *Graham's Magazine* article: "Because universal or even versatile geniuses have rarely or never been known, therefore, thinks the world, none such can ever be." We should beware the author's own misdirection too – this was a man who once claimed to have been born two years after his mother died and to have traveled much in Europe during time spent entirely in America. We would do better to remember the well-spoken and handsome Southerner of contemporary accounts, the man who considered his crowning achievement a serious and prescient 1848 prose poem about science and the unity of the universe called *Eureka*.

Poe's verse, unlike the little-read *Eureka*, has been as popular as his stories, particularly through its impact upon French literature via Mallarmé, Verlaine and Rimbaud, and upon Modernism through T. S. Eliot. He was a clear influence upon the *vers libre* movement, and although poetry's unprofitable nature prevented him pursuing it to the degree he seems to have wished, he produced a number of extremely fine poems: not only the celebrated but uncharacteristic "The Raven" (which follows closely the story format of his prose), but also deeply personal verses such as "For Annie," unforgettable songs of loss like "Annabel Lee" and the highly original sound-experiment "The Bells." His best poems are easily as powerful in their expression of emotional intensity as his prose, and it is a shame that Poe was eventually more keen to comment upon poetry as a concept than to practice it himself.

A few themes recur throughout these diverse tales and poems. Poe constantly returns to the mysteries of the mind and especially the psychological basis for human action. Although he begins with authentically "Germanic" stories of the bizarre ("Metzengerstein"), Poe developed considerably over time through a fascination with science to explore the psyche in a trance- like state ("A Tale of the Ragged Mountains," "Mesmeric Revelation"). Elsewhere, men are locked in a particular state of mind or "monomania" ("Berenice," "William Wilson") from which death provides the only solution. The individual, usually the narrator, and his preoccupations with a single inescapable trauma can be found even in the revenge elements of "Hans Pfaall" and "Hop-Frog" and also in Poe's attempts to get back at individuals (notably Richard Adams Locke who he tried to better with his "Balloon Hoax") and editors that had made his own 'literary life' so difficult ("X-ing a Paragrab"). The enduring theme is surprisingly not so much one of horror, death, loss or madness (though those themes certainly recur) – but of obsession. In his criticism, Poe raises the short story format up for its potential to exist as a single perfect unit of meaning, and this unity of purpose is one he seems devoted to seeking. And so the otherwise disparate "Morella," "The Spectacles" and "The Domain of Arnheim" converge in spirit. They test theories about the fanatical mind and its capacity to focus on a single fixation until suffering or enlightenment. Each tale is complete, a wholly contained parable or mystery requiring neither a past nor a future, because it tells of a unified experience of the extraordinary.

Further Reading

Poe, Edgar Allan, *The Narrative of Arthur Gordon Pym* (New York: Penguin, 1987)

Silverman, Kenneth, *Edgar Allan Poe: Mournful and Never-ending Remembrance* (HarperCollins, 1991)

Thomas, Dwight, *The Poe Log: A Documentary Life of Edgar Allan Poe* (Boston: G. K. Hall, 1987)

Meyers, Jeffrey, *Edgar Allan Poe: His Life and Legacy* (Charles Scribner's Sons, 1992)

Biography

Edgar Poe was born in Boston in 1809 to traveling actors David Poe, Jr. and Elizabeth Arnold Hopkins. Elizabeth Poe died in December 1811 and her husband died or disappeared soon afterwards, leading to Edgar being brought up by foster parents John and Frances Valentine Allan. Poe attended the University of Virginia before enlisting as a private soldier. He published his first poems in 1827 but it was not until he was discharged from the army and won a literary prize for his tale "MS. Found in a Bottle" that Poe started to achieve fame as a short story writer. He began to work as effective editor at the *Southern Literary Messenger* and established himself writing journalism, stories and poems. Poe had his greatest successes in 1845 when "The Raven" and a new collection of his *Tales* were published to widespread acclaim. His wife Virginia died early and this led to the depression and reliance on drink that have scarred his reputation and dominated the interpretation of his work. He himself died in mysterious circumstances in 1849, and the details of his biography remain controversial and disputed.